The Murmur

The Murmur

STEPHEN HUGGINS

Brian –
Hope you enjoy this story.
Hope even more to meet you
some day soon.

Steve Huggins

Deeds Publishing | Athens

Published by Deeds Publishing in Athens, GA
www.deedspublishing.com

Printed in The United States of America

Cover design by Mark Babcock.

ISBN 978-1-950794-29-4

Books are available in quantity for promotional or premium use. For information, email info@deedspublishing.com.

First Edition, 2020

10 9 8 7 6 5 4 3 2 1

For my father, who explored strange worlds
and introduced me to H.G. and Ursula;
Samuel and Issac; Philip and Ray;
Harlan and Robert . . . and Kurt . . .

Nature has left this tincture
in the blood,
that all men would be tyrants
if they could.

—DANIEL DEFOE

Prologue

Parking lot grit bites my cheek. The impression is remote, as if I'm watching the evening news and the reporter has forgotten to turn on his microphone. The mill burns like a funeral pyre, its roar strangely muffled. Its smoke penetrates deep into my sinuses. I comprehend these sensations, but I cannot feel them. All I feel is anguish. The screams of burning children obliterate everything else.

My grandfather, a disgraced AME pastor, used his two beagles, Michael and Gabriel, to police the tomato plants he grew in his backyard. He rejoiced in setting his dogs on the luckless rabbits who crept in to pillage his crop. These grim executions were the only activity my grandfather ever invited me to watch. Otherwise, he ignored me.

When a rabbit feels a dog's jaws close on its throat, it emits a pleading death scream that sounds identical to the shriek of a child, pitiable and piercing. The screams I hear now are thin and high-pitched, but they are not from the throats of rabbits. Nor do they make sense in any world I inhabit. I lie face down in the parking lot outside the Turnell Mill Event Center in Mosby, Georgia, listening to the shrill cries of children burning.

My nose bends sideways against the unyielding surface, but I can't turn my head to relieve the pressure. A terrible gravity redoubles my weight. None of the nerves in my neck respond. I see only those parts of the parking lot right in front of my face, where a fine grit of dry Georgia clay and gravel covers the sun-heated asphalt. Shreds of plastic protrude from its surface, which shines with the iridescent color of a lump of coal.

Only the children cry for help. Why aren't the adults screaming? They must be burning, too.

My right hand is curled as if about to pluck at the parking lot trash, and it might as well be anesthetized. I try to open my fingers. The command short-circuits somewhere on its way to my nerves. But my ears work just fine. A fierce voice cuts through the tumult yelling, "Over here! Bring it! Bring it!" The voice cracks with anguish. The screams go on and on.

The scrim of oily soot that covers my bloodied knuckles makes it appear that I stole the hand from a dead man's corpse. An alien's hand. The blaze singed the small hairs, leaving them crinkled, blackened, tiny snakes fried on a skillet. The soot stain stops at my wrist, where my long-sleeved shirt protects just enough of my skin to leave a thin line. For a moment, the sight of that sand-colored skin breaks my concentration. I ponder the unsolved mystery of my brown mother and my unnamed white father; then a child's rabbit-scream rises out of the chaos and demands that I act.

The scream is impossibly high-pitched. The fire has discovered another innocent in a hidden pocket of the mill. I tell myself that if I crawl back to the mill, join the others, lift the chained door, I might yet save someone. I order my hand to push up from the asphalt. It twitches once, then locks half bent. I send the order again. Nothing happens.

Air wheezes through my crushed nose. It carries the alkaline smell of a hot desert wind, and the gummy calcium in my mouth tastes like a school bully has forced me to eat blackboard chalk. The cry of the dying child washes over me, retreats, washes up again and retreats in never-ending waves.

A hand intrudes to rummage me where I lie. A disembodied voice says, "You're going to be all right." I hear him, but all I can see is the fire's reflection glinting on the plastic trash in front of my face. The voice is calm, even magisterial. God's voice.

"You're safe," he tells me. His caring hand squeezes my shoulder.

The voices of the dying belie his assurance. My mind insists that I am inside the burning event center, watching the children erupt into small torches. Their mouths gape in incoherent terror; their bodies are wraiths lurching through the flames, specters from an old silent movie playing on a screen as red as a setting sun. Lesions open in their faces, blister and break even as the fire steals their breath and sears their cries. Their parents make no sound. They simply stand and burn. To my enduring shame, I know that I could have prevented the ruin of their lives and the needless quenching of so many memories if only I had interpreted the clues and acted on them. But I didn't. I was forever a beat too late.

From somewhere outside my torment, the hand on my shoulder turns me over so I can breathe. The grip is deliberate but gentle. Once I'm rolled onto my back, the odor of asphalt subsides, replaced by the overwhelming smell of burned meat, like a family barbeque left unattended.

The mill entrance is only a couple of hundred feet away. Outside the building, frantic wives and husbands beat on the metal door with scorched fists, pleading with those inside that even now, it's not too late to save themselves. Even now, as the flames crack the panes of the high windows, the corrugated steel roof thrums with the fury of a dozen thundering freight trains, and the sound grows and will not peak until suddenly a massive explosion shreds the sky and blows all thought and hope from my brain, and the dark cloud that blooms from the wreckage takes the form of a humped beast rising through the scorched air to admire its handiwork.

"You can't help them," says the godlike voice. "They're gone."

His reassuring hand wills me to calm my writhing and sink back onto the hard asphalt. The ashes of immolated children choke my lungs. I gag, but there is nothing more inside me to void. I am dried out. The brick building has become an enormous crematorium, a death oven, radiating heat. It sears the hair on my head into tight whorls, but I feel no pain. Only shame.

Much later, I will realize that I have been irrevocably changed. Before the fire, I was a diminished man, constricted by adolescent notions of sin and error. The shock of the Hatch family's mass suicide demolished that creature and created a new Francis Grace, a man with transformed responsibilities and unexplored desires. But now, in this immediate now, I hear the dwindling screams and am ashamed.

"You'll be all right," the calming voice assures me. "You have survived."

1

Even before we deserted our obscure town on the outskirts of metro Atlanta and moved to the inner city, I realized my mother's hold on reality was fragile. With the move, she became unhinged. Someone needed to step in and take command, but I was too young to grasp what her illness meant, and no one else showed up to take responsibility.

To save money, Mom visited the county library every month and bought discarded books from the three-for-a-dollar pile. Her favorites were the vapid formula romances she read to me at bedtime, her mind clutching at baroque images, her imperfect hold on reality sputtering like a broken faucet. The first kid's book she brought home was *The Real Stories of Brothers Grimm*, published in 1922. This was the full-strength, undiluted Grimm, with crow-plucked eyes and children eaten by wolves. Its laminated cover, swollen with water damage, felt creepy to my young fingers, and its lurid illustrations visited my dreams. I especially remember an ink drawing of a ravenous witch pushing Hansel into the oven with a long baker's rake.

On better days, Mom showed up with a discontinued science textbook or a book of revisionist history. These were invariably missing pages or had margins scribbled with uninspired pornography, but I consumed them with a hungry heart, certain I would discover the secret knowledge adults hid from their children. I read Mom these books while she watched daytime TV romances with the sound turned off. She mumbled invented dialogue in which she was the central character, so our voices contested with each other; as I read accounts of a knowable, analytical world, she supplied fragments of thwarted passion and hopelessly broken lives.

One day, Mom brought home *The Perfect Heresy*, the history of a 13th-century Christian sect called the Cathars, who believed there were two gods, one wholly evil and the other wholly good, locked in an eternal struggle. The concept hooked her. She read the book over and over until the pages were tattered. The more she bought into the dogma, the more she insisted that I, too, accept its worldview. The good god created angels and the spirit realms. The bad god ruled the physical world. He imprisoned angelic spirits in flesh to make humans. Our duty was to reject our bodies and deny the material world. Only then could we reach our true potential and return to heaven.

Even at that age, I couldn't buy into her belief system. One god was hard enough, but two? Mom recognized my skepticism and redoubled her efforts. "You listen, Francis Grace. Some people have the Evil One caged up inside them. You can't tell who they are, but they're after you. They want you. He wants you."

"Mom," I'd say. "I think people are nice. No one ever tries to hurt me."

"You just watch out, Francis. Don't let them catch you looking in their eyes. That's how they get into your head. Through your eyes, Francis."

That warning, "Don't look them in the eyes," sounds plain enough, but Mom always delivered multiple layers of meaning each time she said it. Ostensibly, it meant not to meet another's gaze. The real message was in the spaces before and after her words. In these lay the orders to be self-deprecating, humble, noncombative. Especially noncombative. She repeated the message often, sometimes bent over at the waist so she could waggle her finger in my face, other times sitting at the kitchen table, my small hands caught fast in her earnest grip. Most often, she stood behind me or spoke out of sight from the next room. Our dull dialogue was unchanging.

"Why don't we look people in the eyes, Francis?"

"Our eyes are the gateways to our souls, Mom."

"And?"

"And nobody owns our souls but us. We don't belong in other people's minds."

"Because?"

"Because the Evil One created our bodies. Everything that's good is safe inside our minds and our souls."

Our minds and our souls. Her catechism grooved deep. It lay in my mind, dormant, until the screams and smells of the mill fire awakened it.

Mom could not let go of this notion of an eternal battle between flesh and spirit. She drilled me with its doctrines, insisting that I stay away from false friends, sugared drinks, and the internet. Her final meltdown began when I entered puberty. Then, instead of telling bedtime stories, she knelt with me and grieved over the corrupting thoughts she imagined battling inside my brain. "Keep your mind clear, and never, never stare into another person's eyes," she warned, her words edged with dread. I learned to do as she said. I kept my gaze lowered whenever I was under stress, never raised my voice unless I knew for sure I was in the company of friends. It didn't work. As hard as I tried, nothing I did lessened Mom's fears.

I had the normal childhood nightmares of monsters circling my bedroom and hiding under the bed, but when we moved to Atlanta and I started sixth grade, a more menacing pattern emerged in my dreams. It wasn't enough that I owned an authentically wigged-out mom. The curse expanded, and my body began to grow mysterious. I became awkward. I felt sudden rages for no reason. Our new neighborhood was loud and threatening. So, when the shadowy forces came at night to whisper how I could punish my schoolmates with a simple wish, I listened. I savored those dreams of power and infliction. But even the most appalling of these wish-dreams did not prepare me for burning children.

When I got older and came home at night from some after-school job, I would find my mother pacing our small apartment, her eyes watery with fear of the demons hidden beneath the flesh of the next-door neighbor and the teenaged checkout girl at the grocery store. Mom rarely had all four wheels on the track at the same time. I listened patiently as her monologues of accusation unfurled, doing my best to bring her back from whatever emotional precipice she was perched on. I learned to feel satisfied if I could just get her safely into bed without a relapse. It was hard work, but the practice made me good at listening to people and getting them to confide in me.

The part of Atlanta where we lived worked overtime to reinforce my mother's worst fears. We had more than our share of drug overdoses, car-jackings, and drive-by shootings. Whenever I tried to reassure Mom that most people were peaceable and generous, she would remind me of the one time we were seriously in danger, her trump card against my Pollyanna hopefulness.

That particular evening, we had walked to the *carnicería* one block over from our apartment. When we started back with our groceries, someone followed us. At thirteen, I was streetwise enough to spot a mugger. Our neighborhood was a gangbangers' theme park, a hunting preserve for any street punk or wired-up stoner hoping to make a twenty-dollar score. The police picked up the bad guys and kept them locked up long enough for them to set up the next hit with their cellmates; then the courts turned them back on the population. We had so far been lucky to avoid trouble, but that evening our good fortune ran its course. I trusted people in a general, abstract sense, but I was wary enough to spot the exceptions. So when I heard the steps behind us quicken, I knew what I had to do. I dropped back a half-stride, and when the man lunged for Mom, I slugged him in the stomach.

Fogger Grace, the hero. The guy was three times my size. I don't think he even registered my punch, and his one-armed swipe knocked me hard against a parked car. My head whacked into the car and I saw sparks, just like in the cartoons. Mostly red sparks, with a few yellow sunbursts. Mom was mewling for someone to help. There was no one. I was out of the action, *hors de combat*, wrecked.

Then, deliverance. I remember our rescuer only as the

Shadow Man. He appears before I even think to call for help, materializing out of the dusk, suddenly there in our most terrible moment of need, an avenging Batman, a lethal Deadpool. I can't tell you how he looks or how he comes down on our attacker, but he uses his merciless baton to scourge the guy who grabbed Mom. My hero does more than scourge. He beats the man so bloody that when my head clears, the body sprawled on the sidewalk is more an unstrung marionette than a human being. My mother yells, "Stop! Oh, please stop!" but our rescuer is relentless. I remember, too, a white, splintered bone protruding through the material of our attacker's long-sleeved shirt, his pants torn and bunched around his ankles, his face bloodied, both arms bent at impossible angles. The Shadow Man vanishes. We never see him again.

We never saw him again, but he and the mugger became further examples of mankind's evil for my mother to rail against. And that was fine. But I wish she could have reamed the Shadow Man out of my mind. He became another entry on the long list of memories to bury and thoughts not to have.

Mom's constant droning about evil forces was so exhausting that I escaped to the city library whenever I could. I became the reclusive geek who sought refuge in books and music.

Mom's anxieties didn't get any better when I landed a scholarship to Emory University. Every morning when I left for class, there was a breakfast sandwich waiting on the kitchen counter, always wrapped in computer paper, always dense with prayers written in cramped longhand, warning me not to give in to the Evil One. My mother's pleas battered against the lessons of my classes in science and philosophy, which taught that I lived in a world governed by fixed and comprehensible laws. I chose reason.

To remain sane, I had to diagnose my mother's moods and words constantly. In contrast, she had only a meager idea who I was or what I thought. Her imagination played hard on scenarios where demons lured me into crime or what she called "sins of the flesh," but with my keep-your-head-down-don't-look-at-others discipline, those options hardly ever presented themselves. Very few women invited me into their beds, especially because the other admonition that stuck with me was Mom's warning to never have sex with a girl without first asking permission. She didn't actually say "have sex." She called it "doing that thing," but she was adamant that the girl had to ask first. I couldn't grasp why this was so important to her. Meanwhile, I passed up opportunities to sleep with willing girls, girls who, I now realize, were waiting for me to make the first move. Only years later, when the Hatch family burned to death and I met Lauren Klout, would I finally break Mom's sex prohibition.

Hobbled by my mother's phobias, it took me six years to earn a near-useless master's degree in comparative literature. Over time, proximity to students with normal childhoods gave me an understanding of what lay outside Mom's dream world. Although many of the peculiar behaviors she taught me stuck, I learned to separate the black pepper from the fly shit; to distinguish fantasy from reality. Most of all, I made a firm vow never to push people around—or let another person command me.

I broke free from Mom's religious views, but I never completely outgrew her conviction that there is another spirit trapped inside me, a more genuine Fogger Grace, yearning to break free. I see this same delusion in so many of the people I meet—that we have a more authentic self locked inside us—that I think the feeling must be nearly universal. Like Mom's idea of an angelic spirit imprisoned in mortal flesh, there is an alternative version of ourselves who is more worthy, more honest, more moral.

About the time I graduated, Mom's paranoia locked in, and she began wandering our Oakland City neighborhood in southwest Atlanta, warning wary pedestrians to shun the Evil God. Without warning, she would slip into a catatonic trance that left her repeating the same nonsense phrase over and over. Her favorite was, "No voices. No voices," as if she were the priestess of a long-dead religion and had to interpret her own dreams.

I gave up *my* dream of earning a PhD and obtaining a tenured job as a beloved but eccentric college professor. Instead, my teacher's salary at Atlanta Brookhead Academy just covered the cost of enrolling Mom in Magnolia Meadows, an assisted care facility with discreet bars on the windows and electronic locks on the bedroom doors. The Meadows didn't seek the aged and forgetful. Its clients were people who disturbed others with their erratic behavior. Mom excelled at upsetting people.

My mother was not yet fifty. She had borne me in her teens and stuck with me when others might have sought an easier way out. It was my turn to care for her, and I felt proud to have made this sacrifice, even though I could no longer afford to eat out or pay for satellite TV. I didn't realize it at the time, but this elementary decision put me on the path to Turnell Mill, the fire, and to the very confrontation with the Evil One from which my mother had hoped to protect me.

The entertainment I could afford was listening to audiobooks while I jogged. My ingrained practice of avoiding eye contact with strangers made dating problematic, which suited my bare-bones budget. I spent my abundant free time playing Civ 7, a computer game where I got to create a civilization from scratch, dealing with invisible people at a distance, starting wars, and building castles with high walls. The computer gaming trade called this a 3C, for "command, control, and conquer." It was a crutch for a life with very little drama.

So it seemed an extraordinary stroke of luck when my Emory advisor got me a second job writing feature articles for the gradually shrinking Atlanta Journal Constitution. I eagerly traded nights and weekends for a shot at a normal life. My first article—about a "cat whisperer" who could train any species of pet—was an unexpected hit. I was successful as a feature writer because I was a good listener, quiet when others spoke—a self-defense developed as a boy, when attention to Mom's words might help me anticipate her next sideways drift. I chose cheerful interviews where I didn't have to look into people's eyes and where I could use my ability to put them at ease. I churned out a reliable stream of human-interest interviews, perfect for readers wound tight by family stress and office political intrigue.

Then came the Friday night call from Merciless Michelle, AJC's senior editor. A friend of hers from Georgia Tech had recommended I drive out I-20 to cover the Hatch family reunion in the nearby tourist town of Mosby. Her orders were, "Grace, get me a story about goofy, God-fearing country hicks. Something with lots of *y'alls* and broken syntax."

Far from being the liberal paragons most people assume

they are, Michelle and her editorial staff colleagues had a decidedly jaundiced view of humanity, assembled inch by column inch from the stories they reported. Nor did they limit their disdain to people from the great, gray wastelands outside urban Atlanta—which they took for granted was Georgia's sole oasis of learning and awakened social consciousness. For them, a large segment of Atlanta's population was equally worthless, infected with a permanent strain of immorality and inhumane indifference to the rights and sensibilities of others. These attitudes never intruded into print, but the underlying belief was that outside their immediate social groups, most people were better classified as subhuman beasts than as members of the human race.

Atlanta Brookhead Academy was on summer shutdown, so I welcomed the opportunity to get out of the city at the newspaper's expense. The reunion promised to be the hokey family gathering that urban Georgians imagine fill up the rural calendar, with clog dancing and colorful characters and vignettes of quiet life, the standard feel-good assignment I could knock out in a few hours. I already had a contact. One of the Hatch boys had been my teammate on the Emory cross-country team.

But Mom was right. The material world lays traps. By Saturday afternoon, I was mired in a nightmare for which even my mother's grimmest warnings could not have prepared me. The Evil God lurks inside some people, infecting their minds with a desire to harm even those they hold most precious.

2

I had no forebodings as I drove east toward Mosby on Saturday afternoon, no anticipation of the horror that hid in the quiet antebellum tourist town of 4,837 souls. My mother was from nearby Pickett, a town so much smaller than Mosby that her parents, staunchly religious African-Americans, gave up on their fifteen-year-old daughter the moment she gave birth to a whitish outlander. Or perhaps it was she who estranged them; I never learned which.

My grandparents eventually kicked both of us out of their house because Mom steadfastly refused to name my absent father. The solitary clue to his identity is the fact that I am so much lighter-skinned than my mother that people identify me as Puerto Rican, Greek, or Italian, depending on the ethnic assumptions of whoever thinks it's important to classify skin tones. Bottom line: no one could place me by race, and that put me on the outside.

Pickett is downright tiny. Mom and I lived there in semi-rural isolation until I turned twelve and we moved to

Hotlanta (as people who don't live there are fond of calling it), where I grew up with a single mother mad as crackers, surrounded by other fatherless children, and coming face to face with complete families only when I ran long-distance events at track meets. The intact family was an alien concept. The mystique surrounding the Hatch family reunion, and the public's interest in it, was as meaningless to me as the courting rituals of inbred Yankee patricians. So I thought.

I welcomed the excuse to get out of the city into the noiseless world of memory. For the first hour, I was stuck with the I-85 arterials, creeping past the ever-expanding sameness of car dealerships and cut-rate fireworks and franchise hamburger shops. Somewhere east of Covington, I finally broke free of the creeping Atlanta sprawl into land marked by open fields and patches of softwood forest. A theme of recurring crosses marked the boundary between city and countryside outside the I-85 loop. Billboards began to ask me "Where are you Going? Heaven or Hell?"

The weather guaranteed a soggy reunion. The previous night's rain had left puddles thick with puke-orange Georgia clay. A ghostly mist, thin as smoke, hung over the highway and collected in the swales, not dense enough to be called fog but annoying enough to make me set my old Honda's wipers on intermittent. The slow cadence of the wipers so lulled my senses that I nearly missed the minor drama that flashed over the highway about a car length in front of me. A small brown bird broke from the pinewoods and wove through the speeding traffic, jinking and jiving inches above the pavement. Her pursuer, a relentless red-tailed hawk, matched the prey's every terrified lunge so closely that they seemed connected by invisible reins, the hawk steering its quarry in flight. They flashed by for only a few seconds, and even then, the distraction caused me to swerve onto the shoulder, my wheels perilously close to the soft mud.

"Dammit," I muttered. I tapped the steering wheel with my fist. Many times I had worked as hard as that tenacious hawk, right on the tail of a story that might become a masterpiece of story-telling, and then saw the opportunity get away. Well, that wasn't quite right. Truth was, I hungered for a deed that would let me escape my bland, humdrum routine, but no matter how determined I felt at the start, I inevitably backed off just when the job was almost done. I listened instead to the self-doubt that sat like a stone in my chest, speaking in my mother's voice.

I whacked the steering wheel again, harder, then settled down and concentrated on prewriting the day's column in my head. The basic storyline took shape: the contrast between the instinctive distrust of big city residents and the neighborly society of small-town America. There were plenty of places for a guy like me to hide in Atlanta's crowds.

A man who kept his head down could remain undetected his entire life, yet I was already into my thirties and damn weary of hiding. My distrust of others had become hard-wired. I liked people in general, but always felt exposed, as if something threatening lurked on the edges of my experience, honed by eighty million years of killer genetics to pounce on me. That had to change. If I could dump my passive manner and get aggressive, push for the deep story rather than just listen, I might get a fresh start and escape to a higher salary bracket. Sure. All I had to do was change my entire personality.

I switched on the radio and caught the tail end of Lynyrd Skynyrd claiming he was free as a bird. Yeah, I thought, as if. Even Lynyrd had a girl to leave. I had no one.

I dreamed writing a story that could resonate like *Freebird's* lyric, of creating that one awesome break-through article, a piece of inspired writing that would capture national acclaim and launch my career as a writer of unique insight. Just let me find the right subject, the strange and wonderful event that glued readers to my words...a success to free me from the monotony of my life. With success, I could develop a sense of forthrightness, maybe find a woman to fill the emptiness. Long odds that a small-town reunion would deliver that sort of voodoo power.

I had my cell phone balanced on my thigh and when it chirped, I saw it was my senior editor, Michelle, AJC's Iron Lady. I switched to hands free.

"Almost there, Michelle, I..."

"Just listen, Grace. Here's the angle I want you to take. This Hatch clan is the most ambiguously mixed-race family in the state. Got it?"

"Yes, I..."

"Use that word, 'ambiguous.' There are fifty-one adults and thirty children, all descendants of grandsire Furlong Hatch—use that word 'grandsire,' I like it. They sport skin tones ranging from dark chocolate to pasty white, hair that varies from kinky to curly to wavy to straight. No one can identify a recurring racial pattern. Play that up."

"Got it. All different."

"Play up the contrasts within the same immediate family unit. Very today. See if you can find some sort of prejudice inside the clan. That would be smart. You know: parents of two or more different races, children who bear little resemblance to either parent. Old Furlong Hatch was a goat. He spilled himself into a lot of female friends, but his genes express themselves in all sorts of random variations. Take that and run with it. Race, identity conflicts, secrets."

"Sure, Michelle. I'll..." She hung up.

I had already dug out this information. Part of my task in the proposed article was to decide how to discuss this incongruity without using the word *race* or any language a social justice critic might consider judgmental. But race, even though it no longer officially existed, was an essential element of my Hatch family story. This was, after all, Georgia: a state where everyone wants to know "who your people are." The Hatches were a blended twenty-first-century goulash of hyphenated European, African, Hispanic, and Asian Americans. They were the family of the future.

My GPS pinged just as I saw the road sign that announced, "Historical Mosby, Next Two Exits." The first house I saw as I turned off looked like the set for a movie about cavaliers and ladies, or depending on your biases, about plantation privilege and smoldering resentment. Greek columns; a sunken brick driveway. I'd entered Sherman country, land of the March to the Sea, but without the burned fields and starving citizens. From my research I also knew that Mosby had the lowest crime rate in the state, but one of the highest suicide rates. Perhaps one statistic required the other.

The GPS screen took me directly to the Turnell Mill Event Center on the outskirts of Mosby. I stepped out of my car into a pool of steamy humidity just as the 11:30 CSX freight rolled past, its mournful horn nearly drowning out the clatter of steel wheels on steel tracks. I'd stick that piece of nostalgia in my opening paragraph.

I had emailed my college buddy, Grady Hatch, telling him I'd be dropping by the reunion to take photos and to collect a few insider quotes about his vanished grandfather. I spotted Grady unloading hay bales from a pickup. When we ran cross-country together, he was the reliable heart of the team. He'd set a pace and stick with it the entire run, regardless of weather or terrain, clicking off each mile of woods and hills with the same steady tempo he used on a flat track. If I finished ahead of him, I'd always double back to cheer him through the last hundred yards, yelling, "Run away, Grady, they're gaining on you!"

Grady was heavier now and softer looking. When I waved, he looked up, frowned, and stacked another bale next to the event center entrance.

"Grady. Hey. It's me, Fogger Grace. You get my text?"

Grady wiped his runny nose and let his frown solidify. "You shouldn't be here, Fogger. This is a private party. Very private."

Long practice helped me brush aside his rebuff. I looked at my shoes and slipped into my "aw, shucks" disguise. "Grady, buddy, I only want a peek at the scrapbook of family ghosts. Maybe a joke about Sherman's March?"

Grady's expression vacillated between impatience and something more somber. He pointed a finger at my chest and shook his head as if admonishing a child, but before he could speak, a plump Asian woman stepped between us and held out her hand. Her smile was genuine. "Hi. You must be one of the out-of-state cousins. I'm Sue. Is Grady giving you grief?"

"Sue, I'm Francis Grace. I'm not a Hatch, but Grady and I were buddies at Emory. My friends call me Fogger. Or just Fog. Take your pick."

When Sue Hatch laughed, her jet-black bob fanned out to match her smile. She had dyed the last few inches of her hair the orange-red color of a late autumn sunset. "My cranky husband's put himself under way too much pressure to get this party done right. The reunion is Hatch families only, but that doesn't mean you can't join us later for leftovers. Right, dear?"

A confused, forlorn expression washed over Grady's face. "Honey, I haven't seen Fogger in years. I'm sure he wouldn't . . ."

"Oh, you stop, now," she said. Her Savannah drawl clashed with my every preconception of Asian American speech. "I crave chatter time with somebody who's not straight out of the Hatch bloodline." She took my hand. "Honestly, these pure-bloods are treating the reunion like a funeral. I need a muggle smile to drag this party out of the dumpster."

Grady's brow furrowed. He struck me as unfocused, then nodded once and turned back to the pickup. As he did, a girl of about five barreled into his legs with a joyful squeal.

"And this little rabbit," said Sue, "well, this is our next generation. Patty-Ann, say hello to Mister Fogger."

The girl wrinkled her nose and held up her palm for a high five. When I gave her my hand, she chortled, "Mister Froggy," and took a step backward. Patty-Ann judged me soberly for one breath, then lifted her chin and chuckled a loud *ribbit*. She didn't wait for a response, but ran into the interior of the event center to kick at the growing corridor of straw bales just inside the entrance.

"Sorry, Fogger," said Sue. "She's surely not raised right."

"It's okay," I said. "Fog, Fogger, Froggy. I get that a lot. And I won't interfere with the party, and yes, I'd love to have leftovers with you. I'm just going to take a few photos, then I'll clear out until later."

It had been a long time since I'd joked with anyone about my doubly hexed name. Grady's baffling rejection stung. He'd been my best friend at Emory, where my mixed-race identity was often a poisonous undercurrent, threatening any relationship, and he'd encouraged me to unload more than I should have into his sympathetic ear. Where was my comrade of shared doubts and secrets? I took a step back and gave Sue Hatch a self-depreciating smile to thank her for trying to cover up her husband's bad temper, but a quick glance at Grady's hunched shoulders reaffirmed his rejection. Not quite a piss-off, but close.

The shadowed interior of the building was cavernous, over a hundred feet long and nearly half as wide. The old factory bricks had been sandblasted and repointed to look new. No one had turned on the air conditioning, but the darkened building kept the afternoon Georgia heat outside. Patty-Ann played hide-and-seek with three other kids. None of the adults seemed to care, but their laughter made me smile.

I pulled out my Samsung and shot photos of the farm-themed decorations. The decorating committee must have done its shopping at a Cracker Barrel warehouse; the rakes and milk cans and wire-bound stacks of hay threatened design overkill. Someone had parked a dented orange Kubota M-5 tractor with an attached flat trailer just inside the main entrance. I had to step sideways to get around it without knocking over the wall of hay bales. Oil dripped from the tractor onto the parquet floor. Stray bits of straw floated in the expanding inky pool. The event center owner would not be pleased.

Bedsheets covered the trailer's bulky cargo. The words *First and Last Hatch Family Reunion* were spray-painted on the sheets in University of Georgia red and black, someone's idea of a wry one-liner. A stiff, poster-sized black-and-white photograph sat in the tractor's driver seat, a head-and-shoulders shot of a glowering man with full eyebrows and hard cheekbones. His shirt had the blotchy, tie-dyed pattern that shows up in 1980s musicals, all wide lapels and missing top button. The sour expression on his face did not match the exuberance of his shirt.

This must be Furlong Hatch, I thought, the eponymous ancestor from whom these eighty party-goers had sprung. Furlong wasn't happy to be here. His eyes held a blank, unfocused look, what battlefield reporters call the "thousand-yard stare," a warning that some rare trauma had rendered him incapable of empathy. The look belonged to a 19th-century homesteader, not to the grandsire of the laughing children who hid behind the hay bales.

Despite the new track lighting and inlaid wood floor, the event center held an aura of old age. In the deep past, it had been a factory for squeezing the oil out of cotton seeds. Its wide windows, set high in sturdy brick walls, provided light for workers before electrification, while conveniently hiding distracting views of the world outside. The sills at the bottom of the windows were above the height of my outstretched fingers.

According to my hurried morning Web search, the Confederate Army had converted the building into a field hospital during the Civil War. I planned to use that factoid in my article. When Sherman set Atlanta afire, the last fleeing Confederate trains dropped their dead and dying beside the tracks, knowing that Mosby's citizens—or their slaves—would ferry the bleeding bodies to safety. Most had never moved beyond their dump spot; white headstones marked a narrow cemetery only twenty feet from the tracks. Lost Cause believers covertly decorated the graves with the Stars and Bars every April 22, Confederate Memorial Day.

I heard a giggle behind the hay bales, and a taunting voice said, "Mister Froggy, ribbit, ribbit." If I were ever to have a child, I wanted a clown imp, a Patty-Ann Hatch.

Several adults were setting out platters of food on a trestle table at the rear of the room. Traditional southern fare: fried chicken, greens, cornbread—none of it handmade anymore, but purchased in bulk from the Colonel. I didn't see a beer keg anywhere, so I helped myself to a Coke from the single ice chest in the room. Judging from the many ten-gallon cooler tanks marked "Sweet Tea" and "Lemonade," the rest of the party attendees planned to celebrate Baptist-style. There were enough drink coolers to satisfy a battalion of Boy Scouts: coolers under the dinner tables; coolers perched on the hay bales. The Hatches would be sloshing with tea and lemonade by the time their celebration wrapped up.

Each cooler had a piece of red tape covering its spout. Adults stood guard to shoo away thirsty children. I couldn't imagine why they needed to wait to hand out the lemonade. Rural Georgia still was home to born-again Christians; perhaps any beverage was suspect, even at a family event.

I think my unease first ignited when I noticed that both of the large sliding freight doors at the back of the event center had newly fitted steel burglar braces. Sturdy C-shaped retaining locks added to the impression that the mill was fortified against attack. The wide front entrance was now the building's sole exit. An ancient, eight-section metal warehouse door loomed above this solitary entry/exit point, ratcheted up into the roof beams by a sturdy chain-link pulley that hung down on one side. The chain appeared to be the only means of closing or opening the door. My overall impression was of an impregnable feudal fortress with a slow-motion guillotine built in. For sure it didn't meet code, but no one seemed to care.

Late afternoon sunlight streamed through the entrance to highlight the tractor and its covered trailer. Bits of straw dust roiled in the air above the hidden cargo. Why this stifling apprehension?

3

All the people standing outside suddenly decided they were ravenous, or that they desperately needed to get out of the sun, and they surged into the banquet room with the urgency of a mob late for a concert—or a flock herded by an expert sheep-dog. A odd intensity gripped them. Their breath quickened. Their eyes widened. A few adults walked too slowly for their partners and were grabbed and pulled through the entrance.

I saw Grady take his daughter's hand and move deeper into the room. I could not hear what the little girl said, but my friend stopped and spoke sharply to her, then apologetically knelt and hugged her to his chest. His face still held the strange mix of stupefied uneasiness that I had noticed earlier. It was an expression I now saw mirrored on other faces in the crowd, a look I had once seen in a photograph of panicked German pedestrians pushing into a Dresden air raid shelter, infused with suspicion and uncertainty. It was that same look, and it troubled me.

Grady held up his hands and called for silence. "We are

about to begin...to begin our special day," he said, his voice breaking on the last words. "Everyone who's a direct descendant of Furlong Hatch, please raise a hand." He did a quick count, his lips working silently. "We're all here, so the rest of you, those who married in, those who are dating a Hatch, anyone adopted, go wait outside while we get ready. Go now."

At first, Grady's request generated confused laughter, then a low mumbling began, more a murmur of complaint than a protest. A few adults crossed their arms and refused to move. One grumbling male voice caught the mood. "You shittin' me, Grady?" A woman immediately followed with, "Hey. Language. Children here." Several people began to shove their spouses through the hay-bale entrance into the summer heat. In the confusion, a child began to wail.

Some adults—those most vehemently insisting that their partners had to stand outside—were streaming tears. Tears. Their emotions didn't match the scene, which was already weird enough, but agitation and resistance didn't deaden their resolve. They shoved their spouses toward the door, hardly relenting when their uncomprehending partners stumbled and fell and had to be manhandled under the lurking metal door. The entire debacle took less than sixty seconds to devolve into mayhem. A elderly woman fell, her summer dress ripping at the waist, her white thighs shiny with sudden sweat. When a few parents protested fiercely and refused to leave their children, a goon squad of men bum-rushed the resisters through the door and threw them onto the grass outside.

Realizing that I had an honest-to-God news story here, I snapped pictures as fast as my thumb would work. I got off maybe a dozen before Grady Hatch blundered into me and knocked my cell phone out of my hands and I couldn't get to it in the stampede. Grady had Sue's wrist trapped firmly in his grasp. As he pulled her toward the entrance, he grabbed my forearm with his other hand.

"You, Fogger! Sue! Out!" The look in his eyes was alarming. What had I done to provoke him?

Sunlight momentarily blinded me as we stumbled from the building. I grabbed Sue for balance, and she slugged my wrist with her forearm. When I realized she was struggling to escape my grasp, I let her go. My head ached with an unfamiliar feeling. I imagined a new set of nerves clenched into a tight fist at the base of my skull. Adults stood around in disbelief, talking way too loudly. Their jabbering made my headache worse. I wanted to punch someone. A harsh, ratcheting sound penetrated my awareness, nearly drowning out complaints by the others who stood with me.

"... acting strange all month, and ..."

"Not right, not right by a goddam mile, this ..."

"This isn't Sophie. She's never hit me. Not never. I'm going back."

A storm cloud threw us into shadow, but the blood-beat in my head would not relent. The ratcheting sound grew louder. Then I heard voices rising like the first windburst of an onrushing storm—a chorus shouting hoarse variations of the same thought:

"What the hell is this?"

"Hey! What the shit?"

"What the fuck? You can't ..."

The metal warehouse door was unfolding, section by section, to close off the event center. Each section gave a dull thunk as it snapped into place, a sound with the finality of a submarine hatch sealing off an imploded compartment. A huge brawl erupted at the entrance. Bewildered parents outside fought with the ferocity of a street gang, flailing at their resolute friends and in-laws who blocked the way.

I pushed my way through the mob, crouched, and peered under the lowering door. Inside, I could see the Hatch adults silently and methodically emptying the contents of the drink coolers onto the hay bales. They moved with the exaggerated lurching of robots in an old horror movie, obedient to programmed orders though no one had spoken. The children milled about behind their parents, watching with incomprehension, anxiety creeping into their faces. The youngest cried louder, hysterical. Behind the children, the first yellow flames burst forth.

The odor that wafted through the closing door was not lemonade, but gasoline.

The people outside the mill had become a frightened, angry, disorganized mob, baffled by the reunion's swift disintegration into chaos. Now the whiff of gasoline instantly drove them to panic. They surged toward the lowering door, shouting. Not words. Growls. Then shrieks. Animal voices.

The metal door jerked down to five feet, then four, each metal slat snapping irrevocably into place. I watched, stupefied as a man inside the building pulled the bedsheet off the flat trailer, revealing rows of Blue Rhino propane tanks ranked tightly against each other. He grabbed a tank in each hand and lumbered toward the rear of the building. A woman standing near me gasped, and then the crowd crushing outside bulldozed me aside, raised their hands to the door, tried to block its descent. People inside pushed them back from the entrance with farm rakes, knocking their relatives off their feet. The door was still chest height, but no one got under it.

The hay bales began to blaze fiercely. Flames raced across the floor, eagerly devouring the path of spilled gasoline.

Adults outside shrieked as they fought to keep the lowering door from closing completely, but only the wails of children answered from inside the building. The ratchet wheel rasped. The door dropped another foot. I fought back to the door, hooked my fingers around the edge of the bottom section, braced my knees, but the metal dropped, remorseless, pulling me to my knees.

Flame-glow reflected on the parquet tiles visible at the narrowing bottom of the entrance. Then, just before the door thumped shut, Sue Hatch threw herself onto the ground and rolled underneath. The door fell the last foot and thudded into its concrete retaining groove, reverberating like the door of a burial vault.

Too late, I braced my arms against the barrier. The individual slats had locked into place. A desperate woman shouldered her way through the swelling mass of bodies to get beside me. She lunged against the door, her palms splayed flat on the unyielding gray metal, her arms stiff. Two men crowded in between us, their shouts turning to animal grunts as they strained against the barrier to try to raise it.

There was an unmistakable *whoosh* as more hay bales and gasoline ignited inside. The flame-front sped across the interior and hit the door so hard that the metal bulged beneath our hands. The fire's combustive roar smothered the children's screams. Bit by bit, the door grew warm, then hot. I felt hands clutch desperately at my shirt as people farther back in the crowd clawed their way forward to take my place. They crammed those of us at the front against the door until we could hardly move. I could not draw a full breath. I heaved back against the crowd to gain space, dropped my shoulder, and slammed it into metal. My brain swam with animal shouts, with overloaded images of flames, gaping mouths, melting flesh.

The cries inside the mill were no longer human. Except one clear voice close to the door. "Mommy, Mommy! It burns, Mommy!"

We pressed against the door. It creaked, gave no ground. The high, clear voice climbed higher, desperate, panting. "Mom-eee, Mom-eee! It burns!" The door grew hot against my shoulder. The tiny voice carved into my brain, "Mom-eee, Mom-eee-eeee-eeeee," then flew up the scale and was engulfed by the fire's roar.

I stepped back. A sea of hands swirled around me, clutching at the air with fingers outstretched, others with fingers bent into claws, desperate to reach the entrance. Frantic fingernails scrabbled across my head and face, catching on my lips, slashing ruts in my cheeks. Bodies battered me aside, and I stumbled to the edge of the mob. Then a new, crushing pain shot through my head, and my arms fell to my sides as though a poleaxe had severed my spine.

The crowd's wailing turned to shrieks. I heard the pinging of cell phone keystrokes, frantic calls to 911, garbled prayers. The metal door thrummed with the beating of a dozen fists. My mind shouted that I should help, for God's sake, do something! But the pain in my head ruled my body. My arms hung useless.

The brutal blood-beat in my temples felt like flames raging inside my skull. The children's cries crept higher and higher. An orchestra of demonic flutes stuck on third F above middle C, screeching.

I imagined I drove a runaway train, its great wheels grinding and spewing fire, and that I was inside the event center searching for more gasoline to pour on the floor, and that I could see men and women standing stock-still in the ravenous flames while their bodies sputtered and liquefied. Not the children—they jerked and fluttered, moths trapped in an oil lamp's glass chimney.

A pickup truck careened out of the parking lot, scraped the driver's side against the brick wall, came to a halt beneath one of the tall windows. The driver leaped from the passenger-side door, looked about frantically, seized a metal outdoor chair, and wrestled it up onto the truck bed. Another man, grasping his intent, helped the driver climb onto the roof of his truck. They both stood waist high at the window ledge. Orange and white flames danced on the window glass.

The men hoisted the chair above their heads and threw it against the window. Air rushed into the mill, feeding the hungry flames with such force that the suction pulled both men toward the inferno. Fresh oxygen pumped new life into the fire. The flames exploded outward, blasting the men off the truck roof. One fell to the ground and did not move; the other spun onto the truck's rearview mirror. I heard the sharp crack of his ribs over the screams and the guttural sounds of expanding fire.

Yet more people took their place, undaunted. One by one, they climbed to the roof of the truck and reached into the flames, imploring their sweethearts and children to come, come to the window, to safety. Their faces burned raw, their hair crinkled into threads of blowtorched steel wool, but they did not move away until they could no longer see through fear-deadened eyes; then they collapsed into the truck bed, to be replaced by the next cluster of howling supplicants.

Feeling flashed back into my arms. I pushed my way to the metal door and tried to hoist it off its track. Others struggled vainly with me, shouting and sobbing. Their faces, reddened with heat and fear, masked a fever from which they would never recover.

The erratic pulse in my temples was unceasing, and I imagined someone else had taken my mind captive, willing me to abandon myself to the flames. I fought the door until the pressure became so great that it was impossible to hold onto any concept but confusion. I stumbled away from the door, pushed through the crowd of frantic relatives, moaning in self-pity. I surrendered. I left them to burn. All of God's reassurances would never absolve me of that failure.

I blundered into the parking lot, fell, crawled forward on hands and knees, my lungs choked, my head filled with bewildering images. The ground was as sterile as an A-bomb test site. But then I imagined I journeyed across an infinite plain of hard-packed salt. The grit beneath my feet contained tiny aquatic creatures who had died before the first dinosaurs. Enormous animals grazed in the distance, but I knew they could find nothing to eat. They were doomed to perish, unable to adapt. Yet somehow, I was immune. If I said "come," a genie would materialize at my side with a frosty beer and a smile. All I had to do was wish it. Why couldn't I make myself wish it?

My breath caught, filled with the thick, greasy smoke of bacon—a slab of bacon extruding its own fat, sputtering in the pan, shriveling. The smoke congealed. It rose partway up my throat and lodged in a thick wad. I gagged, breathed again, and the smoke was so thick I was drinking it instead of inhaling it. The bacon blackened, shrank, its smell sulfurous. I stumbled ahead on hands and knees. The parking lot's sharp stones dug into my palms, but it was the pain in my head that made me crumple and roll onto my back.

The sun glowed salamander-orange through the foul smoke, yet I could not bear its intensity. The orange light carved its way into my eyes, and I rolled over to hide the sun and the fire from sight. My nose bent sideways against the asphalt. I breathed in a nauseating mash of synthetic tire rubber, hydrocarbons, and oil drippings. When I tried to raise myself enough to move my head, the arm that supported my weight began to tremble, the tremble snaked its way to my neck, and I gave up without getting my nose so much as a millimeter off the asphalt.

A suppressed memory—or the memory of a dream—flashed as my brain switched off. My one temper tantrum. I was five, rolling on the kitchen floor, drumming my heels, insisting that I get waffles for breakfast. Mom patiently explained that she didn't have the right mix. Then I stood up, stamped my feet, and shouted "WAFFLES!" at the top of my lungs. She slapped me so hard that my head bounced off the refrigerator door. "Francis Ogden Grace, don't you ever use that evil voice with me!" Her fingers clenched into a fist, her face contorted with rage, Mom replaced in an instant by a nightmare monster I didn't recognize. That was when I became Fogger: my demeanor kept under strict control; my emotional valence set at zero. Francis Ogden Grace, always in a perpetual fog.

I squeezed my eyes shut against the sights. A distant thunder of screams and moans rolled over me—names wrenched from husky throats, curses rasped between grief-bitten lips. And a calming hand reached through the chaos, gripped my shoulder, and blocked the pain. The maelstrom of noise abated. Reassurance flooded in. "You're going to be all right," said the voice of the unseen hand. "You're safe."

I nestled into the asphalt and let the soothing voice shield me against the turbulence. Then, suddenly, my mind shocked into clarity for a few deafening, imperfect seconds when the fire reached the propane tanks. Rapid-fire explosions blew the event center's transom glass all the way to the Confederate cemetery, shredding the tattered red-and-black battle flags. Tiny beads of molten 19th-century glass combined with the abundant organic carbon trapped in the building, producing an ugly cloud the color of a dry wound. The blast ripped the event center's metal roof into ragged strips. The metal door buckled, but what it trapped inside, stayed there.

4

Someone held a pencil flashlight up to my eyes and moved it left to right, right to left. A woman's voice said, "He don't seem so bad. Come get me if he says anything about the fire." I was not fully awake, but I picked up that she'd said *don't*, not *doesn't*, and it annoyed me, because the owner's voice was seductive.

Christmas lights strobed around me, alternating red and blue, keeping time with the blood throb in my brain. I heard the swoosh and hiss of water being shot into the gutted husk of the building. The sensation that I was four atmospheres below sea level gradually retreated. Voices came and went: hoarse shouts, commands weighted with fatigue. The tires of heavy vehicles crunched on gravel. Minutes passed. Perhaps longer.

The screams of the dead still saturated my mind and I remembered a brown-bag lunch debate I'd had with an Iranian colleague at Brookhead Academy, where we both taught. He told me how the ayatollahs sent child soldiers into the mine fields during the Iran-Iraq War. Roped together to prevent escape, they cleared barbed wire and mines with their bodies.

In my trauma-induced delirium, I remembered saying, "Jesus, Mazyar. That's gruesome. Wasn't there a backlash?"

"Oh, hell no. Child sacrifice is patriotic. Check your Hebrew Bible. Study the Aztecs, the Mayans, the Minoans. Our Gods place heavy demands on us, Francis. The Carthaginians held out against Roman might for more than a hundred years. When Hannibal's invasion failed, and the legions camped outside their walls, they sacrificed their infants to Bal to hold off defeat. It didn't save them."

By the time I was able to move my neck, my Iranian friend had gone silent. Fire trucks had smothered the blaze inside the building; but deep in the woods, persistent tendrils of washed-out yellow fire snaked their way through dry pine needles. False colors marked these rills, as if the tiny flames were fairy lights, the perverse result of a fermenting chemical soup of gasoline, propane-melted flooring, and animal fats. The greasy smoke that blew across the parking lot smelled loathsome. I recognized that I was no longer dreaming but instead cataloging abstract analytical observations of a human tragedy. That callousness was enough to rouse me.

A resonant male voice spoke into my left ear. "Easy, friend. You're coming out of it, but let's wait and be sure." Was this the person who'd carried me from the parking lot? Dragged me? Led me?

I sat slumped against the door of a black car, my head turned toward the wheel well. My view was of a tire with small pieces of gravel wedged into its treads. I tried to make sense out of this, and I tried to turn and see who knelt next to me, but my head was taking no orders. The owner of the godlike voice squeezed calm into my shoulder. I put my trust in him and focused on making the swarming colors resolve into the individual lights of emergency vehicles. I raised my hand and stared uncomprehendingly at the raw knobs of my knuckles. Where was the missing flesh? Oh, right. Baking on the steel door. I dropped my hand into my lap, then raised it again to look. Was this my hand?

"At one point, I thought you were trying to dig through the pavement," said the soothing voice. "I had to keep a grip on that hand to stop your digging."

I mumbled nonsense words in reply. The voice said, "Oh, you tried, for sure. For a while there, you were a man of many turns."

A woman in a blue uniform hunkered down and stuck her face inches from mine. She had a handsome command face, but wide cheekbones prevented her from being conventionally pretty. Skin the color of a light cappuccino. I wanted to drink it, to devour it. Dark, green-brown, fathomless eyes. Short dark-brown hair under a police cap.

"Is he with us yet, Doctor Amon?" she asked the person beside me. Not waiting for a reply, she looked directly into my eyes. I dropped my gaze out of habit.

"How 'bout it? Are you ready to answer questions, Mister Grace?" It was the throaty contralto voice from earlier, the woman with the tiny flashlight. She had my wallet open in one hand. Her flashlight flicked back and forth between my driver's license photo and my face, and I had the feeling that she didn't think they matched.

I slid farther to the right, feeling cool metal against my cheek. The man on my left caught my slide and drew me back to lean upright against the police cruiser. Lights danced across the cruiser's door, illuminating the logo of a stylized, white-columned antebellum mansion and the words *Mosby Police.*

I mumbled, "M'okay." No, I felt dizzy and nauseous. The impression of brain squeeze had warped into a more insidious sensation. Someone was taking a large can opener to my gray matter, determined to scoop out what little sanity remained. I pushed the image away and got unsteadily to my feet.

My benefactor kept a firm grip on my arms. He propped me against the police cruiser, then stepped beside the officer to check me out. A tall, slate-colored guy with Harry Potter glasses, dressed in a mussed white shirt, sleeves rolled to his bony elbows. He flashed a smile, and I saw the lines where other smiles had etched his face. Once his hands were free, he pulled off his striped tie, wadded it up, and stuffed it in his pocket. I teetered, and his hand shot up and steadied me. He was a bald black man with a briary moustache and grizzled eyebrows like fine steel wires. My mind cleared enough for a vagrant thought: how could he see through those tangled, untrimmed wires? Weren't they relentlessly distracting? But that wasn't the point. He had an earnest expression. A kind man, I concluded. The sort who'd befriend a stranger.

"Thanks," I said. "I'm..."

"Francis Grace," the police officer interrupted, "from Atlanta. What are you doing here, Mister Francis Grace?" Blue lights played across her polished gun belt and the laminated name badge on her chest: KLOUT. Mosby's stylized antebellum house was sewn on the sleeve of her blue blouse. She was tall, her eyes just below the level of mine but bright and piercing. I had to blink to focus on her. A caustic film blurred my vision.

"The pretty police lady I will help any way I can." My words brought a look of disbelief to Officer Klout's face. The mangled syntax sounded strange even to me.

Klout stood and stretched her back. She began to say something else, then held back and stared at me with the expression she probably reserved for meeting someone who had just landed his spaceship from the planet Mongo.

"Jee-eez-us. The whole of fucking Georgia is descending on us—TV stations, GBI, governor's office. Swarming in here like flies on shit, and I'm supposed to reassure them that Mosby's a safe little town for Momma and the kids to visit? And you want to flirt? Jee-eez-us."

I must have been dazed, because I asked, "Do you always begin and end your sentences with the same words?"

Klout's jaws snapped shut like a Rottweiler biting through a bone. Her green-brown eyes, which I saw were flecked with gold, had taken on a fevered glow. She anchored her right hand on the webbed belt next to her sidearm, a 9-mm SIG Sauer, and ran the fingers of her left hand over her forehead, brushing aside strands of damp, dark hair. She looked away and spoke into the air. "This is your joking place, Mister Grace? Really? A place for laughs?" She took a half-step to regain her composure, then bent forward and put her face up against mine again. Her glare focused my thoughts.

"Look. I came here to..." My words came out slurred. I cleared my throat and started again, more deliberately. "I'm here to cover the reunion for the AJC. I write a column. Family stories. Human interest stuff."

"Oh, we got that. Yessir. Burned babies. Human interest." Klout took a deep breath to regain her composure. "Okay.

You're upset. I get that." She deliberated for a moment, then reached into the patrol car for her radio telephone. She spoke in hushed tones punctuated by frequent curses.

The tall black man offered me his hand and said, "Al Amon. You feel okay on your feet?" He was my height, a shade over six feet, but with the fat-free look of a triathlete. His white Sam Elliott mustache contrasted dramatically with his dark skin, and the lights of the emergency vehicles sparkled off his polished head. The ragged mustache curled downward at the corners of his mouth, bracketing an earnest smile.

It was a symptom of my stupefied state that I wanted him to start quoting Ginsberg: "I saw the best minds of my generation destroyed by madness ..." Yeah, that fit everything I was feeling.

I took his hand in both of mine. "Thanks, Al. Whatever you did for me, thank you." I sensed, rightly or wrongly, that I could trust him.

Officer Klout surveyed the parking lot. Police and state troopers had broken the survivors into small groups. I had the sense that the interviews had just begun. Many of the Hatch partners were so stunned they couldn't cooperate. One woman with a flame-reddened face struggled to answer a state trooper, her cloth-bandaged hands moving so eloquently that they substituted for the anguished words she could not speak. She began to gulp air, her eyes luminous with grief, taking ever deeper, more desperate breaths until, without warning, she staggered and collapsed to her knees.

Klout sighed. "Here's what we do," she said. "Mister Grace, Doctor Amon, you're gonna stay in town until we can talk. My office checked you out. I have your cell numbers and will get in touch, so no retreating to Atlanta." She hesitated, then added, "And unless y'all want reporters to chew you up, don't talk with anyone about what you've seen."

"Where can we stay, Chief?" Amon asked politely.

"There's a couple of flop motels on 441 next to I-20. Stay away from them. Try one of our B&Bs. Move fast; the media vultures will snap up every room that's not nailed down. Go on, now."

The field swarmed with firefighters, EMS workers, and four kinds of uniformed police. Once more, I flashed on the scene of children burning, flailing. My chest tightened with anger. I gave up holding my breath and gasped a huge lungful of smoke-tainted air. The policewoman's eyes widened. My sudden rage was so pronounced that she could see it. Despite the realism of my convincing dream, I knew I had not collaborated in the inferno; but a residue of imagined guilt urged me to seek a target, someone to lash with my sense of helplessness. I saw no one who looked even remotely evil. No one I could attack.

Al Amon walked with me closer to the smoldering event center, to where I had parked my car. The paint of my beloved Honda Civic was scorched and peeling, the windshield covered with a glistening black membrane that I did not want to analyze. A wicked piece of roof girder pierced the radiator grille. When I retrieved my laptop and overnight bag, the trunk lid left my fingers greasy with soot.

"Come on," said Al, "I'm parked farther back."

My guardian angel pointed to the turbulent ground where the parking lot met the surrounding pinewoods, now transformed into a carnival midway by emergency vehicles and police cruisers. He walked through the colored lights with a deliberate dignity, lifting his knees high, his spine as straight as a diplomat's. We found his white Kia SUV at the edge of the woods, soot-covered but undamaged. The pall of char-grilled meat penetrated into the car.

I stared back at the Event Center as we pulled away. The grounds were dense with people in uniform. I noticed the firefighters first, dressed in high-visibility yellow Nomex slickers and goggled helmets. Many wore breathing gear. Most of the rest were dressed in blue, but at least a half-dozen wore khaki, and more in white EMS garb. A few people in business suits were already there, looking self-important, pointing into the drifting smoke. Many of the responders were women and although Lauren Klout was not the sort of person I would normally notice in a field of uniforms, by the time we left, she was the only one I remembered.

Al and I didn't exchange another complete sentence until we got to the center of town, where he suggested we get something to eat. We found a diner on Main Street. The bar television played a direct NBC broadcast from the event center, where a breathless newswoman admitted that no one knew what had happened, but it was definitely the work of international terrorists or a gas line explosion. We took a booth where we did not have to see the screen.

The menu featured meat loaf and three, paired with service as slow as tectonic creep. A bowl of tootsie pops sat in the middle of our table next to the napkin dispenser. Neither of us had much appetite. Al spent most of the meal reading and sending text messages on his phone, while I pushed congealed brown gravy around my plate. Over coffee, I learned he was a

DNA researcher at Georgia Tech, a specialist with a PhD in evolutionary biology.

I could not follow Al's patient, thoughtful description of his work. Although I could tell he was choosing the simplest words possible, he quickly lost me. Did I know that the chemical bonds that held DNA strands together sometimes slipped? No, I didn't have a clue. As Al grew excited, his voice dropped to a whisper. Did I know that little bits of DNA code could break off and move from one chain to another? Nope. Why was he babbling about these things when we had just watched families burn? I wanted to take a wire brush to my brain to scrub away the sights and sounds of Turnell Mill. When I admitted that I wasn't following him, Al politely changed the subject.

"So. I'm the one who suggested you come to the reunion." He peered at me over the lip of his coffee cup, his expression a message of warmth and honesty. "Your column is a favorite of mine. I knew I'd be coming here and figured it would be a nice way to meet."

Half my attention had been replaying the tape of the fire while I listened to Al's lecture about DNA. His casual comment about involving me in the fire jarred the memory tape off its track. My one talent is an ability to size people up, to read their intentions. Al was a nice guy. He'd helped rescue me, but now he'd admitted a deception. My first impression had been of a man with deliberate, ultra-formal reserve, and I had slotted him neatly into the stereotyped academic profile I'd always wanted for myself: fussy, soft-spoken, anal-retentive. Now I was forced to re-evaluate his candor.

"Wait a minute, Al. Start over. We just watched people lie

to their families, then burn them to death. Klout is right. People are going to hammer us with questions. So you and I need to be straight. You could have phoned me and asked me to come to Mosby. Instead, you went to my editor and suggested a puff piece. What are you not telling me?"

Amon stared thoughtfully into his coffee cup. When he took off his glasses, I saw the stems were too tight and had left perceptible grooves above his ears. It made him appear vulnerable. He gave me a wistful look. I forced myself not to lower my gaze like I normally would.

"Fogger, your work at the newspaper proves you have a special gift for getting people to talk about themselves. You know how to capture the gravity of their lives in a few hundred words. You can sense their arrivals and their departures. I don't know how you do it, but that is what you do."

His flattery didn't answer my question. "I've schooled myself to be as nonthreatening as they come," I said. "Folks open up to me. How that could help your research, I can't imagine."

"I've been studying the Hatch clan for a long time. The variations they exhibit aren't just in physical characteristics. All their behaviors diverge from the general population's. I want to learn why these multicolored people are so keen to match up with dissimilar partners. What explains their ability to influence other people? I thought you could help. Now ..." He put his cup down and spread his hands in a gesture of exasperation. "Now, it's a different mystery."

"I want to help, Al, but my mind is way the hell off track. I don't know what parts of my memory are true and what's nightmare. And, listen, this disaster shit isn't anything like the things I write about. Not remotely."

Al wasn't listening. He had withdrawn into his thoughts. His hands crept up his cheeks to hold his head, his thumbs sweeping the hairless temples, as if to brush away irrelevant thoughts. After a minute of withdrawal, his awareness darted back to me, and he said, "Do you hear it?"

He leaned back in his chair and looked around the restaurant, taking in the customers and waitstaff. A perplexed, mournful look came into his eyes. "Something's very wrong here, Fogger. I don't mean what happened at the fire. There's something wrong with *us*." His words faltered. "Here we are, swapping backstories, talking about our work. We watched people burn, man. Could it be more grotesque? Why aren't we numb?"

He was right. The patrons at the bar traded jokes and sipped their drinks. Although I could not see the cell phones in their hands or the television over their heads, I knew they streamed images of charred bodies and zombified survivors, of grim firemen who struggled not to vomit into their respirator masks. But tonight at this bar in Mosby, at ground zero of a mass suicide, they laughed and drank as they would on any ordinary summer evening. Was this the inevitable consequence of countless years of numbing horror stories, where every hyperventilated TV newscast began with a breathless, "And now, this horrifying breaking news," and where even the most commonplace event was a portent of the apocalypse? Were we now unmoved by real tragedy?

Al made a fist, then bent at the waist until his forehead nearly touched the edge of the table. "I can't stomach this," he whispered. "I can't. All these people watching their screens, spaced out on tragedy. For fuck's sake!" He twisted half around and hit the table so hard the silverware clattered.

I reached for his hand, but he stood and spoke to the crowd at the bar, his voice rising to a growl. "What's *wrong* with you people? Can't you see their bodies? Their burned bodies?"

The patrons stared back at us, incomprehension on their faces. Perhaps fear, too. Al sank back into his chair. His mouth grew tight. "We might as well be mannequins, Fogger Grace. I realize we're in shock, but this bullshit is wrong. We live in a world of strangled empathy, a world where a morally empty man can become president. The infection is catching, dammit." He uncurled his fists and pushed himself to his feet so abruptly that his chair fell over in a clatter.

Al let it stay there. "Families died. Do these people give a shit? This contagion has been spreading through America for years." He smothered a hysterical giggle. "Indifference. It's a plague."

He dropped two twenties on the table and shook his head when I tried to object. "I reserved the last two rooms at the Braxton Bragg Inn while we were waiting for dinner. I signed us both up for breakfast. I'll try to be in better control of myself by then."

I wanted to tell Al that I felt strange, too, as if the fire had swept us into a dimension where the rules of reality no longer worked. I wanted to tell him I shared his unmoored feeling, that the fire from the event center had become a flame in my chest, eating away at the heartwood of my soul. What I said was, "Thanks. Your brain works faster than mine."

"We need to get our brains in synch," he said. "I had a text message from Officer Klout, too. You might not have noticed that she's Mosby's police chief. She says we're to meet her at a coffee shop across from the police station at 10 a.m. Interviews."

My mind was weary and freighted with repellent memories; the smells and sounds of the fire still threatening to smother me. But as we drove the last few blocks in the quiet dark, I sought a sense of calm from Mosby, so much like the small town where I had spent my early years. It seemed at once familiar and calming. There are isolated communities buried inside the Atlanta metroplex that communicate the same aura of make-believe. You see a Greek Revival facade and suddenly you are a character in a favorite movie. You feel immersed in images of cavaliers and the Lost Cause. For a resident, this is simply your neighborhood. For the visitor, even a cream-colored hybrid like me, that white Corinthian column triggers false memories of class privilege and social stratification, where you can imagine yourself descending the granite steps in frock coat and brocade waistcoat, hear the whisper of a hoop skirt on the granite steps, and have your footman help you into a waiting carriage. You know it is fantasy, but it infuses a strange tranquility.

The Braxton Bragg Inn was a modest but pleasant place created by pushing two different 19th-century wood homes together and adding deep, decorative porches to unify them visually. It sat on a quiet, carriage-wide street of modest early twentieth-century homes. My room was larger than my entire Atlanta apartment, with a period four-poster bed and overstuffed furniture. Truth was, I had never been in a B&B or slept in a fine hotel. I felt as if I had stepped into a PBS travelogue about exotic foreign lands, the kind of show that appeals to middle-class retirees who can afford to have smiling, bearded financial planners greet them by name in television commercials. In no way did this genteel room acknowledge the bewildering barbarity that had been my first day in Mosby.

I took a long shower, a very long shower, then washed my hair first with hand soap and then with the little silver packet of shampoo I found on the sink. I expected noxious ash to rinse out of my hair and foam around the drain in a gray pool, but nothing appeared.

After I had lain sleepless in bed for a half hour, I got up and showered again.

Nightmare images beset my sleep. Patty-Ann Hatch runs into the event center, deep in the shadows of the hay bales. I warn her to come back, but she pours a cup of lemonade and wrinkles her face at the taste.

I come partially awake when the CSX freight groans through Mosby in the early morning. Its base vibrations go deep into my chest, beneath my rib cage. The sound is at once mournful and suggestive. It laments, but it also beckons, says it can take me away from Mosby's sorrows. In my half-awake state, the chant of the diesel engine dances broken glass across the gravel between the tracks. Its horn alerts the sleeping dead: both the gray-clad dead, their wounds gone brittle with age, and the fresh, soot-clad dead, baked into reluctant bricks.

5

After Al and I wolfed a hurried breakfast, he drove me to the Verizon store so I could pick up a replacement phone. I had planned to send a quick message to Michelle, but she was way ahead of me. "Stay in Mosby," her email read. "We have the facts. You get the personal stories. Save all your receipts."

This was not my typical story. But as I writhed in bed the previous night, I recognized that the grim fire gave me an unforeseen opportunity to redefine myself. If I could force myself to be assertive and drop the habitual timidity my mother had drummed into me, then the Hatch fire provided my best chance for transformation. I might even find the nerve to revive my comatose novel, make friends and hold on to them, even develop genuine intimacy with a woman. I could hope.

Al broke my head trip by muttering, "Well, shit. I guess emotions are running hot."

We'd reached the town square, and parking space had been sucked up by TV production trucks and police cars. Field reporters shouted angrily about freedom of speech to a small army of state troopers and police who outnumbered them three to one. As we passed the scene, a red-faced reporter shoved his mike too close to one of Mosby's finest. By the time we circled the block, the reporter was braced against a patrol car, his face now purple with indignation. Al was right. Law enforcement was taking no shit from the press.

We parked two blocks away and walked to the coffee shop, passing antique shops and real estate offices. The temper of the press-versus-police scrimmage settled down. The reporter who'd been manhandled grumbled, "Enough of these assholes. Back to the mill." His team loaded up and headed out of town. Two more TV teams followed them.

We had a block to enjoy Mosby, which was a quaint, picturesque town. Crepe myrtles lined the streets, shedding their pale bark in long strips. I knew how it was with old towns. Once there had been oak trees spaced along the sidewalk, but they disappeared with age and high winds, and the town council replaced them with lower-cost alternatives. The midmorning sun glinted through the white and red blossoms, but the trees thinned as we reached the town square, and the temperature rose several degrees.

The square centered on a single-story brick post office, squeezed onto a half acre plot, surrounded on all sides by nose-in parking spots sized for 1920s automobiles. A problem the Town Council had not got around to fixing. Late-model pickups sat with their huge ass-ends protruding hazardously into the narrow roadway. The old buildings that surrounded the square took on a hard-edged appearance in the sun's glare. The Aintry County courthouse, complete with its World War I doughboy statue and imposing brick bell tower, arose on one corner of the square, a teahouse on the second, then the police station, and finally the town's lone coffeehouse.

Al tugged my sleeve and said, "Let's hope Ms. Klout is more levelheaded than her officers. Don't rile her, okay?"

"Riling isn't in my vocabulary, Professor." His suggestion really annoyed me, so I added, "Why'd you say that, anyway? You just worry about yourself."

"Okay, Fogger. The set of your mouth looks tense, is all."

I unclenched my jaw. It was easy to feel tense. Even here, miles from the mill, the reek of burned petrol invaded my sinuses. I worried that the air carried lead paint and asbestos, needing only a drop in temperature to condense the ash of six dozen Hatches into deadly rain, but the slow-moving pedestrians we passed on the sidewalk showed no signs of concern. Unlike Atlanta's wary urbanites, they greeted us with polite nods and greetings. It could be any peaceful day in this picture-book antebellum town, as long as your sense of smell was switched off.

As we crossed the street to the Magic Beans coffee shop, a high nimbus cloud moved swiftly across the sky, darkening the street and dropping the temperature at once. Sunlight filtered through clouds suddenly as thick as potato soup, muting the crepe myrtles into an Impressionist street scene, needing only a strolling Parisian couple to complete the composition. The effect was disorienting. The fickle sunlight played tricks with my depth perception. My foot caught on a poorly set sidewalk brick, and I half-stumbled into the coffee shop's recessed entry. A hand-drawn sign on the door read "'Pull. Don't Push.'"

As I reached for the door handle, a tiny woman seized my wrist and spun me toward her. She jammed her four-legged aluminum walker against my legs. The scuffed yellow tennis balls on the walker's feet glued it to the sidewalk, preventing me from opening the door.

"You stood there," she said. Traces of spittle showed at the corners of her mouth. "My little Karen was screaming to get out. You did nothing. Nothing!"

The woman may have been slight, but her grip on my wrist was intense. Scratches painted the back of her hand. Her chipped and bitten fingernails had made those marks. Fresh scratches overlay older scars and swollen veins blue with age. Behind her on the brick sidewalk, a sturdy-looking man and a woman with equally fierce expressions leaned in, crowding us so close against the entrance that we could not open the door. They had the tousled hair and drawn faces of survivors.

The little woman held tight to my wrist. The fury in her voice stiffened, and her words knifed into my brain, mucking up the careful script I had been rehearsing for my meeting with the police chief. "They screamed to get out," the woman insisted. "My Karen. You could have let her out. You walked away. You sat down. Why didn't you help? You could have done something."

The odd numbness from last night returned, the feeling that a legion of voices swarmed inside me, each attempting to deliver an urgent message. An unwelcome vibe took hold, and I thought if I concentrated on this woman's scowl hard enough, I could cut through the roaring mental tumult before it overwhelmed me. But the woman's voice jumped another half-octave. Her male companion muscled Al aside and shoved me against the door, grinding my back against its brass handle.

"If you want to beg for forgiveness," he growled, "now's the time."

"Hey," Al protested. "Enough already."

The man drew back his fist and I flashed on my face being smashed. Tried to raise my hand to block him, but the tenacious little woman held tight to my wrist. The fist floated toward me in slow motion. I could see the ropy white scars that crisscrossed its knuckles, and I ducked my head and hoped he'd change his mind about slugging me.

And he did. Al shouted, "Stop!" and the enraged man froze his fist in mid-blow. The tiny woman let go of my wrist. Her female companion stepped off the sidewalk into the gutter, a confused frown bunching her brows. The stocky man stared at his fist for a moment, then uncurled his fingers and dropped his hand to his side. All three looked bewildered.

The petite woman searched my face, her eyes narrowing with uncertainty, and a soft exhalation parted her lips, a sound that might have been part of a word. "Wherrr..." She rocked with the reaction of someone doused with ice water, and then, magically, the reflection of the sun off the glass door dappled her face with a sheen of white spots, and she added, "Why, look at you. You could be my own dear Robert. He's with Jesus now." She turned without waiting for a response and stumbled down the brick sidewalk, the window reflections speckling her back. Her escorts stared at us blankly, then hurried away. I began to call after her, to tell her I *was* at the door and I *did* try to help, but she cocked her head as if she'd heard a whispered word, and kept on walking.

"How'd you do that?" I asked Al. He gave me a knowing smile and a slight nod, acknowledging the entire scene with no surprise, but he did not answer my question. I wished I had his skill. All my life I had swallowed anger and avoided conflict. I aimed most of that anger at myself: for failing to break free of my mother's phobias, for suppressing my ambition, for accepting a mediocre job, for leading a life of suppressed desire. How much easier it would have been had I learned Al's command voice.

The officer on the other side of the door checked our names against a list and let us enter the Magic Beans coffee shop. Old building from the mid-1800s: distressed wood floors, pressed tin ceiling, well-worn wooden furniture. A restive teenage boy curled on a scarred leather chair just inside the door. His attention caromed around the room from wall to ceiling to floor. His busy fingers wove a knotted string into a Jacob's Ladder and he stopped only when he saw us enter. He cocked his head to one side, birdlike. He gave a sharp nod as if in recognition; then his concentration broke and he resumed his aimless weaving.

Each of the occupied tables had a uniformed police officer and several shell-shocked people hunched over cups of coffee. I didn't need to catalogue the kaleidoscope of skin colors to know the customers were the partners of perished Hatches. Their conversations, muted and sparse, were so subdued they might have been mistaken for a distant waterfall. Where were the media, I wondered?

Chief Lauren Klout had already commandeered a table. Her blue uniform was crisp, her police cap on the hook beside our booth. She had combed her dark-brown hair straight so it fell just below her ears in a timeless cut. Her eyes tilted at the corners like those of a watchful cat. The puffy skin beneath those eyes confirmed an exhausting, sleepless night. Klout showed no other signs of fatigue, but when she glanced up to acknowledge us, she pressed her fingers hard against her temples, as if a sudden migraine had wound its steel spring inside her head. Klout was early thirties. Her toned body said she was committed to regular workouts, and the set of her mouth confirmed that she took crap from nobody. Despite her air of weary resignation, she turned me on.

I am obsessed with the desire to identify, then analyze, the subtle "tells" that hide within speech and gesture. My talent is to detect these signs and decode your personality by careful dissection. Something about this Klout woman interfered with my cut-and-dried approach.

Yesterday, I'd been overwhelmed and disoriented. Now, my senses restored and focused, I realized that, despite her surname, Klout was at least half Hispanic. The light streaming through Magic Beans' large sidewalk windows made her skin glow so alluringly that I wanted to stroke it. If I was right, Klout was likely Mosby's first Latina law officer and its first female police chief—evidence, in this small southern town, of grit and determination. She would be the woman who dove into the mountain lake headfirst. No wading in the shallows, just right in and head for the distant shore with sure strokes.

Instead of an introduction, Klout tapped the table with a green-polished fingernail. She gave us such a tight smile it seemed to hurt her to force it out. As we sat down, she asked, "You boys pulled yourselves together?"

Al and I replied "Yes," in unison. I added, "Chief, I was confused yesterday. Whatever I might have said ..."

"I get it," she said. "So, how's about we start over?"

"Before we begin," I said, "what can you tell us about the fire?"

Lauren Klout's deep sigh spoke of a long night hunched behind barricades and yellow police tape. She moved her notebook to the windowsill and combed her fingers through her dark hair. I wondered how it might feel to run my own fingers over her head, to trace the fine hairs down the back of her neck. Despite her take-no-prisoners style, I found the prospect of being grilled by this woman strangely arousing.

"I got dog-puke nothing," she said. Her voice was cigarette husky, and I figured this was her natural tone. "No survivors, except the ones were outside the mill. We're looking for an invitation list of who all was in there, but no one's come up with a copy. A body count's, well, difficult."

"The fire took everyone? All the Hatches?"

Klout responded with a hard-edged stare that verged on hostile. Her green-brown eyes turned several shades darker.

"You damn well know the answer to that, Mister Grace. You saw what I saw. The Hatches burned them and their kids down to lumps. Until I find a list with missing names, I'm thinking there's no more bloodline Hatches in Aintry County, just widows and widow-men."

Just then the barista jammed her steam pipe into a latte and opened the froth valve. The explosive sputtering made Al cringe. The vertical lines in his face deepened. "Burning," he muttered.

"Everyone's going to burn in the end," said Klout. "If you got to burn, best you do it with family." She bit the inside of her cheek and gave another deep sigh. "So how come y'all were there to see the show? Luck?"

Al gripped the chipped edge of the table, his body tight but his face as blank as a hospital wall. "I'm doing genealogical research on the Hatch family. I left campus about 3 pm. Got stuck in I-20 eastbound traffic. I saw smoke when I got to the railroad crossing and pulled in to help. The flames were through the roof." Al began to tremble, but Klout either did not notice or deliberately ignored his distress.

"First-rate luck, huh? Maybe kept you from turning into another charcoal briquette. Your office can back you up on that timing?" Klout didn't wait for an answer; leaned forward. "When you saw the fire, did you call 911?"

"I . . . no. I didn't think to. I saw Mister Grace. He needed help."

"Did you use your doctor skills to help the people who got hurt?"

"I'm not that kind of doctor. I'm a geneticist."

Klout grimaced. "Not a real doctor, then. If you didn't help people, what did you do?"

"I found Mister Grace on the ground. His eyes were open, but he wasn't conscious. Kept rocking his head from side to side. I thought he was having a seizure, so I pulled him away from the fire."

"And how close was Mister Grace to the fire, Doctor? Did you smell gasoline on his clothes? Could he have faked his seizure?"

"Hey," I said, "I've never had a seizure. Never. I wouldn't know how to fake one."

Klout put her hand in front of my face, palm first. "Hold on, Bucky. You'll get your chance. What else, Doctor Amon?"

Al clenched his hands in his lap. He squeezed his eyes shut.

"I saw flames in the upper windows. They were fighting each other at the entrance. The children—" He gulped a breath. "The children were screaming. Terrible cries. Just the children. No sounds from the adults. None."

"And?"

"The people outside, they were in a frenzy. They ran up to the building one or two at a time. The heat forced them back, then they'd run up again, back again, up, back, over and over, shouting until they collapsed on the ground. They'd fold over, dig their fingers into the dirt. And they made...sounds. The wailing, the inhuman screeching, even after the screams inside stopped, those poor people on the outside...human beings are not meant to make those sounds."

Sounds, he said. Strangely, the coffeehouse was nearly soundless. From the other tables, there was hardly a murmur. The survivors and their police handlers sat nearly motionless, sunk in collective grief. Many of them had faces scorched by the fire, arms and hands roughly bandaged, but for the moment they were sleepwalking through their morning, barely animated. The only energized person was the young man at the entrance. He rocked back and forth in his leather chair as though riding an endlessly trotting horse.

Al swiveled in his chair, raised his voice. "What's wrong with everyone? Why are they so calm? This isn't a rational reaction. People burned, for God's sake! Am I the only one who hears screams in his head?"

I caught hold of his wrist and squeezed. "They're in shock," I said, "same as we are. Let them be. Dammit, Al, I don't want to remember the screams, either." But I did remember. The word *screams* stuck in my mouth like a bitter seed.

Lauren Klout had a glint in her eye that would have done a Jesuit inquisitor proud. When she rapped the table to get my attention, I noticed for the first time that the chief was missing the first joint of her left ring finger. "What d'you want to add to Doctor Amon's report, Grace?"

I showed her my press card and a copy of the article I keep in my wallet for identification. She didn't even look at them. I told her what I had seen inside the event center: the ten-gallon coolers labeled lemonade and sweet tea, the gasoline that poured out of them, the flat trailer covered with bedsheets, the deliberate, robotic way the adults set the fire. And the damned accordion door, the way it ratcheted down, segment by clanking segment, until there was just enough room for Sue Hatch to squeeze underneath.

Chief Klout shifted her case-hardened gaze. I dropped my eyes for a moment, then forced myself to meet hers. "Mister Grace," she said, "I have a witness who says you were fighting with Mrs. Hatch just before you say she crawled into the building. Did you push her in?"

6

I stared at Lauren Klout a heartbeat too long before I said, "What? No! Absolutely not."

"Did you hold the door so's Mrs. Hatch could get inside? Did you help her set the fire?"

Klout's question startled me. "No, and hell, no. Sue was trying to save her daughter. I'm dead certain of that."

The back of my neck began to warm. As the police chief waited patiently for me to say something incriminating, I fought to hold my innocent expression and keep my mouth shut. I fought against lifelong discipline to hold her gaze and not drop my eyes. And the impulse was especially strong. I couldn't let her interpret my reluctance as a sign of guilt. But when I met her eyes, I felt as though she wanted to dig into my head where the optic nerves are wired into my brain, and ransack my files.

Lauren smiled, then. "You're okay for now, Mister Grace. I have other witnesses who tell the same story about you." She leaned back in her chair and fluttered her fingers in a ladylike wave-off.

That understated gesture transformed my impression of Chief Klout. For the second time, my talent for sizing up people had failed. Misreading Al Amon had made me unsure. Getting thrown off balance by Lauren Klout left me flummoxed and wary. My carefully rehearsed description of the Hatch catastrophe had evaporated with her first question. I looked up at her to see if she had observed my confusion and caught her penetrating stare for the briefest calculated moment.

A sudden warmth spread over my face and down my back. Worse, a growing fullness accompanied the warmth in my groin. I had never experienced such a spontaneous, insistent attraction to a woman, and I winced inwardly that I could have a sexual response under such grim circumstances. Lauren's second sidelong glance—a brief flicker of attention—told me she had picked up on my response. She lowered her chin, and the hint of a smile crossed her lips.

This strong physical response was confusing. I am not experienced in sexual matters. I was still a virgin in my junior year at Emory, when a kind girl took pity and led me through the steps. I didn't disappoint physically, but after the first month of vigorous experimentation, she declared that I wasn't "spontaneous" and gave up on me. I wasn't surprised. I'd had a lifetime of practice suppressing my every urge and reaction. Nevertheless, I kept experimenting whenever I met a woman who showed interest. My friends called this offhand attitude "sport fucking." Sex was always a release, frequently exhilarating, but in the end, unfulfilling. I kept searching for the kind of transporting rapture that seemed to appear only in novels and

Hollywood films. Never found it. So having a sexual response while being interrogated by a police officer was way wide of any experience I'd had before.

Klout glanced out the window and said, "Well, shee-it." Before I could understand her sudden mood change, she pushed her chair back, picked up her cap, and went through the coffeehouse door onto the street. A white van with "Channel 7 Total News" emblazoned on the side was unloading a Steadicam operator and a callow-looking guy with a microphone. Lauren began arguing with them.

Ever since Al and I arrived, a woman had been watching us from behind the espresso machine. Now, she walked over to our table and said, "This should be interesting. If there's one thing the blue bitch is good at, it's misdirection. I kinda hope she fails this one time. We could use the business." She looked down at our baffled expressions and shook her head sympathetically. "You fellows must've been at the mill yesterday. I'm sorry about your people. Can I get you anything? On the house."

She was a large woman with heavy breasts and dyed auburn hair, wearing a tight jacket that pulled across her broad shoulders and slacks that painted her muscular thighs. Her outfit played on the politically correct stocky-but-fit look that New York fashion was beginning to push, as did the tattoos on both her hands, which mimicked black spiderweb lace gloves. In one web, an orange spider spun a small green sack. The woman looked familiar, and as I tried to decide why, she suddenly grinned and said, "Fogger Grace. Honey, is that you?"

I made the connection at once. "I'm good, Cassandra. You?"

"Why, sweet of you to ask, Fogger. I'm just peachy. Welcome

to my shop. I guess you and your friend aren't here about the Hatch fire after all."

"In fact, we are." I turned to Al, who had risen to his feet to look out the window while we were talking. "This is my friend, Al Amon. We met at the mill yesterday. Al, this is Cassie Wrenner. We went to school together through fifth grade in Pickett, a town even smaller than this one."

Cassie gave a deep laugh and boxed Al's shoulder. You might have thought they had known each other for years. "Oh, the pain of fifth grade," she said, one hand on her ample chest as she shared this hilarious memory with a bewildered Al Amon. "Kids turn so cruel at eleven. They gave Francis and me the most wretched nicknames you can imagine."

Al ignored Cassie's attempt to pull him into the conversation. Instead, he stared out the window as Lauren Klout argued the TV news team back into their van. But Cassie wasn't having it. She tugged Al's sleeve to get his attention.

"Poor Francis Ogden Grace—see, I remember your whole name, Fogger—he got his nickname easy. Those terrible initials, plus he always walked around with his head down like his Momma had shamed him or something."

Cassie abruptly turned her profile and good-naturedly puffed out her chest to give Al the full effect. "My nickname was Bubbles. Can you guess why?"

Time softens memory. I remembered Cassie being as dismayed by her nickname as I was by mine. We always sat together in the back of the classroom, Cassie with her arms folded over her way-too-early D-cups, and me staring at whatever book I had propped in front of my face. She had gone right on growing after fifth grade and had plainly conquered her self-consciousness. Her precocious development had progressed from embarrassment to asset. Now it was a trophy she could brandish as a significant feature of her personality. Meanwhile, I remained stuck in a perpetual fog.

I must have blushed, because Cassie said, "Oh, Fogger, you're still the same shy boy."

Outside, the white van drove off toward the event center. Lauren Klout saw us watching through the window and shrugged her shoulders with a self-satisfied wink. Cassie muttered "biker girl," under her breath, but when Lauren came back inside, she said, "Chief Klout. Can I get a cup of coffee and a raisin bagel for Mosby's finest?"

Lauren ignored her and directed her reply at me and Al. "Channel 7 is gonna join the media clusterfuck out at the mill. They'll get stonewalled by the State Police and the GBI, and at five they'll come back here for my press conference. I'm not looking forward to that circus. You guys make yourselves scarce. Let them get their twenty-second spots from us. You stay here, and they'll twist your shit around 'til it's you who burned up the babies. Jeez-us!"

"Why, bless your heart," said Cassie. "What could be a bigger story than the town's most celebrated rainbow family dying together? Get real. You just don't want all that bother, directing traffic and such."

I knew southern speech well enough to translate Cassie's "bless your heart" as "you are a first-class idiot." Lauren Klout might have a stiff manner, but she won my respect right there by not punching my former classmate in the face.

Lauren gave Cassie a look that would curdle milk in the cow, but measured her words. "I hope you sell a load of coffee this week, Cassandra, but we can't let this fire define our town. These were our people who died. Let's respect them." She looked down the street and scowled. "You boys make yourselves scarce. Something new comes up, I'll call you." In spite of myself, I thought her folksy speech pattern was endearing.

Cassie persisted in trying to talk me and Al into staying. She offered us lunch and promised "choice gossip" about the Hatches. Cassie was a toucher. She patted us on the shoulder and called us "dear" and "sweetie," pinched our arms and squeezed our wrists as she badgered us to have another coffee. Al and I claimed exhaustion and got away just as the TV vans returned to fight each other for parking around the post office.

We walked the two blocks back to the Braxton Bragg Inn. White crepe myrtles and dogwoods lined the back streets. If not for yesterday's gruesome events, I would have enjoyed the antebellum nostalgia. I couldn't imagine why my mother had been so insistent on leaving this charming town.

Yellow roses and purple loropetalum snuggled against the inn's postcard-perfect picket fence. Just looking at them made my shoulder muscles unwind. Two elderly golden retrievers crawled from under a porch bench, stretched, and ambled down the wooden steps to greet us. They waited patiently with lolling tongues until we had scratched their ears, then climbed the stairs of the covered porch and flopped back down in the shade.

Al paused on the porch and stared up at the old oak trees that shadowed the front lawn. For a moment, I thought he was drinking in the quiet back street, but he had something else on his mind. "I should show you my research," he said, favoring me with a sly smile. "To make it interesting, I have a bottle of excellent bourbon in my room. Stop by at five, okay?" Suspicions alerted, I agreed.

I had an hour before 5 p.m., so I phoned my mother at the Magnolia Meadows facility. The aide who answered didn't need to ask who I was. No one called Mom but me. I called every Sunday, knowing she would not remember when we had spoken last or how long she had been at the home. I dreaded the day she would not remember me.

The day I imprisoned my mother in Magnolia Meadows, I copied her one family photo and set it as the wallpaper on my cellphone screen. As I waited for her now, I studied the lines of her face in that photo—searching, as always, for the sane young woman she must once have been. Of the three people in the picture, only Mom smiled. My grandfather stared at the photographer, an inexplicable menace burning in the crosshairs of his gaze, his white Kwanzaa hat and the gray fringe of his curly hair framing his midnight-black face. Grandmother, a half-shade lighter and wearing a bright Kwanzaa dress, stood half-turned away from him, one hand on her daughter's shoulder, the other gripping her arm, shielding her even lighter-skinned child from her husband. Mom was thirteen years old, three years away from giving birth to her only child.

The code of that one photo was far too easy to decipher. Before Mom's sense of humor completely disappeared, she would sometimes tap the three faces in order and say, "We're missing the Norwegian in the woodpile," and add a snort. You could say the same for me. The social justice folks will tell you it's what's under the skin and inside the head that matters, but that's not the way I've lived it.

Mom's voice sounded more querulous than usual. "Francis,

when are you graduating from that school?" She always asked this first.

"I did graduate, Mom. I have a job at the Journal-Constitution now. How're you feeling?"

"They don't feed me enough, and there's nothing good on the TV. Come up and take me to a movie. Something with Morgan Freeman. Okay, honey?"

"I'm working, Mom. I got a job in Mosby, next to your old hometown."

Long pause. "Oh, Francis. Son. I know that place. I won't even say its name. No. Not there. You get out right this minute, quick as you can."

I took a chance and asked, "What do you know about the Hatch family, Mom?"

Her pause was longer still, then her voice hardened. "Francis, you just get out. Don't you talk to any of those Hatch people. They're with the Evil One, dressed in the world's flesh."

"Please don't get upset, Mom. I..."

"Don't listen to their words, Francis. Run away. Keep your eyes down." She began a typical rant, sputtering warnings about everything from chemically poisoned vegetables to the devil's agents in Congress. I listened patiently as Mom continued to rehash her complaints, until I heard her aide, a forgiving woman named Mary-Adelle, ask her for the phone; then I heard a thump as it hit the floor. Mom fumed in the background. Her thoughts followed a familiar flight path, performing the outside loops and stalls of a stunt pilot on speed, expressed in her routine mix of mild curses, accusations, and speaking in tongues, all too familiar for me to get excited about. I heard the name Hatch several times. Finally, Mary-Adelle got control of the phone.

"Momma's going to take a nap now, Mister Francis. You call again next week, she be just fine."

Mom yelled a final warning. "Don't look at anybody, Francis. Don't listen to what they say." Then the line went dead.

7

My stay in Mosby promised to be longer than I'd planned, so I borrowed Al's car and drove to the local Goodwill store. It was like shopping on a cut-rate cruise liner. The one other customer exhibited the terminal consequences of America's addiction to high-fat, fast-food diets. She reminded me of my mother, grown soft in her caged middle age. This woman's rear end was swollen to a preposterous width, her thighs as thick as a rain barrel. She rocked along the aisles like a passenger on the deck of a rolling ship. What irresistible voice commanded her to self-destruct?

I regarded the woman with sympathy. Chances were, her spirit of adventure beat as strong as in the next person, but the burden of her shells kept her imprisoned as sure as my mother's keepers kept her at Magnolia Meadows. Chances were, she longed to be walking the deck of a real cruise ship rather than the aisles of a small-town Goodwill store. I wished *I* were on a cruise ship, headed into the Pacific with a woman who looked like Lauren Klout.

I added three changes of clothes to my overnight bag. My new wardrobe was more colorful than usual, but dammit, I almost *felt* colorful. And upbeat. The visit took maybe twenty minutes, and I was back at the B&B with time to spare.

The first thing I saw when Al opened his bedroom door was a large round table with claw feet, covered with a patchwork quilt. Two ladder-backed chairs flanked the table. One had an empty glass and a half bottle of Woodford Reserve parked next to it. Al drained his own glass, poured another inch, and clicked the bottle with it.

"Sit down. I have something to show you that'll deepen yesterday's tragedy."

"That's not possible," I said. "Yesterday was rock bottom."

I poured an inch of Woodford into my glass, neat, and let it cauterize my throat before I sat. The smoky bourbon went down with the texture of smooth cough syrup. The burn in my sinuses cleared my head, so I poured another and said, "You're stalling, Doctor Amon. What is it you're holding back?"

Al opened a scuffed leather briefcase and pulled out a folded document printed on thick stock. When he unfolded it on the quilt tablecloth, it was a poster-sized family tree, rows of boxes connected with bold lines, printed in a cramped, meticulous handwriting.

"Ten years ago, while I was searching for Atlanta-based athletes with excellent genes, I discovered a video of the 2001 Peachtree Road Race. It showed a man named Furlong Hatch running a strong third place overall, matching the leaders up to the five-mile mark, when he suddenly quits and walks off the course."

"The Peachtree's a big party," I said. "I've done it twice.

Sixty thousand mostly wobbly runners. Only a few hundred professional entries. The rest drop like mayflies."

"Yeah? Well, Hatch registered in the seventy-to-eighty age group, Fogger, running against national-level competitors less than half his age. He was on his way to becoming a national sensation. Then he chose not to be."

Al pointed to a box near the top of the chart. The information was spare.

Furlong NMN Hatch

Born: 1926. Died: (?)

There were more than two dozen boxes strung out horizontally beneath Hatch's name, some linked by solid lines, others connected with dotted lines. A few boxes were blank. Those with names in them had more boxes ranked underneath, showing further levels of descendants. Someone had pasted colored dots in each of the boxes. The pattern looked haphazard. In stark contrast to the confusion of colors and notes on the bottom of the chart, the two boxes above Furlong Hatch were blank. Al's mystery athlete was a man without origins. As far as the chart was concerned, he had materialized out of a vacuum.

I pointed to the broad row under his name. "Mister Hatch was a busy guy."

"You could say that," said Al, his smile stiff.

One box in the second-to-bottom row had a yellow index card taped over it. "Who's this?" I asked.

Al dismissed my question with a wave. "Not important," he said. "The significant thing is that although these Hatch descendants stayed well below the radar, unusual traits kept showing up in most of them. In the past ten years, four of them committed suicide because they kept hearing voices in their heads. Got that? But listen, of the rest of this population, none of them has a police record, none got into serious trouble at school, and none of them ever got divorced."

"That's the family I've always wanted. I envy them."

"Okay, but as a group they're statistical outcasts. These green dots are people who exhibited uncommonly good luck. This one refused to get on the school bus with a drunk driver and missed being on board when the bus crossed the median and went headlong into a bridge abutment. This one came home a winner every time she played poker at Harrah's. Another called the police before a looney at Walmart threatened the personnel at the return counter, then tackled him when he drew his gun and held him down until the police got there. The blue dots? These are people whose neighbors described them as their best-ever friends. They used phrases like 'best buddy a guy could have' and 'the one girlfriend who always made me feel better.' People loved them without reservation. And get this, everyone they ever married developed the same lovable characteristics."

Al hovered over the chart, speaking faster now. "Yellow dots? Great at sales—used cars, homemade pottery, real estate, insurance. Didn't matter what. Never a dissatisfied customer. How many car salesmen get one hundred percent customer satisfaction?"

I pushed back my chair. "Honestly, Al. I interview nice people all the time. Most folks are decent and good-hearted. They make good friends and have good marriages."

"You're way too innocent, Fogger. The Hatches are straight out of a 1960s white-bread sitcom. They're too successful, too lucky, too much in control of their flawless lives. Do you know probability theory? No? Well, never mind. These people defy reason. Genetically, they're unique. Statistically, they're a freak fringe."

"I guess they proved the freak part just fine. I tasted their smoke when I brushed my teeth this morning. What happened to the old man?"

"I tracked him as far as 2006, when he fathered a child in Nebraska. Then he vanished."

I did a quick calculation. "He fathered another descendant at eighty? You're right, the guy is a sensation."

Al's smile stretched into a grimace. He poured himself another bourbon. "I've been tracking Hatch descendants for years and there are still a few of them left. Could be I'm about the only one who knows this. So how about we make a cold call on one of them?"

I agreed with Al that the Hatch family couldn't all be suicidal, so we drove his Kia to Lake Nokose to surprise a teenaged survivor. Al didn't give me much detail on the kid, but when we crossed the Nokose Bridge, he took one hand off the steering wheel and waved at the sluggish water, muddy brown with storm runoff. "How's this for a metaphor?" he said. "I'm convinced the mill suicides correlate with the family traits, but it's too murky to comprehend. They murdered their children, for God's sake. They tried to obliterate their own bloodline."

A mist hung over the river, as fine as smoke, turning the disc-like setting sun into a dull aluminum pan. The waterfront homes up the river still had lights shining at the ends of their floating docks, as if their owners were so wealthy, they didn't have to worry about electricity bills. I couldn't decide how to respond to Al, so I substituted a question.

"This kid we're visiting—how come he wasn't at the mill?"

"His name is Ronnie Millman. His mother's dead and his father's an invalid. He's fifteen, homeschooled by his aunt. The county school records say his behavior is unacceptable, whatever that means. His aunt married into the bloodline, but she's as overprotective as any mother. She's blocked every request I've made for a visit. If you play your humble cub reporter act, I might have my best shot at getting to see him. Just keep it low key."

"Al, I'm an expert at playing low key. I learned early that the nails that stick up always get hammered back down. Humble is how I get by." I thought about his description and then asked, "When you say the kid's behavior is 'unacceptable,' what does that mean?"

"Ronnie's aunt claims his classmates worship him. They call him Mister Charisma. But his teachers—they won't stay in the same room with him. They won't even let him in the special ed classes."

"Then I can help with this kid. I know what it's like to be invisible to my classmates. To most of my teachers, too. I know how to decode the way people speak."

"Better be ready to be disappointed. Ronnie's certifiably psycho and proud of it. He thinks everyone else is the problem."

"Insane people are always sure they're fine. It's only the sane people who are willing to admit they're crazy."

"Did you make that up?"

"Nope, that's Nora Ephron. There's a fine line between psycho and just odd. Sometimes all a person needs to know is that there's someone willing to help."

"And you're going to be that person?"

"That woman at the coffee shop entrance was right, Al. I failed at the mill. This is something I can help with. Sometimes, the most important thing in communication is hearing what isn't said."

"Ephron again?"

"Peter Drucker. An expert on lifelong learning."

Al grinned. "Your rhetoric blows pretty strong when you get your wind up. It cheapens the grace behind your words."

"Grace is a naming accident. It's not who I am. I can buckle down when I need to."

"Bullshit. You're an innocent."

"Trying hard to change that."

We turned into a gated golf club community of high-end homes. A sign at the whitewashed guardhouse said, "Reynard's Plantation, Residents Only," but there was no one manning it. Ronnie Millman's house was one street back from the lakefront. The house was white brick on three sides, with an elaborate vaulted entrance, tinted windows, and a mismatched gothic turret that belonged on Edgar Allan Poe's estate, the very opposite of sleepy Mosby. After the doorbell played the opening bars of "La Marseillaise," a woman's voice crackled from a hidden microphone. "What is it?"

"It's Doctor Amon, Missus Hill, from Georgia Tech. We've talked on the phone about visiting Ronnie. Can we speak with him?" I heard a sequence of clicks as the microphone turned off and on several times. When I looked up at the small grille above the door, I saw an inch of round, clear glass. I pointed, and Al took his business card out of his wallet and held it up to the camera, his smile broadcasting sincerity and goodwill.

A short, burned-out woman in a stained housedress opened the door a few inches and took Al's card. She only glanced at it. "I don't suppose it matters anymore. Come in. He's in the family room." She opened the door farther, then turned back and added, "Don't make him upset." The words came out as a plea.

Ronnie Millman was the same kid I had seen at the coffee shop. He had dull blond hair and lips too full for his narrow jaw. Except for an acute case of adolescent acne, his face was pale, almost bloodless. Most boys of this age carry a latent foreshadowing of their eventual manhood in the set of their shoulders. Not Ronnie; he remained in an androgynous state, neither boy nor man, with no visible evidence that he would ever escape his teens.

Ronnie sat in a corner of the room in a large, barrel-shaped chair, his legs tucked tightly beneath him. His pale-gray eyes flicked around the room like a wary bird's. Ronnie had so many warring quirks that I couldn't register one before another took its place. While we spoke, time and again he fitfully crossed and then uncrossed his arms, and when he wasn't twitching about his fingers, he fretted with the arms of his chair.

There was no air conditioning. The air was close and smelled of cat piss.

Ronnie finally drew his gaze down and let his attention bounce from Al to me to his aunt and back to me. "Something happened, didn't it?" he said. "Something you don't understand. Something that makes you afraid." His words came fast. His lips crooked into a knowing smirk.

Al was unperturbed. "Something bad *did* happen, Ronnie," he said. "What do you know?"

Ronnie jumped to his feet, then, without hesitating, sat

back down and stared intently at the ceiling. He began to tap out a pattern on the chair arms, three taps on the left, and then the same three at the same cadence on the right. He made a dissatisfied face and tapped again, trying to get the pattern correct, and while he fought his compulsion, he said, "Are you going to let me back in school? My friends need me."

Ronnie's aunt did not sit down. She stood behind us, ignoring his frenetic behavior. I assumed her exhausted look came from caring twenty-four seven for a personality mired in an OCD swamp. It was obvious why Ronnie so disturbed his teachers.

"No, dear," his aunt said, "not yet. This is Doctor Amon and his assistant. They want to talk with you."

The room was stale and suffocating, and I began to suspect that they had turned the air conditioning off long before we arrived. Al's bourbon sat sourly in my stomach. I swallowed and shivered involuntarily as a bead of sweat worked its way down my spine. My articles for the AJC were feel-good interviews, the kind that started with me asking, "What made you happy today?" My usual approach would be risky here. Playing with fire. No, scratch that simile; rather, it would be *reckless* in Ronnie's unglued world. Without my reliable conversation gimmick, I could think of nothing to say.

Ronnie tilted his head to one side and locked it stock-still, his eyes twitching in time with his frantically tapping hands. Then his voice changed into such a prayerful tone that I overcame my revulsion and sought the source of his desperation.

"You want to help me," he said. "I know what I did was wrong. I won't hurt anyone else. I promise."

8

"Who did you hurt, Ronnie?" asked Al. "How?"

"I only pushed him a little. He said I couldn't go back to school. I only wanted to see my friends. They miss me."

"Ronnie's father," the aunt interrupted, "my brother-in-law, had a stroke while they were having an argument. Ronnie blames himself." Having said that, she left the room without another word.

Al took a deep breath and adopted a new demeanor. His shift surprised me. One moment he was a deliberate, calculating academic, and then, as if a relay had closed, he lowered his voice and spoke in a soothing baritone. I have never been to a therapist, but I recognized his disguise from television dramas.

"Are you a lucky boy?" Al asked in his tranquilizing voice. Ronnie looked at him suspiciously. His drumming picked up tempo. "Do you have a lot of friends at school?" Al persisted.

"You need to pay attention. They're all my friends. They're crazy about me."

Al leaned toward me and said, *sotto voce*, "The high school labeled him 'disruptive,' but they won't say what that means."

Despite Al's attempt to speak softly, Ronnie abruptly stopped his drumming. "Not disruptive." His voice rose. "Not disruptive! You listen, now. I told the teachers. I told my father. My friends need me. Are you going to help?"

"We will help, Ronnie," said Al. "But we need to understand first. Perhaps you'll tell us about your friends so we can understand better." A flick of Al's gaze urged me to step in and help, but my conversational skills had abandoned me. The apprehension in the room made me think of my one abortive free-diving trip, to the meager depth of forty feet. Mask squeeze, tormented eardrums. My head, and this room, could not cope with so much tension.

Ronnie slammed his feet onto the floor and pointed at Al. "I'm sending here!" he shouted. "You don't know how to listen! Pay attention! And this one," he swung his finger toward me, "he has a hole in his head."

Al kept his therapeutic disguise intact. "Okay, Ronnie. How can we hear you better? Give us some help here."

Ronnie thumped the chair arms with both hands. The tempo sped up. "I've been sending you the code. Right hand, English; left hand, Spanish. You don't even get it. And this one," he pointed his accusing finger at me again, "has a *hole* in his head." He dropped his hands to his knees and leaned forward with the word.

"Hey," I said, "I'm sitting right here. What's this crack about a hole in my head?"

Ronnie's aunt chose this moment to push a wheelchair into the family room. Its occupant, a middle-aged man in a bleached yellow bathrobe, was curled sideways, the right side of his face drooping so profoundly that it appeared barely fastened, threatening to slide off his skull. The fingers of his right hand lay upturned in his lap, closed as if he might be hiding something tiny and precious. Or trying to make a fist to protest his affliction.

"Here," said the aunt. "This is what happens. Do you really think you understand about the fire, about the children? What else could they do? They had to escape the voices. My sister-in-law drove her car into the lake. Now they're all gone." Her gaze stabbed sideways at her nephew, then quickly back to us. "All except Ronnie," she added.

The man in the wheelchair hunched forward, demanding to be part of our dispute. He raised his clenched hand and stretched it stiffly toward the boy in a cryptic denunciation. The sounds he made were not speech but a string of guttural consonants. An eye as blind as a burned-out bulb emphasized the sagging side of his ruined face, and when he swung his ravaged head in my direction, his right eyelid, raw and watery, drooped so far that it seemed frozen in a perpetual wink. He did not try to speak, but his teeth snapped together like those of a feral dog cornered in an alley.

His gestures were mere sideshows to the bottled fury of his expression, so it seemed a natural consequence when, his arm still outstretched, he swung his accusing claw at me. The inarticulate sounds from his chest dried up and I think he held his breath, because his fixed stare stilled mine. A question mark solidified on his brows, daring me to explain his condition.

I wasn't capable of handling so much focused attention, so much non-verbal signaling. Low-threat interviews. That's what I did. Ronnie's finger, his Uncle's frozen fist? I couldn't decipher the messages coiled in their furious gestures. I wanted this to be over, but I hung in there.

"Ronnie," I said, "if you want us to come back, we'll be in Mosby for the next few days. We can talk this out."

He made a finger-gun and pointed it at me. "Not you, geek. Words go right through you. Go away."

We were all silent for a beat, then Ronnie said, "Well, okay, then. Say goodbye. I'm hungry."

"Right away, dear," said Mrs. Hill. She spun the wheelchair so abruptly that her brother-in-law nearly spilled onto the floor. "You can let yourselves out," she yelled, and she disappeared into the back of the house, pushing the frozen man and his frozen expression and his frozen arm before her. We left the front door with Ronnie's gaze hot on our backs.

Outside the stifling house, all appeared normal. I had a crashing headache, but the air was fresh, the sunlight muted, the day undistinguished. My job was to report stories about real people, but the performance I'd just witnessed was nothing I could translate for my readers. They would think a hack Hollywood screenwriter had replaced me.

"So, do you see a hole in my head?" I asked Al. "What the living hell was that about?"

He shook his head and said, "Ronnie's upset because we didn't react to his performance. I've always wondered what it would be like to have a conversation with a manic spider. I think we found out."

Al started his car, then sat at the wheel, hands at three and nine, letting the engine idle. When I asked if he wanted me to drive, he got out and walked to my door so we could change sides. He didn't speak as we retraced our route back to Mosby. When we got to the Nokose Bridge, it occurred to me that the river looked exactly the same as when we'd crossed it earlier, a wide, sluggish current of muddy water. Or maybe not. All that runoff dirt in the water let you see each veer and eddy in the flow, so that what appeared to be stasis at a distance was in fact endless variation, a fugue with the same simple elements endlessly recombining, creating unique patterns in each moment. And the sad, sick turmoil of Ronnie and his captive family was another variation in the fugue.

Al nodded at the river and said, "How's this for a murky metaphor?"

"You already said that."

"Did I? Well, I meant it's all murky. The freak explosion, all those people dying together at one time. I wanted to examine their weird behavior. Instead, I got this terrible fluke accident."

I crossed over the center line; quickly brought the car back into the right lane. "*Ac- accident*?" I sputtered.

"What are the odds, Fogger? The day we arrive to check out this Hatch phenomenon, a gas main blows and incinerates everyone. I mean, hell, all the people I wanted to study, wiped out in one explosion. Could we have worse luck?"

I edged over to the breakdown lane and put the car in park. "Accident?" I repeated.

Al's eyes took on an uncertain cast. The vertical creases in his face deepened into dark rifts. He took a shuddering breath and held up a finger to beg my silence and shifted his gaze to the road, focusing on the rise where the road disappeared into the pinewoods. He rubbed his steel-wire eyebrows and pulled in another deep breath.

"Al," I said, "let me ..."

"Wait," he said, "let me do this on my own." He breathed so deeply I feared he might hyperventilate. I tried to imagine all the conflicting facts that must carom around in his methodical brain, each trying to assert its own version of truth.

"That's not right, is it?" he said. "Not an accident."

"No. What do you remember?"

I could see him wrestling with the idea, his lips forming words he did not speak out loud. He raised his hands to his face, peering at me through his fingers, then pushed his back against the car door. "They killed themselves?" he asked. I sensed he dreaded my answer. "Good God. They did, didn't they?"

I nodded.

"Well that kills it. The chips are all on the table."

"I've got no idea what you're saying, Al."

"Someone's thinning the herd."

We sat there, our car buffeted by a string of speeding lumber trucks that blasted past us, their denuded pine trunks clattering against each other, tips bouncing above the pavement, red flags warning us not to get close. Their passing blast blew tuffs of pine needles against our car. One truck pulled across the solid double lines and tried to pass another on the bridge. Neither gave way at seventy as their drivers shouted insults through their open windows.

"Has this happened to you before," I asked, "this confusion?"

Al shook his head, but he let his mouth relax. "I suspect I know what this is," he said. He patted my arm. "Let's go back to Mosby. I want a Magic Beans latte." He pointed down the road with a wagon master's flourish.

I wasn't buying it. "Whatever's wrong with this program, Al, you can't debug it with a cup of coffee. Seriously."

He patted my arm again and winked. "To quote our police chief, hold on, Bucky. I can explain what's happening if you'll give me a little time. Trust me, it's all coming together." Then he turned on the radio and began scrolling the XM channels. "I need some thinking music," he said.

"If it helps," I said. "See if you can find trumpet jazz. Miles Davis, Wynton Marsalis, someone who opens up."

"Nope. Not what we need." Al kept searching until he found the B. B. King station. They were playing "The Thrill is Gone."

"Why King?" I said. "What's wrong with Davis?"

"Metaphor. Every B. B. King song tells a story about his emotions. He convinces us to take on his pain and make it our own. And he does it with invisible electric signals."

I didn't connect the dots between Al's lapse of memory and "The Thrill is Gone" until later. He assumed my silence meant I had bought into his plan. Whatever it was.

"Yes, sir," he said. "Let's see what the good folks in Mosby have to say."

9

The waitress at Magic Beans stuck a paperback book into the waist of her jeans and treated us to an open-mouthed yawn. The bright green wire braces on her teeth added to her childish look. She was about five and a half feet tall, but weighed no more than ninety pounds, tops. The blades of her hipbones were all that prevented her jeans from falling to the floor. "You want coffee?" she asked. "Or something to eat?"

"Two of your best lattes," said Al, giving the girl a blazing smile. "Anything new going on in town?" he asked, as if inquiring about the weather.

"Oh, we got news, all right. You don't watch the TV? We had this really gross accident a couple days ago. Like, it was this gas main exploded and a bunch of people got, like, burned up. Really sick."

"Sounds like a freak accident," said Al. His warning look stifled the protest rising in my throat.

"You got it. Really sick. So, two lattes?" She might as well have given us a baseball score.

I took out my braided wallet, the one I'd made at the Boys and Girls Club on Saturday nights when I was ten, and fished out a twenty. I held it in front of the waitress and said, "Who calls the shots in sleepy Mosby? Who knows how the town works?"

"I'm not from here, so I wouldn't know." Her voice switched gears into a whine. "You want anything to eat, or not?"

"Who does the owner suck up to when the health inspector has a problem?"

"I'll come back when you make up your mind."

I noted Al's amused smile when she walked away. "Hey," I said. "I couldn't let you do all the questioning."

"And you're so good at it," he replied.

"In Atlanta you can buy information as easy as ordering a Big Mac. I guess they have higher ethical standards here."

"Clearly not."

Magic Beans looked like it had been hit with a virus pandemic. We were the only customers. I fidgeted in my chair, still perplexed by Ronnie's comment about the 'hole' in my head. After our coffee arrived, Al asked, "Fogger, what do you know about the myth of Dionysus?"

"As a matter of fact, I wrote my master's thesis on him. God of wine and holy drunkenness. But hold on. Our waitress, she told the same warped story about a gas main explosion. What could ..."

"Bear with me," said Al. "Let's explore a theory. Yes, Dionysus was the god of wine, but also the god of epiphany and ritual madness. He was a well-known hard-ass about his reputation. One day, his cousin Pentheus insulted him, saying he doubted Dionysus was a god. Dionysus drove Pentheus's mother and her Maenad friends crazy, and they tore the poor man apart. Pentheus's mother paraded through the streets of Thebes with her son's head on a pike, not even recognizing what she had done."

I knew all this, so I grasped his analogy, that someone could condemn his foes to psychic dismemberment with a wish. To be honest, I had always longed for that power, but I kept the fantasy suppressed, pushed down with all the other unholy desires that tumbled around in my brain. But I knew that wasn't Al's point.

"Okay," I said. "Mass hysteria. But listen, you bought into it too. You denied the suicide."

"I have an answer for that," he said, but just then Cassie Wrenner pulled out a chair and sat down between us. She laid a framed black-and-white photo on the table. I had an eye-blink vision in which the orange spider on her spiderweb tattoo trembled, preparing to crawl off her arm onto the photograph.

"Since you were asking about the Hatch family," she said, "I thought you'd want to see the granddaddy of them all. If you ever stayed here long enough to pee, you'd see this photo on the wall back by the restrooms."

It was the same grim man whose photo I had seen propped against the tractor seat at Turnell Mill. He leaned against the hood of a 1956 Buick Century, one foot hooked on its giant chrome bumper. The wide-brimmed plantation hat he wore threw his face into shadow, but it was definitely Furlong Hatch, looking annoyed.

"Who's the woman standing next to him?" I asked.

"Dunno," said Cassie. "Old Furlong had lots of 'wives' and

way too many girlfriends. Wasn't a woman of any age that he couldn't get horizontal. That includes church ladies and girls barely out of diapers. Sure it's one of them."

Al gave her a big smile. To me, it seemed forced. "Cassie, would you please help us? As part of our research, we're doing a cross-sectional survey of Mosby's residents. I see a lot of your customers are using disposable coffee cups. When they finish, could you collect, oh, maybe a dozen of them for us? We're only interested in Mosby locals, people whose names you could write on the cups." He squeezed her arm and flashed her another dashing smile.

Every police procedural show I have ever seen on television has a wise old cop getting his hands on a coffee cup so he can run a DNA test on a perp. How could Al be so damn obvious? Cassie might be ineptly confidential and intrusive, but she wasn't a dummy. Surely, she would call him out. But no, she went glassy-eyed and beamed at him.

Cassie covered Al's hand with her own and pressed his fingers into her arm. "Well, I don't know if that would be right. It's an invasion of privacy, isn't it? Wouldn't that be a Facebooky kind of thing?" She didn't let go of Al's hand.

Al squeezed again. "No, Cassie, it's science. It'll be fine."

She hesitated barely a moment. "Well, I guess okay. But you can't let anyone know. I'll do it because you're the one who asked, Al."

"Great. I'll come and look at the cups. Tomorrow, perhaps?" He gave her arm a final squeeze and Cassie nodded, her eyes bright. "But first," he added, "we have a few pressing errands to run. I'll see you tomorrow then."

Al left his coffee untouched and walked out of the shop.

When I caught up with him, he had waylaid two women at the crosswalk. "I hear there was an incident out at Turnell Mill on Saturday," he was saying. "Do you know anything about it?" One woman tightened her purse under her arm and looked apprehensive, but the other began to talk at a breakneck pace.

"Why, yes. I think everybody knows about the explosion. I have a friend whose brother knows someone on the EMS squad, and he says it was just awful. A bunch of people were having a birthday party for their children, and the mill blew up. It just blew up, bam, just like that. They all got themselves killed—the children, the parents, just terrible."

"And these people were ...?"

"I hear they were all part of a religious cult," the woman continued. "One of those strange, Pentecostal splinter groups, the kind without a real minister. Oh, but I don't think that had anything to do with the accident. Jesus just decided it was time for them to go."

Al bounced off a little bow and said, "Thank you, ma'am. You've been very helpful."

"Oh, I can tell you more, believe me. Why, I heard that they were so badly burned that ..." But by that time Al had crossed the street, searching for his next target.

Al next intercepted a balding obese man who had just parked his SUV in front of the post office. "Sir, can you tell me anything about the people who died Saturday at Turnell Mill?"

The man jammed his cell phone into his belt holder and blew through his gray mustache. "You're damn right I can," he huffed. "Somebody needs to pay for this. The owner of the mill, the gas company, the city. Maybe all three. Everyone uses gas in this town."

"It was an accident, then?"

"Well, it sure as hell wasn't a terrorist attack, I can tell you that. Where that friggin' horseshit idea came from, I can't imagine."

"Who died in the fire?"

The man's face was glowing as ruddy as a habanero salsa. "Not a fire. An explosion. I heard a whole family of farmers got killed. It's a damn crime. They should find who's responsible and lock them the hell up."

"I'm with you," Al agreed. He motioned to me, and we crossed the street again to the one-story police station. Behind us, the balding man sputtered more complaints to the empty sidewalk.

"What the hell are you doing?" I asked.

"Just what it looks like. Running more tests."

"That theater piece with Cassie, the thing about the cups—how'd you get her to agree so easily?"

"It takes practice. Charm is a basic life skill. Teach yourself how to fake sincerity, and you've got it made."

"That was more than charm, Al. You manipulated her."

"*Manipulation* is an unfortunate choice of words, Fogger. Let's see what our lady police chief says today. You take the lead. If you haven't noticed, she has a thing for you. She'll respond better to your awkward schoolboy approach."

When we entered the red brick building, Lauren Klout was leaning over the dispatcher's shoulder, staring at a computer screen. She looked up and smiled. "Mister Grace, Doctor Amon. What's up?"

I gave her my sincerest smile and said, "We wanted to check up on your investigation, Chief. Has anything new turned up?"

"Done and done. State forensics has some details to fill in on the explosion, but we've pretty much put a wrap on it. You're free to go whenever you want." She twirled a ballpoint pen in her fingers and spoke into space, not meeting my eyes. Her lips turned upward at the corners, and she added, "If you want to stick around Mosby for a while, Mister Grace, there's a lot of good things to enjoy here."

I ignored the invitation, stared at the floor to recover my focus, exhaled a way-too-melodramatic sigh, and said. "Chief, we need to speak to you in private."

Lauren's smile disappeared. She stared at us and scratched the bridge of her nose. The half-stub of her ring finger made it an arresting image.

"It's important," I added. My voice sounded lame.

Lauren opened her office door and held it until we walked in. When she sat down, her face held the expression of someone putting up with a racist joke. She used a finger to push her cheek into her teeth so she could get a good grip. "Well?" she said through her teeth.

"What happened at Turnell Mill was not an accident." My words sounded strange to my ears. "They set themselves on fire. They did it deliberately."

She gave an amused chuckle and let her smile broaden to show she was in on the joke. Her smile faded bit by bit as Al and I remained silent. She flexed and unflexed her fingers into a fist as she watched me, disregarding Al completely, then stood and kicked her chair into the shelves behind her, tumbling a framed citation and a row of stacked ledgers. Her hand began to drift unconsciously toward her holster.

"What kind of sick game are you playing at?"

A thrill of self-assurance took hold of me. I leaned across the desk to emphasize my seriousness. "This is not some bullshit game, Lauren. Listen. I watched the Hatches kill themselves. You took my testimony about the fire. You recorded Al's, too. Read it. This entire town wants to pretend they didn't kill themselves. They did."

"The fuck you say. The gas main blew up, pure and simple."

"You took notes when you interviewed us at the mill. Go ahead. Check them."

Without shifting her attention away from me, Lauren opened a drawer and pulled out a thick daybook. She held it in front of her nose so she could watch me as she flipped through the pages and read. Her eyes widened. She flipped forward, read further, muttered "Shit," and sank into her chair.

"It's a mass phenomenon of some sort," said Al. "I might discover what it is if we can get your help."

"Right. Hold on, so's I can get my thoughts pulled together." Lauren took a set of stapled sheets from her in-basket and handed it to me. The typed cover sheet read, "Incident Report H3181."

"Read this."

I scanned quickly to confirm what I'd already expected and handed it to Al, who grunted and put the folder back in the basket. The report described a gas explosion with multiple casualties. Eyewitness interviews, including our own, were all edited. They confirmed the sudden and tragic loss of life, but they omitted the strange behavior of the Hatch family, the setting of the fire, and the attempts by those outside the mill to save their loved ones.

Lauren Klout used her knuckles to thump her ledger. "I

sure as hell recognize my own damn handwriting. I dated questioning you at 1832 hours on Saturday afternoon. And, yeah, what I wrote in the ledger isn't in the final report. Hell, it's not in my *memory*." She ran her hand over her scalp, deliberately mussing her hair so a straggling lock dropped over her forehead. "There isn't a person in town, and that includes my officers and the guys from EMS and the state troopers, who doesn't believe this was an accident. But I see my notes, with your words." She swallowed and made a face as if a sour taste had swept into her mouth. "You say you can explain this, Doctor?"

Al's look had more uncertainty in it than I expected. "If I could get a clue about what happened inside the mill, I think I could answer that."

"My buddy, the county coroner is hacking her way through the autopsies. She calls it a Pro Formal. That's Latin words for 'filling out the forms.' If you think it'll help, I can get you in to see the assembly line. She owes me a favor."

I was so far outside my usual limits that I could no longer see the shore, so I said, "What the hell. For sure. Do it."

Lauren turned her back on us while she made the call, leaning over and speaking low into the phone. The elegant curve of her spine beneath her uniform made my breath catch. I pondered her invitation to stay in town. Something about this woman threw me off balance, and right now I needed to concentrate. It didn't help when she glanced over her shoulder and repeated the same knowing smile that had unnerved me earlier. A deliberate, private smile, somewhere between a smirk and an invitation; a glimpse of white teeth between her hungry lips. Damn me, I welcomed it.

Lauren hung up the phone and said, "Tomorrow morning after nine. Meet me here around ten and I'll drive you out there. Ever been to an autopsy?" I shook my head. "Don't eat a big breakfast," she said with a lilt in her voice, never looking at Al.

"Chief," said Al. "While I'm trying to fit all this together, it would help if I could collect DNA samples from people in town. Could you help me set that up?"

"That's a shit idea, Doctor Amon. Getting everybody in a lather while they're still confused about what happened? I don't think so. So, no."

Lauren walked us to the door and held it for a moment. "Look," she said. "These screwed-up stories about what happened. Until we dope it out, keep this confusion to yourself. Way too many versions bouncing around right now." Only then did she push the door open.

As the three of us stepped out of the police station, a breeze wafted down the street, ruffling the crepe myrtles down Washington Street and corkscrewing the umbrellas that shaded the wrought-iron tables outside the coffee shop. The air smelled of pine ash. Cassie Wrenner sat beneath one of the beige umbrellas across the street, watching us with her arms crossed. A man in ivory-colored slacks and a black suit jacket sat at the table with her, eating a sandwich. He could have stepped out of a full-page Armani ad in *GQ* magazine. I thought it odd that he'd wear a sports jacket on such a warm day. As she stood, Cassie whispered something to the man and mussed his hair. She nodded at us and raised one hand in a half-hearted wave, fingers wide, and when Lauren turned away to check the traffic, Cassie made a hasty, invisible-phone gesture and pointed at me.

Lauren turned back and grunted. "Cassie has eyes on you, Fogger Grace," she said. "She has spies all over our little town, bird-dogging your steps. Could be she's craving a change in her dull life." No question, it was a smirk on Lauren's lips. "Could be, too, she's doing damage control. You know she owns Turnell Mill? Owns the city council and the mayor, too."

I cut my eyes back to Cassie on the other side of the busy street. Her frown suggested that she knew what Lauren was saying. A sharp gust made the sidewalk umbrellas jump. The man in the dark suit, oblivious, never looked up from eating his sandwich, and when a second gust began to lift the umbrella partway out of its concrete base, Cassie leaned over and steadied the pole. The canopy popped in her grasp, then the wind blew itself out in a single surge, and the sound of rustling of leaves and awnings died away. In the sudden lull, the grumble of a truck engine made me look toward the intersection, where cars waited for the traffic light to change. Cassie made a fist and raised her thumb to her ear again. She nodded earnestly, as if that would compel me to call. I ignored her.

The sound of motor exhaust rose again, and I realized that the pickup truck waiting at the intersection was gunning its engine, daring the car in front of it to forget the light and get out of the way. The truck was a huge, six-wheeled monster with quad wheels in the back and dual exhausts mounted above the cab. A red-and-black Georgia Bulldog sticker had peeled down from the rhino bars mounted in front of the radiator, blinding the bulldog's eye. For some reason this seemed deadly significant. Engine revs made the windshield shake, concealing the driver behind coruscating reflections. The driver gunned his engine again, and the truck lurched forward and whacked into the rear bumper of the car in front. As it did, it cocked its wheels to the left to prepare for a jack-rabbit launch.

I had a sinking, certain feeling it was aiming at us.

10

Lauren said something about Cassie Wrenner and the property she owned around Mosby. I wasn't paying attention. From the corner of my eye, I saw the traffic light change and the pickup hit the gas. It leaped into the intersection, swerving around an oncoming car that had not completed its turn.

"Hey," I said. "Hey, watch out." Al and Lauren paid no attention.

The deep bass of the truck's engine vibrated in my chest, and I flashed on the image of our bodies mashed into the rhino bars. Without thinking, I stepped forward and threw my arm across Lauren's chest, knocking her behind me. I turned toward her instead of watching the oncoming truck, and when I heard the screech of tires, I braced for impact.

For an instant I thought we'd been hit, and I staggered forward into Lauren. It was all in my head. The pickup slammed on its brakes as an oncoming sedan veered into the intersection from the opposite direction, panicked, and stalled. The pickup driver, a stunned woman with a glass necklace, sat for a moment in front of her steering wheel, covering her eyes with both hands. Then she shuddered, yanked the car into the right-hand lane, and sped away, her diesel exhaust hammering the police station windows, her upper body leaning forward at a forty-five-degree angle against the steering wheel.

"What's this?" Lauren asked, pushing my arm away from her chest with a grin of honest amusement. Her breath smelled of wintergreen.

"That woman," I said. "The pickup. It was aiming right at us." My mouth was as dry as stone.

Lauren bit the inside of her cheek. "Town's full of cowgirls in the afternoon. You get used to it."

"No, Lauren. She tried to hit us. She almost did."

"You're a sweet man, Fogger Grace, but relax. And don't make sudden moves when you're close to me. I'm a trained killer." She added a snort to show she was joking. But I didn't feel at all relaxed. I started to protest her brush-off, but when I looked at her face, I thought better of it. Al and I thanked her, promised we would be back the next morning, and crossed the street while we had a four-way stop.

"Did you see that, Al?" I insisted. "Seriously, you saw that truck try to hit us."

Al was absorbed in thought. He had not seen the pickup truck or noticed it over-revving. When I described what had happened, he, too, brushed me off. The gears were grinding away in his head, and he wouldn't let anything penetrate his thoughts.

Not me. My apprehension amplified the noise of every car behind us, and I nearly pissed myself when a donked 1975 Chevy Impala with twenty-four-inch wheel rims came up fast, first-generation rap music blasting from a 120-watt sound system, the subwoofer pulsing so hard the car's windows boogied with each vibration. After that, I caught myself looking over my shoulder whenever a truck rumbled by.

Al opened up when we got back to his Kia. "I know it's asking a lot, Fogger, but would you go with me on one more cold call?"

"Is it another Ronnie Millman? My fillings ached just to be in the same room with him. He makes me seem normal."

"It shouldn't be anything close to that. These are twin sisters, reclusive types. Only seen once a week in church. Daughters Furlong Hatch planted a long time ago on one of his vulnerable cousins."

"Wouldn't they have been at the mill? We should look for them in the morgue."

"They won't be there. I have the reunion invitation list. They're not on it."

I stopped and stared at him. "The police haven't found an invitation list yet. Are you going to tell me how *you* got one?"

"Not yet. They live north on 441. Not far. Come on; if you're not with me, there's no telling who I'll decide I am or what I'm doing in this dull country town."

Another twenty-minute trip with Al. I listened to B. B. King do three different versions of "Why I Sing the Blues." All three fit my mood.

Mary and Maisie Hatch lived in a gray, double-wide trailer at the end of a winding dirt road. The trailer sat on cinder blocks at the top of a small rise and was girdled by an extensive vegetable garden. When we stopped, the dust from our wheels blew onto a clothesline behind the trailer, where several dresses and towels hung in the late afternoon sun. We walked up the sloping access ramp and stood in front of the aluminum screened door. Through the screen, we could hear an evangelical preacher on the radio asking God for protection against the Antichrist and his earthly representative, the president of the United States. Al looked at me and nodded. When I knocked, the door and the sides of the trailer rattled.

The sisters came to the door together. Both wore dresses that probably looked stylish on Sunday mornings. I wondered if we had caught them on the way out, or if they spent all their time looking forward to visitors. For a moment, I felt that all four of us belonged in an old movie in which two gentlemen arrive to pick up their dates. When we introduced ourselves, they invited us in.

The sisters must have been in their seventies and were a handsome pair. I imagined the days past, when young men would catch their breath as Mary and Maisie walked by. Perhaps even today, an old classmate of theirs would mutter a blessing because he had once imagined himself bookended naked between them.

Al eagerly accepted Maisie's offer of sweet tea. He waited until they sat down, then took a seat on the threadbare sofa next to Mary. He went right to the point. "There was a Hatch family reunion in Mosby the day before yesterday. Do you know what happened there?"

Maisie did all the talking. No, they had heard nothing. Didn't often get down to the city. No reason to, she said. So we told them.

"God's will," said Maisie. "We didn't hold much with the part of the family from down south in the city. Only time they ever came to see us was when someone died and they wanted a carry-in casserole. That, and when they kept pestering about that fool reunion. God blessed us that we didn't give in to them."

"Praise Jesus," said Mary. "He's taken them home." She took a sip of tea and affirmed her judgment with a pigeon-like nod.

I had met several sets of twins while researching a column once. Communication between Mary and Maisie modeled the secret language of other twin pairs, a matter of subtle changes in posture and voice. I picked up on an undercurrent of sadness but nothing that suggested unholy commands between them. We sat in silence for about a minute. Having thanked Jesus for letting them escape the disaster, the sisters had nothing more to say about the death of their blood relatives.

Al wouldn't give it up. "In the last few weeks, did you ever think you might change your mind and go to the reunion?"

"My goodness, no," said Maisie. "Why would we? Those other people have their own lives, same as we do. We don't mess in other folks' affairs. We're sorry they died, but if that's what the Lord wanted…"

"Well, have you been hearing strange voices, people ordering you to do things?"

The sisters sat up straight and exchanged a secret message. As they did, Al casually reached past his own tea glass and picked up Mary's. The sisters looked at each other, and Maisie signaled with a graceful fluttering of her fingers. Mary nodded in emphatic agreement. They gave us wee smiles and stood up together. "Thank you and goodbye," said Maisie. "Have a blessed day."

Al attempted to reclaim the interview. "I'm sorry we alarmed you with the news about your relatives. Perhaps we can come back another day."

Maisie drew herself up and said, "They must lay in the beds they made. They must eat the food they prepared."

I couldn't guess what that meant, but I read the stiffness in their spines. Before I could stammer another question, we were outside and the twins had closed the door. They hadn't noticed Al's theft of an iced tea glass.

Al and I had a late dinner at the slow-motion café. I can't remember what we ate, but I remember Al's evasion. I asked him only once to open up about his theory of the Hatch suicide. He repeated his vague clue about Dionysus but stonewalled on unpacking the idea. I asked again if he was talking about mass hallucination.

"It's not a hallucination," he said. "The Hatches weren't imagining things. They were under orders."

"How?" I sputtered. "What kind of compulsion is strong enough to make a father kill his child?"

He clammed up, refusing to answer any more questions until he had "more data." Maybe tomorrow, he promised, after we saw the county coroner.

I refused Al's offer of another bourbon and instead took a long walk along Mosby's backstreets. Dusk brought a buzz of insect sounds and a mixed chorus from the pine warblers roosting in the pecan trees. These were sounds I never heard in the city, but the past two days had moved Atlanta so far away in both space and experience that I might as well have been walking on Neptune.

I awoke in the night in a strange bed in a town where I

didn't want to be. When I swung my legs out from under the covers and sat on the edge of the bed, the moonlight falling through the bedroom window made an irregular square on the floor, just where I had planted my bare feet. I was thirty-three, but in the moonlight my feet could have been those of an aged man who never took off his shoes: pale and wrinkled and traced with vulnerable blue veins lying just below the skin's surface. Life is a game played at a swift pace. No halftimes.

I gathered up my bedspread and walked out onto the porch where the two retrievers stirred briefly to give me sleepy nods. The air was cool and quiet.

Maybe one day I would escape the restlessness that pulsed in my temples, the feeling that I was trapped in the wrong body. For now, the insecurity made me crawl under the bench and sandwich myself between the Goldens, pulling them close and breathing in their yeasty sent. The female huffed and snugged her head under my arm, more like a cat than a large, shaggy dog. Her warmth did nothing to calm the turbulence in my heart.

Laying there in the dark, I recalled a Byelorussian movie from a film class at Emory. The pivotal scene in *Come and See* occurs when a Nazi SS death squad forces a partisan teenager to watch as they murder all the people in his village. The squad forces the peasant families into a barn and sets it on fire. When the desperate families lift their children to the barn's small windows and push them out, the *Einsatsgruppen* stuff them back into the flames. The roiling smoke takes the shape of a freight train embarked for a place called freedom. And the boy must watch.

That night, in my dreams, I was that boy.

11

The Nazi storm troopers camped all night in my head. I woke face down on the heart-of-pine bedroom floor, one hand tight around the leg of my bed. When I tried to uncurl my fingers, they didn't respond but throbbed as if I'd been in a fistfight with an armored truck. My face was so grooved from sleeping on the floor that when I shaved, I nicked myself. The sight of blood on my cheek froze my hand. I stared into the bathroom mirror, watching the thin streak of red mingle with the shaving cream, thinking how lucky I was to be using a safety razor. What if I'd used an old-fashioned straight razor? It would be easy to draw the blade across my throat and watch the blood gush into the sink. How easy that would be. I could visualize the blade sliding easily into my jugular.

Where the ever-loving hell had that come from?

I banished the image, stunned by thoughts of self-destruction. Something about suicide-plagued Mosby had crept into my thoughts. I pushed it away. The anticipation of pursuing this strange case, and of seeing more of Lauren Klout, let me hope the day would improve.

I ate an all-American breakfast of pancakes, eggs, and orange juice, trusting that sheer calories would allow me to compartmentalize the Hatch suicides. It didn't work. The ghosts in the smoke-filled closet scrabbled at the door and would not stay quiet. I got out my tablet and started a list of questions:

Why the mass suicide?

Why only Hatch pure-bloods?

What perverse chemistry makes Mosby's citizens deny the suicide and insist on accident?

What are Al Amon's real motives?

What does Ronnie Millman's bizarre behavior tell us?

I turned my tablet off when Al joined me. He came to the table with a brisk step and a cheerful smile that made me wonder if he'd once again forgotten everything that happened. Damn, if he didn't slap me on the back! I fought the urge to smack the side of his head to get him on track.

I waited until he got a cup of coffee and a bagel. "Think hard, Professor Amon. Do you remember what happened here two days ago?"

"Okay, Fogger. It's smart of you to check on me, but I'm too happy to take offense." His grin tightened. "So, no, I didn't slip back into the gas explosion fable. I remember everything that happened. But listen, I think I've got a handle on this process we're living through."

"Process!" I said. "Of all the weak words you could choose, you call this a *process*? It's a shitstorm."

"Whatever. Call it a phenomenon or a wonder. Whatever works for you. American families don't commit ritual suicide.

Mass hallucinations just don't occur this way, not so convincingly. Not across an entire population. This is unprecedented, and the reason I came to Mosby, the theory I've been working on for years, is proving out."

"And now you're holding back again, Al. Cut the elaborate happy dance and get to the point. Give me the straight story, or we can part company. I can follow my own instincts."

Al lowered his voice. "Murmuration," he said. His self-congratulatory smile was even more exasperating.

"Speaking quietly?" I replied.

The smile disappeared. "No, dammit. When you see birds wheeling together in synchronized flight, that's murmuration. Lots of species exhibit this behavior. Starlings fly in flocks of thousands. They make split-second, unpredictable changes in direction, swoop and turn and never run into each other. Schooling fish do it, too. Look here."

Al pulled out his cell phone and made a few quick selections, then handed it to me. A video on the tiny screen showed a huge flock of birds moving in an intricate dance, weaving endless, wavelike patterns in the air. The camera zoomed in, and I could see individual birds in the dense grouping, each turning in a synchronized ballet so perfectly they seemed connected with invisible wires.

"Now," he said. "Let's compare." He took the phone back, punched in new instructions, and handed it to me again. This time, the screen showed a foot race: hundreds of lanky women in what must have been a marathon. The densely packed contestants jostled for position, fouled each other, sometimes shoved their competitors aside. I watched as one runner came down on the heel of the person in front, sending her skidding onto the pavement. Another woman tumbled over the first, and soon there were half a dozen bodies for slower runners to dodge.

"How do the birds do this without running into each other?" I asked.

"Oh, that's the rub, isn't it? We've figured out that starlings keep track of the nearest seven birds around them, and their reactions are so fast that they never collide. But that doesn't fully explain how it works, because starlings in other parts of the flock turn at exactly the same moment. There's invisible communication going that we can't see. Other animals—ants, for instance—use different systems."

"They track the other ants around them?"

Al gave an exasperated sigh. "No." He sighed again and thinned his lips. "No," he repeated. "Individual ants are practically brainless, but as a colony they can accomplish complex tasks. They use chemical markers and pheromones to give instructions to each other. That, plus some feedback mechanism we haven't been able to decode. The more pheromones they lay down, the more intense the message becomes, the more the message gets reinforced."

"I get it. It's sort of like when bees tell each other where to find flowers."

"Dammit, Fogger. Stop guessing and listen. Bees communicate with physical signs. They do a waggle dance. It's not the same thing. Ants use chemical messaging. So do humans. We release pheromones. They're like hormones, but they act outside the body, in the air. Men secrete them to attract women, and vice versa. They absolutely affect the behavior of other people." He spoke earnestly, but in an uncalculated way, his innocent delight in his research coming out not as pride, but as intoxicating knowledge he was compelled to share.

I saw where Al was headed, but his theory struck me as feeble. "I've heard of pheromones, but aren't they very weak, like a scent? They don't do anything more than elevate sexual tension, do they?"

"You're right, up to a point. The chemical strength varies with the sender and how much they want someone to get the message. And it's all involuntary. Pheromones are fleeting and volatile, but they permit us to signal each other for sexual intercourse, to exchange emotional information, and—get this—they modify our cognition." Al sat back in his chair and opened his hands as if to say, Voilà! His broad smile returned.

"Neat theory," I said, "but a human being can't send a signal strong enough to convince an entire town that the Hatch family died in a freak gas explosion." Then the full implication of his theory hit me. I thought hard before I continued. "That's not your real point, is it?"

Al waited for me to go on.

"The big issue isn't how the message gets transmitted," I said. "It's what the message makes us *do*. What we're talking about is actually a command, something you must do because you want to do it! You think a pheromone message, from another person, could make eighty people kill themselves." I made this a statement, not a question.

"Go ahead," he said. "Tell me I'm full of shit. Then give me a better explanation."

"But how could a simple chemical message have enough force to make people commit suicide?"

Al's smile dropped away. "It could not be a 'simple' chemical message. The sender would probably have to repeat it many times, put down layers of reinforcement, unless there's a way to boost the signal strength." He drew a halting breath. "The person who sent this message would have to be very strong. Very strong."

No, I didn't think Al's theory was crazy. I had seen his single, shouted word freeze a fist in its flight. Three people who meant to hurt me had suddenly stopped, wished me a nice day, and walked away. And that meant...

"You can do this yourself, can't you? The guy outside the coffee shop—you made him stop with a word. With a command." The statement sounded ridiculous, but I believed it.

"That's what it looks like. I never managed that trick before. But in fact, I got beat up quite a few times in high school because I got girls to pay attention to me when they should have ignored the skinny nerd. You remember how Ronnie Millman's aunt said his nickname was Mister Charisma? That was me. Unfortunately, when I needed to get the boyfriends to stop kicking my ass, the charm expertise evaporated."

My expression must have relayed respect. Al chuckled and added, "If that's what happened. If I got that fellow to stall his punch, it was a first. Could be that stress brings out the talent."

"Wait a minute, Al. There was no time between the start of that punch and the aborting of it. None. Can a pheromone signal work that quickly?"

Al's eyebrows rose, and worry lines appeared in his forehead. "No, definitely not. That's more like the speed of a synapse firing. The mechanism..." He broke off, weighed his thoughts, and started over. "There must be an instantaneous transmission. We've been studying other kinds of signals..."

Al's worry lines were like precise furrows cut by a miniature plow. I waited for him to flesh out his speculation, counting four distinct furrows as a measure of his deliberation.

Al rubbed the top of his head and said, "The mechanism would need to be instantaneous, similar to an electrical burst or…" …his eyes opened wide… "a synapse firing. Like an electrochemical signal in the brain."

He gulped down the rest of his coffee and began to pace the small breakfast room, holding his elbow in the cupped palm of one hand, his finger ticking off his points with abrupt, stabbing motions. I could imagine him lecturing a room of undergraduates with exactly the same mannerisms.

"The brain is an electrochemical device. Every electrical device generates a field. What if the talent permits a person to manipulate others' electrical fields? Dogs seem to know when a master dies, even at great distances. Birds and whales can sense faint magnetic fields and navigate by them. What if a human could do the same thing?"

"Could that explain why the Hatches killed themselves?" I said. "Something like mind control?"

"Mind control! Don't be ridiculous, Fogger. This isn't some science fiction movie with telepathy and lightning bolts shooting out of your ass. The human body couldn't generate signals with enough intensity to take control of another person's body. The energy required would boil your brain. Where the hell are you getting this from?"

"Damn me, Al. You're the one who brought up firing synapses and electrochemical signals. You're the one who claims he can get a woman turned on by making a wish." I had another thought. "A skill like this wouldn't show up without a reason. Maybe this is an evolutionary response to improve the species. God knows, we need improvement. How would this ability make human beings better?"

The look on Al's face told me I had disappointed him again. "Listen to me," he said. "First of all, evolution doesn't have a purpose. That's a common misunderstanding. Evolution doesn't seek to improve anything. It's a crapshoot. Every time a new child is created, our great big grab-bag of genes starts churning."

"I know that. We get a mix of our parent's genes."

"More than that. Chromosomes drop out or get duplicated, or they get assembled in the wrong order. Most genetic mistakes never make it to birth. Two out of three fertilized eggs get rejected in what's called a *spontaneous abortion*. They go down the toilet and women don't even notice it. This is something the pro-lifers don't quite understand. God performs a lot more abortions than people do. But some of these genetic blunders go to term, and if the random variation helps the new individual survive better, then the trait can get passed on. Most don't."

"I get that, but why would an ability to communicate with pheromones, or electrical signals, or whatever it is—why would this help a person survive better?"

Al got a faraway look. "I've thought about this a lot. All I have is speculation, but the world population has doubled since I was born. We've run tests where we let rat populations increase unchecked. Younger rats band in groups and attack others. Males try to mate with other males. Eventually, they cannibalize each other. Denser populations mean more forests get cut down, more plastic gets into the oceans, more economic refugees fight their way to the next border, more people drink up a dwindling supply of fresh water. It's at moments when a population is under extreme environmental stress that the new ability delivered by a random gene can spell the difference between extinction and survival."

"I'm with you," I said. "But would murmuration fix this?"

Al's eyes lost their dreamy look. "A person who can navigate this choking swamp of bodies—with instantaneous communications or by influencing the people around him—would have a big advantage over the rest of us."

"Maybe," I said, "but the real solution is to reduce population enough that we aren't fighting over the last acre of land and the last glass of water. Plagues used to take care of that. What if murmuration is a super-effective weapon to reduce population?"

"Hell, Fogger. If you want to go all doomsday on me, consider this. What if a Hatch with this random gene wakes up to its full potential? He realizes he isn't only lucky, he can give orders to other people that they must obey. He's the alpha member of the pack. What does he think about the rest of us, then? Aren't we just obsolete normals?"

I'd watched too many *X-Men* movies not to know the answer. "You're describing a superman surrounded by annoying chimps," I said. "Chances are, he'd view us with contempt."

Al nodded solemnly. "Right. And that one superman might not want any of his cousins competing with him. We're talking about an ability that's a light year beyond my modest success with women. I can't speculate until I know a lot more about how this new upgrade works. I need more data. Don't take your guesswork any further until we've heard what the coroner has to say."

"This doesn't require guesswork," I said. "History tells us what happens. Someone becomes immune to the plague and survives. Someone else invents gunpowder and kills off the competition. Every time someone gains extraordinary power, weaker people get screwed."

That thought gnawed on me. Humans have preyed on each other throughout history. Track anyone's family tree a few generations back, and you'll find plenty to be ashamed of, especially if you're one of those people who believe in collective guilt, or follow a religion that says you must atone for the sins of some ancestor who lived seven generations earlier. One look at my family photographs confirms that my bloodstream runs thick with both slave-owners and slaves. I have never submitted a sample to one of those genetic testing services, but it's likely that my DNA has traces of conquistadores and Chinese railroad builders, starving Irish immigrants and interned Japanese shopkeepers. My forbears were the African slaves and their European overseers, the conqueror and the conquered. All true, but genes don't define who I am. I do.

In the long history of the human species there have always been people who dreamed of a society where men and women treat their neighbors decently, where what is essential about a person is who they are, not who their ancestors may have been. Sure, I hear you say. Most of those dreamers were flawed. They did not always practice what they espoused. But I wanted the better world they dreamed of. And I could pursue that world, as long as a superman didn't alter the playing field.

We waited until mid-morning before walking to the police station to meet Lauren Klout. As we walked, I might have soaked up Mosby's tranquil streets, so unlike Atlanta's constant buzz, but instead I unclipped my cell phone and googled *murmuration*. I adopted Al's slow pace and stumbled along, the tiny screen held in front of my nose, fascinated by silent videos of birds in flight, tiny beings sweeping the sky in response to obscure programs. The flocks were constantly in motion, weaving one intricate statement after another, never holding a fixed form, as if God couldn't decide what He wanted, and had compelled the flock to dance forever. The designs begged for music, but no tune I hummed caught the sense of balanced control.

12

As soon as he slid into the back of Lauren Klout's police cruiser, Al began to ask about unexplained events in Mosby's history. Lauren shrugged and told him we only had a short drive to the coroner's office, but he pushed on.

"Just give me one incident, Chief. A death that made little sense. People acting out of the ordinary. Anything."

Lauren pushed down on the accelerator harder and kept her eyes fixed on the road. "Well, there was this freaky single-car accident out on the bypass last year. Molly Yearling drove her and her fifteen-year-old daughter into the side of Bob Kenny's dentist office. They weren't wearing their seatbelts. Killed instantly."

"And why did that seem unusual?"

Lauren's sigh made me suspect she might have had a personal relationship with the victims. "The dentist office is three hundred feet off the road," she said. "We had a statement from a customer who'd just been through a root canal and was sitting in her car feelin' sorry for herself, said she saw Molly stop the car, line it up, and drive right over the berm, across the parking lot, and flat into the building. Never backed off the gas. Didn't hit the brakes. But this witness was pumped up with painkillers, so who could be sure?" Although a dashboard-mounted computer screen and a keyboard separated us, I saw her blue blouse rise and fall as her breathing picked up. Al's questioning had pushed on a raw memory.

He began to ask another question, but I beat him to it. "Were this woman and her daughter related to Furlong Hatch?"

Lauren looked at me with undisguised suspicion. She had not made the connection. "No, Fogger. Least, I don't think so, but I get the picture. That what you've been sniffin' after, Doctor Amon?"

Instead of answering, Al put his face up to the wire mesh prisoner screen that separated the front seat from the back and said, "What about other deaths in the Hatch line?"

There was a delay while Lauren decided whether to answer. We passed a dead fawn, thrown from the road and entangled in a wire pasture fence. Its dappled hide showed no signs of damage, but its lifeless legs stuck stiff and straight into the air. The natural imbalances of power that intruded into my thinking were always just a glance away. Half a dozen brown-and-white goats worked the field on the other side of the fence. They had stripped the land bare of all but a few young gingko trees. If someone didn't move the goats soon, they would tug up the roots and strip the bark.

"I got this police chief job three years ago, May 7," said Lauren. "Youngest chief in north Georgia. Same day as that, the high school's senior class president walked right in front of a logging truck on 441. Parked his car on the blind side of a curve and waited, then jumped right into the road when the logger came around the turn. He was a Hatch boy, and that was my first fatal accident. And that's enough questions for now, thank you very much."

We pulled off Greensboro Road at a one-story, aluminum-sided building. A neat, hand-painted sign on the door read, "Gunner's Deer Processing: Hunter's Welcome." The walls gave off a muted ticking sound as they heated in the morning sun.

"Coroner's office can only handle two or three dead at a time," Lauren explained. "We're using Gunner's lockers for the overflow."

The inside of the building was unfinished, its walls decorated with antler sets and mounted deer heads. A man looked up from his magazine as we entered. He pointed to a large door behind a rack of camo hunting suits.

There were about three dozen people inside the twenty-by-twenty cooler. Only three of them were alive. The arctic air smelled as if someone had cooked chili there a week earlier and burned it. Two figures in full bunny suits worked at a steel lab table just inside the cooler door, their gender hidden by yellow breathing masks. I glimpsed a blackened corpse on the table, its arms and legs curled into a fetal position like a child playing hide-and-seek, trying to make itself as small as possible. Coroner's assistants tweezered flakes of charred flesh into Ziplock bags. The cadaver's skull was split open, whether by heat or examination I couldn't tell, but its exposed interior walls were dark with soot, its dreams extinguished. More black body bags lay on the stained concrete floor, jammed so tightly together that I was forced to step carefully to avoid tripping over them.

A short woman looked up from her work and nodded at Lauren. Loose strands of her dull brown hair escaped from under the pink-and-white shower cap pulled over her head. She wore oversized garden gloves and had stuck a peanut-colored cigarette filter into each nostril. A lighted cigarette hung from her lips. The smoke curling up into her eyes made her squint. Her black lab apron had white cartoon stick figures of sprawled bodies on it, a joke of sorts, I guess, because the words underneath the cartoon said, "Our bodies of work speak for themselves."

The coroner paid no attention to me and Al but put her hands on her hips and said, "So here you got 'em, Klout. Twenty fried crispies. Whaddya want to see?"

"Not me, Alice. These guys are with Georgia Tech. They ask the questions."

Alice took a deep puff on her cigarette and winked at me. "Whaddya say, handsome? You're an improvement on my regular visitors. How can I help you?"

When Al stepped forward and held out his hand, Alice raised hers and twiddled her gloved fingers. "Don't think so, lover. Are you the muckety-muck of this team, and if so, why are you here wasting my time?"

"I have a PhD in genetics, ma'am. Have you been typing these people? DNA typing?"

"Bet your ass, Mister Yellow Jacket. State of Georgia doesn't trust dental records anymore. Everything gets DNA backup. Lucky for us these poor critters didn't burn all the way to the core. There's plenty of soft organs we can pull from. We're just about done. Got a business card? I'll email you my records."

"Wait a minute," I said. "Aren't there privacy issues about this? Can we get data that easily?"

Alice squared her shoulders and faced Lauren. "If we're going to pussyfoot around about the details, then fuck it. You said this was off the record. This one favor, you said, and we'd be even."

"Easy-like, Alice," said Lauren. "We can get even if you'll just unpucker. I'll make sure none of this flows back on you. Just answer their questions."

Alice lit another cigarette from her stub and drew in a long lungful. A far-off look shone in her eyes. "Okay," she said. "What else?"

"Cause of death?" asked Al.

"Aha. Ha, ha, ha." Alice coughed and bent over, her arms out at her sides to keep from falling. "Oh, boy. Where'd you get this comedian, Klout? Ha!" She coughed again and followed immediately with another deep drag.

One look at Lauren and she sobered up. "Okay, okay. Cause of death is a total cocktail. You got asphyxiation, thermal damage, projectile damage, and explosive tissue damage. All four in no particular order. Also, some cyanide poisoning. No variation from one body to the next, except for one."

"Cyanide," I said. "Someone poisoned them?"

"Not the way you think, handsome. Not deliberate. Cyanide is a toxic byproduct of combustion. It's normal in house fires and other contained events. Done now?"

"What was the other one, the exception you mentioned?"

Alice shelved the flippant act, dropped her cigarette on the floor, and crushed it with her polyurethane clog, grinding her foot into the concrete floor. "Over here," she said. She walked to the back of the locker and knelt next to a plastic tarp.

I knew there was another body under the tarp. I prepared

myself to face a burned corpse. But my few days in Mosby should have taught me that nothing was that simple. I wasn't ready, and it wasn't simple at all.

Three bodies had fused into a single mass, an interwoven jumble of arms, legs, and heads. I expected to see a sterilized pile of burned sticks, perhaps the pristine white of an exposed bone, but under the blackened crust was the pink of cooked flesh, and the shock of a viscous yellow liquid that leaked from tormented limbs and pooled on the tiled floor.

Sue Hatch had made it to her family before she died. I knew it was Sue because strands of her orange-red hair had, against all reason, survived the heat and explosion. They lay like a shout against the ruin of her blackened head, defying my understanding of how fire consumes. Sue's body had melted into the carbonized side of Grady's larger body, one of her arms fused with his chest so completely that I could not distinguish between them.

I managed to deal with that. Her bravery and sacrifice spoke for themselves. She'd fought her way through the screaming mob to die with her husband. Fine. I could even school myself to accept her sacrifice as a poetic metaphor for devotion and determination. It was Patty-Ann who threw me off. Grady Hatch died with his hands around his daughter's throat. His head was twisted away from her, and although his eyelids were burned off, I felt certain his eyes had been squeezed shut. Grady's fingers had become inseparable from Patty-Ann's flesh, and I knew that if I could see the bond at a microscopic level, I would find the molecules of their cells interlocked.

My thoughts turned easily to homicide. Darwinian

response to senseless death. As it turned out, I was a different man than I had always imagined. A man ready to punish. A man who desired vengeance.

I must have gagged or made a sound, because Lauren slipped her arm around my waist. She took her arm away quickly, but I welcomed her fleeting reassurance.

Al knelt down and touched his finger to the place where Grady's hands wrapped his daughter's throat. "How do we explain this one? He wasn't content to kill his child with fire. He doubled down, killed her twice."

"That's not it," I said. "He didn't want Patty-Ann to burn. He wanted it over as quick as possible." I brooded over the melancholy tableau a while longer, then said, "This was about love."

I guess I was the only one who thought so. They all three looked at me with unmistakable variations of disbelief. Alice pulled the tarp back over Grady's family. "Okay, so it's an unusual example, but not unique. We coroners have our own grisly folklore. Mercy killings under extreme conditions? That's one of them. Doggone, though, if I can figure how a person could keep his mind clear in the middle of a furnace."

"He'd had a lot of time to think about it," I said. "A lot of time to grieve and prepare for what he had to do."

Under my breath, so the others would not hear, I whispered, "Run away, Grady. Run away."

13

As we left the makeshift morgue, Lauren Klout lost her footing on the loose parking lot gravel and bumped my shoulder, and I automatically took hold of her arm, enjoying the fleeting touch of her sturdy bicep. Her eyes locked on mine for an enticing instant, and she smiled. My years of observing people confirmed that this collision wasn't accidental, but part of that peculiar ritual men and women use to signal when they're attracted to each other. I'd seen other people play this courting game. Never experienced it myself.

When we got to her police cruiser, Al got in the back again but Lauren opened her door and leaned on the roof, her arms folded one atop the other. She stared at me across the roof as I stood at the passenger door, as if she had just discovered a hitchhiking penguin.

"I looked you up on the internet, Fogger Grace," she said. "Read some of your stuff on the AJC website. You write sweet stories."

Some hidden meaning played around the edge of her

sentence, but it didn't come across as a compliment. "I write human interest stories about ordinary people," I said defensively. "It's my specialty."

"Uh-huh. Like I said, sweet." She spoke without taking her eyes off me, measuring the effect her words were having.

"I think you honest-to-god *like* these people you write about," she added. She opened her arms and used her fingertips to tap a brief rhythm on the roof of the car. I had a quick flash of Ronnie Millman's drumming, but this wasn't the same. Lauren was rolling something around in her head.

I met her gaze. "I do," I said. "Why not?"

"You really care about these burned people."

"Well, yeah. I could have been one of them."

"That's not the same thing," she insisted.

"No, it definitely is."

"Fogger Grace, you're for sure a piece of work." With that, she lowered herself into the cruiser and hit the ignition. I barely got inside before she floored the accelerator, spraying gravel against the aluminum walls of the meat locker.

Our visit to the deer locker-morgue undercut my growing attraction to the police chief. I sat in the front of the cruiser as we drove back, steadying myself with one hand on the hinged computer screen attached to the dashboard. I sensed Lauren was mildly annoyed that I held onto her computer, but she didn't protest. I tried to focus on the landscape, determined to get the image of Sue Hatch's orange-dyed hair out of my mind. We passed a chain-link fence overgrown with smilax vines and honeysuckle. A faded sign said this was the Mosby Industrial Park, but the field behind it was a nirvana for starving goats, thick with kudzu-choked trees and dotted with fire ant mounds. The body of the mangled fawn was close by. A trio of buzzards spiraled above it like sheets of burned paper.

Whatever I looked at generated some negative image. I focused on the road ahead, where it disappeared into a distant line of trees, submerging my imagination in the unknown woods beyond. Thunderheads to the west had slid so low that only a sliver of lighted sky was visible between them and the horizon. Ever since Al had shared his speculations about murmuration, I'd been brooding over the frightening implications. Al didn't appear worried. He sat in the back, ignoring us while he scribbled in his notebook. Occasionally, he muttered a soft "yes" or "uh-huh."

Finally, Lauren reached over and gently removed my hand from her computer screen. "You need to chill, Fogger," she said. "It's hard to make out the mercy in that poor man back there with his hands around the little girl's throat. You saw it. For sure, you got inside their heads. If you'd tell me what you think was happening here, I might put myself in there with you."

There it was again. Maybe I couldn't correct her syntax, but I wanted her to help us find a solution to the suicides. Murder, I reminded myself, not suicide. Whichever it was, I welcomed an excuse to spend more time with Lauren Klout.

"We discovered two Hatch relatives who live about halfway up the road to Walker's Crossing. Mary and Maisie Hatch. They hadn't heard anything about the mill fire. Didn't give us much reason to believe they cared, either. Anyway, they survived."

Lauren's only outward reaction was to raise her eyebrows. "I'll ask the Creek County sheriff to keep an eye on them. In case, you know, they start acting funny. What else?"

I gave her a condensed version of our murmuration theory, waiting for Al to correct me from the back seat. He let me finish and then summarized. "Human murmuration: coordinated, instantaneous, directional communication. Oh, and you can add the word *compelling*. Or better yet, *coercive*."

"I've heard tell some animals can get their prey to hold still while they're tracking them," Lauren said. "Some snakes do that with birds. Hypnotize them, get up close, then bang. That what you're talking about?" She looked in the rearview mirror and saw Al shaking his head.

"That's another thing altogether," said Al. "There's an animal called a stoat, a member of the weasel family, that hypnotizes rabbits by doing a dance. The prey gets mesmerized by the dance until the stoat can get close enough to immobilize it with a bite to the back of the neck. What we're talking about is even more effective. We're describing a form of instantaneous control that the prey can't shake off."

Lauren listened carefully, her eyebrows raised and her lips puckered, but nodding to get across that she didn't consider our idea completely unzipped. "Then you're talking about telepathy, same as on that Netflix series?"

Al was more patient with Lauren than he had been with me. "This is more in the nature of a command. I say, 'Pass the salt,' but I don't move your arms to make you do it. Instead, I send a message that makes you determined to get the salt to me."

"So, telepathy."

"Not exactly. If you have this ability, you can't read minds, but you can plant ideas and compulsions. Perhaps you can interfere with emotions or intentions, I'm not sure. More than likely, it's related to empathy. Even people with no talent for murmuration get feelings of empathy."

"Somebody put this crazy idea in their heads, and that was enough to make them kill themselves?" she said. "And kill all their kin? That's not what I think of when I hear the word *empathy*. And besides, how strong would the message have to be to make that stick?"

"Imagine a set of controls that squeeze so hard they make you want to kill your entire family," I said. "Every last one of the adults was part of this—all the directly descended blood relatives of Furlong Hatch. Families can be screwed up." I thought of my own botched childhood. "But they rarely murder their own. I can't imagine how the survivors, the ones who married Hatches, are going to live with that knowledge."

Al quietly closed his notebook. "It's not like they chose this. Someone took control and directed them to kill, forced them to do it. That's the part about murmuration that's still a mystery. The group communicates by some unseen means, and they all act together. And mobs make strange decisions. Hey, don't shake your head at me, Fogger. You understand the implications, don't you?

"Jonestown, back in 1978," he continued. "Hundreds of families took poison, parents and children together. Nearly a thousand dead, a third of them children."

"You're misremembering, Al," I said. "Jim Jones forced his congregation to drink poisoned Kool-Aid. His guards held guns on them. He might have called it revolutionary suicide, but it was a mass murder."

Lauren cleared her throat. "Far as I know, you can't fucking separate murder from suicide. When it's eating a hole in your head, you do what you have to so's it'll stop. My mom killed my dad when I was thirteen. Sat him in a kitchen chair and pushed a shotgun against his chest and pulled the trigger. He sat there and waited while she fumbled with the shells. Waited for her to do it. After she blew his shit all over the refrigerator, she offed herself. And they loved each other. Didn't keep them from killing themselves."

The silence stretched out. "And don't you worry about the survivors," she said. "They'll learn to get by."

We drove in silence for another mile, then she asked Al, "Your DNA magic, can it tell us who has this power to make people believe?"

"Pretty sure."

"And you're sure it's Furlong Hatch who made this happen?"

"Seems he's the one."

"But there's all sorts of nitty-gritty mystery stuff in our DNA," said Lauren. "Maybe there's others out there besides Hatch."

"I think that's unlikely, Chief. These sorts of changes are random. They appear in response to evolutionary pressure. It takes time for them to prove they're a survival advantage and then spread."

"Couldn't they have been there all along?" I asked. "I read that we all have some bits of Neandertal in our DNA. Maybe this is a lost talent."

Al leaned forward again. "Yes, we have small amounts of Neandertal and Denisovan genes. There're even signs of other almost-humans in our blood, the so-called 'ghost' hominins who bred with our ancestors, but nothing that suggests this sort of ability. This is an all-new vector, and it would be so dominant that we would notice it."

Lauren shook her head. "I'm still not buying all the way into this horse-hockey theory, but if this person *did* exist, he'd keep his special power hidden. Just saying."

My cell phone buzzed. The caller ID immediately told me who was calling, and I knew she'd be unglued. I got as far as, "Hi, Michelle," before she tore into me.

"Where's my story, Grace? We've got a chance here to put the AJC back on the map, and you go radio silent? The first damn thing you learn about journalism is, get the damn story. Survival of the fittest, Grace. Get your ass in gear!"

I switched her to speaker phone so I could hear over the road noise. "Things aren't what they seemed at first, Michelle."

"What kinda crap are you slinging, Grace? Biggest accident in Georgia in thirty years, and the competition's pushed it to the back burner. You sent me an email saying it was a suicide. A mass suicide, for God's sake! NBC says it was a gas explosion. So do Fox and CBS. Are they wrong?"

"I'm working on it now. I'll have something for you tonight."

Michelle roared ahead as if she hadn't heard me. "I wait, and I hear nothing from you for two days! Two days! If everyone else is having a major brain fart, we have a chance—one chance—to scoop this story. Do you have a story, or have you been injecting direct?"

"Like I said, Michelle, it's complicated. I'll have something for you by tonight, I promise."

"How complicated can this be? Did they kill themselves, or did they just blow up? I'll be sitting here at my desk until you get back to me. And listen, I don't do waiting. Sort it the hell out." She broke the connection.

Lauren shot me a glance. "Any story's gonna be tough to come by," she said. "'Specially when we can't sort out what we got here."

"Between the three of us, we've got more than we think we do," I said. "We just need to knit it together, sit down and map out the clues."

Lauren shook her head. "You get started without me. I got a touch-and-go with the GBI in Conyers that'll tie me up for a couple hours. You can use my office till I get back."

As we got out of Lauren's cruiser a few minutes later at the Mosby police station, she turned to Al and said, "You hold here a couple minutes, Professor. There's something I want to show Mister Grace."

I followed Lauren into the office, and she shut the door behind us. "All right, Mister Fogger Grace," she said. "Whatever this weirded-out attraction is, it's aggravating the both of us. Let's just have ourselves a little taste to see if we want to put your quarter in the slot."

I was still processing those words when she stepped forward, put her hand on my chest, and pressed her lips against mine. The tip of her tongue slid over my teeth. Her tight stomach muscles thrust against my groin. My body twitched as if I'd bitten down on a poorly insulated electrical cord.

It took only a breath for me to follow her lead. There was a subtle shift in her posture and I leaned into the kiss. Her claim settled on me, infused into me. She had a smell about her. Not perfume, something muskier, less contrived.

Lauren's fingertips brushed the back of my neck. The

feeling of her scarred missing digit on my skin was electrifying, then her mouth opened, and she bit down lightly on my lower lip. Our tongues met, but when I dropped my hands to her hips and felt their sharp points against my palms, she stiffened and took a step back to break the embrace. I could see the pulse beating in her neck.

"Hold on, Bucky," she said. "So far, we're just trying on for size." She stepped back and licked her lips with just the tip of her tongue. "I figure you're a white chocolate with extra sprinkles. Interesting, but we need more time to be sure."

When we returned, Al was lounging against the cruiser, hugging his notebook. He wore a bemused expression. The cruiser's air conditioner was still running, its windows misty with beads of condensation. Lauren got in and lowered her window. When I leaned over, she gave my hand a hard squeeze. "Let's see if we can fit in some one-on-one time," she said. "You should try sticking your nose into places you can't find on the map. You agree?"

"Yeah, definitely."

"Smooth talker," she said. Then she switched on the red and blue flashers on the light bar and drove west down Main Street.

14

Al and I had no sooner sat down in Lauren's office than my cell phone buzzed again. "Mister Grace, this is Mary-Adelle from The Meadows. I been trying to reach you about your momma."

"Is she okay, Mary-Adelle? I'm tied up right now."

"Your momma's been in bits and pieces since your last call, Mister Grace. That's why we're coming to Mosby to see you."

"My mother hates Mosby. She doesn't want to come here."

"Well, we turnin' off I-20, so you be ready to change your mind."

"This is a bad time, Mary-Adelle. Turn the car around and take Mom back to The Meadows. I'll see her as soon as I can. That's an order."

"I hear you, Mister Grace, but your momma, she's my client. I do what she say, so long as it don't put her in the danger. So, too bad."

I raised my voice. "Mary-Adelle, I pay the damn bills."

"Yes, sir, but rules is rules. She gives the orders and I drive her. Besides, we in the town now. I passin' a Dunkin' Donuts right now. Where we gonna find you at?"

I gave Mary-Adelle directions to Magic Beans and walked across the street to find a table. The sound system was playing "Hotel California" and had reached the part where one of the all-time greatest guitar riffs hits its crescendo. The system had a loose wire somewhere. It emitted random spiffs of static and sometimes dropped out for a full second before regaining the track. The sound quality was second rate, but it was marvelously loud.

It wasn't long before Mom thumped her walker into the coffee shop. She wore her usual frazzled look, but her lipstick was straight and she had on a clean dress. She gave me a fleeting hug and kissed my chin when I bent down. I settled her and Mary-Adelle on a couch near the front window.

"Be a good son, and buy Mary-Adelle a coffee with whipped cream and lots of sugar," she said. "Order one for me, too, and a bran muffin." She kept her lips compressed in a straight line until I spoke to the waitress, then gave me her sternest look. "I vowed I'd never come to Mosby again, Francis. You do realize that."

"Yes, Mom. I remember."

"I'm here because you are."

No matter how unbalanced Mom got, she always tried to be there for me. My fondest memory was of when I was fourteen and Mom finally took me to Six Flags Over Georgia. I rode the Dare Devil and Goliath and Acrophobia while she stayed below, silently mouthing incantations against the Evil One, her face as flushed with believer's fervor as mine was with exhilaration. She risked her soul so I could see how other kids lived every day.

She fretted with the hem of her dress. "You're not safe in Mosby. I've told you that. You should not be here, but here you are, anyway."

"It's my job, Mom."

She watched me from the corner of her eye, uncertainty furrowing her brow. "You know that I love you."

"Always, Mom." Today, I could believe her. There had been so many other days when she was a foreigner, a stranger from a strange land, transported here unaware of our ways and incapable of communication. But today she was here, risking her soul. I welcomed the freedom of talking with her, mother to son, without the steady barrage of insanity. Without warning, she picked up on her old refrain.

"There are evil forces in this town, people who hurt other folks just for the pleasure of it. You need to leave before ... before ..."

"What happened to you here, Mom?"

She steepled her fingers in front of her lips, then pushed them on either side of her nose up her forehead. Her eyes grew moist with memory, but her face hardened. "Your father," she said in a whisper. "Your father lives here. Lived here."

At last, I thought. "What about him, Mom? Why did he leave you; leave us?"

Her smile was unreadable. I guessed she was unsure how to answer. "All these questions," she said. "Your father never saw you, Francis. He was here and then gone. He had other things he had to do."

"More important than you? He just dumped us with Pastor and Grammy and walked away?"

"You mustn't get angry. Don't use that voice."

Mary-Adelle was making a good job of pretending to study something in a magazine. I had known her for years and didn't care if she eavesdropped on our conversation or not. I sat back in my chair. "Mom, you're not answering."

"These days, I can't fully remember how he looked. But I remember his touch."

"Mom," I insisted.

"Don't you use that tone with me. It's hard to remember. It was a long time ago."

It wasn't a long time ago. Mom wasn't yet fifty, but her past was clouded by dementia. She had been shrinking away from me for years. One day she'd bundle her phobias and superstitions and lock herself in the closet with them and let herself collapse like an exhausted, imploding star, until nothing was left but my memories of her. And when I was gone, she'd disappear.

Her eyes took on a clear, tuned-in look, and I witnessed one of those rare moments when sanity paid a brief visit. "Families get caught up in patterns," she said. "We repeat the same mistakes; children reworking the same stupidity as their parents. I didn't want you to get trapped, to carry on the same way." She gave her words a finality that said she had explained everything, then her eyes drifted away into the far-off.

"Who was he, Mom?"

"Ohhh ..." She drew the word out. "He was a man of God, like your granddad. Was the priest at the Episcopal Church here in Mosby. He was a smart man, a proud man. And the good Lord punished his pride, the same as he punished your granddad. He wanted to love me, Francis. Disgrace and ruin was what he got."

She looked up at me, her eyes tearing. "Your father loved me, Francis. We kept it secret for months, hiding our times together. Those were wonderful times, before the evil came."

I held my breath, expecting Mom to launch into one of her familiar rants about the Evil One and his plot to enslave the world. Instead, she stumbled into another moment of clarity.

"I made the same mistake my mother did," she said. "When I found out I was pregnant, I told him he had to marry me. And I think he wanted to, but he told me I was a sweet girl and sent me away, back to my mama and papa."

"What happened to him? Where is my father now?" I didn't know what I would do if she gave me the information.

"They told me that the day after he sent me away, he lost all his reason. He tore up his rectory, then he killed himself. Now, that doesn't sound quite right to me, but that's what they say. He went and killed himself, is all I know. Papa wouldn't let me go to the funeral. There was evil got into your father that made him do that. The more I looked, the more I could see there was evil all around. After that, Papa kept me away from other people."

Mom stroked my arm. "You don't need any more than that, Francis. He's been dead for years. But the evil that wormed its way inside him, the thing that made him kill himself instead of choosing me, it's still here in this terrible town. Come back to Atlanta. Don't stay here."

Someone gave the balky door a violent tug and stepped into the shop. Mom cringed into the sofa. For a moment, she seemed ready to bolt. Her hand slid to my wrist and gave it a gentle squeeze. "You won't listen to me," she said. "My warnings slide off you, like always. For once, son, will you pay attention?" Mom's voice was so matter-of-fact that I could almost believe she had both oars in the water. "I want you to come back to Atlanta. We can leave right now."

"I'm not in the right mood for this, Mom."

"This town has evil in it. It has always been here. Come back."

"I can't. I finally have work that's serious, Mom. And there's another thing here that's just as important." It was Lauren I was thinking of. I had never felt an attraction as vital—and as essential—as the charged connection I had with her.

"It's a woman," Mom declared. "You found a good woman, didn't you?" Irrational, yes. Maniacal, yes again. But when she wanted to, Mom could put the wackiness aside and see into my heart.

"You got it, Mom. I'm not sure yet, but as soon as I am, I'll bring her to see you."

The waitress brought our coffee and muffins, and Mom decided to go silent. Mary-Adelle dug into her whipped cream, humming softly with each spoonful. Mom emptied three sugar packets into her cup, continuing the foot race between diabetes and dementia to see which one got her first. She watched me with a nobody's-home expression and stirred her coffee, then held her spoon halfway to her mouth and stared out the window at the post office square.

"I used to love coming here and walking around the square," she said. "There was always a festival going on in the park—Chili Cook-Off, July 4th, Founder's Day. You remember? No, of course not. You were later, but I met him here, just down the park by the fountain. I met your father at the Firefly Festival."

"Tell me about that."

A girl of about two ran through the shop and threw herself onto the floor nearby, screaming bloody murder about something I couldn't make out. I looked back into the shop, where her parents sat with a second child in a portable car seat, reading cell-phone messages. They ignored their daughter and let the screaming go on and on. Their detachment from the world and their indifference to the rest of the patrons were so entrenched that it had become a learned behavior, a social disease. They no longer viewed others as worthy of consideration, and they were teaching their daughter the same lesson.

Al and I were chasing someone infected with the worst extreme of these values, the same arrogance, the same contempt for one's equals. Conceit exists in many of us, but daily reminders of our personal weaknesses typically limit it. With some people, not so much. The world is always vulnerable to narcissists who imagine they are immune to the laws of reality and the rules of conduct toward others. People who think this way are delusional. But what if an assembly error in a minor gene sequence nullifies our laws of reality? Then all bets are off. The old rules don't apply to someone whose powers obliterate all the limits.

My mother stood and trudged over to the table where the young couple sat. They sensed her approach but continued to stare at their phone screens. When she swatted the father in the back of his head, the glass he held to his mouth sloshed iced tea onto his grilled cheese sandwich. Mom pointed at the girl on the floor, who had gone suddenly mute.

"Do something about that," she whispered. "You're in charge."

She came back to our table, sat down, and turned her judgment on me. "You get your woman out of Mosby this very moment, Francis. Don't let the Evil One find her. He will crawl into her and ruin her. If you love her, you save her."

This was the old-school Mom. Her anti-Mosby diatribes were a staple ingredient of my life. A phrase or two might change order, but she never added new details. Her warnings had a permanent home in my head. But I would not leave here, and that meant I couldn't let her distract me.

"Mary-Adelle, take Mom back to The Meadows. She's ready to go now. You drive safe."

Some unintended edge in my voice got through to my mother. Her mouth opened and closed in silent protest; then she took a folded paper out of her purse, crumpled it into my hand, and wrapped my fingers around it. She gave me a cheerless smile, got to her feet, and let Mary-Adelle lead her out of the shop.

15

I waited until Mom and Mary-Adelle were out of sight before I read her note. It was the sort of message I had unwrapped from my school lunches, year after year. "Let every man be swift to hear, slow to speak, slow to wrath." She had sent me this one so many times that I automatically recognized the quote. *The New Testament*, James 1:19–20. Don't get angry. Yes, Mom. It's a fine homily, but the ground is shifting under my feet, and if I need to get wrathful to find stability, so be it.

I sat back down, pulled out my cell phone, and began to compose a column for my editor. I fudged the entire question of how the Hatch family had died and instead wrote about the peculiar citizens of Mosby and their strange indifference to the deaths at the mill. It was a darker piece than I had ever written, but I had plenty of material to work from, and when I hit 'save' forty minutes later, my phone was almost out of charge but I was smiling and feeling downright proud of my work.

As I got up to leave, I saw Cassie Wrenner come through the bamboo curtain at the back of the shop, where a small sign said "Private." The man with her had the flattened nose I associated with cage fighters. He wore aviator glasses and crisp white slacks and a black blazer so tight over a black tee shirt it made his upper body look like the obelisk in Kubrick's *2001*. He walked through the room like he owned it.

I turned to go, and Cassie boomed out, "Fogger, honey, hold on!" She came straight to my table, but her friend followed at a measured pace, stopping along the way to speak with patrons who stood to shake hands with him. I waited for him to reach us, annoyed that the delay was preventing me from seeing whether Al had discovered anything new.

When the man got to us, he waited until I held out my hand. I kept it simple, said, "Fogger Grace," and gave him one shake. Only then did his lips part in a smile that was more a grimace, revealing large, square teeth. He was in his mid-fifties, his body toned but somehow tightly packaged in his clothes like a shrink-wrapped piece of meat. His handshake was more than firm. He pressed his thick thumb into the back of my hand, seemingly intent on squeezing the marrow from my bones.

"Fogger, I thought you'd want to meet Norman Garrison," said Cassie. "Norman is a leader in the Mosby community and the principal of Aintry County High School."

Garrison let a false smile crawl across his face, but it disappeared somewhere around the bridge of his nose. His eyes were dark points behind his aviators. When Garrison still didn't speak, Cassie began to add details, like a press agent trying to cover for her arrogant boss.

"Norman is our local success story. He grew up here and did his degree up at UGA. Got his PhD in psychology and came back to share himself with our little town." The sidelong look Garrison gave her stifled anything more she might have said.

"I've been wanting to meet you and your associate," he said. "Cassie tells me the two of you were at the mill when the unhappy accident occurred." There was something annoying about his voice. I guessed he always spoke in a stilted, condescending tone. "Perhaps we could get together from time to time and share news? I'm an authority on everything that happens in Mosby. Nothing escapes my notice."

And nothing bites my ass worse than a blowhard, I thought. "Well, perhaps you could tell me about the Hatch twins up in Walker's Crossing. They were the only ones to miss the fire at the mill."

"Oh," said Garrison. "You mean the suicides." His heavy-lidded eyes avoided mine and searched the room, taking inventory of who was ignoring us and who was taking notice.

"No," I said, "You're confused. I mean they weren't at the mill with the others."

Garrison didn't suppress his triumphant smile. "As I said, Mister Grace, I'm very much up on all that happens around here. Mary and Maisie Hatch may have missed the explosion, but they are most definitely suicides. Sometime last night, for sure."

I believe I let my mouth hang open for an instant. I stared down at the table and scratched my ear. My voice faltered. "I saw them just yesterday. They seemed anything but suicidal."

"You saw them? Whatever for, I wonder? Their place is quite off the tracks, isn't it?"

"How . . . ? Are you sure of this?"

Garrison's smug smile spread. "The Creek County sheriff stopped by to check on them this morning. He found them slumped side by side in the backyard of their trailer, noosed on a clothesline. They didn't stay inside and climb up on a chair and jump off with any proper sense of dignity, just slipped the line around their necks and sat down in the dirt."

Garrison gave a chuckle. "Can you imagine anything more homespun? Just the sort of hayseed act the rest of America expects from country folk. A rather tasteless way to go, don't you agree?"

He spoke with the indifference of someone who has watched a classic film so many times he has the dialogue memorized but no longer cares what emotions the words express. Damn if I didn't want to cold-cock the bastard right there. Didn't, though. I held my peace and forced a phony smile. Garrison was so used to insincerity that he didn't notice how much effort it required for me to do that.

"So, as I said," he continued, "I am rather the expert on whatever's important in our town. I long for intelligent conversation. Why don't we meet—you, me, and your friend—so I can keep you up to date?"

"We might make that happen," I said, "but, fact is, I have to meet Doctor Amon on another matter right now. I'll see what might work for him and get back to you." I pulled open the balky door and stepped out onto the sidewalk, my thoughts filled with a picture of the twins. Were they permitted a last "God bless" before they sat down in the grass, noosed together as they had been in life? Garrison followed me out, and when I turned back to face him, he pinched the cuff of my shirt with two fingers and didn't let go.

"There's been a strange undercurrent in town since the accident," Garrison said. "I wonder if you and Doctor Amon might want to discuss it. I know more about Mosby than anyone else. For that matter, I believe I understand the people here better than anyone." As he spoke, the photogray lenses in his glasses darkened until his eyes became invisible.

I took a step back to break his grip on my shirt, but he held on, oblivious to the implied insult, so I reached up and gathered his fingers into my fist and pulled them away, bending them backward just enough to reinforce my message.

"I'll let you go now," he said, his eyes shimmering with annoyance. "When you and the doctor are ready, Cassie can tell you how to contact me."

I have interviewed enough neurotic community activists to recognize Garrison's type. I wished I could reach into his brain and repair its wiring. These grandstanders take over communities. They hunger for recognition and deference and they seize on the passivity of well-meaning people. They are incapable of performing their work in the background, preferring instead to move to the front and inflame sensibilities. The few who have genuine charisma more often use it to silence and overawe than to lead.

When their need becomes desperate, charismatic leaders persecute the innocent, shamming righteousness as they destroy lives. The Cotton Mathers and Joe McCarthys and the White League deflect their own terrified self-doubts into witch hunts and foreign wars in which they momentarily become superstars. And when they falter there is always someone waiting to seize the microphone and aim the mob at the next target. I didn't have time for the Norman Garrisons.

When I got back to the police station, Al had his Hatch family tree spread across Lauren's desk. He had used colored pencils to connect the boxes with new, looping lines. He made no protest when I peeled off the yellow index card that covered the one box in the second-to-last row. As I suspected, Al was mixing his theoretical research with personal motives. It was his own name in the remaining family tree box. To what degree were his conclusions being contaminated? I tapped his name with my finger.

"That's right," he said. "I'm one of the bastards."

"And you're tracking him down?"

"It started that way. It's a mystery to me, how fifty per cent of me is Furlong Hatch, yet I look nothing like him. My mother's husband is black, but my half-sisters are lighter than I am. My mother's people are South Sudanese. I got intelligence and skin tones from her. All I got from Hatch was a middling ability to make friends. You can see why I wanted to figure that out."

"Your ability to make friends," I asked. "How does it work?"

He shrugged. "All I have is suspicions. I know how murmuration works in animals. In humans, I'm still trying to sort it out."

"You can do it, too, Al. The murmuration. I saw you do it with that guy who wanted to deck me."

"If you'd been paying attention, you'd remember I told you that was a one-of-a-kind performance. For all we know, the man decided on his own not to hit you. Look, I'm not saying I don't have a talent. All of us in the Hatch bloodline inherited something from Furlong, but what I do—what they can do—is modest. I've always had a minor ability to charm people. I don't know how it works, but I do know it's limited to that. Charm."

"Then take a guess, dammit. Somebody in this town has a whup-ass talent, and he's using it to kill people."

Al traced the curving lines on the chart with his fingertips. "The talent manifests in different ways, Fogger, and it's held in this small group that I'm a part of."

He paused for a moment and grunted. "Yeah, a small group! It's much smaller now." He sighed. "This is why I focused on evolutionary biology. I have a personal interest in cracking this nut. I'm another of the old goat's bastards, so I got what he had. The Hatch family line is a classic closed-hereditary community. Whatever the driver of our talent is, it's embedded in our DNA."

Thanks to Garrison's insufferable posturing, my temper was boiling. I let the anger come through in my voice, harsher than I intended. "I've figured that much already, and I don't have a PhD. How does it work, man?"

"Will you listen? I don't *know* how it works. It's not pheromones, because they can't work that fast. It's not high-frequency sound, because our experiments don't detect it. At one point, we thought it might be some sort of alignment between neural nets, but we haven't figured out how to test for that."

"But animals do it. You told me sparrows communicate with each other this way."

"Yes, yes," Al made a dismissing motion with his hands. "All true, and yet it's not an answer. One sparrow decides to change direction, and instantly all the sparrows in the flock take the same compass reading. Even those a hundred meters away move at the same time. The very same time, Fogger. You know the word *charm* originally meant, 'a practice with magic powers'? It might as well *be* magic."

"Black magic, Al. I ran into a friend of Cassie's named Norman Garrison on my way over here. He says the Hatch twins hung themselves soon after we visited them."

"So soon?" He squeezed his eyes shut before meeting my stare. "Damn. I thought...I hoped...we'd figure out how to neutralize whoever's doing this before he got to the sisters. I failed them."

I gave him the sketchy story Garrison had told me. "Do you think we led the alpha to them? Are we responsible for Mary and Maisie hanging themselves?"

Al shook his head. "I won't blame myself for things I can't control. There's way too much we don't understand yet. A person with this kind of ability? An adept who's manipulated people for years? He might be able to track someone the same way police track a cell phone to find out where a criminal is. Even if you don't turn the phone on, you can determine where it is or where it's been."

He studied the look on my face and said, "And just maybe, I could be wrong about how this all works. Maybe he can listen to what we're thinking." Before I could react, he said, "But that's preposterous. When starlings murmurate, they send messages. They damn well don't read each other's minds."

"We're a different species, Al. Bigger brains. More complex."

"Nonsense! It has to work the same, regardless of species."

"Why? And if it isn't different for this Hatch master-mind, how did he track us to the sisters?"

"Not enough data, my friend." His scowl deepened. "Tell

you what I *do* want to believe in. Karma." A tremble ran over his shoulders. "I hope someday that bastard gets an ice pick stuck in his transmitter."

"That would be in his head, Al."

"Right. Karma."

I had one more question. "Is there ever an alpha sparrow? Has one sparrow ever gotten the rest of its flock to commit mass suicide, to land in front of a bulldozer or crash into the side of a building?"

Al propped his chin on his hand and stared into space. His face reminded me of Leonardo da Vinci's famous self-portrait, solemn eyes that held a world-weary disappointment, lines etched by everlasting disillusionment with humanity's sad performance.

"No," he said, "but that's what we've got here. A Judas sparrow."

16

All we had to go on was a locker full of burned bodies and Al's theories about murmuration. That, and an improbable hunch about an "alpha" Hatch. Nothing else to tell us why a whole family had decided to slaughter themselves.

When we needed a more permanent space to work in, one of the officers moved us out of Lauren's office and into a windowless room used for records storage. Al taped his blood-line charts to the walls, then we added post-it notes with every additional piece of information we had collected. We worked the rest of the afternoon searching for ways to uncover the identity of the mystery alpha Hatch. We got nowhere.

Our hopes hinged on the idea that Al's DNA screens would reveal a clue. He stalked around the office, poking his cards with a stiff finger and adding notes in his spider-like handwriting. I received a one-word rebuff to any suggestion I made. When the coroner sent Al an email confirming that she had forwarded her autopsy files to his Georgia Tech office, his immediate reaction was to demand that we get another latte at the coffee shop.

"I've been mainlining caffeine ever since the fire. Another cup will zone me out."

"I insist," he said. "It's time for you to make a sacrifice for the cause of science, my friend."

Al gave his usual order to the skinny waitress at Magic Beans. He hummed along with the piped-in 90's music while we waited, but he gave me no clue about what he wanted me to do. When the waitress returned with Al's latte, Cassie followed her, carrying a cardboard box filled with Styrofoam go-cups. Each cup was labeled with a name and date. Cassie's hand lingered on mine when she handed me the box, and when I pulled away, she added a wry grin, miming that we were both in on a ridiculous joke. "I hope you boys find what you're looking for in these dirty cups," she said. "Just stay put here for a minute."

Al closed the cover on the cardboard box and watched her go. "This thing between you and Miss Beans," he asked without humor, "what is it, exactly?"

"Childhood crush," I said, hoping it was no more than that.

He made a looping gesture in the air with his hand. "Could be a point of leverage for us. Think about it."

Cassie came back with a bran muffin for Al, then set a cup of coffee in front of me. She nudged the cup toward me, paused a beat, then moved it another inch closer.

"I didn't order this."

"On the house, Fogger. For old times." Cassie's face wore a sheen of expectation, her smile stretched thin, showing too many teeth.

The thought came into my mind that I definitely did not want another coffee right now, but I poured cream into the cup anyway, not wanting to appear ungracious. A disconcerting vibe rolled over me as I watched the almond-white cream swirl clockwise in the cup. It looked like a photograph of a distant galaxy, cold and unreachable. I had the sense there was something indefinably wrong, that the cream was curdled, that the coffee would be as bitter as a sucked nail.

"Thanks, but not now." I pushed the cup away, and when Al looked up, I raised my chin and said nothing. He narrowed his gaze, then the skin on his face tightened with comprehension.

Cassie stood with her hands on her broad hips, her lips closed over her smile, eyes drifting in and out of focus, obviously baffled by our rejection. She held the same pose my mother used when exasperated by my inability to remember a catechism. Finally, Cassie gave out a soft sigh. She reached for my coffee, but her hands shook and she knocked over the small vase of roses in the center of the table, splashing water over the surface and spilling blood-red petals into my lap. She ignored the mess and reached again for my cup, but gingerly pulled back her hand, as if touching the saucer might scald her skin. Finally, she picked it up.

"Maybe later, then," she said. She swept up Al's coffee and took both cups behind the counter, poured the coffee into the sink and turned on the hot water full blast. A cloud of steam rose from the sink.

Al pulled a half-dozen napkins from the dispenser and mopped up the spill. "Your voice changed," he said. "Like there was another man inside that nonchalant disguise."

Coming from my new friend, that hurt. "I have the same

voice for everyone, Al. Same face. I don't change accents or use double negatives to fit my audience. I simply listen to a person and hear them the way most people don't, because I pay attention. It's a reporter's trick."

"Don't think so. This thing with the coffee. I don't like what it implies."

"Just a hunch. Something about the way she fixed her smile. She doesn't even understand what happened."

Al nodded slowly. "Perhaps."

We took the box back to the police station and stored it in a corner of the records room. Al phoned and confirmed that one of his grad students would drive straight to Mosby to pick them up. His team would spend the night in the Georgia Tech lab, breaking down the gene sequences and noting anomalies.

As we left the police station, Al stretched his arms and looked up at the cumulous clouds. "Don't know about you," he said, "but I need a break. My momma always told me, no matter how dark it gets, you need to stop and smell the roses."

"I don't feel I'm in a smell-the-roses moment," I said. "More like standing at the bottom of a deep well that someone's pissing into. That kind of moment."

"I saw just the place when we drove in." Al pointed and led me a block down Jackson Street to a shop with a huge ice cream cone above its door. Inside was a child's dreamland: infinite varieties of candy; perhaps three dozen flavors of ice cream. Behind the old-fashioned cash register was an authentic 1950s advertising poster: a boy and a girl ran across a meadow, their cocker spaniel puppy yapping at their heels. "Candy gives kids energy," the sign said. "Be sure to put it in their lunch every day."

Al made the store his private playland. He ordered a waffle cone with three scoops of bilious-colored ice cream that looked like someone had scraped it off the palette of a crack-addled artist. I searched in vain for plain chocolate. I might as well have been trying to find a straightforward flavor in the Ben & Jerry's section of a grocery store. My frustration duplicated our failure to unravel the alpha's identity. Every flavor was a problematic mixture of multiple tastes and textures. Nothing simple. Nothing plain. I settled on coffee mocha chip with almonds.

It wasn't half bad, but it didn't lift my mood. I pointed at an array of wax candy shaped to simulate buck teeth, huge mustaches, and fat red lips. "Here you are, Al. Mosby and its disguises. Things go on beneath the surface, people die, and the town hasn't got a clue."

"That's an excellent simile, Fogger. This town gets its name from John Singleton Mosby, a Confederate partisan ranger. His men would strike Union outposts, then blend in with the Virginia locals so well that the Federals couldn't identify them. Union troops called him the Gray Ghost."

"This guy—this alpha Hatch we're looking for—he might as well *be* a ghost. He could be anyone on the street; anyone here having ice cream. None of my experience works here and I'm scared, Al. Honestly."

Al took a large lick from his cone. "The alpha is an ambush predator. All the prey can do is be on guard and watch for small hints. This is a *small* town, a one-room schoolhouse town. I don't see this guy staying hidden for long. Just having us here will draw him out."

"That's why I'm terrified. He's very practiced, Al, and he's a survivor; top of the food chain. He doesn't have to track down his prey. He destroys their defenses. Throws out weak trouble-makers like unwanted scraps."

A smear of blue and green fringed the bottom of Al's mustache. He looked years younger than when I'd first met him. "You spend way too much energy trying to force a solution, Fogger. Eat your ice cream. If there were only pain around, life wouldn't be worth the effort. Sometimes the simplest wonder—rich Superman ice cream, for example, clears your mind; reminds you to treasure joy when you find it."

"Dead kids," I said. "A mass murderer who has us on his list."

He wouldn't give up his smile. "Nothing new there, my friend. In case you haven't noticed, there are millions of people working every day to shorten your life. The only way to handle constant threat is to adapt. I've made a career studying evolutionary biology. There's always a stronger life form waiting to pounce on you. But in the long run, evolution responds. A new danger shows up and voila! Life adapts to meet the challenge."

"The murmuration? How's that supposed to help?"

Al stopped and raised his ice cream cone as if it was the answer to my question. "If people could talk to each other with their minds, holding nothing back, wouldn't that be a better world? Speaking true; meaning what we say."

"But that's not the way it works. This alpha Hatch you're looking for, he's not speaking true. He's putting lies in people's minds. He's gluing up their thoughts,"

"It's a natural ability, Fogger. If we could control it; turn it to good."

"No time, Al. Evolution's a long-range process, and we're

living right next to a lethal superman. We need to short-circuit him right now."

"Yeah, yeah. So right now, the alpha looks unbeatable, a perfect apex predator, but there will be a correction. It probably won't be us who resets the balance. But someone will."

"And while we're treading water with the shark," I said, "waiting for that next evolutionary hiccup, what do we do?"

He took a big lick of his cone. "We're still in this fight, my friend. Meanwhile, nothing prevents you from seeking joy. Look, even I can spot the way our Police Chief wiggles her eyebrows at you. Pay attention. Buy a wax mustache and go see her, will you? Life would be dismal without joy and discovery."

"That obvious, huh?"

"Oh my, yes. Both of you are signaling to beat hell. You don't need to understand pheromones with all those visible cues flashing."

I gave myself a few moments to think about Lauren's kiss and the taste of her mouth, but a nagging thought intruded. "I don't understand how you can recover DNA from a coffee cup," I said. "I mean, it must get all mixed with coffee and diluted and contaminated."

Al shook his head. "We've come a long way since the early 2000s," he said. His condescending smile so reminded me of Garrison that it nearly torched me off again, but I held my temper. "If you tear open a packet of Sweet'n Low with your teeth and then give me the wrapper; I can tell you who your great-great-grandmother slept with during Wolrd War I."

I made the mistake of asking Al what he was looking for in the DNA. In a few sentences, I was once again way the hell out of my depth. Proteins control our physical characteristics and traits, he explained, and DNA carries the design information for making proteins. So, the genes in a person's DNA are building instructions. They encode nucleotides in certain amounts and in a specific order to determine each of our traits, like how big we will grow or how well we can see in the dark. There are about three billion building blocks in this human Lego set, and random variations occur all the time. Individual DNA molecules, what we call chromosomes, often get some of their codes transposed, or deleted, or even scrambled. And our bodies make copies of copies of copies of genes, each repetition providing a new chance to bungle the job. The average person has several hundred abnormal genes. Most of these random variations don't survive a single carrier. Others, if they are beneficial, can get passed on to future generations. This is what we mean when we talk about evolution. Got that? Me neither.

In desperation, I asked Al if anything we'd learned came close to explaining the horror we'd seen at Turnell Mill. He finished off his cone and swiped his hand together in a gesture of "all done."

"I've been studying a mutation called the p2 forkhead-box protein that might give us a lead. P2 has striking evolutionary implications. In humans, the mutation causes problems with language development and facial movements, but when we introduced the p2 into mice, they exhibited accelerated learning, unusual ultrasonic vocalizations, and unusual growth in neuron length and flexibility."

"So, we're dealing with something like that?"

"Now you're grasping again. It's probably nothing of the sort. But it tells us how much we don't know about the potential of a random gene hiccup."

We strolled back to the police station through freshening summer air. I suspected Al was setting me up for something, but I wasn't going to push him, so I concentrated on finishing off my mocha chip cone. It did taste awfully good. Once again, Mosby with the heat burned off had all the qualities of a charming, small-scale town. If not for Mom's vague-but-lurid concerns and the glaring handicap of a homicidal phantom, it would be a nice place to live.

The grad student's lab report would take at least the entire night to complete. Meanwhile, Al and I had nothing to do but sit around the police station and speculate, and that was where Lauren found us when she returned in the late afternoon. She stood in the doorway of the records room we'd turned into our office. With her hands stuck flat in her hip pockets, she asked how we were doing. Straightaway, I invited her to dinner. She tilted her head to one side and didn't answer, and I had to stand there, having delivered the seven-word sentence I had practiced in my head, and wonder if I had bobbled the invitation. Her smile began so slowly that I expected a turn-down. Then the smile moved all the way to the corners of her mouth and she said, "Sure, let's do that."

Lauren suggested an Italian restaurant in a remodeled icehouse on the edge of the town park, four blocks from the station. I had just enough time to return to the inn for a shower and a change of clothes.

A strange email announced itself as I was dressing. It was from my editor, Michelle, and it read: "Yr new column cooks. Nice dark turn. Explosion is old news. Give me more dark stuff. Sent a bonus to your account. Take couple weeks off with pay." Bonus? Weeks off with pay! It had only been a few hours since she reamed me out. Where had her demand for sensation gone? I knew my editor, and I knew someone had worked on her to get this response.

An unexpected bump in wealth was great, but this sudden windfall added another dimension to Mosby's lethal environment. A being who could infect lives seventy miles away in Atlanta was a lot more powerful than someone limited to a single rural town. Whatever the cause of Michelle's about-face, it was one more bad vibe I didn't have time to think about. My plate was already full of threats.

17

A transformed Lauren Klout came to dinner. Her police badge and name tag were missing. She still wore her uniform, but she'd discarded her cap and sidearm and unbuttoned the top button of her blouse. The low lighting in the restaurant gave her skin the color of fine olive oil, golden and molten, and the sheen in her hair drew tones so deep black it shone purple. The tones cascaded when she moved her head quickly, as if her hair was a colony of underwater creatures, gentled by a current.

Lauren caught me looking at the vee of her breasts, where the shadow of her blouse darkened her skin almost imperceptibly, and the faintest flush momentarily colored her cheeks, as it must have colored mine. When she greeted the waitress by name and ordered a Moscow Mule, I had hopes that we might forget the past few days and simply enjoy each other's company.

Fortunately, there was no piped-in music at the restaurant to make us strain to hear each other. We started with the usual first date questions: who are your people, and where did you grow up? We learned that my early years on my grandparents' modest vegetable farm were not that different from hers living with parents who ran a drugstore together; but for both of us, life had changed at about the same time: mine with a sudden move to Atlanta, Lauren's with the haunting death of her parents.

Conversation stalled, our drinks arrived, and Lauren deftly broke the lull by asking if Al and I had made any progress with our private investigation. I sketched out Al's speculation about murmuration and electrochemical signals and the rest, holding nothing back. Lauren seemed to grasp the concepts better than I had. She waited until I ran out of gas, then gave me a wry smile.

"A Hatch Alpha, huh?" she said. "You know, I believe in space aliens with tinfoil helmets, but people sending kill orders with their brains? Whoa there, Fogger. That's still a stretch too far for me. But sure as hell *something* stinks bad in my town."

Lauren swished her drink around in its copper mug. "If there was a man with the power to make folks do what he wanted, why wouldn't he come out and say so? Run the whole town and make no apologies for it. That's what I'd do." She fished the lime wedge out of the mug and licked it with the tip of her tongue. "And for that," she said, "Mosby's a nice little town; but a man with that much power, he'd be an Avenger superhero in a big city, cash in on his powers big time. He wouldn't stay here."

She was right. Why would the hypothetical Hatch alpha remain anonymous? If I had been born with that talent, I would have reprogrammed my life. All those moments of insecurity, times when I might have chosen different outcomes, I'd have controlled them as though I were the director of my own epic movie instead of just letting shit happen.

Only once had I ever entertained such a fantasy: in fifth grade, on my back in the dirt under our one pathetic playground pine tree, a crowd of my cheering classmates bunched around us, a nameless boy pummeling me with beefy fists. He was a soft butterball of a boy, his face as empty of expression as a bowl of mashed potatoes, a boy who probably had never had the balls to bully anyone, and he picked me. And I know why. I was Fogger, the boy who kept his eyes on his shoes, the shy boy who kept always to himself.

I cried and I begged, tears running down my cheeks and snot running into my mouth, and his blows didn't hurt nearly as badly as the shame and despair in my head. I wished myself far away, hidden in the school library or at home safe in my bed, but wishing couldn't make it so. I cringed in the dirt with my forearms locked over my face and suffered his blows while I waited for him to wear himself out. My tormentor gradually slackened his attack, his blows running down like a mechanical toy with a weak battery until they stopped altogether. I pulled my crossed arms away from my face and looked up to see him straddling my chest, snot on his lips, wearing a look of dumbfounded surprise, as if the angel I'd been praying to had finally landed a blow square on his temples.

"He hit him," said a voice from the crowd, a little awestruck. "Fogger hit him." He might well be in awe, because landing that blow was a first for me. And a last. Spooky behavior for me. Creepy, even. The kid crawled off my chest and walked away, astonished that I had fought back. That was not how people expected Fogger Grace to act. And it wasn't how I reacted to violence after that. Even then, I wished for the magic power to punish my tormentors, but I was no Hatch alpha. I could only rely on the rare lucky punch.

This memory played out in the few seconds after Lauren guessed how the alpha would act, and it took me to my own unexpected answer. "Mosby would be the perfect place for the alpha. It's got a population large enough to satisfy all the basic needs. More important, it's far enough off the grid that the outside world would overlook bizarre incidents. He'd have plenty of time to clean up his mistakes. And if he needed something Mosby couldn't provide, he'd order a few puppets to go get it. It'd be Shangri-La."

"That doesn't work, Fogger," said Lauren. "Little things stand out in a small town. Everyone knows your business. You start herding people around like you're a sheepdog, it'd get noticed for sure."

"The person who's doing this has had lots of practice," I said. "He put a lid on the mill fire. He put a new fake story out in less than twenty-four hours, got it to the reporters, your police, everyone the state sent, and the town's entire population. Got them all to believe it. I'd say he's managing just fine."

Lauren narrowed her eyes. "Yeah," she agreed. "Lots of practice. If there was a man had the power to do this—and I say *if*—that could explain what's going on. Let's you and me pretend I buy your story. What if Mosby's the bush league, and your alpha man, he's sharpening up his skills so he can move up to the majors?"

I didn't have an answer for that, but Lauren didn't want one. "Listen, now, I want a dinner where we don't talk about men with scary powers," she said and blinked at me. "Men without powers are enough trouble."

Dinner came. I don't remember what we ate, because I caught her sneaking looks at me between bites, a barely concealed smile on her lips. Just as often, Lauren caught me surveying her. There were a lot of silences where we might have spoken but didn't. I leaned forward without meaning to, closing the distance, wanting to peer under her brows and do what I had always schooled myself against: hold her gaze and see into the complex brain working behind those green-coffee eyes.

I found myself talking more than listening, and Lauren seemed okay with that. I told her about growing up in Pickett, about my crazy mother, my boredom with teaching smug know-it-alls at the academy. I told her about my desire to shed the newspaper column and write the Great American Novel.

Lauren finally held up her hand and said, "Take a deep breath, Thoreau. I don't need a data dump. Tell me where these come-on flutters are coming from. What's that all about?"

I took a mouthful of wine to cover my hesitation. Truthfully, I had no answer. My brain was in turmoil. My body was another matter. I ached to be alone with her.

Lauren was way ahead of me. We were only halfway into the meal, but she drained her wine, dropped her fork onto her plate, stood, and said, "Okay, Fogger, let's go. My place." I could do nothing but throw some cash on the table to cover our meal, and rise and follow her.

Lauren told me her condo was above a jewelry store on the other side of the park, and she took off fast, walking three steps ahead of me, taking long strides. Cicadas droned in the night, a sound never heard in the urban world I came from. The park itself was dimly lit by old-fashioned globe streetlights that softened its features: the band shell with its fluted white columns; the chain-suspended porch gliders standing empty around the periphery of the lawn, creaking faintly in the breeze. The night was pleasantly warm, and for the first time since my arrival, I let the small-town tranquility of Mosby fully reveal itself.

Lauren paused in the center of the park beside a tiered metal fountain and waited for me to catch up. "You think maybe we could move a little faster?" she said.

"Don't you feel it?" I asked. "Doesn't everything feel . . . magnified?"

"Magnified?" she laughed. "A girl can hope."

She stood with one hip cocked, arms akimbo, fists on her hipbones, waiting for me to do . . . something . . . and she stared impatiently into the night sky. The light shone softly on her hair and brightened the metal figure atop the fountain, a slender woman who held a vase on her shoulder. I suspected the sound of trickling water came from that vase, but in the dimness, I could not tell for sure where it spilled from, just that water splashed softly from one tier to the next, pooling in the fountain's dark, octagonal base. Tree frogs wump-wumped from their hiding places in the nandina bushes. A sense of expectation hung in the air.

My desire rose with the throb of a tuning fork struck hard by an eager hand. I should act. It was my place to speak, to step up and embrace her, bury my face in the seductive notch where her neck swept into her shoulder, but I was lagging behind her in many ways, and I let ambiguity drop over us like a cloak.

The distant streetlights caught the merest glint of green in Lauren's gaze. She gave a little huff and strode off toward the condo, moving with a certain glamour, a dancer performing a seductive pavane. I felt her pheromones working overtime, compelling me to keep up.

There was jazz playing when we entered her condo, but Lauren immediately commanded her Internet link, "Svengali, play Smetana, 'The Moldau'."

"I'm fine with jazz," I said, realizing at once how lame I sounded.

Lauren pursed her lips in a deliberate smirk. "I've got this, Fogger. Follow my lead."

"Playing Smetana, 'The Moldau'," said a disembodied voice, and the music began. It was rich, slow, and dreamy, and although I didn't know the piece, I sensed it was telling a story I should understand.

I searched for the signs that would speak to me about Lauren Klout. I had not given thought to what her condo would be like. If I had, I would have got it wrong. A floor-to-ceiling bookshelf covered one entire wall, crammed with hardbound and paperback books of all description, some racked in upright rows with pristine covers, others tattered and worn, wedged into whatever space was available. More books lay on the floor next to an oversized reading chair.

She caught me studying book titles and said, "Really, Fogger. We have our evening mapped out from here on. You won't need a book of instructions, will you?"

"I'm still numb that I got this far. Let me go slow."

"We don't want you numb, do we? You settle back and let me know when you're ready."

There were no live plants, but a high-quality artificial flower arrangement on the small dining table kept the room from looking austere. The artwork that covered the condo walls looked expensive; I had no real familiarity with good art and couldn't be sure.

All of Lauren's paintings were abstract except for one, executed in a hyper-realistic, almost photographic style. I say "realistic," even though the creature shown emerging from a green, storm-tossed sea was unlike anything I had ever seen in film or print. If a dolphin had a giraffe's neck and tapering fingers at the end of its fins, it might approximate this fantastical creature who arched over the waves with its belly exposed to the storm like a primary deity from some ancient, vanished culture. A pod of identical creatures swam in the deep background. I turned to Lauren and smiled my approval.

"My working title for it is *The Escape*," she said. I thought a better title would be *Expectation*. The painting asked a question, one left hanging unanswered in the suspended arc of the creature's exultant emergence into the air. Then I noticed an easel that held a large canvas, perhaps three feet by four, masked by a protective cloth. It sat between two front windows that would give a view of the park had Lauren not covered them with wooden plantation shutters. I nodded at the painting with its exotic sea creature. "Then you're the artist?"

A narrow crease appeared between her brows. "If you can't at least guess . . . ," she said, and it finally registered that since we had entered her condo, Lauren's diction had subtly changed.

I didn't ask permission but walked over to the easel and raised the cloth to look at the work in progress. The bottom half of the canvas was the same light green as the sea in the painting I had admired. The top was sky blue. A simple black line divided the two halves. A horizon? Too early to tell, unless this was a completed abstract work.

"Are we here to study my paintings?" she asked. She slid her hand up to her throat and unfastened another button of her blouse.

That was all it took to derail my thoughts of a gradual approach. I took her in my arms and buried my lips against the curved spot at the base of her throat that had tortured me throughout dinner, let my hands trace the firm sheath of her ribs, slide down her back to grip her buttocks and press her body against mine. My hardened desire pushed against her waist. We clung together briefly, exploring each other with our hands and lips; then Lauren broke away and began to dress a chair with her clothes—precisely, unselfconsciously, as only a woman can do, pausing only once to run her fingers through her hair, shaking out the tousled strands until they swirled around her head like the tendrils of a dark aquatic plant.

When she finished, she stood with a perfect stillness, the sort a doe manages when you look up from your walk and realize she has been standing there, unnoticed, for minutes, expectant. The lights from the park squeezed through the slats of the plantation shutters, casting horizontal streaks of glimmer onto her skin, turning her body into a latticework of shifting curves and lines. In seconds, my clothes were on the floor. We pressed together, flesh against flesh, hand and tongue: tasting, smelling, savoring.

Somewhere in the background, "The Moldau" began to mount, flute and clarinet building slowly and languidly, then quickening, becoming a wave that lifted and enfolded. More instruments entered: a violin, more violins, a harp, improvising and enhancing the theme that swelled into a base wave, taking us with it. We began on the chair; with a few deft movements she guided me in, and I found not the scorching heat I expected but the warmth of some enchanted material, both pliant and resilient. Her most secret parts slipped beneath my fingers like the inner skin of a ripe mango. She exuded a potent musk, thick and sweet and wet, and the scent made me giddy.

We moved onto the floor, drove and plunged and rolled our way to her bed. Something fell with a crash, and "The Moldau" stuttered in mid-crescendo before regaining its momentum. Lauren bore down on me, showing hungry teeth. And her voice, low and urgent, hoarsened on my name. I sensed she was scarcely more skillful than I, but her hunger was immense, a great whirlpool at the bottom of the falls, taking in everything that entered her domain.

Instead of the familiar feeling of spring-tightening pressure, tension, and release, I felt flooded with well-being and acceptance. I had limited experience as a lover, but I welcomed the sense that I was being altered, realigned. When the violinist gets deep into his performance, he rocks back and forth, gripped by the passion of his total abandonment to the music. That was how I threw myself into Lauren. The wave lifted us up, crested, slid down into a trough, lifted and peaked again. We were always part of the wave, always in its embrace.

And when we finished, somehow back on her bed, tangled in wet sheets, my nose deep in the dark dream of her hair, smelling the salty sweetness of her scalp, I realized that whatever woman I touched hereafter, or entered, or tasted, she would be as a child's clumsy nursery song compared to the hymn that was Lauren. This one encounter ruined me for any other woman. I did not care.

I wanted to hold her until dawn, but she turned away from me and switched off the nightstand lamp. "That was nice. I'll see you tomorrow," was all she said. Her breathing leveled out, and she was quickly asleep. I lay there, listening to her steady breaths, until "The Moldau" began playing for the third time, then quietly dressed and let myself out. The clock in the courthouse tower said it was only ten p.m.

The streetlights washed out most of the night sky, but as a city boy I was used to light pollution. I could make out the most obvious constellations. It comforted me to know that Orion would rise every night, Bellatrix and Betelgeuse in their immutable locations on each of his shoulders. This at least I could count on, even as the world of men and supermen fragmented, and reformed with complete disregard for any sense of harmony and stability.

18

The two retrievers at the inn acknowledged me by lifting their heads a meager inch, thumping the porch with dutiful tail wags, and then flopping back into sleepy disregard. I knelt and scratched the female behind her ears. She yawned and stuck her pink tongue out between her teeth.

The reproduction carriage lamp above my door was shining. Beneath it, a single white moth did pirouettes, stroking its wings against the glass. Enough light shone through the drawn window shades that I could see someone waiting inside, and when I cautiously opened the door, I found Cassie Wrenner sitting on the edge of my bed. She had pulled up one corner of the bedspread and was worrying it with her fingers. She looked up briefly to check that it was me, then dropped her gaze to her lap and continued to fray the edge of the bedspread. I left the door open. Cassie's demure demeanor was so calculated that it pissed me off.

"This looks like one thing," she said, "but that's not the

reason I'm here. You need to understand about Lauren Klout before you get in any deeper. She's not someone to run after."

"There's nothing you need to tell me about Chief Klout, Cassie. She's helping me look into the Hatch deaths. That's all there is to it." I pulled a chair beside the bed and pointed at it. Cassie slid off the bed, but instead of sitting down, she walked around behind the chair so it stood between us.

"I'm not a stupid person, Fogger." Her lips made a determined line. "I watch the *Law and Order* reruns. Don't you assume that I don't understand why you wanted those cups."

"Al Amon asked for the cups, not me."

"But you're working together, and Lauren doesn't know anything about that, does she?"

"I'm not sure what Chief Klout knows or doesn't know, Cassie. As far as I can tell, she's a competent woman."

Cassie's lips formed a smirk. "Oh, competent. For sure, she's competent. When she sets out to do something, she always manages to get it done. Mosby is a small town, Fogger. Anyone who hasn't already heard where you went after dinner tonight sure as hell will have by noon tomorrow."

I pushed down my anger. "Go home, Cassie. If there's anything we need to talk about, we can do it tomorrow. I'll come by your shop."

Cassie circled around from behind the chair and dropped into the seat. Her skin was as pale as eggs, and she rolled her shoulders and hunched over to make herself appear small and vulnerable. "That's why I'm here, Fogger. Nothing happens in Mosby without Lauren knowing about it. We need to work together to bring her down. I can help you."

Reading people is what I do, and Cassie's version of a

sincere delivery played false. "It's funny you should say that," I said. "Lauren thinks you're the one who runs Mosby. You want to bring her down. Why?"

Cassie hadn't expected me to throw the question back at her. She twisted around in the chair and said the first thing that came into her head. "Lauren signed the permit for the reunion. She knew all about their plans. Every detail."

"And you own the mill, Cassie, don't you? How much of the reunion idea was yours? And you catered a lot of the food. How about the drinks? Did you supply the lemonade?"

Her eyes grew large, and she pulled her arms protectively across her chest. "No! Look here, Fogger. I did let the family use Magic Beans to plan their reunion. I don't remember whose idea it was. Not mine. But that's part of what stinks with this whole story. The Hatches were all hopped up about having the reunion at first, but once they got the permit, and the more meetings they held, the more cousins showed up, and the more their mood turned sour. The planning went on for half a year, searching out relatives. Lauren's police helped them track down the missing cousins."

Cassie's argument was full of holes. She dismissed her own participation in the reunion planning while inflating Lauren's minor role into a conspiracy. Would Al think this made her a candidate for Hatch alpha? What better role for the alpha in Mosby society than owner of a shop nearly everyone visited at least once a week? Chances were that Cassie was acting out some petty turf war between small-town power brokers. At the least, she was raising doubts about the one person I trusted most. I decided to humor her.

"I have no reason to suspect Lauren of anything, Cassie,

but you can still be part of our investigation. We need to talk to Hatch survivors, the ones whose partners died in the ... fire."

She inched forward in the chair and pointed an index finger at her temple like a child playing a guessing game. "I've got just the place. There's a survivors' group meeting at Liberty Temple tomorrow morning. I helped set it up. I'll tell them to expect you."

"Okay. That's a help. I'll see you at Magic Beans tomorrow."

Cassie had my thanks, but she wanted more. She walked to the door, turned back to me and said, "Steer clear of that witch. Lauren Klout's as fake as they come. If you want to unwind while you're visiting Mosby, someone you can find comfort with, I have a cozy place in town, too. You just let me know."

I gave Cassie time to get away, then stepped out into the night. The air had suddenly become heavy with the cool, close humidity that precedes a summer storm. The cicadas thundered in anticipation, and in the distance, heat lightning flashed behind low-hanging clouds I had failed to notice earlier. The male golden retriever raised his head and waited, counting off the seconds until the distant thunder rolled over us; then he stood and peered into the night, and growled.

When it came, the storm gave no preliminary warning but burst upon the town in a cascade of rain and thunder. The effect was exhilarating. Raindrops hammered the porch roof. There were cobwebs between the pickets of the fence railing, and the spray off the porch steps caught on them, glistening in the light from the carriage lamp. The blowback from the steps drifted into the covered area, spotting my shirt and slacks with drops the size of tears. I stood where I was, letting the wetness build until I could feel the condensation begin to run down my cheeks. Then the downpour increased, and the rain blew onto the porch and began to saturate my clothes.

A bright flash pierced the low northern clouds, then a wait for two, three, four seconds, and the thunder blast rattled the door to my room. I felt it echo in my chest like I was sitting in the front pew for a Bach organ concert. Street and house lights flickered and a series of companion flashes played behind the clouds, casting momentary images of imaginary beasts.

I held onto a post and leaned out from under the protection of the porch roof. Heavy drops pounded my palm. Then, for no reason I could explain, I tramped down the steps into the drenching dark, flung my head back, and watched as electrical flashes illuminated the clouds. I half-expected the retrievers to follow, but they stayed on the porch, pacing circles in their small world, heads down, searching for a dry spot to bed down.

The rain came hard, and I let it soak me. An aroma like fresh laundry rose in the air. The rain striking my head and shoulders made me think of the taps my mother used to give me when she lifted me from my bath, her fingers dancing over my skin while she whispered, "Here, and here, and here." And with that memory, in the downpour, Mosby lost its menace.

A streak of lightning sped across the cloud front a quarter mile above the town. It did not touch down, but when the thunder cracked, a huge limb tore away from the pecan tree at the end of the block and crashed onto the road, and I flinched. The sound rolled over me like the opening cannonade of a Napoleonic battle. For some inexplicable reason I felt exhilarated. A strong smell of ozone permeated the air, mixed with the sweet vanilla of tea olive flowers torn from their branches. The inn's swollen gutters overflowed into the bed of mondo grass beneath the porch overhang. A hiss like radio static rose from the road, but I could hear each drop as it struck the asphalt. The individual impacts were as distinct as fingertips playing Prokofiev's *Seventh Piano Sonata*, full of anger and aggression, heading for a showdown with divine will.

I was nowhere near ready for a collision with a heavy-weight sociopath, but so what? My worries dissipated. I stood drenched in the cloudburst while the drowsing dogs watched my strange behavior through heavy-lidded eyes. Lightening split the night sky, and it made me think of the galvanic charge in Lauren Klout's kiss.

19

Enterprise Rent-a-Car dropped off my loaner Toyota first thing in the morning. My sturdy old Honda was a total loss from fire damage at the mill fire. It would be a while before insurance got settled and I got myself a new ride.

The sky had cleared to a pale blue sheen. Leaves and small branches littered the sidewalk, and raindrops ticked quietly out of the trees. For a few minutes the calm held; then a chainsaw shredded the peace as a road crew began to dice the pecan limb that had fallen during the storm. I went to the breakfast room but had little appetite, so I grabbed a bagel and got on my way.

I drove north to the survivors' meeting at Liberty Temple, about fifteen minutes outside of town on Nokose River Road. The drive was pleasant. I passed a field of grazing cattle, acres of pulpwood pines planted in neat rows, a single house with a large mailbox held between the teeth of a welded metal T-Rex. Pine trees swayed in an unseen breeze. I rolled my window down, drank in the fresh air, and thanked nature for giving me a time-out to enjoy life beyond the reach of the alpha.

Normal was an experience I could no longer take for granted.

I passed no other cars on this country road. A familiar apprehension washed over me when I saw the church. The term *survivors* already hid a lot of dark baggage. Experience had taught me that with the grieving, even the most tactful question could trigger an overwrought response. When I do interviews, most of the people I meet long for a civilized world where folks treat each other with respect and restraint. Some, however, are convinced that life has betrayed them. Their desire to revenge themselves is insatiable. Someone is to blame for their rotten luck. Find that guilty person. Punish him. I often have to scrub entire paragraphs of discontent before I can craft a feel-good column from my raw material. I hoped these survivors would not be awash in grievances.

"Everyone keep it low-key," I said under my breath, not sure who I was speaking to. A prayer to the good spirits who hovered outside the church, perhaps.

It wasn't concern about the survivors' interviews that was causing my underlying disquiet. That foreboding went deeper, but it was easier to label. Now that I had accepted Al's theory of human murmuration, I saw the deaths at Turnell Mill as more than a mass murder. They violated all the values I cherished. That one person would use his power to control others? Obscene. People weren't harnessed oxen to be used against their will. My entire life, various forces had shackled my right to be who I wanted to be. I had let the constraints pile up: my grandparents' indifference and petty cruelties, my many self-inflicted impediments, my mother's screwball behavior, her well-meaning but bizarre religious beliefs—until I had lost control over life itself. I often felt like a survivor myself, chewing on bones of injustice.

The temperature had reached eighty-six degrees when I pulled into the parking lot. I parked next to a Dodge minivan with the figure of a praying Snoopy stenciled on the back window. Nearly all the cars in the lot had bumper stickers that advertised their owner's Christianity. Three crosses stood on the artificial berm in front of the parking lot. Two were creosote black, the larger central cross was white, with a deep purple cloth draped limply over the horizontal arm, sodden from the perpetual rain that followed Easter.

Liberty Temple, a modest one-story building of lapped fiberglass panels, followed the model of an enlarged double-wide trailer. Its roof was flat except for a single low-pitched section over the entrance, so out of proportion that I imagined the parishioners must have run out of money during construction. The church had no steeple and no ornamentation other than a rough sheet-metal cross bolted to the exterior wall. Although it was already midmorning, naked hundred-watt bulbs shone brightly behind the arms of the metal cross, which had the same slapped-together look as the dinosaur mailbox I had seen earlier. The same metal artist?

The church didn't skimp on air conditioning. The temperature inside hovered somewhere in the mid-sixties, a shock after the eighties of the parking lot. A stainless-steel coffee urn sat on a trestle table in the narrow vestibule. Empty Styrofoam cups filled the trash can under the table and spilled onto the floor. I got the message—more people had arrived early, inhaled a hasty cup, testified to their sorrow, and split before I got here. Sure enough, only three survivors sat in the pews.

Two of them craned their necks to check me out as I walked down the aisle. The other leaned forward, clutching the back of the pew in front of him, perhaps praying that the universe would reverse course, start over.

The altar was plain shellacked oak covered by a beige hand-embroidered tablecloth. Next to it a beat-up, bright-red Fender Stratocaster leaned against an abandoned drum set. The survivors waited for me to sit down. I took a seat in the front pew and half-turned around to face them. In the subdued lighting, the three reminded me of the painting known as *Whistler's Mother*, whose official name is *Arrangement in Grey and Black*. That was what I saw: three people who exhibited a color spectrum, from anemic white to coal black. We studied each other in silence. A fierce-looking white woman spoke first. She verged on obese, but if she had combed her hair and straightened her clothes, I might have called her attractive. She had pulled her long hair back from her forehead and tied it with a rubber band, leaving a thin strip of pale skin above her tanned face. Anyway, she didn't care what I or anyone else thought about her appearance.

"We're here as a favor to Cassie," she said. "She says you have questions. Ask them."

"I'd like to know if your spouses acted out of character in the days before the accident at the mill," I said, keeping my voice as neutral as possible. The three shifted their weight in the pews. The fierce-looking woman eyed the other two, nodded, then gave me a thin smile that held back an impossible volume of pain.

"I always felt safe around my Tom. Other wives complain about meanness and battering; not me. He never gave me reason to fear—until that day, when none of us wanted to go except him, and he pushed us into the truck and drove to the mill so fast you'd have thought we was in a race, kids cryin' and me asking what's happenin'. Then the explosion took him and Autumn and little Joey. And now I'm left. Just me, here alone. That enough for you?"

I could think of no way to take the bite out of this woman's heartbreak. Whenever I'd met this kind of reaction in the past, I would shift to a less painful subject. This time, I pressed on. "You say Tom acted different that day. Did he do anything that made you suspect he didn't want to go?"

"Like I said, he laid down the law to us. He kept telling us how much he loved us, over and over, but how we just had to get there. Listen to me. I love Jesus, but I'm angry. Who'm I s'posed to be angry with? I'm s'posed to say 'praise Jesus,' aren't I, but he's the one let this happen. That gas main, it might have picked any time to blow, some hour deep in the night when my babies was asleep, not when all our folk was there. Jesus let it happen. He let my babies die."

"Oh, hush, now," said the man on her left. "We're in God's temple. Don't you say that here." He was maybe sixty, his eyes swollen and discolored, but I couldn't tell if this was his regular look or an outward sign of grief. Another point on the color scale: pink but with mocha-tinted splotches on his face and neck, a body that could not decide how to paint itself. He wore a sport shirt with green and red parrots that looked straight out of a Jimmy Buffett revival, but it lent no joy to his disposition.

"One thing Martha says, we all agree on," he said. "Those people we loved, they weren't there that day. I let on as how I lost my wife, Seppy, at the reunion, but that weren't her. No, not that day."

"How was she different, sir?" I asked.

The splotchy-skinned man pondered for a moment and said, "You'd a thought her radio got tuned to the Doomsday Channel. Everything just down, down, down, like she got hooked onto public radio or something." His gaze drifted off toward the altar. I waited for him to start up again.

"Seppy," he sighed. "She was the kind of woman was always on top of things, a chicken nailed down on a bug. I loved her for that. Depended on it. But that last month before the reunion, she couldn't focus on anything more'n a few minutes. She'd forget to make dinner, started dressing all sloppy. No, sir. That weren't Seppy atall."

"What sort of person was your wife?"

"We didn't have kids together. Both of us widowed, past the age to start a new family even if we'd wanted to. She had a boy, a fine boy, got himself killed by a logger truck out on 441 a few years back. Knocked him right out of his shoes, back into the trees. When we married after that, the neither of us wanted children, but I sure always wanted her. Fell in love with Seppy back years ago. Waited for her when she married that no-account house painter; waited more years while she got over him. I miss her terrible bad." He drew another deep breath.

"If you're searching for strange," he went on, "then that day the explosion happened, Seppy sent me off to Athens to find her an ice cream maker. Didn't need no fancy ice cream maker. We got a Dairy Queen just down the town. So I think that errand was for this—she planned it so's I wouldn't get back in time. She had a warning from God, and He told her not to have me there. And that's what's the hardest thing. I wasn't there for her."

"Y'all had a lot of planning meetings at the coffee shop," I said. "Did anything happen during those meetings that seemed strange to you? For example, did anyone seem to be in charge?"

The angry woman crossed her arms. "Ha! Nobody was in charge. Talked the plans to death, is what happened. Talk and more talk. Mostly the diehards searched for more relatives. Found some. Rounded 'em up like they expected somebody'd be handing out lottery tickets. Got one man to come down all the way from up in North Carolina, didn't even know he was a Hatch until they told him."

The blotchy-faced man chimed in. "What I remember is lots of talk about food—who was to bring what, those things wives talk about."

"Who supplied the lemonade and the iced tea?" I asked.

"What a fool thing to ask! We ordered drinks from the coffee shop. Who cares? Fact is, our wives died, our kids and our family. If'n this is where your questions is gonna go, I'm done."

After that, I didn't know how to put the conversation back on track. I couldn't ignore the pain I was inflicting on these people. I had already guessed what they would say. Everything confirmed what Al and I had pieced together. Somehow, the Hatch alpha had wormed into the minds of his victims, suppressing their judgment and their natural desire to protect family, ruthlessly selecting the Hatch descendants for death but allowing their non-Hatch spouses to escape.

I was ready to give up on this charade when the third survivor, a quiet, dark-black man with scarred forearms, sat up as if waking from a deep sleep. He took a sip from his Styrofoam cup and wiped his lips with the back of his hand. Scores of shallow cracks lined his sun-hardened face, but his smile was genuine. The fingers on the hand that held the cup bent sideways at an acute angle, the souvenir of an old accident or a virulent strain of arthritis. "You'd be Flo Grace's son, Francis."

"Yes, sir. You know her?"

He gave me a satisfied smile and flipped the fringed leather on his motorcycle vest as if to say it was his answer. The vest looked like a costume from a high-school musical. The gothic lettering read, "Up-Top Riders. We Got It."

"I courted Flo-Flo way back then," he said. "Back before." Before what, I wondered, but I waited for him to continue.

He sat there with a slight grin and said nothing more, so I asked, "Sir, do I look that much like you remember her?"

He squinted. "Thing is, you've got too much Wonder Bread in your sandwich. Could be I see a bit of Flo-Flo in there, but hardly a penny's worth. Not as pretty, but she's in there, way deep. What I see the most is *his* cut in you, Francis. That highly agitates me, but that's not a stain on you. You be you."

I thought hard before I asked, "Do you know him, sir—my father?"

"I 'spect you call everyone sir or ma'am, don't you? Flo-Flo would have taught you that."

"Yes, sir, I do. Unless they give me a reason not to. And my father?"

He turned his head to the side when he replied. "Oh, he's long gone now. Long gone and good riddance."

"I'd appreciate anything you might tell me about him."

"Not for me to say. If Flo hasn't told you 'bout him, it's not my place." He exchanged frowns with the other two. There was furious signaling going on that I couldn't decipher.

"I get mixed up about him, but I can tell you, he might've called himself a minister, but he weren't no man of God. No, sir. Only honorable thing he ever done was kill himself." He pointed his bent fingers at the blotchy-faced man. "No, don't you tell me I can't say that. I'll say it again. He should've done right by Florence. Killed himself instead, the coward." He turned back to me. "You been fine so far not knowing about that. You be fine going on, now." The set of his jaw had finality in it.

My question about heritage shut down the interview. The three offered nothing but dead-end regrets and indignation. I looked at the empty cross on the wall and decided to make a long overdue visit.

20

My father.

Even at a young age, overhearing voices broken off in mid-sentence through the thin walls of my grandparent's house, and observing how certain words triggered a sharp rebuke, I learned he was a forbidden subject. Later, when we lived alone in Atlanta, my mother never tolerated questions about him. Unattended, I speculated wildly about his identity.

When I was very young, I fantasized that I was a star-child, fathered on this insignificant planet by a passing space explorer. When I grew old enough to need a more down-to-earth dream, I decided that he was a Special Forces hero killed on a world-saving mission kept secret by the government. Still later, I became the offspring of a tragic love affair in which my father had had to move to a distant land, never to return, never to know that he had fathered a son. None of these head trips ever satisfied my yearning to know my true identity.

I had not seen my grandparents since I verged on

adolescence. My last memory of them was of the day they turned us out of their Pickett home, my mother crying, almost hysterical, while Pastor and Grammy stood resolutely on the porch of their small wooden house, their arms defiantly crossed against their daughter's heartbreak. There was always an invisible barrier between us. As a boy, I was not permitted to call my grandfather any cute nicknames—not Grampy or Pop-Pop or even Grandfather. Our relationship was far too distant for that. He expected me to call him Pastor, and I did.

On that last day in Pickett, I sat in Mom's sparsely packed car knowing that my world had irrevocably changed. Pastor locked his eyes on me and, for perhaps the first time in my life, held the stare. He walked slowly to the car and put both hands on the lowered window.

"God's testing me, boy. I don't hate you, but you are the offspring of someone who aims to harm my bond with God. I got enough stress on that relationship already. You stay in the city with your people and don't come back."

My people. I had no idea who my people were. Only that they were not in Pastor's house.

I don't know what caused the final break with my grandparents—some new outrage by their batty daughter, amplified by the continued aggravation of a bastard grandchild? Who knew for sure? A final, unacknowledged worsening of their child's mental illness had pushed them too far. The embarrassment they had put up with for so many years had to disappear, so they abandoned her to their angry God.

The meager connection that defined my relationship with my grandparents ceased altogether after we moved to Atlanta. No birthday cards, no inquiries about how Francis was doing in grade school or college, no anonymous Christmas presents. Over the years, memories winnowed themselves down to a few: exploring the woods with Pastor's two beagles, helping Grammy can vegetables in glass jars, listening to Pastor say grace before dinner. He could turn any grace into a ten-minute jeremiad against any of the thirty-two deadly sins. After more than two decades, my trip to Pickett would be as much a trip back in time as a call on my estranged family.

Pickett lies a short drive from Mosby on a two-lane state road bordered on the southern side by a mix of small farms and mini-developments. The road had lost the densely wooded acreage I remembered. Some parcels were so new they were just bare lots with the trees scraped off, waiting for cement and cinder blocks and bricklayers. The relentless sprawl of Atlanta had overrun Conyers, submerged Covington and Social Circle, and was lapping against defenseless Pickett. Mosby would be next in the path of the great urban overflow.

Railroad tracks bordered the north side of the road. Curiously, the grassy verge between my lane and the track bed was chock-full of billboards. I couldn't picture how the traffic on this country back road justified the expense of so many ads. The State of Georgia makes no pretense of trying to save roadside views. Acres of trees are clear-cut to provide maximum viewing intervals for advertising. Drivers can read the messages from a quarter mile away. On the interstates, electronic billboards are rapidly replacing the traditional 14x48-foot models, multiplying the opportunities for distracted driving. They can arrest you in Georgia for texting while driving but not for flashing glassy-eyed drivers with ads the size of a motor yacht.

The billboards along this stretch all used the old-fashioned "bulletin" format, and they all advertised the same service. One after another, they pleaded with me to sue someone for something, anything. An up-to-date game plan for success. The nicknames of the personal injury attorneys were familiar to me from their relentless television ads on Atlanta TV. The short drive to Pickett featured seven different bidders for my business, including The Bulldozer and Mister Massive Settlement and The Insurance Agency Assassin. I imagined them each having part-time jobs on the WWE wrestling channel, with feather-encrusted tights and wicked tattoos. My favorite billboard showed an attorney standing on the prow of his ship, aiming his harpoon at a whale that spouted a stream of hundred-dollar bills. The string of negative images put me in an unsettled mood for my visit with my grandparents.

Cynicism had a good grip on me, but it disappeared when I saw flashing lights in my rear-view mirror. Not a blue-and-white Mosby police car, but a black cruiser from the county sheriff's patrol. I checked my speedometer, saw I was well under the limit, and pulled over onto the verge.

I watched the rear-view mirror and after a long wait, the cruiser's driver-side door opened. The red-and-blue light bar continued to strobe. I turned off my engine, but no one got out of the cruiser. When no one emerged, I waited another few minutes, then got out and began to walk back to see what the problem was.

"Stop right there!" a loudspeaker barked. "Show me your hands. Keep your hands where I can see them."

"Sure thing," I said. "I understand. What's the problem?"

"Back up slowly to your vehicle. Keep your hands up. No sudden moves."

"Officer, I…"

"No talking. Put your hands on the roof of your vehicle and lean forward."

The officer got out slowly, deliberately, never letting his gaze drop. A small, stiff man with glowering dark eyes. His jaws worked continuously, as if he were chewing on a large wad of gum. It wasn't his expression that communicated menace. The threat was from the Remington Express shotgun he held at ready position; the barrel pointed at the ground. My bowels roiled over.

I turned slowly to face him, hands open, fingers spread. "Look, Officer, I don't know what's going on, but I've done nothing wrong." And I watched, horrified, as the barrel of the shotgun began to rise.

"Hold on. Please stop. I have my hands up, see? This is a mistake."

The shotgun faltered as the officer cocked his head sideways and stared at me. He took one hand off the gun and keyed the microphone attached to his shoulder. I couldn't hear what he said or make out the response, but he took a step back and lowered the shotgun so it once again pointed at the ground.

"A mistake," he said. His voice was mechanical. "You're free to go."

I stood until the cruiser's taillights had disappeared and for a long time afterward. When my pulse had fallen back to normal, I started the engine and resumed my drive. By the time I got to Pickett, I felt calm enough to confront my grandparents.

I parked on the grass swale in front of the house in which I had lived for my first eleven years. The yard was brown with summer drought and pockmarked with holes left by armadillo snouts. There had never been a doorbell, so I knocked, waited, and knocked again. I heard nothing but the musical trill of tree crickets.

I found my grandfather in the backyard, perched low on the railroad tie border of his raised vegetable beds. He wore what had once been a respectable Tilley hat, now beaten and shabby. It went well with his baggy-ass jeans and rundown sneakers. I guessed the white shirt he wore had been part of his Sunday service preacher's uniform. It bore stains left by years of home repair tasks and yard duties, but the contrast with his dark brown complexion still made his appearance snap as if he'd stepped out of an old photograph. I felt nostalgic when I looked at him, although not in a good way.

"Hello, Pastor. It's Francis Grace. How are you?"

Pastor had a wire basket on the creosoted railroad tie next to his knee. It held a mix of red and yellow heirloom tomatoes, some stringy peppers, a few onions. He didn't look up but pulled another yellow onion out of the bed, knocked off the dirt, and added it to the basket. "I heard you were in the area, boy. What made you come on out here?"

"A visit, Pastor. It's been a long time. I wanted to see you and Grammy."

He reluctantly glanced up at me, pulled the brim of his hat down to shield his eyes. "You are still too white, boy. You should stand in the shade, so's you don't get sunburned. The good Lord only knows why he condemned our family to get lighter skinned with each generation."

My grandfather leaned over and placed both his fists on the railroad tie to push himself up. When I took his arm to help, he swatted my hand. "Not so ancient as to need that," he said, then hoisted his basket of vegetables and weighed them before making a decision. "It must be about noon. I'll be having my lunch. Imagine you'll be wanting some. You come up to the house."

When we got into the small kitchen, Pastor pointed me to a chair and shambled over to the old porcelain sink to wash his hands. He washed for a full five minutes, never saying a word. He opened the refrigerator and took out a loaf of bread and a jar of peanut butter, then put the jar back in the refrigerator and pulled out a Tupperware bowl. Lunch was pimiento cheese sandwiches on white bread with the crusts cut off. My grandfather didn't ask what I wanted to drink, merely poured two glasses of sweet tea and sat down at the kitchen table. He took a small bite of his sandwich and chewed for a long time, grimacing when he swallowed. I pictured his throat raw from the thousands of damning dinnertime diatribes he had blasted at me during my childhood.

Pastor stared at his plate, chewed another bite, and never met my eyes. "So," he said after a long while, "how is she?"

"Sir?"

"Don't you play smart with me, Francis. You were always doing that, hiding behind your wide-eyed, innocent disguise, acting the stupid white boy God never intended you to be. Don't you do that, now. How is Florence?"

"She's in a special home for people who have emotional problems, Pastor. She has this twisted idea that her parents don't love her. Never loved her." That wasn't true, at least not the whole problem, but my grandfather had always been a sonofabitch, and I wanted to hurt him if I could.

"Ah," he said, and took another bite of his sandwich, chewing deliberately. Pastor Ogden Grace had preached against Satan for thirty years, warning his flock of the wages of sin, sermonizing to one-up Jonathan Edwards about sinners in the hands of an angry god, sinners whom God holds like spiders over the pit of a fiery hell. Then his unmarried daughter became pregnant, and his lake of eternal torment sprang a titanic leak. The catastrophe took his career with it. My grandfather's simple "Ah" carried a deluge of regret I could not hope to sort out. Nor did I want to.

"I'm in Mosby to report on the fire at Turnell Mill. It wasn't an accident. Someone made it happen. Someone who controls what people do; controls them."

"You know who that is, boy. Satan has had his way with this family. You are familiar with his work."

"I mean a person, Pastor. A flesh-and-blood evil; not an abstract."

"Devil's never been abstract, Francis. He's in everyone who doesn't follow the Lord."

"I'm trying to sort out who controls things around here. You'd know. Who pulls the strings in Mosby?"

"There's different types of controllers. Some of them are obvious and don't care who sees them pushing folks around. That devil tax assessor, for one. And the people sets the prices at the grocery. Their day's coming and the Lord will take them down."

"Okay, but . . ."

"The ones to watch for are the hidden ones. Those who lurk beneath the surface, pushing the fears and the hates with their lies and their insinuations. Every town has 'em. The stealthy ones. They're the ones you don't see. But you remember they're just the puppets. The puppet master's always the same."

Those were the most words my grandfather had ever said to me at one time. He was right in his way. The alpha was a puppet master, and as evil as the spirit he feared. When it was clear he had nothing more to add, I asked, "How is Grammy?"

Instead of answering, he took a gulp of iced tea, swished it around in his mouth, and stood, pushing himself up again with his fists. He walked back to the sink and washed his hands again for another five minutes, his back turned to me, never saying a word. I knew better than to interrupt his inflexible ceremony. It had always been this way.

Pastor finished washing and dried his age-cracked hands on a dish towel. He turned and walked out of the kitchen. I hesitated, then followed.

Grammy sat in her bedroom in an overstuffed Barca recliner, watching television with the sound turned off, just as my mother used to do. She looked withered and wasted, about twenty years past her expiration date. The threadbare pink bathrobe she wore awakened memories from long ago. It now engulfed her. I remembered watching her bustle around the kitchen in that robe when I came back from school, waiting for her to put dinner on the table, hoping she might tell me to set the table or ask how my day had gone. That happened so rarely that I could recall the specific words and gestures of the individual times she had inquired.

Grammy didn't react when I leaned over and gave her a hug, but she asked, "Who is this boy, Ogden?"

"It's your grandson, Francis," I answered. "I came to visit you, Grammy."

She laughed at something on the television, a commercial showing carefree seniors playfully dealing with their emphysema. I moved around her recliner and crouched on the floor in front of her. She craned her neck to see the television screen over my shoulder. "That's nice," she said, then after a while she asked, "Who is this, Ogden?"

"It's Flo-Flo's boy," he replied in a flat voice, "that's who." I felt his eyes on the side of my head. I did not give him the satisfaction of turning to look at him.

"That girl who had the devil's baby?" asked my grandmother.

"The very one," he said.

"There was that boy who came here. Then he went away."

I put my face up against hers. "I'm right here, Grammy," I said.

"Oh, not you. The father of that girl's baby."

Pastor walked out of the room. Grammy saw something move on her silent screen and smiled. If she was aware of me at all, it was as a faint distortion in the ether. The Grammy I remembered, the woman who sometimes gave me easy tasks to perform so I could feel useful when my mother's brain skittered off the frying pan, that woman had walked away a long time ago. This fake Grammy laughed at her mute TV, never taking her eyes off the glowing screen.

I stood and forced out a deep breath. A large, invasive creature had taken residence in my lungs, and I might dislodge it with enough effort. I tried again and realized I was gasping, becoming lightheaded. My grandparents' indifference had always hovered around me. I had simply forgotten how it could suffocate.

Grandfather waited for me back at the kitchen table. He

wore a holier-than-thou smirk, savoring my discomfort. I waited for him to speak so I would have something to fight against, but he didn't. This was the past I remembered from childhood: the studied disregard, the barely buried resentment.

"I didn't choose this," I said. "I just got born, Pastor. That's all I did." His smile hardened, so I pushed him. "Name him. Name my father. Was he from here in Pickett?"

Ogden Grace shifted his bony ass in his chair and let out a choleric sigh. I turned his smile back on him, satisfied that I had gotten under his skin.

"You don't get to ask me that," he said. Spittle flecked his lips. The veins in his neck swelled with blood. "I didn't even know he was around here until he planted you in my daughter."

"So it's easy. Tell me who he is. Tell me and I'll go. You don't want me here, and I don't want to stay any longer than I have to."

Satisfied that he had regained control, Pastor settled back in his chair. He looked away from me and addressed the kitchen wall. "Don't stay, then. We haven't missed you. Don't need you. Go."

Now, because he had yet to answer me, I leaned forward and spread my fingers on the tabletop and arched them, knuckles rigid, feeling my impatience grow like a fever. I didn't like this mounting sensation of outrage. It threatened my every discipline of self-restraint. "I'm part of your blood, Grandfather. Tell me who he is."

"You are not my grandson. There's none of my blood runs through you. We are not your people. You don't have any people. Get your car off my lawn. Go."

The drive back to Mosby took a lot less time than the drive

out to Pickett. The backsides of the billboards read the same as the fronts. I sensed the Hatch alpha's pathology in the ads. Was it all nationalistic braggadocio, those ideals to which people pledged their lives and sacred honor? Had that country ever existed? Modern textbooks tell us that there never was a land of the free; that there never was a culture that valued individual responsibility and civility; that we have been stealing from each other since the inception, undermining and lying to each other from the get-go. Others argue that our country might once have had ideals but abandoned them a long time ago, that the world we should have is one where someone else is always to blame for our faults and our misfortunes, and that someone should pay the bills to satisfy our desires.

As in my childhood, Pastor Grace had done a number on my temper. That was all on him. I yawned to unclench my jaw, and made a point of looking at the daylilies by the roadside, but their random beauty didn't bring peace of mind. Once again, I vowed that I wouldn't let my grandfather keep his hooks in me. Pickett was my past. Keep it there, frozen. If I wanted to live in a different world, I'd have to keep on building it.

21

Despite my best efforts, my temper threatened to boil over as I drove back to town. If I met anyone associated with the suicides—no, the *mass murder*, I reminded myself—I would be at risk of breaking orbit and going completely off into deep space. The danger was real: I was no longer the meek, confused Francis Grace who had been exiled from Pickett twenty years ago, nor was I the Fogger Grace who had lived an unassuming life ever since. If I found someone guilty of the merest trespass of any kind, I wanted to lash out, to do real damage.

Sure, I could blame my anger on my grandfather, but my unrelenting conjectures about how murmuration worked made it worse. Murmuration forced its victims to remain in the mill fire even as the pain became unbearable. Did it also steel them to the reality of their deaths, of their own willing murder of their loved ones? I hoped so. What thoughts had reeled through their minds as they stood, mutely burning? Did the alpha blank their minds to the odor of their burning flesh? Did he blind them to the sight of the fat bubbling and sloughing from their bones? Did he orchestrate their senses so they felt no pain? I hoped so, but I suspected he did not.

What of my friend Grady? He must have schooled himself, over and over, to seize Patty-Ann and choke out her life when the fire started, to shorten his child's agony, and I'm sure he shouted that he loved her. But this took only part of his attention. What else flickered in his brain as it sputtered and melted? Our minds are wondrous instruments, capable of processing a multitude of simultaneous thoughts. Surely, Grady thought about other things. But what? I think he wondered what he might have done to avoid this terrible end, and remembered the words he regretted saying or not saying in his life, the love not given, the good deeds not done.

Did he think of God? Or did his mind shut down and deny it all, expecting to awaken from the nightmare? Run away, Grady.

I have a sure-fire way to clear my mind. The ache to live demands that I run. It is my greatest joy: running the streets as a boy, running cross-country in school, jogging as an adult. All I need is a pair of good running shoes.

My regular shoes were back in Atlanta, so I pulled up to the ATM at the Bank of America and withdrew four hundred dollars. My receipt showed a balance of $14,722. There had never been that much money in my account, not even close.

Whatever change Michelle had intended to make in my pay, Accounting had made a whopping mistake, but I wouldn't take time to sort it out now. Instead, I drove to Fancy Feet, a store I had seen near the post office, and bought a pair of New Balance running shoes. They were a hideous, baby-poop green, but they were the only pair in my size. Five minutes later, I parked my car at the B&B, changed into shorts and my new running shoes, and set out at a fast pace along South Avenue, following signs pointing to the John Lewis library.

The temperature had held in the eighties, and I could taste the humidity with each breath, but I kept my pace up, and soon my body relaxed into the familiar endorphin burn that signaled a runner's high. As I ran, the town's postcard flavor gave way to a more familiar mix of architectural styles. I felt as though I were running in one of Atlanta's tree-lined suburbs of heavily shadowed lawns and brick sidewalks buckled by aged oak tree roots. My preoccupations with the Hatch family and my overdue AJC feature columns melted away. I lengthened my stride, heading for the US 441 bypass on Mosby's southern border.

My body fully warmed up, I fell into a runner's trance, the side of distance running I most enjoyed. During cross-country races, I'd use that twenty minutes to go deep within myself and think about why the hell I was punishing myself this way. What was the point? Cross-country is an individual sport, but we all ran together along the same path. I'd worry about my fellow American's propensity to choose sides and fall into line, running lockstep toward conflicting goals that have the same finish line. The alpha. Had I honestly figured out *his* goals?

The road ran downhill from the Aintry County Courthouse before turning south and leveling out for the long run to the bypass. A postage-stamp-sized lot at the turn contained what must have been one of the few statues of Robert E. Lee not yet defaced by the forces of the righteous. My own racial heritage was decidedly mixed, but I didn't understand the mania for destroying memorials. Years of rain and frost had blotched

Lee's stone face. Beneath this camouflage lay sorrow. When the war was lost, he had said so, and he'd urged his fellow white Southerners to turn their attention to rebuilding. He prayed in church that they would not hold a grudge for the devastation of their land and hopes. Instead, far too many of them joined the White League and the Klan and bought into the fiction of the noble Lost Cause, making Bobby Lee a stone saint.

South Avenue meandered through a mixed neighborhood of homes that spanned two centuries of architectural history. Twentieth-century bungalows and ranch-style homes now and again intermingled with stately two-hundred-year-old patriarchs. The oldest homes had street-side plaques proclaiming the year they were built. These homes were more modest than those along Main Street, but each had its own name: The Hutch, The Grievers, Yancy Miller's Ivy House, The Shipwright House.

One large house stood out from the rest. Chances were good that all the land now filled with later-style homes had once comprised the estate of this commanding building. A long *allee* of huge old oaks and dense shrubs led to a single antebellum residence set well back from the road. Before the Civil War, this opulence had announced a landowner of importance, perhaps the owner of one of the many cotton plantations that once surrounded Mosby. Many people who bought homes like this today—in particular, wealthy northerners living out a Scarlett O'Hara fantasy—remained so ignorant of history that they would not stop to ponder that slave labor had built the house, truss by truss and brick by brick. Even longtime southerners rarely mulled over this aspect of the past. But in its time, this multi-winged house and its tall Corinthian columns had asserted an unambiguous message of control, authority, and obedience.

Now, in the twenty-first century, a person with an invisible, haphazard gene was exercising a similar power of control, authority, obedience. His supremacy wasn't artificial, imposed by superficial differences in skin color or a temporary surplus of wealth. It derived from a more insidious source, anchored in evolutionary superiority, in the ability to make people do his bidding merely by convincing them to want it. Al Amon hoped that human murmuration was evolution's response to overpopulation, that instant communications would somehow free people to work out their most vexing problems. Wishful thinking. Murmuration didn't improve communication; rather, it made the master–slave imbalance of power absolute.

The estate's irrigation system was running. The inconsiderate owner didn't care that his Rain Bird sprinklers overshot the holly hedge that bordered the sidewalk and drenched my path. I had to swing wide onto the road shoulder for a dozen strides, then duck back onto the sidewalk. Just as I did, the crunching sound of tires jarred me out of my musings. I overreacted and jumped sideways into the hedge. When I turned, I saw a Mosby police cruiser creeping along beside me, blue lights flashing. Lauren Klout faked an effort to conceal a smile behind her cupped hand. I took one look at the thin scrape marks on my right arm—damn, holly cuts stung worse than razor cuts—and smiled foolishly at her.

Lauren put the cruiser in neutral and lowered her passenger-side window to lean across her computer console. "Sorry I spooked you," she said, "but I was eyeballing your tight ass." She added a smirk to show she enjoyed my awkwardness.

"Lauren," I said, "last night was . . ."

"Nice. You were going to say *nice,* weren't you?"

Actually, I'd been searching for the right superlative. I wanted a word that meant *transcendent*, or *out-of-body*, or *world class*, but a word that wouldn't come across like a needy puppy. *Nice*, she said. I held my tongue. To repeat that tepid word would have been false, so I just nodded.

"I've been thinking we should get together. You free tonight?"

"Al and I are meeting to go over his files. It won't take long. His work is way over my head. So, what, dinner?"

Lauren pushed her finger into her cheek. "Dinner's good. Not much else to do on a date here in Mosby, 'less maybe you got some better ideas. I'm thinking a repeat of last night's tryout would be a good place to start. Got a few twists we might study on. You stop by about eight." She slipped her cruiser back in gear and took off before I could agree. She knew I would.

Sexual intimacy was an under-explored part of my life. My few experimental hookups, satisfying in a one-off way, had satisfied my physical needs, but I'd never been fortunate enough to find someone in whom I could drown myself. My inhibitions always blocked that final barrier of full commitment. My one night with Lauren had been the otherworldly experience I'd craved—a rapture, to be honest; a feast. The prospect of a second chance with her added energy to my stride, but I jogged only a few steps before growing pressure in my bladder signaled that I had to find a restroom, fast.

Up ahead was the county library, a modern building of glass and wheat-colored brick. I sprinted across the road, my urge cresting, then slowed to a brisk walk, determined not to look silly. A cast-concrete statue of Joel Chandler Harris's Tar Baby sat to one side of the library, partially hidden by a screen of inkberry and yaupon holly. Br'er Rabbit had a foot and one fist sunk deep in the Tar Baby's body, his other fist waving in the air as he debated the risk of throwing another punch. Should he keep trying to defeat this soulless creature, or should he admit defeat and yield? Rabbit was not just trapped. He was being sucked into his anonymous antagonist. I'm usually fond of artistic metaphors. Today was not one of those times.

As I passed through the library's sliding doors, I saw Cassie Wrenner unloading a canvas bag of audio CDs into the book return locker in the library drive-thru. She'd parked her silver Lexus 570 obliquely. Its air conditioner labored to keep the car cool with the door open. Apparently, I couldn't put my Mosby connections behind me, not even for as long as a run. First Lauren, which was okay; then Cassie, not so okay. I noticed a sign that announced, "Do not leave audio books in the locker. The heat will damage them." I could have stepped back outside and pointed this out to her, but I didn't want another conversation, not now.

The restrooms were down a side corridor near the drinking fountain. I took a long, languid piss, leaning over the urinal with one hand braced on the wall. My morning had been a real pisser. I'd gotten my mainspring wound up at the survivor's meeting; then Pastor shoved me into a time machine to revisit a past that could never be the loving childhood fantasy I had always craved. All I'd wanted from him was the recognition that something related us, but even now he couldn't give it. Mosby was adept at withholding information. It appeared everyone except me had well-founded suspicions about who my ghost father was.

I exited the restroom and bent over for a drink at the water fountain. When I straightened, Cassie Wrenner stood on the other side of the fountain, much too close. She took a step forward, and I backed against the wall, keenly aware of the stink of my sweaty Emory Eagles T-shirt.

"You're not a good listener," she said. "I made my invitation clear enough."

22

Cassie wormed her fingers under my shirt and slid them up my belly to the center of my chest, sneaking past my personal perimeter. She pinched my chest hairs and when she twisted them, I flinched and stammered, "Whoa, Cassie, this isn't a good idea."

She smelled of Oblivion, the one perfume my mother always insisted on wearing, and the scent was so heavy it made my head swim. Her hand had to be slick with my perspiration, but instead of withdrawing it, she pressed her palm flat against my breastbone. Her presence seemed to fill the space around us. When she looked up at me, her glinting blue eyes shone with a mixture of desire and some other emotion too impenetrable to identify.

"What is it with you, Fogger? All those other boys in school wanted to get their hands under my shirt. You're the one boy I wanted to go there, and you never tried." Her fingernails scratched ever so lightly on my chest. "I thought about you all through middle school and high school. All those other hands but not yours, and now here you are."

"Look, Cassie. This is awkward. I can come by your shop later, and we can talk there."

"I have a nice room just above the shop. It's private. I'm the only one who's ever there. If you came, we could have a celebration. You know, a reunion party." She emphasized her message by dropping her other hand onto the small of my back and rocking her breasts against my chest, eagerly nudging me against the wall. Whatever she wore under her blouse, it was as stiff and insistent as a bulletproof vest. I didn't imagine Cassie could be more emphatic, but then she slid her hand down my chest and cupped my shorts between my legs. Despite myself, I felt a surge of response.

"Not now, Cassie," I said. "I'm on a run." I stepped sideways and slid along the wall until I was free of her embrace, then I was through the sliding doors, past the still-idling Lexus, and across the street before I cleared the Oblivion from my head. My suddenly tight shorts were so twisted around that I had to self-consciously tug them into place. Too many confusing thoughts, too many competing propositions I would have welcomed even a week ago.

"Get with it, Fogger," I muttered. "Pull up the anchor and go." Great. Now I was talking to myself.

I completed the next mile at a solid pace, but a strange sort of wildness seized me and I increased tempo, reaching further with each stride. The warm concrete flashed beneath my shoes. The sensation was of flying smooth and effortless above the sidewalk. When I reached the final quarter mile, I began to run full-tilt toward the highway and it was only with effort that I managed to stop myself before plunging into traffic.

My breathing was holding steady. I felt great, as if I had never quit training for cross-country. In fact, I had never felt better. My cheeks burned with excess energy. Someone had plugged my spinal cord into an electrical outlet. The back of my neck tingled with excess voltage. I watched the high-speed traffic hurtle along the bypass, twenty miles an hour over the fifty-five limit, and yet it seemed woefully, laughably slow. Migrating dinosaurs, taking their time on their way to electric car extinction.

I caught brief glimpses of drivers as they blew past me. Nothing here of the friendly Mosby finger-waves, the polite stopping for pedestrians at crosswalks. This was like Friday afternoon rush hour in downtown Atlanta: vibes of homicidal urgency and impatience, white-knuckled grips on steering wheels, jaws clenched with internalized resentment. Too many cars, too close together, moving too fast. Hulking SUVs dodged around overcrowded sedans with blaring radios, the drivers' lips moving soundlessly behind their windshields, wishing pain on the dumb bastards ahead of them, the one poking along at the speed limit, and the semis and logging trucks hulking behind them a yard off the back bumper. Not the sedate flow of downtown Mosby, but not a challenge for an experienced urbanite like me. Not a problem for Fogger Grace.

Speeding traffic flurried road-dirt onto my sweaty legs. A mini-van rushed past me a yard away. The driver was a pretty brunette with vivid lipstick. Behind her, two toddlers in car seats faced the following traffic. One of the boys appeared to be crying but the woman paid him no mind. Her red, red lips moved in silent conversation with her linked phone, speaking to an invisible friend, and she didn't even see me poised at the side of the highway as she blew past, driving much too fast.

A new thought: Why not have fun with solemn Mosby? Play a joke. I could dance through this plodding, predictable traffic and never get scratched. Dance like a butterfly, wasn't that the saying? Just wait for the next big car, its half-aware driver looking down at her lap checking emails. Better yet, one of the lumbering semis, its exasperated driver an hour behind schedule, trying to reach the Amazon distribution center within his time window, cursing himself for being drawn into this nowhere town. I balanced on the curb, preparing for my epic sprint through the traffic.

Are you insane? Stop!

A box turtle lay on the verge of the road near my feet, its shell splintered into a brown and yellow mosaic, its just-visible pink flesh shining glossy in the sunlight. The impact that crushed its case had thrown the animal onto a patch of hard-baked clay. A red trail showed where it had crawled no more than a foot before surrendering. I watched the shell shards slowly rise and fall and even as I watched, the movement stopped. I felt a momentary twinge of regret, then tensed for my heroic, eyes-closed leap into the maelstrom.

For shit's sake, Fogger!

I had a clear view down all four lanes. A white semi crested a rise a quarter-mile away on my left. Dense, dark diesel smoke poured from its overhead exhaust pipes. The driver leaned on his accelerator, crowding the old Jeep ahead of him, daring the poor sucker to move over or speed the hell up. The gap between the two was just about right. I could do this.

No! You can't dart through high-speed traffic. It's suicide.

I teetered on the curb. The spacing between the semi and the harried Jeep was just about right. My calf muscles tightened with anticipation.

I stand in the sand of the Barcelona arena and watch the *banderilleros* with distain. They run up to the bull's blind side and jab their barbed sticks into his hump, hoping to enrage him. I am the non-violent alternative, the *recortador*, dressed in spotless white shirt and slacks, a red bandanna tied around my waist, facing the charging bull unarmed. My athleticism and daring against the beast's mass and momentum. Thousands in the arena cheer my name. The crowd's roar obliterates my fear. I bounce on my toes, timing my leap over the bull's wicked horns. I have to get this just right.

Stop!

I plunged in. Three lanes of east-bound traffic in a blur. Hulking shapes; startled car horns, engine rumbles lost way down in the base notes, no music. The wind blast from the truck cab buffeted me as I cleared its front fender, and I lost my stride as I crossed the uneven median strip. I stumbled, spun in a 360 still moving forward, and ran on. Three more lanes, heedless drivers hurtling west, radios tuned to political outrage, blind to my passing blur.

The semi's infuriated air horn didn't even register in my ears until I hopped, triumphant, onto the far curb. I gave the semi driver a chummy high-five and waited for his recognition that we were part of a daredevil fraternity, but he had his hands full wrestling his trailer out of a nasty fishtail. The driver of the semi behind him was not so kind. He flicked a stiff middle finger and gave me the full blare of his angry quadruple air horns.

The traffic hadn't slowed. I had flashed across the Valley of Death too fast for them to react, and man, I felt great. I mimed a Gene Kelly tap dance I had seen in an old TCM movie. A week ago, I would have been too self-conscious to put on such a grandstand display, but today I was the invincible hotdogger. I could make the run again. Right now.

Next time, I'll die.

The background stammering in my ears became the buzzing of a raw electrical short. I swayed on the curb. The fingertips of my right hand were slick with road grime. From the corner of my eye, I had seen the Kenworth logo on the semi-trailer's hood as I dodged across the highway, reached out and brushed my fingers over its right fender. No way. I could not have done that. I was fast, but I could not have flitted across the lethal space between car and truck and survived. But the oily glaze was there, coating my fingers, damning my pretension of cool wisdom. It had the slick feeling of clotted blood.

My thoughts froze like a dove shot in flight.

My knees suddenly gave out. The blood drained from my head, and I dropped onto the concrete curb so hard that the shock sped up my spine and slammed into the base of my skull as if a dump truck had hit me in the ass. The ammonia-sharp odor of spoiled cottage cheese rose from my armpits. A trickle of urine seeped into the crotch of my shorts.

It wasn't only that I had gambled my body against a force that could never react fast enough to avoid turning me into bloody hash. I had risked the lives of the semi driver, the families in the cars nearby, probably the lives of blameless people on the other side of the median. My stomach heaved, and I bent over the gutter to vomit. I held the position and filled my lungs with exhaust-flavored air, taking deep gulps, but nothing came up. My throat was as dry as an Andean mummy.

A steel-gray Porsche Carrera came over the hill where the semi had emerged. It drove straight and clean, cutting the air like a scythe, headed toward a distant retreat known only to its pilot. When it passed, the driver flashed his high beams once to warn that he saw me sitting on the curb. I raised my hand waist high to signal that I would stay put. The Porsche downshifted into fourth gear and accelerated away, its rear end squatting momentarily with torque response. The exhaust's base rumble blew back against me, playing deep in my chest. The Porsche drove down the road, rounded a curve, and vanished. It should have been me behind the wheel, driving away from Mosby with Lauren in the seat next to me, headed west with Norah Jones playing on the radio. A new Fogger Grace in a new car with his new love, headed to a new start.

Until coming to Mosby, I had never seen death laid out on a grand scale. The sounds and smells of Turnell Mill filled that gap. I had seen human frailty in all its snake-bitten vulnerability. I looked again at the road grime on my fingers. Why wasn't this my blood? Why wasn't the liquid sack of my guts spilled out on the highway, tracked over with the squiggles of indifferent tire treads?

My leg ached, and when I looked down, I saw that one shin had been scraped raw from a collision I couldn't recall. How close. How goddamn mortally close.

I didn't have to think hard about what had happened. Sometime during the past days I had met the alpha, and he had planted a subtle directive. An image matched to my deepest need for recognition, the image of a man in a glamorous *recortador* costume, challenging death. Daring. Romantic. An applauding crowd. Run through traffic. Don't question it. Just do it. You'll be fine. A dead ringer for the irresistible command that told Grady Hatch to take his daughter into the flames.

But it wasn't the same.

I had survived my brainless stunt. There was no way I would go on repeating it until I became roadkill. Somehow, I had short-circuited the alpha's command. Al Amon had missed an important element in his analysis: that some people—Fogger Grace, for one—could refuse to obey the alpha. I might not know how to send commands, but I could sure as hell repel the impulse to follow them. With absolutely no justification, I decided the universe had adopted me as its pet. I could beat this.

I recalled a memory technique from an episode of the BBC series *Sherlock*, where the great detective creates a "mind palace" in his imagination, in which he stores all the details he needs to recall later. Well, dammit, I could invert that concept and create a place to lock up the alpha's commands. In my imagination, I walked into an impervious stone bank vault, opened a safe-deposit box, and shoved the *recortador* madness inside. The alpha's tinny voice protested for a moment in a small corner of my mind. Then it went silent.

When the traffic was clear, I crossed to the other side of the bypass and began my jog back to Mosby. If I stayed in this town, I would need a lot more safe-deposit boxes. Bigger boxes with sturdy locks.

23

Al opened my door to find me laid out on the bedroom floor, staring at the ornate plaster design that surrounded the ceiling fan. The memory of dodging high-speed traffic lingered in my mind, and I felt better on the solid floor than perched up there on the bed where I might try a double Salto dismount with a full twist. When I told Al about my dance with the semitrailer, he merely snorted.

"Once the alpha learned about our investigation," he said, "it was a sure thing he'd try to take us out. The traffic angle is ingenious. Fits a pattern, doesn't it? He wants his murders to look like accidents." He put the stack of loose-leaf folders he'd been carrying on my table and began to sort them into piles.

My temper erupted. "What the fuck, Al! I nearly get pancaked, and you call it ingenious? You're missing the point. When his trap didn't work the first time, I severed the command. I cut it off, killed it! Where does this come from?"

Al pulled out a wooden chair and sat on it backwards,

leaning his forearms on the backrest. "I can give you a guess. The guys over in Neuroscience have this theory that human brains have three different operating systems, each evolved in its own time. The most ancient, they termed the lizard brain. It controls our instinctive behaviors—aggression, dominance, territoriality. The next to evolve was the limbic system, responsible for emotions—reproduction and courtship, parenting, feeding behaviors. They call the most recently evolved part the neo-mammalian complex. That's where we developed the higher-order functions—language, abstraction, planning, the things that make us human."

"Lizard brains!" I sputtered. "Fucking great! What am I supposed to do with this? I'm trying to survive. Where does my ability to block the alpha's commands come from?"

"This three-brain concept is just a simplified model, Fogger. Most scientists don't hold with it anymore. But if it has some bearing on how you've survived so far, I'd expect to find the ability buried deep in the lizard brain, down there with the dominance and basic defense skills. Congratulations. It appears you can access those primitive functions and push back against whatever the alpha wants to make you do."

I chewed on this for a while, then said, "If we all have a lizard brain, then anyone can learn how to block his commands. You, for instance. I can show you how to conjure up a mind palace. It's just a matter of building one in your head."

The expression on Al's face was one of infinite sadness. He reached out and patted my shoulder. For a moment I felt I was back in the parking lot outside Turnell Mill, and he was reassuring me that everything would be fine, even as the Hatch families breathed their last lungfuls of fire. But my expectation of normal had changed. I could no longer pretend his gesture promised protection to either of us.

"My friend," he said, "you believe I'll be able to save myself just by thinking hard on it. That's not how it works. Obviously, some people are born with this gift. You were. I wasn't. The alpha will come at us again, and he'll keep coming until he gets it right. I hope you make it. Me? I'm burnt toast."

I had expected Al to congratulate me for not getting myself killed. I'd been sure he would think of something to do with this discovery, but rather than celebrating, he was giving me jack shit vibes full of self-pity and capitulation.

"You're missing the point, Al. This damned alpha doesn't want us to find him. He tried to kill me outright. I blocked him. If I can do it, so can you. Instead of wracking your brain, you're waving the white flag. Enough with the scientific abstraction. Give me something concrete."

Al pulled two black and white photographs from a manila folder and laid them side by side on the table. "This genetic aberration is certainly not abstract," he sighed. "He's a mass murderer as real as a Hitler or a Stalin or a Mao. It's time we started naming him like we would any other world criminal. He's Alpha with a capital 'A.' A for abnormal; A for Alpha."

"And for amoral," I said. "My gut tells me me your cousin has killed more than just the Hatch family."

Al put his hands flat on the two photos. "No guessing how many. He can cover his tracks by mucking up our memories, so maybe hundreds. The usual label of sociopath doesn't apply to him. He's a society of one, so far outside that he slides off the scale of human taxonomy." When he looked up at me, his eyes were tearing with an emotion I couldn't fathom.

"My lab serfs finished the DNA runs. This," he said as he tapped the photo on the left, "is a view of a normal chromosome six. Our scanning electron microscope makes it easy to see the details." He tapped the right photo. "This is the same view from the number six of one of the Hatch victims. This bulge on the end, here, is a telltale gene aberration." He clapped his hands in satisfaction and made a "there you are" gesture, then awaited my applause.

To me, the chromosome images were pairs of lumpy black and white sausages, twisted from having stayed too long on the grill. But, yes, on the right photograph there was an additional bulge, a stunted, club-footed appendage protruding from the bottom of the sausage "leg."

Al didn't expect me to comment. He slipped into lecture mode. "Chromosome six has more than 170 million base pairs. That's an almost limitless pool of possibilities for variations and mistakes. Chromosome six controls the immune response, and it's where epilepsy and Parkinson's show up, but there's a lot going on in there that we haven't sorted out yet." He selected another folder. "Group A, the results from the coroner's samples. Every one of her samples shows the same bulge, except for one." He pointed to an entry labeled *Deep Mutational Scan: Sequence 4 of Female/31-33/ Marker: a 14, cc 07, 2 Betris, Clear, No suspect Alleles*—"It's this one, for Sue Hatch, who was not a direct descendant of Furlong Hatch. She's the only one who lacks the marker."

"What about your DNA, Al? You must have seen this Hatch bulge in your own blood."

His smile took on a grim quality. "Yeah. I discovered it about twelve months ago, but I wasn't sure what it meant until now. These Furlong Hatch people? They're all my cousins. We were all part of one big, aberrant family. Not many of us left now. Cousin Alpha saw to that."

Al selected another folder. "I haven't looked at the Group B results yet—the samples from Magic Beans. Shall we?"

After only a few minutes sifting through the photos and charts, Al made a sound like someone had punched him in the stomach. I looked over his shoulder and couldn't see the reason for his reaction. He closed the folder, pondered, then opened it again and slid another electron micrograph onto the table. "You see this?" he asked me.

"Shit, Al. I got no idea what I'm looking for. What is it?"

Al tapped the micrograph with his fingernail. There was a noticeable tremor in his hand, so I examined the photo closely. The image was a near match to the other Hatch samples. It had the same ugly bulge at the bottom of chromosome six. When I sat back and shrugged my shoulders, Al nodded at the micrograph and said nothing, so I studied it again. The protrusion attached to the side of the gene was actually different from the other Hatch samples. It appeared swollen, deformed, almost mangled. Its four distinct lobes gave it the look of an ugly heirloom tomato.

"All the samples from Magic Beans are normal," he said, "except for this one."

"And this is all it takes to make a monster? It's so…microscopic."

"That's how nature works. Little changes; big effects."

"Okay," I said. "I see distinct lobes. What does that imply? More powers? How does someone get four lobes instead of one?"

"Your first question is indeterminate. This might be as simple as an assembly error. I would need to see the genes express themselves before I'd know if they carried new traits. Maybe none. Hell, Fogger, I have no idea." He pushed the micrograph away and lowered his head into his hands. He stayed this way for the better part of a minute until I cleared my throat; then he held up his hand.

"Your second question? That's easy. You get two carriers of the single-lobe marker to interbreed. That would compound the mutation, reinforce it." Al pawed the photo back with both hands and began to make tongue clicking *tk-tk-tk* sounds under his breath.

"Who does this sample belong to?" I asked.

Al looked deep into my eyes, his brows furrowing in distinct unease. I had learned that he was given to fits of sudden inspiration and unexpected kindness. He could also be infuriating, secretive, and insensitive. Like now. He handed me the cover sheet for the sample and in a flat voice said, "Cassandra Wrenner."

The cover sheet was meaningless to me: *Deep Mutational Scan: Sequence 4, Female/33-35/ Marker: c 04, bb 08, unknown, unknown, aberrant, Suspect Alleles in 6, 9, 17, 21*. My mind rebelled at the implications of Al's hypothesis. In my confusion, I reached for the last of his manila folders, labeled "Group C." He cut me an annoyed look and tugged the folder away.

"Give me that," he said. "You've got no way to interpret what you're reading. It's all statistics and factor analysis and micrographs."

He stood and pulled his chair up to the table and sat down facing me. As soon as he began to read from the third folder, the frown on his face intensified. There were only three sheets in the folder. Al kept flipping back and forth between them with such vigor I feared they would shred. His frown became a grimace. He glanced at me, then stared at his shadow on the floor with the focus of a surgeon wondering where to make his first incision.

After a few more grunts and *tk-tk-tk* sounds, Al collected the folders into a stack and stood. "This is all technical stuff," he said. "I need time to study it." He let his gaze sweep over me without lingering. His bleak expression gave me no clue, but something in what he read had shoved him into an especially dark space. When he turned for the door, I took hold of his arm, and he flinched.

"These extra lobes on Cassie's marker, does that tie it down? Is she the Alpha?"

Al wrenched his arm out of my grasp. "There could be a lot of people with this marker. Got that? More unsuspecting Hatch cousins with latent murmuration abilities. Most of them are going to be harmless, like those poor, dull souls who burned. Cassie's a suspect, but so are the ones we haven't tested yet. The marker doesn't prove she's the guilty one."

"What good are DNA photographs if we can't tell who the Alpha is?"

"It *will* tell us. It's just—I simply don't have enough data yet."

"But you have a guess. Those extra lobes suggest something. Take a guess. What do they mean?"

"Incest."

He read my frown and repeated, "Incest." Realizing that was not enough, he added, "Two people, each carrying a Hatch gene, breeding together. Potentially reinforcing the trait. That adds an uncharted variable to a random mutation we don't yet understand. It's a whole different ballgame now." He yanked the doorknob. I stepped into the doorway and spread my arms to stop him.

"Don't be in such a goddamn hurry," I said. "Help me think this through. If the Alpha knows I've learned how to block his commands, how will he come at me next?"

"You're standing in his way, just like you're in my way now. He'll come at you harder until he overpowers you. That's all you need to understand. Step aside, will you?"

"He has a weakness, Al. He's all alone. Isolated. Afraid. He manipulates everyone around him, but he can't experience the joy of simple friendship, can't trust anyone. He can never be sure there isn't another superman out there, gunning for him. His fear is our advantage."

"Two Alphas?" Irony colored his laugh. "How about three, or ten? Furlong Hatch fathered a lot of children. If he slept with one of his bastard daughters, why not more? Am I really that far ahead of you now? Stop and think."

"So maybe there are more, and he's paranoid. We can use that." I put my hand on the doorknob to keep him talking.

Al stepped back and his hands came up defensibly. Did he think I would hit him?

"This is about you as much as me," I said. "I can block. But you're the one with the Hatch gene; number one on the hit list."

"Me? I'm just a hairless academic. I don't have the defenses you do. He doesn't want me."

"Don't say that. It's bad luck. And you told me you were burnt toast. Remember that?"

Al wiped his mouth with the back of his hand. He looked over my shoulder and said, "Luck is the name we give to probability. The probability is that we're both fucked."

"Al, please. How will he come at us next?"

"How the hell should I know?" he said. "You figure it out." He pushed me aside.

After the door slammed shut, I did just that—tried to figure it out. I paced the room and made lists of various scenarios, and in all of them I ended up dead and forgotten. The effort got me nowhere. There was still too much I did not understand about my own abilities, and about how far the Alpha's mastery extended.

My train wreck meeting with Pastor had rekindled a lot of old, suppressed questions, the questions I had repeatedly asked my mother until she stopped responding altogether. It had become second nature not to acknowledge that our family had a past. Mom had suppressed these questions, just as she had squelched my other queries about life's mysteries, fearful that any examination of the past would release the demons from Pandora's box. No more. I opened my laptop and began to assemble Pastor Ogden Grace from the bits of information in the electronic ether.

Forty-plus years ago, Ogden Grace had built a successful career in the AME church he helped build in Greenville, South Carolina. Two months after he married Grammy, he abruptly left Greenville and moved to the tiny backwater town of Pickett, Georgia. His only daughter, Florence, was born three months after that. There, in a few minutes on the Internet, I had learned that my grandmother was already pregnant when she and Ogden married. Did Pastor know at the time?

Given his strict beliefs, you could bet he didn't. Later, when his daughter extended the curse and added yet another unwanted child to the family, he must have felt his god had abandoned him. The church in nearby Mosby where Ogden Grace preached was small, but this disgrace was enough to blow his career to pieces. It was resentment, onions, and heirloom tomatoes after that.

Formal laws serve a good purpose, but it's the unwritten Darwinian rules that keep people from bumping into each other and abrading sensibilities. We depend on these innate rules to avoid conflict. The Alpha and his contempt for boundaries made a mockery of human nature. He was no longer *our* kind of human.

What else might I discover? I stared at my laptop for a while, then typed in Lauren Klout's name. A lot more data this time. Born Sofia Luciana Ortiz. Soon after her birth, her mother marries Deacon Klout, and Sofia's name gets anglicized. The murder–suicide of her parents is a two-day news bomb in Athens, Georgia, but when no relatives come to claim her, Lauren disappears into the maw of the Georgia Division of Family and Children Services. She emerges at age seventeen, graduates high school with honors in academics and Army JROTC. Two years at Georgia Military College, two more at Georgia State with a degree in Criminal Justice, then more of the same: U.S. Army Intelligence, an early out, then Georgia State Patrol in Mosby. Then a surprise appointment as chief of police, one of the youngest ever and, yes, the first Latina chief.

On impulse, I typed Cassandra Wrenner's name. More information but less interesting. Her parents ran the Mosby pharmacy. Cassie had played the role of small-town belle: Football Queen, Chili Cook-Off Queen, Miss Aintry County Cotton Queen. She had been one of the few to stay in a town whose young people typically left for the faster pace of Atlanta or Charlotte. She became active in local politics. The local paper showed her chairing events at the Cultural Center, receiving awards from the Mosby Development Association, organizing election campaigns for the governor and a state senator. A force in the provincial community but nothing to suggest unusual influence or abilities.

Despite my research into Pastor and Grammy, despite my anger and disappointment about family, I had neglected my regular phone call to my mother. I checked my watch. Four o'clock. Plenty of time. To be honest, I hadn't thought of her for days. I'd check in with Magnolia Meadows, but I wouldn't tell Mom about my visit to Pickett.

A new voice answered the office at the Meadows. When she asked who was calling, I said family, and she put me through to Mom's room. Another unfamiliar voice answered.

"Where's Mary-Adelle?" I asked.

"That woman resigned day before yesterday," the aide said, sounding both indignant and officious at the same time. "She didn't give no notice atall. Just walked out on us."

"I'm sorry. She was a good-hearted woman. Can I please speak with Mrs. Grace?"

There was a vexed "harrumph" in my ear laced with barely concealed animosity, then I heard my mother say hello. Her voice quavered.

"Hi, Mom. Sorry I haven't called. I've been really busy."

"Who?" she asked.

"Called you, Mom. I'm sorry I missed our regular call."

"Who is this?"

"Mom, it's your son, Francis. I'm working here in Mosby, remember?"

I heard her breath catch. "Mosby? I don't know anyone in that awful place. Why are you calling me? Who is this?"

"It's Francis, Mom," I said, relying on years of practice to keep my voice neutral. "It's your son, Francis."

Mom let out a single stifled sob. "I don't know anybody named Francis. No. I had a baby boy a long time ago, but he died. Please, please, no more voices. Don't you call me." She began to weep, making catlike snuffling sounds. "My boy. He died so long ago."

The officious aide took the phone back. "Listen here, you. Mrs. Grace doesn't get calls. You got to be some kind of bent-up animal to call an old lady and pretend to be family, making her all hysteric. Mrs. Grace, she don't have a family. You call here again, and I'll sic the police on you." The line went dead.

I put my cell phone on the table and slouched in my chair. I didn't need Al to tell me what had happened. The Alpha's methods were much more calculated than we'd suspected. He had visited Atlanta, or somehow gotten within range of my mother, and had sent the messages that erased me from her memory. Not erased, exactly, so much as masked. The Alpha couldn't empty my mother's memories. Instead, he'd locked them behind a permanent barrier. Mary-Adelle had gone, too. There was no one to convince Mom I'd ever existed.

I had another sobering thought. There was no way to change this. I had no power to recreate the memories that murmuration had sealed off. My mother had been disappearing, little by little, for my entire life. Now she had vanished altogether, and it was permanent.

Actually, I was the one who had been, in a very real sense, erased. There was nothing to be done about it. An anonymous someone was writing my column for the AJC. Someone kept depositing money in my checking account, but I had not heard from my editor in days. Links with the past were being warped or severed. I felt so liberated by this knowledge that a surge of self-reproach washed over me. It only lasted a few seconds. I would puzzle over the implications of my new independence some other time, but right now I welcomed the new freedom. I was certain I'd adapt.

24

I didn't want to stay trapped in the B&B. Too many thoughts tangled in my mind. My flirtation with the Kenworth semi had gutted whatever relaxation the jog might have delivered, and the stiffness in my neck and shoulders persisted. I showered and left to explore Cemetery Road toward the railroad tracks.

I kept hoping the CSX would rumble through town and blow its nostalgic horn: three long, two short, one long, one short. The horn blew five times each day and once every night. The first time it awakened me in the night, it had triggered migraine flashbacks of the mill fire. But over time, the sound evoked a sensation more akin to sentimentality. Each time it returned, Mosby became the comforting oasis tourists wanted it to be, the folksy town I yearned for. But right now, there was no train horn, only the raucous cicada song that signaled the coming of dusk.

I entered the elegant limestone gate of the deserted cemetery and strolled among its monuments. Mosby's founders located their cemetery on high ground with a far-off view of four different church steeples and, more distantly, the courthouse clock tower. The crypts in this choice spot were the earliest, marked by monuments that resembled elegant, multilayered cakes topped with sorrowing angels. Others celebrated prominent families or dimly remembered and discredited wars. One monument defied tradition with a five-foot recreation of the *Nike of Samothrace*, with the decapitated head and missing arms of the original. I wondered what the devout citizens of nineteenth-century Mosby had thought about the thin veil covering her breasts, the triumphant, outspread wings announcing the victory of a pagan god. Was she a trespasser in this corner of Christian contemplation? Perhaps two hundred years ago, there had been another secret, seditious mind in Mosby, someone determined to throw a wrench into the machinery of a stable, God-fearing society.

A soulful electric horn announced the 5:30 CSX. It clacked by at a jogging pace, the cadence of its wheels as regular as a heartbeat. Many of the freight cars bore reporting marks stenciled on their sides that ended in an X to show they were privately owned rather than part of the railroad fleet. All these cars and their hidden contents would spread out from pint-sized Mosby into the vast rail network of North America. No matter what Al might argue, I didn't think his Alpha would be content to remain confined to this antique backwater town.

The lowering sun shone through clouds like a dull gray coin. Fresh-cut cemetery grass turned emerald as the light waned. More recent twentieth-century graves spread out down the slope on a manicured lawn, marked with unpretentious ground-level headstones. Every one featured a socket to hold a vase of bright artificial flowers. This gaudy display clashed with the otherwise serene expanse of St. Augustine grass and marble markers. Few Yankees decorated their dead so vividly. Plastic flowers were a distinctly southern custom.

The elevated railroad right-of-way bisected the burial grounds, and on the distant side of the tracks, I could see a small thicket of red and white. When I reached them, I discovered nineteen simple Confederate headstones, each with its Stars and Bars flag, marking another location where an escaping troop train had dumped bodies in November 1864, when John Bell Hood fled the fires consuming Atlanta. Someone had faithfully tended each grave, clipping the grass and brushing off the bird shit. When I bent to study the engraved inscriptions, I saw that one headstone bore the legend, "Colored Hospital Attendant." Who knew? These hasty graves might contain several distant cousins.

The battle I now found myself in was also a civil war, a war among people who looked the same but shared opposing beliefs as to who gave commands and who followed orders. If I ended up dying in this war, I didn't want to be an anonymous fatality. I wondered what this "colored" man had done. Saved lives perhaps. Defended someone he loved. Cared for men he secretly despised.

"At least you earned a marker," I said to the headstone. "Good for you."

To be cherished in someone's memory is the only reward most of us can hope for. The undetected war being waged in Mosby was as crucial as the one that had killed this man. If I was on the road to a dusty death, I needed to believe my journey would make the world a better place and that someone would put up a nice marker on my grave, without the plastic flowers. But regardless, to please show I had not died for some banal reason, some petty grudge or solitary, unintended offense.

Small orange-red mounds spotted the gravesite, spoiling the reverent mood. The grass had been recently mowed, but each of the mounds had grown to six to twelve inches high, rebuilt overnight by the industrious fire ants that infested Georgia. Minute balls of clay like congealed rust, positioned carefully, hid the queen who spent her life below the surface, sending orders to her workers. I took a step back, not wanting to get the clay gummed into the treads of my running shoes.

As I stepped back, I looked up from the graves, back a hundred yards along the footpath that meandered through the cemetery. A slender figure stood in the shadow of a giant water oak, leaning with one hand against an obelisk-shaped monument to catch his breath. He glanced in my direction and started forward in a shuffling trot, looking less like a genuine threat than a winded child struggling to catch up. The light in the cemetery had softened with the onset of dusk, blurring the sharp edges of the monuments. The effect would have been calming under other circumstances, but the stiff, shambling gait of that distant figure ruined it. His dogged determination radiated menace.

My cheeks tingled with the same itchy burn that had preceded my dance in traffic. I didn't want to appear panicked, so I squared my shoulders and took a side path that branched off from the main road. Thick tree roots thrust through the much older concrete surface, breaking it into large, uneven slabs. At first, the path paralleled the train tracks, then dropped away into yet another community park, this one dense with ghost ferns and drooping clusters of purple wisteria.

After the manicured symmetry of the cemetery, the park's wild neglect grated on my senses. Its tree canopy trapped humidity, creating the sense of enclosure in a tropical forest. I turned twice to glance back up the path, hoping I wouldn't see the person I had spotted under the distant oak. There was no one there. I followed the path as it continued downhill, steeper and more serpentine as it wound through kudzu-covered chinaberry trees.

At the bottom of the path was a two-acre pond. A spectral blue heron stood motionless in the shallows at the edge of the pond, his pencil-thin legs spread at an awkward angle. He peered into the thick, pickle-green scum, tuning his senses to discern which of the tiny algae mounds was a chorus frog hiding beneath the surface. Dragonflies swept off the pond in spontaneous confusion. They did not murmurate but darted and swooped aimlessly. One of them blundered up the path, whirring close enough to tangle its wings in my hair, and I wished an opportunistic barn swallow would swoop down and snatch it out of the air.

A rapid flapping sound alerted me in time. I turned, bracing one leg against the downward slope of the concrete path, and got my arms up in front of my face. A maniacal stick-woman careened down the path toward me, her flip-flops slapping her heels as she staggered to keep her balance.

It was the anorexic waitress from Magic Beans. Her skin was slick with sweat, and she ran with her left hand hooked into the waist of her jeans to keep them from sliding off her bony hips. Her right hand grasped a small steak knife, held high above her shoulder like the deranged murderer in *Psycho*, and I swear she made little *eek-eek-eek* sounds that mimicked the violin score of the bloody shower scene. I felt almost embarrassed by the feebleness of her attack.

I was never in any real danger. The girl's dazed look told me she was flying blind, navigating on instruments. The mechanical, stabbing motion of her knife hand had no real force, and I easily trapped her wrist. She gave up without a fight. I threw the knife into the deep brush and let her go.

Big mistake.

The girl was still under the Alpha's orders. She uttered a ghastly screech, lunged like a pouncing civet cat and grabbed my shirt collar. Using the collar as a fulcrum, she whirled onto my back. I reached back and grabbed a handful of hair; and as I pulled, she sank her teeth into my ear. The pain was so sharp that at first, I thought she'd found a second knife. I dropped to one knee and dragged her off my shoulders onto the path, my hand still knotted in her hair. I got her on her back and put my knee on her chest.

For the tick of a single heartbeat I saw myself as if from the eyes of a distant observer, far up the slope, hidden behind a bleak mausoleum, and I marked how my body bent over the wraith raving beneath me; how my face contorted with a hostility I never imagined I could experience, and I was stunned by the violence of my expression.

"STOP THAT!" I shouted. The out-of-body image stuttered; snapped off.

Fear and outrage made my voice sound as if I spoke from

the depths of a chest much broader than my own—almost my own voice but more resonant and lower pitched. I tasted my morning coffee in the back of my throat when I swallowed. It burned like a mouthful of spoiled wine. I fought a momentary impulse to rip the girl's head off; stood up and clutched my fists in flat shame.

The lackluster sheen went out of the girl's eyes. She blinked rapidly and made fending-off motions with her hands. The Alpha's command released. Now I was the attacker, the girl my victim. My cheeks no longer burned. I'd beaten the sonofabitch again! I'd defused his order, erased it, and filed it in the memory vault. Threat over.

But the Alpha had left his mark. I raised my hand to my ear, expecting to find it torn and ragged, but it hurt so acutely that I stopped exploring. My fingers came away with a faint smear of blood. It hurt like hell, but it was better than a steak knife in the jugular. And it was far too easy to picture such a knife slicing into my throat. That realization, or maybe the mauling I had received, caused me to lose balance on the sloped path. My leg-bone twisted hard, my foot skidded sideways on the mold-covered concrete, and I performed a graceless pirouette and went down hard. The impact shocked my left hip as if the knife had found its target. I lay there, afraid to move, certain my body was irreparably damaged.

The bewildered girl rolled over and crouched on her hands and knees. We were both sprawled on the concrete path, our faces a few feet apart. The girl's eyes held the same leaden deadness as a marble angel on a cemetery crypt, and for that moment there was no more thought behind them than in a statue's stone head. Her vague gaze slid over me; then she looked away and stared into the dense undergrowth. I had slipped out of her mind, dissolved into the kudzu. Ignoring me, she crawled to her feet, meandered off the side of the path, and began to pick blooms off a magnolia. She stared down the path at the green pond and its equally hypnotized heron. In another hour, she would snap out of it, dumbfounded to find herself in the cemetery park in the deepening gloom.

A gaunt girl with a tiny knife? This had not been a calculated attack. The Alpha was mocking me. He knew I had broken his code, and he didn't care. This little theater piece was a taunt. He figured he could turn off my lights any time he fancied.

If the Alpha had hoped to intimidate me, he'd blown it. He'd let me identify one more of his techniques. His attack was weak and crudely executed. Was his imagination that limited? Why not have the girl choose a more public setting, then scream rape? His failure encouraged me. If he didn't step up his game, I had a chance of outlasting him.

By the time I got back to the inn, sundown had crimsoned the cumulus clouds to the west. For a moment, the colors gave me a false sense of well-being. The front desk had taken a message from Lauren. "Can't make the calendar work tonight. Will insert you tomorrow, same time, same place."

The lights were on in Al's room, so I phoned him to see if he wanted to have dinner. I heard the faint buzzing of his phone from the next building, but there was no answer. I stepped out onto the porch. The air was thick with the aroma of tea olive trees, so sweet it felt like breathing candy floss. When I walked over to Al's wing, I nearly stumbled over the female retriever. She was licking a smear of light-green fluid off the floorboards of the covered porch, lapping so eagerly I feared she might get wood splinters in her tongue.

Al opened the door with a smile. The sour mood that had earlier driven him into his room had vanished. His voice was so unruffled, I thought I might have disturbed him at a secret meditation. Al seemed the sort of man who would meditate, but his brown eyes told a different story. They darted with suppressed energy.

"I've been waiting for you to stop by," he said. "I've made a discovery about murmuration you'll find intriguing. But first, a celebratory toast."

"Wow," I said. "I don't think I've ever heard the word *celebratory* used in a sentence before. What are we toasting?"

"Hey, we made it through another day in Mosby, and we're still breathing. That's worth celebrating. Anyone ever make you a grasshopper? You know what that is?"

"Yeah, I know. Crème de menthe, crème de cacao, regular old cow cream, chilled. Way too sweet for my taste."

"Well, that's because you haven't tried my special recipe." He stepped into his bathroom and fetched the two glasses he had sitting in his sink, packed in ice from the machine on the porch. He handed me one, already filled with a creamy green mixture. The cold glass was slippery with condensation, and the green liquid looked like a child's medicine. Moisture dripped onto the table, leaving a trail of tiny drops.

"The grasshopper," he said, clinking his glass with mine, "one of the true southern traditions. Drink up."

I reached out and took his glass, set it on the table next to mine. "Where is it?" I asked.

Al looked down at his drink, dumbfounded. "What?"

I capped his glass with my palm, wrapping my fingers firmly around it. The steady voice that came out of my mouth belied the dragonflies in my stomach. "Where's the container your grasshopper came from?"

25

Al reached for his glass. I pulled it away. "The container, Al. I saw where you spilled some on the porch. Where did you put it?"

"You want more ice?" he asked. "It's better when it's ice cold."

I was losing patience. Al slid his eyeglasses off and polished them on the tail of his shirt. The jitter in his eyes evaporated. He put his glasses on the table, poked them with a finger, took them back, and held the lenses up to the ceiling light fixture.

"Not seeing so well today," he said. "Glasses are dirty. Very dirty. I need . . ." Al let the sentence trail off. He kept on polishing, his breath coming out in a train of stifled moans. Finally, he stopped polishing and gripped the plastic frame in his hands and twisted, deliberately snapping off the temple pieces one at a time, and stuck them in his pocket.

"Shit," he said at last. "The Alpha. Was I going to drink it?"

"Yeah, you were. Where's the container?"

Al crumpled into his chair and stared at the two glasses of

green liquid. He ran a thumb across his lips and said, "In the bathroom. Under the sink."

I took our glasses to the sink, pulled out the plastic container of antifreeze, and emptied the green poison back into it, taking care not to spill any. I screwed the cap on tight and wrapped our glasses in a towel, then opened his door and threw it all in the trash bin outside. Sure enough, the female retriever was leaning against the porch steps, her eyes watering, green saliva dripping from the corner of her mouth. Muscle spasms rippled down her back. Her partner stood nearby, his head bobbing in puzzled concern. He stepped forward and sniffed his mate, then snuffed and lowered his muzzle to the porch and backed off.

I turned away so I wouldn't have to watch the retriever's misery run its course. The sun was in its final minutes of setting. The reddened orb flattened against the horizon with a sense of finality that made my mouth go dry. I called the front desk and reported that one of the porch dogs was acting strangely. A few minutes later, anxious voices sounded outside our door. The voices became urgent. Steps thudded across the porch. I heard the sound of a car racing away, then silence.

As this mini-drama played out next to Al's room, he sat at the table with his chin cupped in his hand, looking toward the door when the noise outside peaked, then back at his mangled glasses, utterly withdrawn into himself. When the clamor outside stopped, he lifted his leather briefcase onto the table and zipped it shut. The entire time, he never looked at me once.

"Here's the funny part," he said in a gruff voice, speaking to his briefcase. "I planned to climb the courthouse clock tower tonight and look at Mosby while it slept. When I thought it through, I realized the tower's not tall enough. I should drive into Atlanta and take the elevator to the top of the Westin Peachtree. It's over seven hundred feet high. I know the manager of the Sun Dial restaurant. There's a great view of the city from up there."

"I get the picture," I said. Hell, yes, I did. After all, I had tried to dance with a forty-ton truck. Al expected to dance with the birds. Same derangement, different setting.

"I planned to invite you along," he added. "I decided you need a break as much as I do, and I would have done it, gotten up there and looked at the city, and ..." He stood and walked to the antique rococo bed and fell back on the lacy pillows. "Why not? Wrap everything up nice and neat. A simple command to one of my grad students: erase everything. Poof! No more clues. Twenty years of research, gone. Then I, too, would go poof! Completely disappear from the university records, become a nonperson."

Al pushed off his shoes and crossed his ankles. After a while, when his stockinged feet began to move, I realized he was humming to himself, keeping time with his toes. The tune was an old Bob Dylan standard from before I was born. I knew the tune and began to sing the words about an ominous spinning wheel that would eventually name someone, but no one knew who'd win the raging battle.

Al sat up in bed. "Almost right," he said. "I was remembering the stanza about drawing lines and casting curses. This sonofabitch has us bottled up in this room, scared to leave. He's outside planning a massacre. There'll be another attack, and another, until he scratches us off, or we figure out...

something." He slumped back onto the pillows. "Why didn't he wait for me to go to Atlanta? Could have wrapped it up for him. Skydiving has a nice, smashing finality. Why poison? That's not final. Not by half."

I told Al about the attack in the cemetery and reminded him of my earlier compulsion to dodge semis on the bypass. I described the warning sensation that numbed my cheeks and made my neck feel on fire.

"He's trying variations of the same basic themes," I said. "We have him worried. This antifreeze thing is a knee-jerk move. A desperation ploy."

"Crap. If you hadn't showed up, I'd be finished. So you learned how to anticipate him. Hooray for you. Me, I'm ready to jump off the Westin. I'd say his command system is in fine shape. He hasn't found the right button to push yet, but he's working on it."

Al swung his feet off the bedspread and opened a drawer in the marble-topped dresser that stood next to his bed. He took out an unopened bottle of Woodford Reserve, broke the seal, and poured two inches into his last clean glass; held it out for me until I took it. He shrugged, saluted me with the bottle, and tilted it back for a long hard swallow. Bubbles rose into the brown bourbon at the neck of the bottle. When I reached across the bed to take it away from him, he lowered the bottle and screwed the cap back on.

I left my glass untouched. "We can't anesthetize our brains," I said. "If his commands can still get through to us, we need to learn how to block them."

"Sure enough, *I* won't be learning that trick. And you don't need to. You were born with an ad hoc defense."

"Damn it, Al. It's you who freezes the fist in the air. If anyone can block the Alpha's commands, it's you."

Al used a thumb and finger to smooth down the edges of his moustache. He squeezed the bridge of his nose and ruefully shook his head. "No," he said. "Between us, you're the special one. I know I said this wasn't mind control, but it might as well be. We don't know how the Alpha sends his commands. They worm into our brains and force us to act against our better judgment. But Nature always comes up with a solution. Every time random mutation creates a new apex predator, that same random chance comes up with a new defense. You've got it."

"I can't tell you how depressed that makes me feel."

"This isn't some Las Vegas magic act with wires and mirrors, Fogger. You asked me if this murmuration ability was evolution, and I laughed at you. I'm sorry. Truly. I've given this a lot of thought, and yeah. So, yeah, Fogger, I'm betting this is evolution. And so is your ability to block."

"You interfered with a command. I saw you do it."

He shook his head again. "I no longer believe that's what happened. I can wish that a person will like me, and sometimes that message gets through, and maybe I get a smile. That's the outer limit of my ability. Stopping someone from wanting to hit me? I couldn't make that work in high school. I've tried to replicate what happened at the door of the coffee shop. Can't do it. I sit in Magic Beans and send messages to the customers: bend over, order a sandwich, raise your hand. They don't hear me." Al looked at me and recognized my incomprehension.

"What happened that first time was a fluke," he said. "Hell, I no longer believe that miserable, pissed-off man was acting under the Alpha's orders. He was overheated, and for an instant he wanted to hurt someone. It's a natural PTSD response to the catastrophe at Turnell Mill."

"You're wrong. I blocked the command to commit suicide with a truck. You can learn how to do it, Al. It's going to take practice, but I can show you how. You'll never take a nosedive off the Sun Dial restaurant. Forget it. That shit's behind you."

The harder I pushed Al, the harder he pushed back. "You haven't thought this all the way through to the bone, Fogger. I'm only shielded as long as you're around. You have the gift of blocking the Alpha's commands, not me. If I go back to Atlanta alone..." His fingers drifted onto the bourbon bottle cap, then he blinked and put both hands in his lap. "If I go back alone, I'm going to fly off the Westin."

"Al, I'm a thirty-something guy who can't even keep a girlfriend. I write a human-interest column with an emotional spin. Soft news, that's what I can do."

"Bullshit. You're a natural blocker. With enough warning, you can intercept the Alpha's command and turn it off. I guess you weren't paying attention when I talked about random mutation. You've probably had this ability all along, waiting for the moment when you'd need it."

"I'm not special."

"Goddamn it! Yes, you are! Why are we having this argument? We're chimpanzees playing with a loaded gun. One of us has figured out how to pull the trigger, and one of us—that's you—has learned how to hide when the trigger's pulled. Be thankful. Don't block that, too."

That night I dreamed my mother was trapped in the mill fire. I fought my way through the blaze, past the flaming hay bales, past the Hatch children caught in their parents' embraces, burning like Marrano Jews in a Jesuit auto-da-fe, and I found her at last, sitting at her kitchen table, reading her dog-eared copy of *The Perfect Heresy.* She looked up and shook her head emphatically, not recognizing me in my fireman's breathing mask and fireproof coat.

"Not me," she said. "Go find my boy. Save Francis."

26

Al and I had no clear plan for the next day. Well, not exactly—I was eager for my dinner date with Lauren and the opportunity to see if we could build on the promise of that first, intense encounter. I needed reassurance that it wasn't a fluke. As for figuring out how to keep the Alpha from getting to us, I had nothing.

Al and I took my car for an early lunch at a Mexican restaurant near the I-20 on-ramp. The walls were decorated with flat ceramic suns, each with a multicolored woman's face painted in the center. Some faces smiled, others were pensive or bored or indifferent. The women in my life had personalities just as diverse. Lauren, my mother, my editor Michelle, and even Cassie were mysteries I despaired of ever understanding.

Oddly, "Hotel California" was playing here, too. Our waitress showed up as the Eagles' song pondered whether we lived in heaven or hell. Her smile revealed brilliant white teeth; she was tall and lean, and when I looked at her glowing skin, it was Lauren I saw.

"Hi, guys. What'll y'all have?" she asked. Her north Georgia accent broke the spell. We ordered enchiladas and a pitcher of Tito's margaritas.

Al drained his first margarita and poured a second. "Drinking tequila is one of the stupidest things we could do," he said. "But fuck it. I have no plan and no future." He picked a kernel of rock salt out of his mustache and topped off my glass. "The fire's burned down, we're out of wood, and the wolves are circling. Saludo."

"Will you please stuff that woe-is-me crap for a while?" I said. "We've got a shot at beating this guy because you figured him out. You did that." I clicked my fingers on the ceramic mask hanging on the wall. The multicolored woman stared into space; her expression opaque. "Billions of people in this wide world, and you tracked him down."

Al took a deep pull on his margarita. "I tracked him to Mosby. That's all."

"Wake up, man. You showed me how Cassie's chromosome six marker is more complex than the rest of the Hatch samples. We need to figure out what that extra part does. So, I've been thinking. Cassie's been coming on to me ever since I got here. I can use that to get close to her. Let's work with what we have."

The enchiladas arrived. We ate in parallel for a few mouthfuls, then Al said, "All I can say about Cassie's DNA markers is that she's got Furlong Hatch genes from two people, so it's a given she has the same ability to influence people that the others had, at least on some level. Does she have a double dose? We don't know. She can probably sell a cappuccino to someone who'd rather have a regular coffee. Maybe she could get herself elected mayor. What the extra lobes mean, I can't guess."

I didn't like Cassie. She was too damn aggressive. Too superficial. But I couldn't think of another way to flush her out, so I volunteered to encourage her. If I could get Cassie to reveal an unknown aspect of the Hatch gene, we had a starting point.

Al was skeptical. "I had the same idea a day ago. Now I'm not sure."

"Well I'm ready to try anything, and she's clearly putting moves on me."

"Look," he said, "if she's a regular Hatch, she isn't even aware of what she can do. She thinks she's lucky or that everyone's attracted to her boobs. That fits what we've already seen from her. But if she's the Alpha, you can't expect her to put on a demonstration. That's not how the game works."

"Do you have a better idea?" I countered. "Time is on her side. We need to perfect our defense, and that only happens when he—or she—is trying to manipulate us. If we go together, and Cassie is the Alpha, I can block her while you look for new abilities to emerge."

Al looked at me as if we were friends meeting after a long absence. "You're a good man, Fogger Grace. A brave man. I wish we had met some other time, long before this."

"You wouldn't have been interested. Before this, I was a nerd. Invisible."

"Probably you just didn't know who you were." Al filled his lungs and forced all the air out in a wheeze. "Okay. That's ... it ... then," he said, spacing each word out for dramatic effect. "Let's go roll the dice."

The lunch crowd at Magic Beans had taken all the tables except the large one that looked out on Main Street. The featherweight waitress took our order with a heavy dose of apathy and without even a blink of recognition that she had earlier tried to stab me to death. We didn't have to wait long before Cassie brought our coffee to the table.

"Fogger, sweetie," she said, "how good of you to stop by. And Doctor Amon." She put Al's cup in front of him, then walked around to stand behind my chair. "What can I do to make sure you gentlemen get my very best service?" When she leaned over to put my cup on the table, her breasts nudged me first on one side of my neck, then the other. She held her position for an extra heartbeat before pulling out a chair and joining us.

"Fogger, honey," she said, "your ear is all red and angry."

"I bounced off a wall that wouldn't budge, Cassie. Just a scrape. Listen, I was thinking about our conversation at the library. I'd like to take you up on your invitation to see the upstairs apartment." Her eyes brightened. "Once we finish our lattes, I'm free all morning. Why don't you sit with us until then?"

When Cassie smiled, her lower lip pulled back and her incisors flashed. I have seen this done in B-rated vampire movies, but never so effectively. If she was the Alpha, her gesture was way too practiced and over the top. A revealing tell would be hard to find.

Only Lauren Klout knew that we suspected a superman lived in Mosby. Cassie, if she wasn't the Alpha, was convinced that a gas explosion had caused the disaster at Turnell Mill. The locals believed the same, and that the team of Grace and Amon were conducting an arcane academic study of small-town America. Even if Cassie was the Alpha, there was no reason for her to know we had identified her.

"I was wondering about that photograph of Furlong Hatch you keep in the back hall," I said. "Are you related to him?"

Cassie guffawed and put her hand on her chest. "Oh my, no. Our relationship is all formal. Furlong is my business partner."

"Isn't he dead?"

"Probably. I don't know that anyone's seen the old coot for almost twenty years. But when I bought the Beans, it came with a built-in minority partnership. I get the building rent free. Furlong, or his trust, gets twenty percent of my pretax earnings every quarter, right off the top."

I hadn't seen Norman Garrison, the arrogant school principal, enter the shop, but when I glanced up, he was striding toward our table, bent forward at the waist as if pushing into a strong wind, his arms crooked and his fingers balled into fists. I stood to show him I wasn't intimidated. This time, Garrison held out his hand first. "Grace," he said, managing to make it sound like a mild curse.

His grip once again insisted that he was more of a man than me, but I was prepared. I got my thumb into the back of his hand and squeezed the nerve enough to make him wince. As soon as I let go, he turned to the table and leaned his bulk toward Al, ignoring my friend's offer to shake hands. "Norman Garrison," he said, suggesting this was all the introduction Al deserved.

Garrison waited a second to let the fact of his dominance sink in, then appeared to rediscover Al and said, "So, this is the celebrated Doctor Amon." He removed his glasses, buffed them on his sleeve, and slipped them into his shirt pocket. "I've read some of your monographs, Doctor. As a PhD myself, I admire your ability to hit the high spots of a complicated issue and bring it down where the man on the street can comprehend."

Al immediately caught on to the hollow bravado. "Really?" he said. "What's your doctorate in?"

"Psychology. Undergraduate in communication studies."

"Ah," said Al, and let the word lie on the table like a horse turd.

A slight flicker of Garrison's mouth betrayed his irritation, but he said, "I thought your paper on chromosome migration added something to the larger scholarship on genetic drift. Where do you stand on the structural aberrations observed at NIH?"

Al sat back in his chair. "Cassie, I'd like to treat everyone to one of your exceptional lattes. Would you please put in an order for us?" Cassie left, and Al fixed on Garrison. "I'm not aware that there is a 'stand' you can take on a structural aberration, Mister Garrison. It simply exists. It's like asking me to take a stand on a cat. Where do you want to go with this?"

Garrison looked disappointed. "Well, if you don't want to discuss the issue, I can understand."

"Oh, I'm perfectly willing to discuss your question once I understand what it is," said Al. He tore a blank sheet out of his notebook and pushed it in front of Garrison. "If you would sketch the phase movement you're concerned about, perhaps I could get your point."

Cassie and the emaciated waitress arrived with four more lattes while Garrison glared at Al. "Here's to science," said Al, raising his fresh cup in salute. "And empirical evidence," he added.

Garrison pushed his cup away, sloshing coffee, and took a half step back from the table. I read the disappointment on Al's face and realized the only reason he wanted the insufferable know-it-all to stick around was to see the man put his lips on the cup. Al pulled a napkin from the dispenser and mopped the spill. He kept his mouth shut and dropped his gaze, staring at Garrison's coffee cup. Too obviously, I thought.

"The AJC wants me to write an article on the mill accident," I said, hoping to drag out the conversation long enough for Garrison to take a drink. "I'm looking for bad luck stories about the Hatch family. Know any?"

Garrison recovered a little and said, "The Hatch family has had more than its share. For example, there was ..."

"Yes, we know about the boy killed by the logging truck, and the woman and her daughter who ran into the dentist's office out on the bypass."

Garrison's frown signaled that he hated being interrupted. "There was the Millman woman out at the lake a few years back."

"Right," I interrupted again. "She drove into the lake and drowned."

The skin of Garrison's face infused with blood. It was easy to read his mind. Interrupted by this nobody a second time! If I pissed him off any more, he'd stop talking and leave.

Garrison pulled a handkerchief from his suit pocket and wiped his face with it, studying me. "Well," he said, straightening his jacket, "how about the Hatch relative from Gainesville who came up here three, four years ago?"

"I don't know that one. Please, go ahead."

The confident smile returned. "He was doing a genealogical

study of the Hatch family tree. He was a good listener, and he was happy to take my advice. I straightened him out on several false tales he had picked up along the way."

I gave Al a quick glance. He encouraged me by lifting his steel-wire eyebrows. We were on to something here. "And what happened to his research?" I asked.

"Well, I thought that was what y'all were after, the bad luck. There was one of those freak accidents, an eight-year-old boy playing with his father's pistol. The shot went through an open window and hit the poor man right in the neck. He died in minutes."

"Please sit down and have your latte with us, Norman. I'm sure you've got a lot more material I could use in my article."

Garrison fished his aviator glasses out of his pocket. "Not today, I have a meeting to attend. Cassie? I'll see you later?"

"For sure, Norman. I'll be waiting."

Al watched the stuffed black jacket step out into the sunlight. "I'm sure there are psychology PhDs with brains, but that's the problem with make-believe doctorates who never do real research," he said. "UGA hands out soft science degrees like Halloween candy. Guys like Garrison waste their time playing one-up games, then fold as soon as you push them. Take a 'stand' on structural aberrations? Give me a frigging break."

I didn't understand Garrison's byplay with Al and said so. "Help me out here. What was the mumbo jumbo about aberrations supposed to mean?"

"What you saw was a worn-out academic having a five-minute pissing contest with a skunk. There's nothing to understand. He downloaded a few papers from the internet and did a superficial read, then tried to bluff us. Standard psychology PhD bullshit. Garrison doesn't understand enough of what he read to frame a decent question. Got the jargon right, but otherwise he scored a clean miss. My question is, why did he bother?"

Garrison had enough on the ball to refuse your offer of coffee, I thought, but kept it to myself. I turned my attention to Cassie. "If you're tired of watching grown men hassle each other, Cassie, maybe we can get back to a more elementary conversation."

"I wish you'd be nicer to Norman," she said. "He's the most respected person in Mosby. He donates to all the causes, chairs the Boys and Girls Club fundraiser. His house is the most historically important in town. You were jogging right by it when I saw you out near the library."

I derailed. "Garrison owns that slave-owner house with all the columns? On a principal's salary?"

Al put us back on track with a different approach. "Cassie, the first day Fogger and I came here, there was a strange young man sitting up front in that leather chair. Is he a Hatch?"

I stymied the impulse to frown at Al. We'd met Ronnie, been subjected to his weird drumming and disjointed accusations. I realized Al was fishing for how Cassie would react to the mention of someone we knew to be a Hatch.

"Sure enough. That's Ronnie Millman. His mother was a Hatch, but she died. Ronnie lives with his crippled father out at the lake. His aunt takes care of them both; drops Ronnie off here a couple times a week while she does yoga at the gym." She plucked Al's sleeve to make sure she had his attention. "I don't believe in that yoga hooey. Just between us, I think Ronnie needs it more than his aunt does."

"Yoga can generate powerful effects," said Al. "In fact, Fogger and I were betting each other that if we concentrated hard enough, we could make people do what we wanted." His shift was so clumsy that I thought Cassie would immediately call him on it, but she just looked at him and snorted.

"No, really," said Al. "We were just about to give it another try. Right, Fogger?"

I had agreed to test Cassie, so I went along with the shtick. "Oh yeah, absolutely. Al can make people admire him just by concentrating on them. Watch." Here was the test I wanted.

Al played it out for maximum impact. He spread his fingertips on his temples, Professor X style, and stared at the patrons in the shop. Nothing happened. Cassie chortled under her breath. I felt the slightest flush in my cheeks. Not a warning flush that signaled an attack, but from embarrassment at our ludicrous experiment. Then, while we watched, several people turned around in their chairs and smiled at us. A couple at the next table waved a subdued salute.

Cassie looked over her shoulder and said, "Hey. Nice trick. How'd y'all set this up?" Her smile flickered on and off, a faulty neon sign flashing uncertainty.

I already knew Al's chromosome six gave him some slight ability to influence behavior, but this was a major-league performance. Even Al looked surprised. He had sent a wish, and we had both seen it fulfilled. Cassie wasn't buying into any of it. If she was the Hatch Alpha, she gave nothing away. Time to push the envelope.

"That was impressive," I said. "We should concentrate on something bigger. Let's order your customers to make a big noise." Al looked at me in disbelief. Cassie shrugged her shoulders and put her elbows on the table, mimicking Al's fingers-on-the-temples pose. It was worth a try. I counted on Al's murmuration powers being limited to just what he had demonstrated, a modest ability to generate goodwill. Any unusual noise from the patrons would mean that Cassie shared the murmuration ability. Regardless, the chance that she would fall for such an obvious trap was remote.

Although the coffee house was nearly full, the music loop playing on the overhead speakers muted the surrounding conversation. "Hotel California" began for the umpteenth goddamn time. A woman next to us accidentally clicked her coffee cup with a spoon, and the sound was loud enough to make me flinch.

Then it started.

27

The Eagles sang a few more stanzas and got to '...my head grew heavy and my sight grew dim.' The clumsy patron hit her coffee cup a second time and apologized to her table-mates. They laughed, picked up their spoons, and began to tap their own cups. Cassie tapped her cup, and then Al did, too. None of the vibes registered with me, but I joined in, and in a breath the entire coffee house was reverberating with the sound of spoons on coffee cups, water glasses, salt and pepper shakers.

The clinking and chiming gathered volume until it drowned out the shop's piped-in music. The joke kept clanking along far too long. I wished that whoever was driving this would bring the experiment to a screeching halt. Then, as suddenly as the cup concert started, it hushed, and we heard the Eagles launch into the song's iconic last line, reminding us that checking out was easy, but we could never leave. The sound of nervous laughter floated over the tables.

Cassie clapped her hands in a little gesture of applause. It was a convincing act. "Hey," she said, "you fellows went all out with this joke. I'm impressed."

I felt nauseated. This had been my idea. I had the answers now and I didn't like them one bit. One of the people here had flaunted his power with no effort to camouflage it. Cassie? Or perhaps he hid just outside the shop or sat at one of these tables, in easy view of us. He yanked the strings and the marionettes danced. Was he mocking me? The bastard had convinced me to dance in traffic. This time I was his collaborator, his accomplice.

Al looked at me hard. His eyes were bright. "There's the evidence, at last," he said. "This ends the old debate. A lot of my fellow evolutionists will tell you that life climbed out of the tidal ooze, a few billion years passed, and as if by magic, here we are, top of the food chain. They forget that there are still new forms crawling out of the sea every day, on and on, ad infinitum." He cleared his throat and turned his attention to the street scene outside the big window. "Didn't you say that you and Cassie had things you wanted to discuss? Me, I'll sit here and think about what we just witnessed. You two go on, now."

Cassie's smile widened. My keyed-up imagination made it a wolfish grin. She stood and walked straight toward the rear of the shop. Al continued to stare out the window, but with a flick of his hand, urged me to follow her.

People have always been willing to tell me their life histories. My experience transcribing those stories doesn't cover many years, but it includes a lot of different timelines. It's my observation that our lives are not the boring, linear journeys they appear to be. It's an illusion that we travel inexorably from a starting point to an inevitable finale. Our blind spot is that we assume, when we step back at any point along the path, that each moment led to the next with unswerving, Newtonian cause and effect, to get us where we are, like a locomotive on a single set of tracks. The life stories I've listened to contradict the deterministic view of the people who lived them. Without realizing they're doing it, each person tells me about the multiple switch points they ignored, the chances to shunt their train onto a different track, the opportunities missed through inattention, neglect, or a willful fascination with self-destruction.

I was as guilty of self-deception as the people I'd interviewed. I thought I'd fake enough interest in Cassie to make her confident of a seduction, then trick her into revealing herself. I thought I'd get away with it. So I followed her, weaving my way around the coffee tables, past the rest room and its framed photo of Furlong Hatch, to the back of the shop.

A curtain of bamboo beads hung just beyond a sign that read "Private." I parted the curtain and found Cassie at the bottom of a narrow stairwell.

"Here?" I asked.

"Here," she echoed, like a trained bird. "Right here and right now." When she leaned forward and brushed the side of my neck with her fingertips, her lips parted with a shuddering indrawn breath, as if the touch had triggered a suppressed hunger.

The space at the bottom of the stairs was as dark as the inside of a steel helmet. Clinking coffee cups roiled in my head, and as Cassie disappeared up the stairs, I waited for the burn to begin on my cheeks and neck. Nothing happened, but my hand hovered over the wooden banister, as though if I seized it I would be committing an irrevocable error. This was my chance to shunt my train onto another track. I didn't have to do this, yet I followed.

I hesitated again on a landing halfway up, where the stairs turned back upon themselves in the narrow, shadowed stairwell. Nothing Cassie had done suggested she had special abilities. After all these years, she still imagined her strongest asset was her tits! And here I was, pretending to have the hots for her to trick her into revealing who she was. The Judas sin.

I emerged at the top of the stairs into a room brilliant with migraine-level light. None of her second-floor windows had drapes or shades. Cassie caught my hands and brought my arms around behind her back, pressing into me, her mouth opening under mine, her hot tongue probing. This was the plan, to get close enough that she would reveal her true self, but it felt more like I had climbed aboard a runaway train.

"Hey," I said, "slow down."

She tugged a button at the bottom of my shirt. "I've got this," she said. "You just let me do it."

Her hunger was contagious. Despite myself, I hardened .A passion curiously like shame washed over me.

Cassie worked her hands under my shirt and ran her fingernails up my back. I winced when her tongue traced the outside of my ear, worrying the spot where the anorexic girl—her own damn employee—had bitten me. Cassie piloted me over to a couch and fell onto it, pulling me down on top of her. Her tongue never ceased searching my mouth. Animal desire took me. I pulled her skirt up to her waist, then hesitated as the headlong momentum of her charge registered. Cassie reached down to unbuckle my belt and when I let go of her skirt and put my hand on her shoulder to push her back, she squirmed out from underneath me. She stood by the couch just long enough to unbutton my shirt and pull down the rest of my clothes.

I let it happen.

Urge competed with contempt at my weakness. This was not the plan. Moving too far; too fast. Questions flashed through my mind: how many lovers Cassie had brought here, and was she somehow pushing me with her Hatch abilities, and where was a condom, but she was moving too fast, and my body responded too enthusiastically.

"Ha," she said, her voice harsh with triumph. "I knew I'd get you, Fogger Grace!" She twisted her dress the rest of the way over her head and shucked her underwear. Then she swung her body over mine and straddled me on the couch, her strong thighs gripping my hips, her hands seizing my shoulders. "You pretended you didn't give a damn, but you wanted me all along, didn't you? Even back then." Her breasts splayed across my chest, heavy as bags of with wet sand.

"Now," she said, "you want me now, don't you?"

And yes, I wanted her, the way a disembodied phallus might instinctively seek a warm cavity to empty into. I dug my fingers into her rump as she lowered onto me. I retained enough of my senses to realize that, as intense as this coupling was, it had none of the complexity I'd shared with Lauren, nothing of the sense of merging. Cassie pumped rhythmically against me with the indifference of a milking machine. After the first few minutes of her thrusting and biting, I just wanted to be done. So, I punched the clock and finished.

A strange lethargy gripped my body, and it wasn't the routine post-ejaculatory fatigue. I felt more like the exhausted castaway who struggles to the breakers at the edge of the shore and clings tightly to the rocks, gathering strength to pull himself out of the sea. A sense of betrayal—of Lauren, of my own values—deepened my weariness.

Cassie stood gazing down at me, hands on her hips, shifting her weight from one foot to the other. She raised her chin imperiously. Her lips stiffened. "I got you," she said. "After all these years, I put you down and laid you out."

The feeling that washed over me was a sleazy mixture of humiliation and loathing. Fogger Grace, stud bull. No, too grandiose. Stud rooster. Cassie didn't care that our tryst had been a cold-hearted quickie devoid of any sensation but lust. For her, it must have been an act close to masturbation. What she savored was something resembling victory. I half expected her to break into a touchdown celebration of lewd gestures. Her behavior was downright unsportsmanlike.

We dressed in the grim acknowledgment that this was a one-time event. When I got over my sense of being used, I realized that at no time had Cassie used any murmuration skills to manipulate me. The telltale burning of my cheeks and the coiled feeling at the base of my skull were absent. Still, the Alpha wouldn't reveal himself so freely. He was too cunning.

Cassie turned her back on me and marched down the stairs without the merest sign of affection or recognition. I didn't want to follow her. I found her bathroom in a corner of the studio, washed myself and glared in her mirror. It didn't help. I couldn't get clean.

When I re-entered the coffee shop, Cassie was in her position behind her hulking brass espresso machine, smiling broadly. I ignored her and walked back to our table by the window. A tall Asian man with shoulder-length hair stood next to Al, who had just handed him a small package wrapped in a paper bag. The man was in his early twenties, dressed in a brown T-shirt that said, "I Aim to Misbehave." I assumed he was another of Al's grad students.

"Thank you, Henry," said Al. "Get back to me as soon as you finish the series." The young man made no reply but dipped his head in a formal nod, then turned to me and made the same discreet gesture of respect. I returned his nod. Al and his student beamed as if I had joined a secret society. After my near-humiliation with Cassie, this simple courtesy went a long way toward restoring my sense of balance.

Al leaned his head in Cassie's direction and said, "Get anything?"

"Nothing," I said.

"I doubt that very much," he replied. Then the door opened behind us, and he smiled.

Lauren swung into the chair next to me and gave me a hard stare. She twisted around and scanned the room. As she did, her leather belt and holster creaked, and her nose wrinkled as if she'd detected a stench. I wondered if she could smell my betrayal.

"You get my message?" she said.

Before I could answer, Cassie came out from behind the espresso machine and stationed herself possessively behind me, her hand on the back of my chair. "Chief Klout," she said. "How good of you to honor us with your business. Do you see anything in my shop that you'd like to sample?"

"I can't stay, Cassie," said Lauren. "I just need some words with Mister Grace."

"Well, then. Guess you did that. We're busy today. I'll get you a free cup of coffee and send you on your way."

I thought I knew what this was about, but the fierceness in their eyes worried me. My aim was to pinpoint the Alpha and stop him. Feminine competition was a dangerous distraction, and it was entirely my fault.

"Your shop is a public space, Cassie," said Lauren. "I'll leave when I'm ready."

"That would be . . . now."

"It's tiresome, the way you always think you give the orders around here."

Cassie showed her incisors again. "Don't I? It's sure not you, honey. Your shiny badge is just something the mayor gave you. It doesn't come with magical powers."

Lauren gave a master class in self-restraint. She ignored Cassie and said, "Read my message, Fogger," and left. Cassie waited until Lauren had crossed the street back to the police station before she returned to her place behind the brass machine.

Al held back a smile. "I think I have the answer to my question," he said in a whisper. "You didn't find out if Cassie has Alpha powers, but you definitely found something." He looked out the window at the police station. "And I'm not the only one who can figure that out. You be careful. The ice under your feet is getting thin, my friend."

I dodged his insinuation by checking for cell phone messages. I had two. Lauren's read: "Mosby in May festival tonight. Meet me at my table. I've got dinner."

The second message was from my editor: "Great article yesterday. Another bonus headed your way." This made no sense. I had not filed a column.

I went to the serving counter, collected the shop copy of today's AJC, and flipped to Section C. Sure enough, there was my column, a soft piece about a couple adopting a three-legged dog from the DeKalb County Animal Shelter. Problem was, the column had run in last December's paper. Michelle would know that and would never have made such an amateur mistake—unless someone was secretly guiding the Iron Lady's thoughts. That was the only explanation of why I still had a job, why I was still getting paid despite doing nothing to deserve it. The Alpha wanted me to stay here in Mosby, where he (she?) could keep watch.

Where he could blot me out.

28

In the history of romance, Fogger Grace's story is a series of dead-end dry runs. A serious connection? Never. Honest attraction with a woman? Impossible. I was condemned to be forever hermetic. Then I'd stumbled on Lauren and fell hard, so sitting at the table between her and Cassie left me feeling like I'd masturbated in front of an audience. I felt sullied.

Needing distance, I left Magic Beans and headed down South Main, away from town square, away from my guilt. The path led slightly uphill toward the distant rumble of the I-20 on-ramp. Neoclassical and Victorian homes sat behind iron fences and yards heavy with magnolia and plume grass. The roots of ancient water oaks heaved the sidewalk into fractured chunks. A hundred years of acorn stains discolored the concrete with browns and blacks, and my easy betrayal of Lauren seemed equally contaminated.

In old southern towns like Mosby, the unmuted dead have their own kind of murmur. It saturates the soil; breathes in the air. The dead sang to me from the wide trunks of trees and from the old brick. Like a liturgical prayer, the words were not distinct, but their meaning intelligible. Some asked for justice, others for absolution. Most simply wanted to be remembered.

Three long blocks from the square I came to a turn-of-the-century schoolhouse, red brick and steepled, set well back from the sidewalk. A sun-bleached sign told me this was the Mosby-Aintry Cultural Center. The smaller sign underneath announced, "Special Showing, Shakespeare's Otello, Aintry County Thespians, 3:30."

Otello was my least-favorite Shakespeare, right down there with Timon, but I damn well needed a diversion. A few acts of the paranoid Moor of Venice might just budge me out of the blind alley where I was trapped. Besides, the old schoolhouse was a safe harbor. I doubted if the Alpha would spend his time watching a creaker like this ancient parable of race and treachery. I bought my ticket just as the loudspeaker gave the ten-minute warning. The one-sheet program bragged of a "gender-enabling performance," whatever that was. Mildly intrigued, I found a seat close to the back row.

The theater had been the old school's auditorium. My seat was authentic 1920s wood and cast iron, with gouged arm rests. It creaked under my weight. Maybe a third of the auditorium was filled by a retirement-age audience, the kind who might actually have read Shakespeare in their youth. And I realized with acute amusement that when the schoolhouse was new, my darker skin would have denied me this seat. I would have attended class outside town, reading second-hand textbooks with torn and missing pages.

Lauren slid into the seat next to me.

"You got time to get all culturated?" she asked.

"Hey. If I'd known you were coming, I'd have bought an extra ticket."

"My Police Chief's uniform gets me a free pass 'bout everywhere but the coffee shop. I'm just here so's the citizens can see me doing my civic duty. You watch. Intermission comes, I'll disappear before the next act."

I felt a rude bump on the back of my head, turned, and saw a horse-faced sixtyish woman plop into the last-row seat behind me.

"Oh, do excuse me, sweetie. So sorry." On closer inspection, her face had more the look of a self-satisfied sheep than a horse. Pleasantly homely. She wore a dull turquoise necklace as wide as a conquistador's breastplate, heedlessly gaudy. Her accent was old Georgia, slow and syrup-smooth.

A familiar voice said, "Scoot over there, sugar. I want to speak with Mister Grace." Norman Garrison took the seat immediately behind me, so I had to twist around to see him. He was dressed in a black crew neck and black blazer, like a sinister mob boss from a Scorsese movie.

"I'm offering one more chance, Grace. I'll help you with your investigation. If you want a good story for the Constitution, you'll need me to guide you to the right people."

Sheep-face interrupted and leaned forward, coming so close that her necklace clinked against my wooden seat back. "You must be that Atlanta reporter Norman told me about. You came to our little town about that terrible accident, didn't you?"

"Fogger Grace, Ma'am. Actually, I came to see my old college friend, Grady Hatch. He and I . . ."

"Oh, those poor Hatch people," she said, "one tragedy after

another. His pretty little Asian wife and their sweet daughter. But you knew that." Her necklace clanked into the back of my chair again. I caught the vague smell of Cointreau on her breath from the double Cosmopolitan she'd apparently had before coming to the show.

"Nothing but death with those Hatches," she went on. "Grady's all-so-ordinary sister shot herself in the head back two years ago. Did you know that? And his father, he was a no-good low country skunk for sure, but he went and drowned out at the lake just a year later. Not fair even if he was a birdbrain. You knew about that, I suppose?" Sheep-face charged ahead, her questions not expecting an answer, her voice raised in a breathless monotone that pretended to be a stage whisper. She flicked her eyes left and right to see who might be enjoying her monologue.

The house lights saved me by dimming. Sheep-face cut off in mid-sentence.

Lauren sat silently; a bemused smile clamped on her face to let me know she had enjoyed my torture. The pupils of her eyes glowed in the dim lights, her eyelashes long and incredibly curled, as if she'd walked in from one of those gauche television commercials, where perfect eyelashes promise bottled innocence and seduction. She caught me watching and pinched the back of my wrist.

The curtain went up. A nearly all-female cast launched into a gender-reversed version of Shakespeare's play. Doomed Desdemona was a frail-looking teenage boy with a breaking voice; Iago a thin woman with flame-red hair who strode across the stage with her shoulders hunched, as if she was playing Richard III as well as a scheming plotter. The only black member of the cast was Otello, played by a large black woman who spoke her lines in British-accented English, her rich alto resonant and threaded with resentment deep in the blood.

When scene two began, Lauren whispered "See you tonight," patted my arm and quietly slipped out the back of the auditorium. She'd done her civic duty. I settled down to let the bard's words draw me away from the mill fire, Pastor, the Hatch curse, the whole catastrophe.

We were well into scene three and "I hate the Moor," and the player's gender flip was working for me. Lanky Iago had convinced me that she would do anything to destroy her admiral, when I felt an insect brush the back of my neck. I snapped my shirt collar and it flew off for an instant, then returned, its tingle just delicate enough to irritate. I scratched my fingertips across my neck. Nothing there. Yet it was still there, scurrying on tiny, whiskered legs. A spider, for sure. A brown recluse or a hobo. I palm-slapped it.

"Hush," Garrison's companion said in her stage whisper.

The phantom spider returned, tip-toeing at the top of my spine where the atlas vertebrae locks into the skull. I brushed my neck again. Nothing. It was an imaginary spider, I decided, but it felt as if it was trapped *inside* my body, between skin and bone. I asked my brain to ignore the sensation, but it didn't help. I lost track of the play and concentrated on not thinking about the furry-legged spider.

So I thought only about the spider.

Slowly however, and irresistibly, the spider-tell morphed into a premonition, a convincing fantasy that Norman Garrison, sitting in the dark behind me, was stealthily screwing a silencer onto the barrel of his Walther 22Q pistol, loaded with hollow-points that would rattle around in my skull and make pudding of my thoughts. It was a thoroughly convincing image. Even as I argued to myself that this was bizarre, irrational, I imagined I was an unsuspecting Lincoln waiting on the assassin's bullet. I could see Garrison steadying the gun, hidden by his black jacket, waiting for a burst of applause to fire his weapon, and I replaced my silent incantation against spiders with a mantra of "don't fire, don't fire," as if an imaginary command could defeat an imaginary bullet.

The lights would come up and the audience would shuffle out. And maybe someone would notice the one figure slumped in his seat in the next-to-back row of the theater, a small hole in the back of his head right at the atlas point, leaking a trickle of blood onto his wilted collar, and no one would remember who had sat behind him, and maybe there'd be a brief commotion. But before long, the story would be that this strange Atlanta interloper—what was his name? Grease, Grape?—had suffered a heart attack, and wasn't it sad, coming so soon after that terrible fire at the mill?

Iago stepped forward into the footlights:

'The Moor already changes with my poison:
Dangerous conceits are, in their natures, poisons.
Which at the first are scarce found to distaste,
But with a little act upon the blood.
Burn like the mines of Sulphur.'

I stumbled from the theater before Act III was over. Piercing daylight scrambled my thoughts. The tops of the water oaks moved in an unseen breeze that did not reach ground level, where the air was still and close. The air was thick in my lungs as I walked back along the root-cracked sidewalk. Back in the air-conditioned coolness of the B&B, I put my head under the sink tap and ran the cold water at a slow trickle.

I couldn't be sure, but it felt as if I'd dodged the speeding semi one more time.

29

That evening, Al and I walked down to the town park under a sky as hard and white as a motel bathtub. The air temperature hovered in the high eighties. A mild breeze blew over the park, but it wasn't enough to cool us or the people who unfolded their sports chairs and spread their blankets on the grass in front of the bandstand. The crowd was festive. Laughing children, back-slapping adults, hugging each other. Georgians accepted humidity as a natural property of summer, not worthy of complaint.

A team of city workers connected amplifiers to chest-high loudspeakers spaced between the bandstand's white columns. Grade school kids stood on the grass with their chins on the stage, asking questions. A worker in an Atlanta Braves cap adjusted an amplifier, and a teeth-clenching electronic screech ripped across the lawn. Younger children jumped and spun as if this was part of the entertainment. Adults gave a smattering of good-natured applause, and the man responded with a mock bow.

My stomach gave a turn. The Hatch families had prepared for their reunion with the same calm demeanor. But there were scarcely any Hatches left. They would not be celebrating. These happy people, with their blankets and picnic coolers, handing out sandwiches, would not be on the Alpha's hit list. I so wanted this to be a pleasant small-town summer festival, a chance to enjoy music with the woman I hoped to mesmerize with my anemic romantic skills.

Norman Garrison came up behind me and hooked my elbow in a tight grasp, spoiling my mood. Al turned back to see why I'd stopped, then turned away when he saw who had intercepted me.

Garrison leaned close. "Mr. Grace, could I have a word alone with you? We need to talk about the accident at Turnell Mill."

"You can say whatever you want right here, Norman."

He looked over my shoulder at Al, narrowed his eyes and whispered, "What do you know about your colleague, Professor Amon?" He didn't wait for an answer. "I've checked with people I know at Georgia Tech, important people, people in authority, and they tell me he is viewed with suspicion. There have been serious charges that he's falsified his research. Then he shows up in my town just as the mill burns down. All those poor people. Suspicious circumstances."

I freed my arm from his grasp. "I'm a good judge of people, Norman. I like Al Amon and I trust him. Can't say the same about you."

"I'm talking about survival here. What happened at the mill was no accident. I've spoken with Chief Klout and told her about my fears."

Al edged closer to us and caught Garrison's last words. "Do you have specific information, or is this just more moonshine you've brewed up?"

Garrison pulled himself up with all the gravity of a Baptist preacher interrupted mid-sermon. "Sir, I'm having a private conversation with Mr. Grace."

"In a crowded park? Not likely. If you can tell us why Mosby's residents keep killing themselves, then let's have it. Otherwise, you're just bullshitting, aren't you?"

Garrison's throat bladed with pink streaks of anger; his jaw muscles clenched, but he plowed ahead. "I am willing to share what I know if you will include me in your deliberations. As Voltaire said, 'No problem can withstand the assault of sustained thinking.' What he meant was, we should listen to those with special knowledge."

I had reached my limit with Garrison. He had the patina of an educated man. He'd learned to parrot some of the books he'd read, but never absorbed what they meant. He'd learned to fake gravitas without paying the dues the way Al had. "There are no deliberations, Norman. We're here for the festival. Music, food, good times."

"You're making a big mistake. 'It is the province of knowledge to speak. It is the privilege of wisdom to listen.' Oliver Wendell Holmes said that. He was Chief Justice and he knew the value of knowledge."

Al laughed deep in his chest. "Holmes was never a Chief Justice. He was a member of the Supreme Court and *acting* Chief Justice for two short months. Memorized oratory is cheap, Mr. Garrison. Maybe you should quote Einstein. He said, 'Any fool can know. The point is to *understand.*'"

We'd pushed Garrison too far. "Are you laughing, sir? People welcome my assistance. Without question."

"I was laughing," said Al. "The stage amplifier ripped out another screech while I was listening to you. An irritating noise without any content." He patted the top of his bald head. "I'd rather enjoy the waning sun than listen to random noise. I love nature. It's going to be a nice evening here in the setting sun."

"That's all for us, Norman," I said. "We'll pass on your help."

Garrison fumed. "You're out of your depth here, Grace. This town is my universe. I've looked you up on the web and you are just a lump of city trash. You'll blow through our streets and be gone before we need to sweep you up."

We could have gone on exchanging insults, but there was no point. Al and I simply walked away. Garrison was a street performer and a bully. The people of Mosby were too kind to peer below the surface of his act. Garrison lived in fear that they'd discover how shallow he was. And he was just the kind of man who would hurt them if they figured it out.

A long berm across the back of the park, reinforced with a retaining wall of decorative concrete blocks, separated the open grass lawn from a raised patio. People had already claimed tables on the patio, from which they could look out across the splashing metal fountain to the stage. Slanting sunlight glimmered on the fountain. Twin ramps started just behind it, rising from the grassy area to the patio. A waist-high, wrought-iron fence discouraged children from playing along the edge. I found Lauren's table there, marked by a paper sign that warned, "Reserved for Chief of Police." I motioned for Al to sit, and he took me up on the invitation.

Cassie Wrenner was apparently the master of ceremonies.

She strode to the microphone and led us all in the Pledge of Allegiance. Cassie wore a tight dress that emphasized her breasts; she turned from side to side half a dozen times to profile her major attribute. I had the sense that she was speaking directly to me when she introduced the country-and-western trio that led off the program. The trio wasn't half bad, but they had the distinct sound of local talent, hesitant on the harmonies. Their half-dozen songs were familiar enough that the audience helped them through the refrains.

Lauren showed up just as Cassie introduced the second act, a six-piece jazz band whose trombonist was skunk-drunk. Cassie chose the moment to aim her comments at me. "For those in the back who aren't paying attention," she said, "here's a group that will help y'all unwind from today's hard work, y'all who've been doing the pushing and up and down 'til you're worn out."

Yeah. She meant that for me.

Lauren unpacked a Subway footlong and a tray of hummus and mixed vegetables. "Doctor Amon," she said, "I didn't know you was to join us, but we can cut this sub in three pieces."

"No, thanks. I just wanted to enjoy the local talent. I'll eat later."

"And you, Mister Grace," she said with a wink, "I believe you're planning to put in some extra hours tonight." Her eye narrowed, and she nodded at my ear. "You okay, Mister Grace? Seems some animal's been chewin' on your ear." She snapped her eyes toward the stage and Cassie Wrenner. "I think maybe you've been spending too much time at Magic Beans."

"Thanks for noticing, Chief. I went jogging and had a run-in with a tree branch. It's nothing that will slow me down."

Lauren's eyes sparkled. "You be careful now. There's lots of things you can chew on aren't so dangerous."

Al gave the smallest of grunts and I began to unwrap my sandwich, certain that if I looked up, my smirk would set him to laughing. I folded back the top of the cold-cut sub and looked at the mound of onions and yellow peppers, then at the garlic hummus. I caught Lauren's gaze and said, "I left my breath mints back in my room. I hope I won't offend anyone this evening."

Lauren dipped a carrot in the hummus and licked it before she bit off the tip, chewing wholeheartedly. "Never pass up a strong spice, Mister Grace. Try the Greek dip. It'll cover up whatever you have planned. Maybe even give you an idea or two."

Al ignored the two of us as we exchanged clumsy double entendres. My friend was intently watching a boy who rocked on one of the two-person gliders next to the bandstand, a teenager who could not stop lurching the swing back and forth as he tried to match the jazz band's phrasing. The chains that suspended the swing heaved erratically in their overhead frame. Al took a celery stick from the platter and used it to make a covert gesture at the boy, adding, "Ronnie Millman."

"Oh," said Lauren, "our Lake Nokose cannonball."

Ronnie fixed on the jazz band and on Cassie Wrenner, who stood at the edge of the bandstand shaking her head at the wasted trombonist. The player's sloppy tonguing and slurred riffs played hell with the band's timing. Ronnie thrummed his hands on the metal swing, as if he wanted to override the trombonist's miserable performance. When Cassie could take it no longer, she walked up to the microphone, clapping loudly, and thanked the sextet for their performance, then rushed her introduction of the main act, a five-man doo-wop ensemble. They immediately launched into a solid rendition of "Unchained Melody." Ronnie's scowl said he was not happy with the change. He wanted to lurch his swing faster than this down-tempo oldie would permit.

I didn't hear the ring, but Lauren put down her sandwich and pulled out her cell phone. She gave a grunt and said, "Got some security horse hockey up at the square. Couple of our local boys parked their muscle car on the courthouse steps. Fogger, you know where to go when this is over. Doctor Amon can have the rest of my sub." She moved off toward the courthouse square at a brisk pace, adding a skip every half-dozen steps.

The doo-wop group sang a cappella with genuine panache. When they began a song called "Little Darlin'," the crowd reacted with applause and whistles. I had never heard the song before. I guessed that ninety percent of the audience hadn't either, but you would have thought they were singing the national anthem.

A few people rose to their feet and began to dance to the music, raising their hands over their heads and swaying from side to side with exaggerated body language. Ronnie Millman stood and joined them. He moved with jerks and tics, more paroxysm than dance, but he was into the moment.

Despite the obvious enthusiasm of the dancers, I have always been suspicious of this kind of display. There is something too deliberate about it to be a true expression of inner abandon. No one acts spontaneously. A selfie-dance looks hip to others. It draws attention, but I have a hunch it's a performance *for* the crowd rather than *with* the crowd.

But then Cassie Wrenner walked back onto the stage and joined in the performance. I couldn't tell if she was leading the crowd or tuning into the vibe. She swayed her Rubenesque hips with the grace of a samba dancer. More people near the stage got to their feet. They swung their arms back and forth above their heads in an expanding synchrony. Participation spread out from the stage like ripples from a brick dropped into a pond. More people stood and joined in.

The unmistakable warning sign of an attack began to tingle in the back of my neck. It seemed only seconds before everyone in the crowd was swaying in a synchronized pattern. Small perturbations in the pattern warped through the crowd, changing and combining in an endless choreography of swirls and eddies but never interrupting the basic design. The effect duplicated what Al had shown me in his murmuration video: coordinated, ever-evolving movement within a flock of starlings.

Before I could put it into words, Al grunted, "Oh, shit. Murmuration." He slowly lowered his sandwich and scooted his chair back from the wrought-iron railing that separated the retaining wall from the grassed area below. The way he leaned forward, his fingers curled over the scrolled metal chair arms, the muscles in his forearms swollen with tension, made me think he was about to bail on me.

"Is this it?" I asked. "Is Millman the Alpha?"

"If he were," said Al, "Mosby would be a perpetual shit-storm. Ronnie doesn't have enough self-control. He's too unstable."

"But his power, Al. Look at them. Everyone's dancing except us."

"Can't be him. The commands come from someone who's cool enough to keep everything under control. Ronnie's an amplifier. He boosts the signal. But, Fogger, he's not strong enough to break through your wall."

I didn't know that at all. Al had only guessed what I might be capable of. If he was wrong… I dreaded what was unfolding. Without warning, a viscous cobweb fell over my face, clinging to my eyelids and lips. I ran my hand over my eyes, but there was nothing there. My cheeks blazed as the brute force of the Alpha's call washed against my will, resolute.

The doo-wop backup quartet quit their intricate dance routine and fell silent. The lead singer's voice ebbed away, then stopped altogether. The sea of waving arms lost cohesion as individuals went out of synch. Then, as we looked on in disbelief, the crowd stiffened, and all of them lowered their arms in unison and performed a military about-face, locking on us eyeball-to-eyeball, their faces fixed, full of moronic menace. The mob bunched closer together and took a step forward. No one jostled another. The spacing between each person was precise. Another step. Then another, quicker, and a thrill swept over them, and I knew they were about to stampede up the ramps and smash into us.

For the space of one deep breath, I welcomed the clash. I'd felt it coming all day, a wave of inevitability, building toward face-to-face confrontation. Here it was. I was ready.

I closed my eyes, concentrated, and my confidence died. The bastard was already inside my head. His signal was immense, and it was not the gentle suggestion that Al had supposed, but an all-out attempt to suffocate me, to wipe me out.

Alpha hit me with the full force of his powers, and it was as if a giant hand squeezed my brain. The pain was unlike anything I had ever experienced, a migraine of brain-splitting force. He dug in. I pushed back, hammering against his signal. His commands didn't waver.

Nearby, someone blundered into one of the metal patio tables, scraping its feet over the tiles. The screech tore at my eardrums. Silverware clattered onto the tiles. Garbled voices made inarticulate sounds that were not words but a susurration of brittle, mashed-up half-words, a flurry of dry leaves tumbling across the grass. I kept my eyes closed, fearing that if I opened them and stared into the crowd, my concentration would break. Fatally.

Without volition, excitement coursed up through my body like the fierce flow from a firehose, full of urgency and dread. My lungs felt encircled in tight bands, and my breath came in short bursts, as if I'd mis-timed the closing sprint at the end of a marathon.

I snatched for a way to focus. I pictured the battle between us as flashes of spasmodic movement rippling across a computer screen. But dammit, this was no idle simulation; the images in my mind were tangible, lethal forces. I know the brain has no pain nerves, but mine felt a remorseless, crushing pressure.

The imaginary computer screen flared. My blocking command was a pulsing electronic field, its surface roiling with eddies of energy. I held that frontier in place by sheer will, and it strained against an opposing field of matching strength, the interface between us blazing with shredded neutrons.

I was in serious trouble. The Alpha's commands weren't getting through, but he was relentless. The force of his assault pressed like the huge weight of some infernal torture machine. I cracked my eyes open for a moment. No fluctuating force fields crackled in the air, no arcs of incandescent energy. All that was an invention of my overheated imagination.

My enemy's commands pulsed as they beat against my blocks, and when I squeezed my eyes shut again, I remembered the coiled fields from a grade-school experiment using a bar magnet and iron filings, forces invisible but deadly. The two of us possessed sweeping powers. Our fields intersected, but we didn't communicate at all. We were two blind knights in heavy armor, bashing each other, never knowing where the next blow would land.

My brain began to stutter, as if it were being ransacked. Random images sped across my consciousness: a snapshot memory of young Fogger hunkered down in the woods, his book of Norse folktales clutched against his chest; an injured dog writhing in the street; an older boy, sobbing, cradling his fractured arm, the ulna piercing the flesh above his wrist, his bleak stare accusing me of his wound.

The blow came with no warning.

The person who tackled me was big, and when he hit me low in the legs, we fell hard onto the patio. He rolled on top of me, using his weight to bowl me over. His face slid against mine; coarse sandpaper whiskers scraped over my cheeks. He wrapped his arms around me and locked his hands together in the small of my back.

Big man. Strong.

I struggled to breathe. I concentrated on my command: *Stop. Back off.* He wavered, but he didn't let go. I slid one arm out of his grip, shoved my fist into his open mouth, trying to drive it past his teeth, all the way down his throat. His breath on my fingers was hot, clammy.

If the guy had bitten down on my hand, he would have had me trapped, but he wasn't thinking, only following imprecise orders to cripple me. I rammed a savage knee into his testicles, and when he didn't let go, I hit him again, aiming to drive his balls all the way up to his lungs. He wavered just long enough for me to squirm free. But before I could regain my feet, a second man piled on. He was smaller, but the punches he rained on my kidneys made me gasp and open my eyes.

A short man. Old. Maybe seventy. His groping eyes were as slick as peeled eggs.

Feet scraped and shuffled around me, waiting their turn to kick me to death. A shoe banged into my already damaged ear. I heard the seam in the back of my jacket give way. The second man shot another stinging blow into my kidney, and I felt my concentration slipping. I forced my eyes closed and blasted my plea, *STOP*, giving it all I had.

Even as the Alpha's goons pounded my body, my silent battle with him never ceased. I sensed the growing confidence of his commands, his joy at knocking aside my defenses one by one. Another jab smashed into my ribs, hard.

In desperation, I targeted a narrow front of his attack and pushed as hard as I could. Fire coursed through my bloodstream, a pumped-up five-cups-of-caffeine, steroid burn. Urgency overtook reason. I bore down on my block. He relented, drew back, then rebounded. My body began to spasm, the prelude to a total shutdown, but I held on.

Then, without warning, just as he seemed poised to shatter my resolve, he faltered.

The jabs into my side stopped. My assailant slipped off my chest. No one took his place, but the sound of scuffling feet continued. I opened my eyes for a quick look toward the lawn. The mob had stopped advancing on the patio, but I sensed it was about to regain cohesion and would pound up the ramp at us in a few more seconds.

I crawled over to the fence on hands and knees. I think I sobbed, waiting for the next blow. My ribs throbbed, but I pulled myself to my feet and seized the decorative finials, a sinner at the prayer rail, pleading for rescue.

"Al," I gasped. "You all right?" When he didn't answer, my lizard brain took over. The white noise roiled out of its deep hiding place at the base of my skull.

ALL STOP. BACK OFF.

As I snatched another look, a pod of six people stiffened and crumpled to the ground. No one moved to catch them. They lay as if suddenly gassed. Beyond them, near the stage, another platoon went down hard, then another. I pulled back on my command.

The invisible force field disintegrated. There was no blast of apocalyptic trumpets, no bright lights, no sense that I'd landed a blow; but deep in my head, a massive pulse detonated, and the urgency of the Alpha's commands snapped off.

Silence descended on the park. I hadn't defeated him. This wasn't the end of our battle. It wasn't a truce or a draw. He wouldn't burn out.

30

The mob remained frozen. The slightest movement stood out like a miniature wind wave on a flat sea. A head twitched here; a hoarse cough broke on the stage. Otherwise, silence.

Below me, on the steps, a large man in mussed clothes unfolded himself and rose partway to his feet, holding his groin. He gave a pitiable groan and puked up something thin and brown onto the step above him, then slumped back to catch his breath. No one offered to help him. He stretched out a hand to touch the stairs, at a loss to explain how he got there. His muttered "Motherfucker," was not a curse but an expression of utter surprise and incomprehension. He had to be wondering: What am I doing on this step? Why do my balls ache? I'm struggling here, why doesn't anybody notice?

My nervous system screamed frantic distress signals. My vision blurred. I couldn't be sure if my blocking message would hold; the thumping pulse in my ears was a premonition of total shutdown. I held fast to the fence and doubled down.

I AM NOT A THREAT.

The doo-wop singers started up a new song, haltingly, their voices joining in one after another, seeking harmony. The song they chose was "The Great Pretender." The man on the steps stood and looked around, embarrassed by the shambles of his clothing and by the spreading urine stain on his pant leg. I closed my eyes, let my hands float up off the iron railing, and imagined all that hostility compressed into a ball I could hold. I let the white noise subside, opened the deposit box in my memory palace, and locked the ball inside.

All my fury condensed into a tight knot in the center of my chest. I took a halting breath and held it. Held it. Then an urgent cramp doubled me over, and a huge belch burst from deep in my stomach, a sound so viscous and organic that it would have sent folks running from the park had the place been quiet enough for them to hear. All that came out was air or gas, but in my near-delirium I imagined I was Saturn vomiting up his children. A taste of dirty pennies filled my mouth.

When I opened my eyes, the crowd was still tottering on unsteady legs, but their attention was no longer aimed at me. They looked dazed, like people awakening from a deep sleep. A few raised their arms and tried to restart the murmuration. After an uncertain wave or two, they dropped their arms and stood still.

I had made this happen. Me alone. The power that surged through my veins! I had performed an astounding act of magic, worthy of Penn and Teller at their Las Vegas best.

A dull ache spread across my kidneys. My Goodwill jacket had split part way up the back. There was blood splatter on my collar and I was missing the top two buttons of my shirt. I couldn't see a wound anywhere, but when I wiped sweat off my brow, my fingers came away smeared with red. Yes, I had a cut on my eyebrow, but it had already stopped bleeding.

I sat down hard in my metal chair, sapped. I checked my one ally. Al's face had the glassy patina of an antique doll. A spot of drool hung on his lower lip.

"Hey," I said. "Al Amon. Come back. It's over."

Al's consciousness migrated back from whatever distant place it had retreated. His face was ashen. "That wasn't me," he said. "I couldn't have done that, ever." The tight lines in his brow shouted apprehension.

"Dear god. How did you . . . ? You blocked him. You blocked all of them."

Sure. I had done that. Blocked them. But my self-assurance was about to dissolve into tears. "What do I do now?" I asked. "If this is all I can do, if I can only stop the Alpha once he makes his move, we're screwed. I can't win if I just counterpunch. Sooner or later, I'll miss. I have to get on the other side of him *before* he sends a command." Even to me, my words sounded more like a plea than a request.

Al rose and walked to my side. He leaned his full weight on the railing, cleared his throat, and spat a thick wad onto the grass below. "Wait. Just hang on a minute. Jesus, Fogger. This was a war." He bent and picked up a water bottle that had rolled under our table. "A goddamn war," he repeated. He drank the entire bottle without taking a breath, then crushed it and threw the empty into the sea of heads, where the crowd still stood straight and expectant, waiting for orders.

"This was a blitzkrieg," he said, turning back from the railing. "A full-tilt, snakebit battle. You might just outlast the war, Fogger. You might survive this shit. Me, I was lucky to be standing next to you when the bastard pulled our levers."

I was about to complain that he hadn't answered my plea when Al turned his attention back to the mob. His back straightened. His hands tightened on the top railing. "Something's happening," he said.

As Al spoke, the mob regained cohesion and rotated together to face the area where Ronnie Millman's glider lurched back and forth like a defective metronome. Ronnie looked up, stopped rocking and brought the glider to a halt. He rose slowly to his feet and took a tentative step toward the stage, then a tremor ran through the mob. I heard a gentle sigh from a hundred throats.

Ronnie suddenly bent at the waist and wacked the side of his head with the flat of his hand, as if he'd just climbed out of a pool and was attempting to clear his ears. Whatever his intent, it didn't work. He rocked on unsteady feet, struck his head a series of faltering blows; gave up, started toward the stage again. He darted his eyes toward Cassie, frantically seeking her help. She turned away, and I couldn't tell if her move was deliberate or accidental.

The mob took a collective, shuffling step toward the gliders. Ronnie retreated, gesturing wildly with both hands to ward them off, but to no avail. He backed up as far as he could, until the back of his knees hit the swing, then he collapsed into it and drew his knees up to his chest. I watched his expression shift through so many conflicting emotions; expectation, doubt, fear; that his face looked like an elastic mask.

The mob closest to Ronnie compacted. He made a final desperate gesture toward the stage, then disappeared from sight. All I could see was a growing knot of people where he had been, fists rising into the air, falling savagely, hacking at the spot where Ronnie had stood. The glider swing thrashed at the end of its chains.

The lead doo-wop vocalist started singing again. His backup quartet executed their synchronized dance as if they still had an audience. The crowd, silent except for the scuffling of feet and the sound of their blows, packed tighter and tighter around the glider. I heard cracking sounds like those I'd seen on a YouTube video of amateur snipers hunting feral pigs. They hunted at night with thermal imaging and telescoping sights and each crack was answered by an anguished squeal.

I'm sure that at some level I knew what was happening, but I didn't block the Alpha's command. I made the decision in a split second. Part of me relished the idea that Ronnie was getting the hell beat out of him. At least, I deceived myself that this was what was happening. Later, I became convinced that I'd known he was being dismembered, just as the mob tore Pentheus apart when he disrespected Dionysius.

"Can't you stop them?" asked Al. I ignored him.

The mob dispersed. They walked back to their blankets, lay down, and began chatting with their neighbors. The doo-wop lead man began another song. For the people of Mosby, nothing unusual had happened. Only I, Al, and the Alpha knew we had just witnessed a lynching.

I lowered my head. Al was on the same wavelength. "Ronnie disappointed his master," he said, "and his master destroyed him."

I didn't care that Ronnie was dead. I didn't feel guilty about not helping him. This might be the break we needed. "Lauren won't be able to deny it this time," I said. "The Alpha's unmasked. The whole town's a witness."

Al's look was compassionate but curious. "Jesus, Fogger. You're still trying to find Mosby on the map of rational thought. It's not there. The only rules that apply here are the ones the Alpha makes."

"There's a bloody smear under the swing, Al. Pieces of Ronnie. It's like there was an explosion. I don't see his head. These people are listening to the concert now, but when they sober up and see him, see the blood on their hands and their clothes, they'll want to know what happened."

"No, they won't. Are you trying you deny how this works? Ronnie will end up in a dozen trash bags in the town landfill. In a couple days, no one will remember him. Not his school friends, not his father or his aunt, no one. There won't be any record that he ever existed."

I looked out at the people sitting closest to the muddy stain that had been Ronnie Millman. Their heads bobbed in time with the music. Al had it right: this was the way the Alpha's world worked. And my mother had been right about the Good God and the Evil God. I welcomed the knowledge that Ronnie had been eliminated. I wished it didn't please me so much.

"If we've learned anything from this," said Al, "it's that you're evenly matched. Next time you meet him, it can go either way."

"I don't think so. I'm still learning. Getting stronger. He's not used to having competition. That gives me an edge."

"Brother, you can't beat him playing defense."

"I'll get around that."

The crowd chatted and listened to the music. I hoped that somehow, they felt the same dull anger that plantation slaves felt, the resentment of troops forced out of the trenches to storm machine guns, the impotent rage at having moved, unwilling, across the chessboard. I hoped their hearts were filled with enough confusion that they'd wake up and remember what they'd done.

"Are you religious?" I asked. "Do you believe in redemption? A final judgment?"

His laugh had acid in it. "The Apocalypse?" he said. "Sure. I was married once. My wife went horseback riding every week with three friends. They'd drink wine and make lists of the sheep and the goats. I was number one on the goat list."

He saw I wasn't smiling. "Don't even go that way, Fogger. This isn't Biblical punishment, it's a natural phenomenon. Maybe we don't understand it yet, but we will."

Al faced me and sawed his hands in the air in a wait-a-minute gesture. "I'm not blowing smoke. I honestly believe that. We'll figure this out. You'll survive. But sure as hell, I don't have a clue how to tell you to do it. I'm heading back to the B&B to think this over."

I stuffed my torn jacket into a trash can, took a step and then turned back to retrieve it. "You should stick with me, Al. In case he tries again."

"He planned this attack in detail, and it didn't work. Oh, he's certain to try again, but not right now. He'll need time to sort out why. We should have a breather before he comes at us again."

"He's a cold son of a bitch. He was here, watching us from somewhere close. Then 'poof,' he was gone, like Keyser Soze in that Kevin Spacey movie, *The Usual Suspects*. I felt him, Al. He's scared."

"And all alone. He's got no one to talk this over with."

"Irresistible murmuration, and he uses it to kill. And gets blocked by a rookie."

"Don't give me the 'with great power comes great responsibility.' Spiderman never had this kind of test. And don't feel sorry for the Alpha. He's a high-functioning sociopath."

I looked out across the lawn where children rolled in the grass. "He's squandering a king's gift. The good work he could do if he wanted."

"Maybe he amuses himself by making a teenager help an old woman across the street, because it momentarily makes him feel like a good little demigod. Problem is, he'd rather force that kid to jump into traffic. Maybe he wants us to worship him. Who knows? He inflicts himself on us because he can. Because our misery pleases him."

"Yeah. That's how I read it."

"In any case, it'll take him some time to regroup, so you should make time for your date."

I wanted Al to be right about the Alpha taking a break before having another go at us. My next task, and it seemed as essential as life itself, was to lock down my relationship with Lauren. Let the Alpha plan his next attack. Whether he sent an army or deployed his foot soldiers one at a time, I would take him on. I would stay in Mosby and fix the bastard once and for all. After that, I could sort out this strange new Fogger Grace I had become, a guy with a grip on his life and a sense of who he should have been all along. A guy who might find a partner with whom he could enjoy that new life.

I lingered, fascinated by the sight of families lounging on the grass next to the smear that had been Ronnie Millman. They sat in the twilight and sipped their sweet tea and clapped politely for each song, satisfied that their children were safe and that the world was in its rightful place at the center of the universe. It was a lovely evening to lie on the grass and listen to music in Mosby, a neighborly country town.

One child rose from his family blanket and walked up the ramp toward me. His gait was wooden, his young face empty of emotion. He stopped at my table and said, "That was a close one, wasn't it?"

Before I could recover, he added, "You're thinking we're evenly matched, out here in the open where we can both see what's going on. You'd be wrong. You're just a half step above these animals." The boy turned away. There was another child waiting behind him, an eight-year-old whose reddened knees shone angrily below her Peppa Pig shorts.

"I've been working this control thing for years," she said, deadpan. "Years of practice. You just started. Keep pretending you know what this is all about. It won't save you, fucker."

The child's flat empty voice immobilized me, not because it confirmed the Alpha's mastery, but because the words were so damn dismissive. Then, as the child turned away, she looked back at me with her dead eyes and said, "You're weak. You might have had a chance if you'd started earlier. But you didn't. You're too slow."

31

I left the death show, rose out of the benumbed mob and made my way to Lauren, amazed that my heart was still whole to give to her. The door to her condo was unlocked.

No sensual classical music this time; the speakers pulsed with a driving *nuevo flamenco* tune, all flurried notes and strumming attacks. The slow-fast-slow guitar rhythms fit Lauren's character. She, too, was composed of mercurial passions. I ached to immerse myself in her heat, to revel in her uninhibited seductions and surprises.

I wanted all that, but for the moment I was a wreck. My breathing was not under control. My thoughts leaped in fits and starts, so I paused in her living room to calm down and straighten my clothing. It worked. Merely being in Lauren's room quieted me. The books on her shelves were not chewing-gum novels but an eclectic mix of odd classics and nonfiction. A copy of Robert Heinlein's *Stranger in a Strange Land* lay open on her dining table. I smiled, recalling the book's peculiar story of romance between lovers from mismatched backgrounds. If I lived with this baffling woman, I could expect wonder to fill each day.

The cloth easel cover lay on the floor. She had added more detail to her painting. There was a rough, sketched-in area in the sea-green bottom half of the canvas, perhaps a rocky shore or a gathering wave front. I wondered where Lauren found the time to paint. For the rest of the world, she might pretend to be the hick sheriff from a 1960s movie, complete with wrong verbs and broken syntax, but when she was alone, inside the four walls of her condo, she was complex and erudite.

I hoped one day I'd understand her. Our minds have an infinite number of rooms, some as large as an arena, others the size of a broom closet. Some have no doors. Others are so well shielded even the owners can't open them. We count ourselves lucky if we can see into even a few of these rooms, but we will never glimpse what's hidden in the most thoroughly protected. I longed to explore the rooms inside Lauren's head.

The bathroom door opened, and a puff of steam drifted into the bedroom. I heard water gurgling into a tub. Lauren stood in the doorway in a cotton bathrobe, brushing her teeth, a bit of white paste on the corner of her mouth. I might have taken her photo at that moment and exhibited it as a Renaissance masterwork. Being Lauren, she broke my reverie by pointing her toothbrush at me and saying, "Get out of those clothes. I can smell her funk on you."

I had no doubt what she meant, but I couldn't think fast enough to mask my guilt.

"Oh, don't get your shorts all knotted up," she said. "This is how Cassie Wrenner works. There's not a man in Mosby can resist climbing up to her hot-pillow room once she decides she wants him. I don't hold that against you, but that doesn't mean I have to put up with you smelling of her."

I replaced the lame excuse I had cobbled together with a simple question. "How did you know?"

"Ha! Cassie told me in her own special way. I'm in my office filling out overtime requests, and I get this flash urge to walk outside and enjoy the humidity. Cassie's second-floor hump pad is right across the street from the station, and when I look up, I can see her head bobbing up and down above the windowsill. All I see is her head, like she's posting on a bouncy horse, up and down and up and down on a nice, hard saddle. Her mouth is all puckered up, but she knows to look down at me, and I swear she smiles."

"I can't explain it," I said. "Believe me, it doesn't mean anything."

"Well, you damn sure won't let it happen again. She set it up so I'd get the message. So I'd be certain she'd got to you. And now you're finished with it."

"I'm done. You're all I want."

"Shut up."

Lauren gave me a more thorough examination. "What's with the mussed-up scarecrow look? Now you been rolling around on the grass with somebody else?"

"I fell down the stairs at the park. I'll tell you about it later."

"Suit yourself." She went back into her bathroom and rinsed her mouth. "Now, get out of those clothes and get your body in here."

It took only a minute for me to do as she ordered. Her tub was a cast-iron relic that in all likelihood had never moved from the bathroom since it was first installed. White porcelain inside, coal-black outside, wide and deep enough for both of us. Lauren was already in the tub, leaning back against the rolled rim with the water lapping her chin. She gave me the once-over as I lowered myself into the nearly unbearable heat.

"Fogger, honey, you look like a long night on a park bench."

I started to explain about the festival concert, but she cut me off. "I don't want you to say anything more about her. Past is past. This is you and me." She let her legs float up past my hips and put her feet on the top of my chest, squeezed her toes to grasp the skin on my shoulders. She squeezed so hard that the tips of her toes turned white. Lauren's smile said she got a kick out of how this little gesture affected me. When she leaned back to stare at my reaction, the dark hairs of her pubis rose above the surface of the water, a soft, mysterious island to explore. How could I hope to understand this woman?

I guess she felt the same. "A strange creature you are, Francis Grace," she said. "I read my Jane Austen and my Emily Brontë, and all their heroes are cold and remote and impossible to make sense of. The heroine works hard at it, and by the end of the story she's turned her lump of a man into a manageable, caring lover. Not you. You started out the shy, sensitive nerd. Now you're becoming somebody different, aren't you?"

I slid my hands up to her ankles and pressed my thumbs into the soles of her feet. The warmth of the water penetrated my muscles. I might lie here with her, my desire suspended between expectation and action, perfectly content if it were not for my own questions.

"And which Lauren Klout is sharing this tub with me?" I asked. "The redneck girl who curses and mispronounces her words, or the painter who reads Heinlein? Which one is the disguise?"

Lauren sat up partway and put her hands on my knees, forcing them wider; then she slowly leaned back against the rim of the tub. She gave me a gentle push with her toes.

"Everyone wears a disguise," she smiled. "Voters don't elect people to public office whom they think are too smart, or suffer them to stay in place once they reveal themselves. Who was our last intelligent president?"

"I can't think of one."

"You'd have to go all the way back to Thomas Jefferson to find one with an IQ in triple digits. The smart ones never make it to the playoffs."

She leaned forward again, her hands on my knees. "The public version of Lauren Klout, the tough, fair, but sexless woman? She's the one who gets to keep her job. That other version, the one who sometimes still calls herself Sofia Luciana, she retreats in here to be with her books. She paints and shares herself with no one." Once more, she leaned back. "Except now."

She was right. Blow away the mill fire, murmuration, whatever errant abilities I could discover. None of these things mattered.

"What secret test did I pass?" I asked. "How did I earn the right to be here, naked in this tub with the hidden Lauren?"

For an answer, she slipped her feet off my shoulders and slid them bit by bit down my ribs until they got to my hips. Her lips pouted, and she arched her neck and back, lifting her hips partway out of the water. The fragrance of rose-scented soap filled my nose, beneath it a musky insistence. Her dark mound shone with drops of moisture, and I reached out to cup it in my hand. The hard edges of her hipbones crested momentarily before sloping away below the surface.

The irises of her eyes expanded until only coffee-green showed. "We've got this private wavelength," she said. "There right from the start. Not at the mill. You got me hoppin' mad, then. But when we sat together at Beans next morning, it came on me. I've stared down bad-assed crack cooks and made them piss their pants, but you sat there making puppy-dog faces at me, so I realized it was mutual."

I chuckled. "Puppy-dog, huh? For me it was more like anticipation. I went to the Beans expecting to tell you about the fire, but my thoughts kept getting jumbled up. Looking at you now, it's that same reaction. I don't think right when I'm with you."

Her smile was pensive. "The other night, with you here, I thought I'd fuck this mule-stubborn feeling out of my system. Use you up. Screw you blind and be done with it. Didn't happen. A colossal failure."

"No, it wasn't. Not a failure."

"I haven't had that much sex in my life, but I can tell when it's special, Fogger. Honey, your flavor's nowhere near ordinary. So far from ordinary that I need to hold onto it, tight."

"That's what I want," I said. "Sincerity. Intimacy." And so I told her everything. I told her she was unique, and that I didn't want other women, and that I risked staying in Mosby because I needed to be with her. And I confessed all that I had hidden from her, including what had just happened at the concert, how I had raced across the highway daring the traffic to run me down, how I had watched Cassie—or someone—make the patrons at Magic Beans keep time on their coffee cups. And the antifreeze. And the attack in the cemetery. All of it.

The water temperature had dropped to blood-warm, but my skin was fevered. I worried that I had blundered, that my delayed confession would convince Lauren that I didn't trust her. She put one hand on her forehead and wiped it down her face, mussing her thick eyebrows and pulling her eyelids closed. She kept them closed and spoke to me in an even, measured voice.

"I hear what you say, Fogger, but I haven't seen *any* of it. You say the people at the festival scared the hell out of you and Doctor Amon, but you also tell me that if I asked them, they'd all deny that it happened. You say you danced through speeding traffic and got clean away with it. The way you tell the story, you should be dead. And then you go and tell me you have a special power that lets you block mind control orders from a secret superman."

"It's not mind control," I said. "It's more of a shield, a barrier."

Lauren sat up in the tub. My confession had quenched our foreplay. Our expectation of passion had turned as tepid as the bathwater.

"Let me get this all out," she said, "and you listen to how it sounds. Here's what I believe. A lot of unlucky people died at Turnell Mill under suspicious circumstances. I read my notes from the scene, and I admit, something is wrong when no one remembers that day the way we do. That's what I can be sure of. These other things you say happened, I didn't see any of them."

"I didn't imagine these things, Lauren. I experienced them."

"Nothing you've said changes the way I feel about you,

Fogger. That also happened, and it's real, too. But please listen while I feed this back to you. Can you hear how far-fetched your stories sound? The way you tell it, no one will ever be able to confirm that these things happened. As terrible as the mill deaths were, I got to believe we'll find a logical explanation for them. We don't need a bogeyman with evil powers."

"Al was there. He and I have been in lockstep on everything that's happened."

"Exactly."

Lauren stepped out of the tub onto a sisal mat. She took a bath towel from a shelf and held it, stiff-armed, until I heaved myself out to join her. She was achingly beautiful. Beads of water shone on her breasts, clear, miniature gems on bronze-brown hills. I picked up another towel and began to dry her shoulders. She stepped back and shook her head.

"We can still get to that, Fogger. Believe me, I want to, but you need to listen." Lauren wrapped her towel high around her breasts so it hung down to her knees. She walked back to her bedroom and sat on the edge of her bed. She pointed at the easy chair next to it, waited until I sat down.

"Was Doctor Amon with you each time you went through one of these far-out incidents?"

"Not all," I said. "I was alone during some of them."

"Well, had you been with him just before these things happened, or did you speak with him right after?"

I saw where she wanted to take this, and I didn't like it. I was certain about what I had observed. I'd seen the Kenworth semi's oil grime on my fingers. I'd poured the antifreeze back into the container. But I had to say, "Yes. He's been with me through all of this."

"So, for a moment, let's say your hypothetical superman exists." Lauren saw my attention waver. She pulled the bottom of her towel across her lap to hide her thighs. "Let's pretend there is someone who has the power to do nothing more than influence your memories. A someone who can plant false memories in your head. Why wouldn't that person be Al Amon?"

"I was there, Lauren. The wind from the semi buffeted my shirt when I ran in front of it."

She ignored me. "What if this one dippity-doo professor has the ability to make you imagine you danced with trucks? What if he convinced you that a crowd of hundreds of people stood up in the middle of a summer concert and almost—that's *almost*—committed murder? Wouldn't your story be the same as you told me?"

"I trust him," I said. "He's the one who figured this all out."

"And he's the one who got you invited to the Hatch reunion on the very day they all died, and he's the same man who showed up when someone needed to pull you away from the fire. Hell, Fogger, he wouldn't need magical powers. A guy with a university lab and brainy friends to call on would be able to drug you and program you with these stories. I learned that in the Army."

Her logic threatened my notions of the past week's nightmare. I'd read the articles in *The New York Times* about government brainwashing techniques and implanted memories. Okay, my memories could have been manufactured. Could have been, but I wasn't ready to give them up. They were too concrete, too detailed, too real.

Lauren slid the towel off her lap and rolled over, her

stomach flat on the bed. "You can chew on that idea later. Right now, we can find better things to chew on."

Making love with Lauren was different this second time. The sound of flamenco guitars and hand-clapping accompanied our coupling. The pulsing rhythms and furious note flurries didn't send me on a magic carpet ride. I didn't imagine myself a musician in a symphony orchestra. None of that, but the sense persisted that despite all the stroking and plunging and seeking of new positions, we were totally immersed in each other. There was no studied maneuver, no exploit lifted from a favorite movie, no play-acting.

When Lauren began to peak, her speech underwent a transformation, and she urged me to "get it, get it, get it." I didn't understand exactly what it was she wanted me to do, but I must have got it right, because a few minutes later she bit my torn ear and demanded, "Again, like last time."

This time, Lauren did not turn away when we finished. She pushed her pillows off the bed and lay on her back with one hand resting lightly on my forehead, drawing small circles with her fingertips. Her deep breaths were the only warning of the weighty debate going on behind her green-brown eyes. She bit down on the inside of her mouth, pushing her cheek in with a finger to get a tight grip. She held it for a while, staring at the ceiling.

"Give it up," she said finally. "Send Amon and his superman babble back to Georgia Tech. Stay here with me."

"You don't want to hear this, Lauren, but the superman is real. He isn't some benevolent creature from a distant galaxy, here to help us pitiful humans. He's a monster, and he thinks we're an inferior life form, and he's ready to sacrifice all of us to keep his power hidden. If we don't stop him now, then in any future I can see, we're his slaves. Or his sport."

Her hand slipped off my face. She stretched her arm above her head and studied her fingers as if she hadn't seen them before. After a long pause, she dropped her forearm over her eyes.

"When I was a little girl, my stepdaddy used to take delight in telling me that he wasn't my real father, because God decided to play a mean trick on our family. I didn't have a real father, he'd say. But when I got older, he said God never makes a bad decision, and there was a good reason for us to not be the same blood. Then he'd lock the door and do things to me."

Geez. I knew I had to decode Lauren's statement and respond with compassion and understanding. I wanted to. It's what a sensitive man would do. "Lauren, I don't know about God, but none of that is on you. Sometimes the people we should trust the most hurt us the worst."

"There's a bitchy God out there, Fogger. He doesn't tell us what he wants. He just messes with us and watches us squirm. Like that Jesus story about an enemy planting weeds in your wheat just to mess you up."

I didn't recognize that allegory and it annoyed me. My mind was zeroed in on a perverse evolutionary aberration who wanted to murder us. Getting from that emergency to Lauren's parable about God was too hard, and I told her so.

"You're going ahead with Amon?" she said. "With his hunt for brain-eating zombies with spooky powers?"

"I don't get where you're going with this. I want to stay here with you, but we have to face this monster head on. We do that, or he wipes us out, one massacre after another."

Lauren rolled off the bed and turned away so I couldn't

see her face. The light from her bedside lamp framed her body. Wisps of damp hair stood out from her nape like delicate sensors, tasting the air. She had a faint port-wine birthmark at the base of her spine, centered over her buttocks, a delicate birth-bruise in the shape of a thumbprint. Earlier, I had run my hand and my lips over it, marveling at the distinct edges and trying to compose a poetic way to compliment her about this one trivial departure from her taught skin. The birthmark grew darker and more mysterious in the lamplight. Only this little red circle, no bigger than my thumb, interrupted the fine glow of her skin, and it captured my attention. I wondered if she even knew it was there.

"I don't want to talk anymore about supernatural powers," she said. "I got enough of that from my daddy. When you can give me something concrete, fine. Until you do, leave me out of it. I want our time together to be about us. Only about us."

I told myself I could pick up our disagreement later, when I could prove the Hatch Alpha was real, but at this moment, the thing that urgently called for my attention was that small reddish circle at the base of her spine. That was where my scrutiny and my lips belonged.

"Come here," I said, and she did.

32

I got up at first light and quietly left Lauren's condo. A faint buzzing sound echoed across the park. A man in a Mosby Maintenance T-shirt had finished packing the bandstand speakers in plywood cases. Now he sat on the edge of the stage, having a smoke. The droning came from the leaf blowers two other men were using to round up festival trash. I crossed the park to the side of the stage. A fourth employee stood by the swings with a garden hose, directing a stream of water at a trampled section of grass.

"Looks like the folks at the festival made quite a mess," I said to him, more a statement than a question.

"Sure did. Mosby families are considerate people, but even the nicest folks get careless at a picnic."

I nodded at four black, heavy-duty plastic bags stacked beside the swing. "Lots of trash," I said, keeping my voice flat.

"More'n usual, but we all agreed to get on it bright and early. Can't have the town park looking sleazy. This is a tourist town, y'know."

I pointed at the mire his hose had made of the matted grass. The water was a muddy orange streaked with red. My gag reflex triggered, but I swallowed hard and choked out, "Did someone have an accident here? The water has a strange color."

"Looks like some hot sauce mixed in there. Some family brought barbeque for dinner. It'll soak in. You won't never know it was there."

I bent down to pick up a beer bottle the cleanup crew had missed. I stared for a long time at the plastic bags I was certain contained the shredded parts of Ronnie Millman, then I threw the bottle on top. "Here's one you missed," I said.

"Thanks, man," was his reply.

Just as Al had predicted, Ronnie Millman was on his way to the dump. His Alpha cousin had already scoured him from Mosby's memory. No one understood the strange kid and his weird behavior. Now he was forgotten garbage. Unlike his Hatch kin, Ronnie knew he had a special talent and he fought to bring it under control. His struggle was heroic, but he lost.

People who have special abilities can only stall the inevitable victory of the self-appointed autocrats and saviors. I would be happy to live with a system run by the elites of which Thomas Jefferson wrote, "... a natural aristocracy based on virtue and talents," but more often those in charge are merely the ones who learn how to manipulate the architectures of control—the dictators and congressmen, the religious leaders and supreme leaders.

Most people are ethical and compassionate. But some are born irreparably flawed and twisted, and they are a mortal danger to the rest of us. Perhaps depravity is embedded in their DNA and revealed at birth. Perhaps it's imposed by dysfunctional childhoods or by failure to embrace a moral system. Does it matter? Despite our efforts to eradicate it, immorality persists.

I once interviewed a retired policeman who had seen so much inhumanity that it played continuously across his face. Grim memories of arbitrary cruelty saturated his words and inflections, and I didn't need to see the photographs from the crime scenes he'd worked to know that he had peered into the desecrations of the depraved and had learned that, given power over others, some people will despoil their fellow creatures and wreak vengeance on them. That certainty permanently damaged this good man who hoped to be a friend to the powerless.

During the night, as I lay awake next to Lauren and listened to her steady breathing, running my fingers over the ridge of her shoulder and the swell of her hip, I made myself several promises. The most important was to ensure that Lauren became a permanent part of my life. She underpinned what I now saw as the new, revised Fogger Grace.

I had also resolved to protect Al, so now I walked back to the Braxton Bragg Inn, showered, and woke him for breakfast. We had time to talk, but neither of us wanted to discuss yesterday's events. I decided not to tell him about watching Ronnie's blood being hosed out of the park. That picture would not help his mood.

My recommendation for the morning was that the two of us visit the town archives in the basement of City Hall for clues to Furlong Hatch's origins or anything else that might help us devise a defense against the Alpha's murmurative powers. I remained on full alert for the warning signs that signaled an Alpha attack, filled with renewed confidence that I could deflect anything he launched at us.

The morning was full of promise, but it did not go well. We never made it to the archives. The attack came so suddenly that the Alpha nearly won.

We had just parked at City Hall when a warning flush spread across my neck. At the same instant, a battered Subaru Outback made a reckless left turn, crossed the median stripe and slammed into Al's half-open car door. The Alpha's timing was off by a millisecond. Al had just begun to get out of his Kia, one foot out on the pavement and his hand on the door handle. A second later and he would have been pulped. The Subaru's front bumper glanced off the fender of Al's car, crunched into the open door and wrenched it off its hinges. The Subaru plowed onward onto the sidewalk, ricocheted off the statue of a World War I doughboy, and slid to a hissing standstil.

I didn't see the ragged metal hinge from Al's door punch deep into his thigh, but I immediately sensed he was hurt. I think he was the one who choked out a single "Ugh" as he went down. Might have been me.

The impact yanked Al out of his seat, onto the road. He landed on his hands and knees, staring dumbly at the ruin of his car door. By the time I scrambled around to his side, blood was seeping through his pants leg. I pulled my belt off and tightened it around his thigh.

The Subaru had come to rest with its front bumper hung up on a sidewalk bench. Its driver, a young man with a barcode neck tattoo, ran back to us, his face ashen. "I . . . I . . ." he stammered. "I was just . . . I don't know why...he just stepped out."

"Call 911," I said. "We need to get to a hospital."

"He just stepped out. I never saw him."

"Shut up and call 911." The guy stopped excusing himself and made the call.

Al tapped the ball of his fingertip on the widening stain. "New slacks," he said in an apologetic voice. "I bought these just a week ago. I never spend that much on slacks. Never."

"Easy," I said. "You're in shock. It looks worse than it is."

"Isn't this how we met?" he said, and chuckled. "Some role reversal, huh?"

The blood seeping through Al's pants leg didn't appear to be spreading. I loosened the belt long enough to see the flow start, then tightened it again. I placed a quick call to Lauren. It went to voicemail, but as I hung up, a police cruiser braked and pulled diagonally across both lanes of traffic. A husky officer flung his door open and sprinted over to us. He took a quick look at Al's leg; then, satisfied, he gave me a thumbs-up and said, "EMS is on the way. Five minutes, max." He turned his back on us and started directing traffic. The young Subaru driver began a long, rambling explanation of the accident, swooping his arms to show how none of this was his fault. The officer ordered him to sit on the post office bench.

Al clutched my hand. His grip was so intense that at first, I thought pain had replaced shock. What I read in his face was far more complex. "You didn't block this one, did you?" he asked.

I bent down so only he could hear me. "No time. He was too fast."

"But you *could* have blocked it. You felt his plan unfold. You're as fast as he is."

I started to tell Al that I wasn't sure I could do that—act fast enough to block a strike as soon as an attack unfolded—but as I began, his gaze turned inward and his grip on my hand tightened.

"Listen," he began, "if I don't get back from the hospital..."

"It's not that bad, Al. I'm not bullshitting. You've got a severe cut. Stitches for sure, but it's nothing to lose sleep over."

"Shut up and listen. Go to my room and rescue my notes. Now! Keep them safe. If I don't get back from the hospital, if the emergency room decides I need an urgent heart transplant, if a nurse makes a mistake with my medication, if anything takes me out of the picture, you give them to my team at the lab." He took a trembling breath. "Promise."

The EMS vehicle pulled up, siren warbling. Within two minutes, the paramedics had Al stabilized, on a stretcher, and being slid into the ambulance. He raised his head and gave me an "okay" gesture with his thumb and forefinger. His words did not match this small sign of bravado.

"You find all of it," he insisted. "Get it to someplace safe."

I nodded my promise as my cell phone rang. It was Lauren. "I got a report from my guy. He says Al will need stitches. Nothing more."

"The Alpha did this. It was a deliberate hit. I want a police guard put on Al's hospital room."

"That again?" she said. "My guy says this is a case of distracted driving. We'll charge the driver, impound his car, jam him up good. But treat it as attempted murder? Thank you, but I don't think so. The mayor would start looking for a new chief."

"Then don't make it official. Put someone in Al's room who's off duty. I'll pay for it. Don't make me beg."

"You're a damn fool. I'm a double-damn fool, but goddamn, all right. I'll work something out, but you will owe me, big time. And listen, Fogger. You need to get your shit together. Al Amon's got your head screwed around backwards. If this mind-reader superman ever existed anywhere but in your juiced-up imaginations, he'd have snuffed you a week ago when you first started nosing around my sleepy town."

Lauren made a vague promise to see me later and ended the call. The paramedics had left with Al while we spoke. I decided not to follow them to the hospital but to return to the B&B and retrieve Al's files before I did anything else.

I took the files back to my room and locked the door. While I understood that he wanted me to protect his lifework, it was also an invitation to snoop around. There was one file in particular I hoped I could understand. When I had returned from challenging semis out at the bypass, Al had shown me the results of the DNA analysis of the samples from Magic Beans—all but the one yellow folder marked "Group C." Al had looked at it, blanched, and refused to share the results with me.

The yellow file folder was the top one in his briefcase. The subject line on the identifier cover sheet said "unknown." The lab codes on the rest of the sheet resembled those I had seen on Cassie Wrenner's DNA sheet: *Deep Mutational Scan: Sequence 4, Male/32-36/ Marker: a 11, dd 02, unknown, unknown, aberrant mode B, Suspect Alleles in 6, 9, 17, 21*. Meaningless, but the words *aberrant mode* told me there was a second person with the yet un-decoded extra lobe.

Cassie wasn't the only candidate suspect for Mosby's homicidal Alpha.

At first, the accompanying electron-microscope photo looked familiar. The bottom of chromosome six had the same misshapen bulge. But when I studied the grainy image, I could not count distinct lobes. Even in black and white, it looked loathsome, like a badlands landscape viewed from outer space. My sense of foreboding reignited. I knew how to counter an Alpha attack if I reacted fast enough. But *two* Alphas?

And, yes, I knew there was another possible interpretation of these lab results. I shunted that speculation straight into the memory palace and locked it up.

I thought I heard a knock at the door, but when I opened it, there was just the male golden retriever standing at the top of the porch steps, his eyes wet and drooping. He sniffed the spot where his mate used to lie, and huffed. He looked up at me and huffed once more, so hard that the gray hairs above his lip stood out from his muzzle. I thought of the retriever bitch, poisoned in my place. Even though I had seen her only a few times, my eyes moistened with childish emotion. I bobbed my head at the vacant space next to the male and said, "Good girl."

I sent out for a Greek pizza and then stayed in my room, where I attempted to drag fresh meaning out of Al's test results. Ignorance defeated me. Next to a PhD specialist, I was a grunting proto-human, unable to understand the simplest terms of his language. I thought for a very long time about the fate of evolution's attempts to upgrade the species. The first experiments died out when they couldn't adapt to a changing environment. Others fell to fists and clubs, eradicated by later models. Early modern humans bred with vanishing Neanderthals and Denisovans, so that all of us carry trace genes from our heavy-browed precursors.

When they coupled, did the early moderns feel compassion for their less evolved cousins? Was it just a hit-or-miss screw with a creature from farther down the sentience ladder, like having sex with a farm animal, or did they share a sense of empathy and wonder?

About eight, I stepped back onto the porch, into the cicada-loud evening. There was no sign that the male retriever or his mate had ever slept here in the drowsy shade. Down the street, a child was dancing in the thin breeze, twirling around in the perfect joy of movement. I heard her song but did not recognize it.

That was when I saw Mosby's starlings as they lighted in the trees, gripping the pine branches so tightly that they might forget their songs forever. They hesitated, irresolute, for only a moment. Then they lifted and thronged into the dusk. There were hundreds, sweeping in constantly morphing patterns, an air music transmuted into elemental forms of vortex and cascade. I wanted to believe they performed their intricate dance just for me, but they flew for reasons known only to each other, speaking a language I could not fathom, their wings whirring with the murmur of a Doomsday machine hidden under a heavy blanket.

33

The memory of the spiraling starlings seemed like an omen, and the image of their gyre remained with me throughout the night. Murmuration replaced my typical dreams where I played the hero in a favorite movie, defeating the bad guys and winning the love of a horny Venus.

I awoke before first light but stayed in bed and watched sunrise creep through the window curtains and onto the carpet. I waited in vain for the thunderbolt of insight that poets write about. No thunderbolts struck. I believe that dreams are suppressed metaphors trying to express themselves, metaphors our subconscious uses to communicate with us, if only we would interrogate them and reveal their hidden truths. But truth had been absent ever since my arrival in Mosby.

Although not quite. My metaphors shared a theme. They all contained imagery of things illuminating me. Moonlight falling on my waxen feet in the middle of the night. Streetlights shining through the plantation shutters of Lauren's condo and cutting my body into imagined slices. Dull gleams hiding behind the glazed eyes of a mob intent on my death. All these hinted that I was guilty of an unacknowledged fault. I analyzed others for a living, but my own self remained a mystery.

I phoned and learned that the hospital would discharge Al at noon. Time had run out. Today, we'd have our final showdown with the Alpha, of that I felt certain. A dramatic day, Wagnerian, so I dressed in my black Goodwill jeans and a black shirt with pearl buttons, sleeves rolled up to the elbows. But a glance in the mirror told me I looked like a cross between a Johnny Cash impostor and a Clint Eastwood impersonator, so I put on my baby-poop green running shoes to temper the impression. My torn khaki Goodwill jacket went into the back seat of my rental car. I parked at the post office and then killed time with a bowl of eggs and grits at Magic Beans, sitting in one of the stuffed chairs near the entrance, brooding over the DNA report on the second Alpha.

Norman Garrison found me there.

"Mister Grace, are you ready to accept my offer to help your inquiry?"

"Just about, Norman. I'll be in touch as soon as I wrap up a few things today. But before that, I'd like to test your comprehensive knowledge of Mosby history."

Garrison sank into the chair next to me, his face beaming in expectation. Just for a moment, he reminded me of my junior-year homeroom teacher, a priggish twit who insisted that each of us recite a poem once a month with our hands folded in front of our chests as if we were shaking hands with ourselves. I practiced Yeats's *The Second Coming* until I could do it in my sleep. When I recited it flawlessly, he criticized me for selecting a poem "you cannot possibly comprehend." His problem was that, for all his pretense, he was deaf to the meaning of the simplest poem. I tried to explain that the poem was about Europe lurching from one world war to the next, but with him, I was fishing in a teacup.

"Norman, can you tell me about an incident that happened here back thirty, thirty-five years ago?"

"What would you like to understand, Mister Grace?" Garrison's smile was so phony I wanted to scrub it off with a rat-tailed file, but if he had what I wanted, I would pretend he was the all-knowing Oz.

"The minister of the Episcopal church," I said, "the one who committed suicide. What was his name? And can you tell me anything about him?"

The smile slipped from Garrison's face. His brows knitted. "Trinity Episcopal Church was built in 1842, and it's been in continuous operation ever since," he said, his eyes half-lidded like a wrung-necked chicken. "The current priest is Tom Booker."

"Okay, but thirty-five years ago, who was the priest who killed himself?"

Garrison's frown spread. "I can't imagine where you got that idiotic idea. Tom came here straight out of the Sewanee seminary forty years ago. He's been in charge of the parish ever since."

"I understood that there was a scandal at the church, that the priest and an unwed mother . . ." My sentence tapered off.

Garrison rose to his feet and stared down at me. "Nonsense. Trinity is my church. I've been attending since I was a toddler. I see perfectly well what you're trying to do, Grace.

You can bet I won't be wasting any more time on you or your insufferable partner." He wrestled open the balky door and stalked out of the shop.

An elaborate network of lies contaminated everything I knew about Mosby. And about myself. If Garrison's story was true, Mom's story about my absent father was another dead-end scam. The Alpha had implanted an alternate history, one that appealed to Mom's sense of fantasy. She believed a phantom priest had fathered her child. So did the other people the Alpha had indoctrinated in case I should come in contact with them. And even that fiction was obsolete; my mother now believed I'd died in infancy. A child who didn't even have a name. If I lost my battle with the Alpha, I'd disappear completely.

I drove my rental Toyota to the hospital, paid the off-duty cop posted to Al's room, and checked my friend out. The discharge desk offered him a cane. Al refused and walked through the automatic doors with a pronounced side-to-side roll.

"What's the damage?" I asked.

"Physically, I have thirty-seven stitches and the mother of all bruises," he said. "The fatal damage is to any of my surviving illusions about having a future. You know that verse about tomorrow, and tomorrow, and tomorrow, and all our yesterdays lighting fools."

"Sound and fury," I said, "from Macbeth."

"Right. I've been bullshitting myself that I'd figure a way to survive this crossroads. Not going to happen. When I try to look forward, all I see is a blank screen tuned to an empty channel. Blotto."

I had to prompt Al twice to buckle his seat belt. He stared morosely out the car window, his attention turned way inside himself. If we were to make it through this day, I needed to jolt him out of it.

"I read the lab results for Group C," I admitted. Al said nothing.

"So, okay, there's a team of Alphas," I continued. He remained silent. "I've learned how to block them. I'll be fine. It's time for you to get back to Atlanta. I'll be staying here. You tell me what to dig into. I'll collect the information and send it to you. You do the crunching in your labs."

Al unbuckled his seat belt so he could turn toward me in his seat. "Fogger, sometimes you demonstrate the judgment of a senile old man. A dull one. Quit looking for a happy ending. I have twenty-four hours at most. Not enough time to get away, even if I tried. I've thought about this from every angle. I'm resigned. All I want is for my work to survive. I phoned the lab and told them you're my beneficiary. Send them whatever you find here. They'll share their results with you.

"Here," he said, pointing to the side of the road. "Pull over here."

We were on the 441 bypass near where I'd had my dance with traffic. I pulled into a dentist's office parking lot and turned off the engine.

"Seriously, Al," I said. "Drop the trumpet-of-doom attitude. If you want to be of any use, snap out of it." But I'd wasted my words. Al's patient nodding meant only that he'd heard me. Nothing I said would bring him back. He had already capitulated to the Alpha.

"Two decades," he said. "That's how long ago I identified the murmuration phenomenon. For a few years, I convinced myself I was a god. Damn, that was a good time! Then I learned there were other people with powers like mine, and realized that if there were, some of them would be stronger, just like all the people who were physically stronger than I am, smarter than I am, handsomer than I am. I've seen this day coming for a long time. I've earned the right to be cynical. Fatalism is my religion."

He clenched his fingers and lowered his hands to his lap. "Can you imagine how I felt when I first realized how murmuration worked? I thought I had a unique power. I daydreamed about all the things I would do once I learned how to control it, how to strengthen it. I'd change the world. Maybe rule the world. But it turned out I had only one trick: a modest, hardly detectable talent for making people like me.

"I traced my roots, searched for others like me. I didn't find anyone else until I stumbled on Furlong Hatch, the lech of Mosby, Georgia. It took more years before I realized he was my one-night-stand daddy. But that told me there were others out there, half-brothers and half-sisters who might give me a family. They could show me how to cash in on my talent. I dreamed of learning how to become an Alpha. Instead, I've helped expose one. And, brother, it's damn clear he doesn't tolerate exposure."

"I can keep you safe, Al. Just stick close to me."

"What? For the rest of my life? Seriously, Fogger, you have enough of a challenge just to protect yourself."

"I'm confident about my ability to block his attacks, Al."

"Bullshit. Your whole life you've trained yourself not to question, not to fight back. You're hell-bent on ignoring the implications of what's right in front of us. Look at yourself, man. You can get people to reveal their secret feelings, but you . . . ." He left the sentence unfinished, as though he expected me to connect his condemnation to some revelation.

"You're the only person with a hope of defeating this monster," he said. "When I'm dead, you'll be the only one who even realizes that he exists. And I mean the *only* one. All my lab team knows is that they've found a peculiar node. Without reading my notes, they'd never suspect there's a world class superman hiding in Mosby."

Al reached into his hip pocket and pulled out a sheet of paper, dog-eared and folded into a tight packet. He held the paper with his thumb and first two fingers. It might have been a hot coal the way he waved it in front of me. "Henry visited me last night with the test results from a DNA sample I gave him the day before my accident. I needed to re-run it to confirm what I suspected."

When I refused to take the paper from him, Al stretched across the divider and patted my arm. "Did you think it was coincidence that brought me to Turnell Mill the same day you were there to see the suicide?"

Well, no; even before Lauren alerted me to suspect Al of masking his intentions, I had thought of it.

He read the accusation in my expression. "No, Fogger," he sighed. "Don't you even *think* I would have done that if I'd known the Hatch family was going to set themselves on fire. But, yes, I worked hard to get you here. I've studied you a lot, your crappy childhood, your loneliness, all of it. I've read all your columns. When I asked you about Dionysus, I knew you had written your thesis about him, but you didn't challenge me on it. Coincidence? You ignored it. I imagine you've practiced ignoring clues ever since childhood. Tuned them out, pushed them down."

I felt bone tired. I settled back in my seat and let Al plod on toward the conclusion I didn't want to acknowledge.

"Once I sorted out that Furlong Hatch was the first to exhibit the murmuration ability," he said, "I began to track all the births around Mosby when he was active." Al put air quotes around the word *active*, a thing I had not seen someone do in a long time.

"It took more years, but I got blood samples from birth records all across Georgia and South Carolina. I got results for single mothers and their children. You can access a lot of private information by being charming," he said, giving me a self-deprecating smile. "Charm, and flashing a business card with PhD abracadabra on them; that works like a charm, too."

He smiled, and for a few seconds there was a different Al Amon there: a younger man, confident, filled with a hunger to know, to sort out who he was and what he might accomplish. Twenty years ago he had been like me, but without the self-doubt. He quested after signs of the brothers and sisters he knew must exist. He assembled the clues, studied the data. But when he found another, it was a twisted, implacable version of himself.

Al still held the folded paper in his fingers. "One of the first sets of records I found were my mother's. There were a lot of bastard births in Aintry County whenever Furlong was around. And I discovered a quiet preacher's wife in Pickett, Georgia, who had the Hatch gene. There's no sign she ever used the murmuration ability, but she passed the gene along."

I pressed my fingers into my temples. I dreaded a Hatch connection, but getting it confirmed this way was too blunt and raw, too painful. Furlong Hatch was my grandfather. He was the real reason for Pastor Grace's disgrace, for Pastor's move to Pickett, the reason my mother had been disowned and unloved. My mother was not Pastor's child; he had known it within weeks of marrying Grammy, when he learned she was already pregnant.

Al raised the folded paper again and waited for me to take it. I knew what the lab report would say.

My suspicions began when I blunted the Alpha's first attack. I'd refused to concede the obvious. Oh, I was good at suppressing unwelcome thoughts. Long practice, drilled into me by my mother. Repeated internal commands. Disciplines that became mantras. Don't look them in the eye. Keep your gaze down. Don't use that tone of voice. Don't get angry. And it had worked.

I unfolded the report. It was a duplicate of the one I had read in Al's yellow Group C folder the previous night, except for one change. Instead of "unknown," the subject line read "Grace, Francis O." Furlong Hatch was my grandfather.

He was also my father.

34

The report for Fogger Grace is a string of Delphic identifiers: *Deep Mutational Scan: Sequence 4 of Male/32-36/ Marker: a 11, dd 02, unknown, unknown, aberrant mode B, Suspect Alleles in 6, 9, 17, 21.* Not so unknown now. Aberrant, yes. Abnormal, certainly. But not unknown. We knew all we needed to know about this sinister person.

"From my coffee cup," I said, not needing Al's confirmation.

"This is my final gift to you, Fogger," he said. "The raw data says you share an extraordinary ability with one other person out of seven billion. It's up to you to learn how far it can go."

I didn't tell Al that I already knew the punch line. The truth hid in the memory of my fifth-grade recess fight, the annoying video clip on perpetual rewind that dogged my nightmares. It kept repeating because it held the secret of my identity, and I didn't want that box unlocked. Resurrecting the event, seeing it as it had actually played out, would compel me to face my abnormality. And my guilt.

I couldn't deny it any longer.

Blows rained down on my face, arms, and chest. I begged the bully to stop. The crowd of laughing classmates circled around us, eager to see someone hurt. They cheered for him, not me. Snot ran down my nose and into my mouth. The pressure in my head hurt more than the punches to my face. My cheeks grew hot with shame. And I *pushed*. Not with my hands but with my will. His blows weakened, ran down; stopped. I pushed harder.

The bully scrambled to his feet, his face blotchy with bewilderment and suppressed anger. He hesitated for only a second, looking anxiously around the playground. Fear crept into the boy's eyes. A whine climbed out of his chest, pinched and threadlike. He searched over the heads of our perplexed classmates until he found what he needed right next to us.

The boy stepped back a few feet, the whine rising in his throat until it rasped my ears. Then he squared his shoulders and ran full tilt, face first into the ailing pine tree, his arms held out stiffly behind him like an old man struggling for balance. His potato face crunched into the rugged bark. He made no motion to protect himself, no effort to slow, but charged the tree as if he hungered for the impact and the pain. He staggered back and turned back to me dumbfounded, his nose streaming blood onto his Atlanta Braves shirt. Not dumbfounded, exactly; more like he couldn't absorb what had happened to him.

Our classmates hushed, also unable to assimilate what had happened. They watched as the bully sized up the tree, planted his feet, and ran at it again, headlong. When he fell back the second time, he left a rust-colored chunk of his cheek embedded in the rough pine bark. The strip of skin was as bloody and ragged as a squirrel flattened by a motorcycle gang. He fell back, dazed, beneath the tree, and began to sob.

I had a dim awareness of what I had done and I luxuriated in it until I got home, and Mom challenged my skinned palms and the blood on my shirt front. She bought my elaborate story about falling down the school steps. After she stopped asking questions, I called on all my long-practiced skills of repression and buried the knowledge so deep that even I could not remember it.

The kids in the mob shifted their feet. They spread apart, looking at one another with suspicion. Finally, one of them came up with an answer. "He hit him," a girl said. "Fogger hit him." I had accepted that version all these years. Until now, when all my memories were suspect. What I remembered were not recollections of actual events but contorted screenplays, the facts rewritten to deny my murmurative abilities. Nostalgia plagued me, a hunger for my world of false memories.

"Fucking Furlong Hatch," I said.

"Got that right," said Al. "But you might as well curse fate. He's in our blood."

"I don't buy that. I've managed to keep him down my whole life."

"He's installed in our DNA, Fogger. Can't do anything about that. And you got a double dose of his genes."

"Furlong Hatch is only a trace inheritance, like an allergy to shellfish. I'm not him. I'm not predatory. I don't harm people. I'm no more Furlong Hatch than you are."

I knew I could control my ability because I'd had it as a child. The other Hatch descendants felt their powers ignite at puberty. They imagined themselves lucky, or blessed, but they never understood their unique ability. My talent surfaced the moment I shocked my mother by screaming, "Waffles!" She recognized my power because Furlong Hatch had used it against her. So she taught me to deny it.

In a moment of clarity, I realized that the constant barrage of my infantile demands had shredded my mother's ego. I felt the shame, now, of understanding her erratic behavior. She had experienced the murmurative power firsthand, first from Furlong Hatch, then when her own tiny despot began to send commands. Mom started early to teach me how to suppress my abilities. She knew that when her son reached puberty, he would discover the capability to inflict incalculable damage. The evil she feared had a handhold from birth. She did her damnedest to keep me from surrendering to it.

I didn't have to strain to come up with more examples that should have been warnings. At the head of my list was the Shadow Man, who had protected me and Mom when I was thirteen. The legitimate memory unfolded, no longer smothered by years of denial and catechism. The mugger attacked. I broadcast a demand for help.

The Shadow Man. I summoned him forth out of my rage. My plea was neither fine-tuned nor focused but raw and insistent, propelled by the undiluted force of my panic. It conjured a flash mob of wrath. People ran across the street to smother our attacker. They rushed out of their apartments, stopped their cars in the street to protect my mother and her sucker-punched son.

It was short and brutal, and I directed it. My mother pleaded with me, "Stop! Oh, please, Francis. Please stop!" but I shut her out. I ordered the mugger's arms broken and rebroken, his eyes gouged out. I had them kick his stomach until it leaked fluids like the runoff from a chemical spill. I commanded them to break his hands and feet, to jam his upper jaw on the curb and stomp his head until his neck broke. And when it was over, I told them to stuff the pieces in a dumpster and blot out their memories. Then, petrified by my obscene power, I forced myself to store it away. I buried my ability to wreak vengeance on the vulnerable.

The taunts I'd endured as an abstracted teenager, the hassles I'd shrugged off, the single bar fight I'd lost at twenty-three, all these had brought temptations to lash out. Mom's constant drumming about inner angels and self-control kept my emotions dampened, kept the darkness suppressed. But the malevolent chimera that lived inside me, barely stayed in check. All Mom's lectures failed to reprogram my fundamental character. I'd have to do that myself.

"I mean it, Al. The Alpha uses his power to hurt people. If I can beat him, I'll turn this curse around; use it to do good things."

"You *can* beat him, Fogger, but this thing in your blood doesn't change who you are. You're still human, with human weaknesses. Unlimited power over others doesn't make you a better man."

"I have a conscience. I have someone who loves me. I'll be a moral person for her."

Al looked very old sitting there, belted into the car seat, the white hospital identification band still on his wrist. Old and shrunken and sad.

"Conscience and moral certainty have never changed the world one jot, Fogger. The crusaders had good intentions. They ended up plundering Constantinople and slaughtering everyone in Jerusalem. Every generation, we get reformers with the best intentions. The world goes on its way, ignoring all their importations. The Pope calls for peace every Easter. How's that working?"

That first morning at the Magic Beans coffee shop, it had been I who stopped the fist an inch from my nose. Al was right to deny that ability. He was not strong enough or quick enough to send that command. And when all the patrons in the shop played a tune on their coffee cups, that was me, too. Had there been other times? Of course, there were. I played the puppet-master, then buried my guilt under a mountain of deformed memories.

Al was my half-brother. I might have him for only a few more hours. Thanks to Furlong's incest with my mother, I had inherited a double dose of his random gene—and along with that gene, all the infernal talents it carried—and still I could not help him.

I squeezed Al's arm and he took a ragged breath. His eyes remained fixed on mine, his expression changing from sadness to resolution, then his throat muscles tightened as if he were about to cry.

"You're way into alien territory, Fogger. I can't teach you anything."

"I'll figure it out. Any advice?"

"The real question is, what do you want to *do* with this gift?"

I had thought this question inside-out for years, fantasizing, as everyone does, about having extraordinary powers. Now, face to face with real-life potential, I could be sure of nothing save the one promise I'd already made. "I won't be another Alpha, pushing people around. There's too much of that in the world already."

"Yeah? Well listen," he said. "You're more strong-willed now than you were when I met you at the mill fire. When I first discovered my modest ability to charm women, I had no problem convincing myself that using it was ethical. All I was doing was pimping up what was already inside me. I never thought of it as pushing women around. But that's exactly what it was. You'll learn to live with it, brother. You're much tougher than I ever was."

"How tough do I need to be?" I said. "The Alpha's ability is stronger than yours or mine. And it's much more seductive. It must be like a drug for him, messing with people's lives, playing God. If I ever get anything close to his skill, I don't want to fall into the same trap."

I believed there were people with a moral compass and that I was one of them. But my experience interviewing people had taught me that even the nicest folks suffered moments of venality, times when desire overwhelmed their better natures. How many had told a lie calculated to harm someone who had angered them? Perhaps some politicians go to Washington planning to restore a civil society, but how many enter Congress in debt, yet exit millionaires? Power corrupts in ways small and large. We all face the daily temptation of small sins. If my powers were anything close to those of the Alpha, how long could I resist using them to satisfy my most fearsome desires?

We sat there in the parking lot, each calculating the possibilities. Cars flashed by along the stretch of road where I'd flirted with suicide. So I could cancel the Alpha's commands. Big frigging deal. No one ever wins a purely defensive war.

"Look," said Al, "I'm not religious, but every religion tells us that a person seeking revelation must isolate himself and walk in the wilderness. Odin crucified himself on a tree called Yggdrasil for nine days so he could learn how to control the nine worlds of men. Jesus starved himself in the desert. Moses and Mohammed went to the mountain to receive wisdom. Gilgamesh walked into the wilderness and under the mountain while he searched for the power to defeat death."

"I'm serious about figuring this out, Al, but not by hanging on a tree."

"Come on, Fogger. These are all metaphors for clearing your mind. Whatever powers you have, they're buried in there, in your gray matter. What you need is time alone to sort them out."

"Meanwhile, what do I do?"

"I'd start by making a big withdrawal from the bank. No? Okay, you don't want me to joke about it."

He pondered for a couple of seconds, then said, "Before you go up against him, you need to calibrate how strong you are. Run an experiment."

"How about I experiment on you? I'm serious, let's see if you'll follow my commands."

Al held both palms in front of my face, thumbs interlocked. "Please Fogger, no. If we are friends, don't. I mean it. The time I have left, I only want my own thoughts in my head. Run your experiment somewhere else."

The thought of playing God with people's lives nauseated me. Or maybe the air inside the Toyota was uncomfortably warm. I started the car. The simple twist of a knob dialed up the air conditioning. Would it be that easy to push people around?

"If it were you," I asked, "how would you do it?"

"Test yourself with a larger group. I've seen you convince a couple dozen people to make an empty-headed orchestra with spoons and cups. The Alpha and Ronnie choreographed hundreds at the festival. You stopped them. The question is, can you give commands with an even stronger force than you block with? Keep it simple. Learn how to make a crowd march in a straight line."

"See, that's exactly what I don't want to do."

"Well, then damn me. You're not taking this seriously. If I had the potential you have, I'd have a May Day parade down Main Street. No, wait, I wouldn't. You don't want to make this obvious. You can't let the Alpha know how strong you are."

"And if it turns out I can control a group to do more than make music with their spoons, what then?"

"I can only guess, but sending a command to an individual must be different from directing an entire group. Figure out how you did it before, and build on that. This is to the death, Fogger. It'll come down to a battle between you and the Alpha, one on one. Like it or not, you'll use other people as your weapons."

My arms and legs were stiff from tensing my muscles. I stretched against the seat back, and my foot accidentally flattened the accelerator. The engine raced to the rev limiter. Both of us jerked at the sound, and I hit the accelerator again. Same reaction. We exchanged rueful smiles.

"Can you help me figure out where he'll strike next?" I

asked. "He knows I can sense when he's giving a command. He knows I can block. What's his best shot at taking me out?"

"I think you just answered that. The only thing that will work for him is an attack where there is no command given, where you can't block because you don't have time."

"Then I'm safe, aren't I? If he doesn't give a command, I don't have to defend myself. Or you, Al."

Al made a dismissing gesture. "Think about that first day at the mill. The Alpha set up his commands months before the reunion. Everything was preprogrammed. All he had to do was sit back and watch."

Al was dead on. Even if my ability to read the commands had been active, I would not have known that Grady Hatch planned to murder his daughter. The Alpha had planted that command long before. The fire and the explosion would have played out in exactly the same way. "So," I said, "he sets up a situation where there's a posthypnotic signal, and his puppets launch an attack before I can see it coming."

"It's not hypnosis, but you got the idea. And a good attack will have numbers. Three people, six, maybe more, all of them programmed to go at once."

"So, all I have to do is stay alert for anything and everything. I'm not getting a good feeling here."

"Welcome to my world," said Al. "Get somewhere alone and think this through. You're an intelligent man. See if you can control murmuration. If you can, then sit down and decide what it means to be a god. That's a question only you can answer."

35

I took Al back to the inn. In a gesture most like a caress, he brushed my chest with the back of his wrist and said, "From here on this is all you. Nobody should give advice to someone with skills they don't understand."

"Skills I may or may not have," I said.

"The skills are there. You just need to calibrate them. And control. You need to learn how to control them." He held his hand out and waited until I understood that he wanted me to take it, then closed his other hand over mine. His grip was firm and warm, his tone wistful.

"You're the brother I always hoped for," he said. "See you on the other side, Fogger Grace."

I nearly told Al that I wished he had been the sheltering father I'd never known. I let the opportunity pass and instead took a slow walk to the center of town, doing my best to enjoy the beguiling peace of Mosby. The people I met smiled and gave me friendly waves. The quiet streets seemed idyllic, but I had watched too many Spielberg and Tarantino movies not to know that when the protagonist rides into the quiet Midwestern town or hikes into the picturesque Tyrolean village, no matter how beautifully the shaded sidewalks and flowering hedges frame his arrival, there's a sniper hiding on a rooftop with the crosshairs centered on the back of his head.

I walked over to a small deli that stood between a boarded-up funeral home and a closed bank on the far side of the town square. The brick sidewalk in front of the deli had three round metal tables with umbrellas. It was too early for the lunch crowd, so I took one of the outdoor tables and turned my chair to watch the sidewalk traffic along two sides of the square. I ordered a hot pastrami and a root beer, and, for the hell of it, added a sack of boiled peanuts, the "caviar of the South." First time for everything; I might not have the chance again.

My laid-back attitude didn't match my exposure, but I felt a stirring of confidence. I struck the pose of a relaxed man on holiday in an exotic foreign country. I tried a boiled peanut and washed it down with root beer. Nope. Not for me.

Tourists strolled past the small shops that faced the square, peering into display windows. A few others, probably townspeople, walked past me with more purpose, on errands or late for work.

I waited until half a dozen people were within view, took a deep breath, and thought, *There are hundred-dollar bills on the sidewalk.*

Each target stopped, bent over, and searched in vain for the imaginary bills. All along the square, other people hustled out of shops and began searching the sidewalks. Two cars nosed quickly into parking spaces next to the post office. Their drivers got out and joined the hunt. The kitchen staff from the deli came out and circled my table, one man in a white apron even getting down on his hands and knees to peer under my chair. I sent, *False alarm. No money. Forget it.* My original six targets straightened and resumed their ambling. The rest of the troop went back inside their shops. The drivers returned to their cars.

Murmuration—what a turn-on! An almost erotic exhilaration flooded over me. I'd made a wish, and people had acted out my desires! It was, in a sick sense, the same beast as my old ego crutch, the Civ 7 computer game: command, control, conquer. But no longer a fantasy competition with the computer! A brief pang of remorse warmed my face. My lips went dry, but the feeling passed. I savored my power. What else was I capable of?

I finished my breakfast sandwich and planned my next test. The other street-side tables had filled, but I ignored the people sitting at them and looked farther down the sidewalk. Nine people were in my field of view. I sent the same message about the dropped hundred-dollar bill but concentrated on just four targets out of the nine. My new pawns stopped and searched in vain for the dropped bill. No one else reacted. No one emerged from the shops. No cars slammed on their brakes. I cancelled the image and reveled in my success, until I realized that I'd thought the word *pawns* to describe my targets. The normals had become nothing more than toys. So easy.

Two men stood next to my table, holding sandwiches and bottles of Coke. They looked edgy, and I realized they must have been standing there for some time, waiting for me to surrender the table. The bigger of the two put his paper plate on my table. He raked his lower lip with his upper teeth. "You going now?" he asked. The way he said it sounded like an order.

"Maybe," I told him. "When I'm ready."

"Well, how about you make it now? We've been waiting here, all sociable, and you're just staring into space. My drink's getting warm."

Who the hell was this annoying guy? I wielded the power to make people jump through hoops, and this yahoo wanted to bully me? Me!

"Why don't you shove your drink up your ass?" I said.

Both men began to unbuckle their belts. The big guy had his zipper halfway down before I pulled the plug on the silent command I'd sent. I apologized and got to my feet. They took the table, only to look into their laps with baffled expressions.

I joined the strolling tourists, escapees from frenetic Atlanta and Augusta trying to squeeze a week of decompression into a few hours. I sent trifling commands as I walked among them. *Tie your shoelaces. Brush the bug off your shoulder*. It got easier. My commands held focus and didn't bleed onto unintended targets. I learned to cancel a command as soon as my victim carried it out. It didn't take long to attract attention when a tourist bent over to tie the shoelaces on his loafers.

I avoided Magic Beans. I needed anonymity, and too many people there would recognize me. Also, it had too many windows facing the street. The post office, however, sat in the lot in the center of the square, surrounded by old oak trees and defended by a wall of cars parked nose-in to the sidewalk. It was small and rarely visited, kept open to provide government jobs.

The interior of the post office was about the size of a small motel room. Banks of obsolete five-by-five-inch post-office boxes framed the walls. Each had a tiny window where you could see whether you had mail.

A woman with a pale blue USPS blouse stood behind a narrow counter, waiting on an elfin woman who looked as withered as an old apple. A third woman waited behind her, absorbed in a video on her cell phone. Perfect.

I positioned myself on the far side of the glassed-in entrance. Then I thought, *Huge alligator on the floor. Jaws yawning. Teeth like daggers.*

Their reactions were instantaneous. The USPS lady froze and let out a birdlike squawk. The woman with the cell phone dropped it and mashed her back against the bank of old P.O. boxes. The big surprise was the wrinkled old woman. She tried to get one leg way up onto the countertop, failed, and then threw herself headfirst over the counter. So much desperation electrified her leap that she fell hard onto the floor on the other side, dragging a trail of stacked mail behind her.

The third woman made ominous gagging sounds. Her face turned cardinal red as she tried to use her backbone to bore a hole in the wall of P.O. boxes. The USPS lady had her cell phone out, tapping frantically at the keypad. I sent a command, *No cell phones*, and she put it down. Her squawks took on a higher pitch, pulsing out of her throat in short bursts.

I had let my attention slip. I turned to look back at the old woman just as she pulled a small-bore automatic from her purse, leaned over the counter, and sent three hurried shots into the floor. She would have emptied the clip, but I recovered and sent *No alligator*.

All three women visibly jerked at the command. I wasn't sure whether they recoiled from my release message or panicked at the sound of gunshots. Their expressions, mixtures of fear and incomprehension, were slow to respond.

I sent a revised message: *Nothing happened. Everything is fine. Everything is normal.*

The effect was immediate. The woman who had been up on her toes against the P.O. boxes slumped back down onto her heels. Behind the counter, the withered woman saw the gun in her hand and hurriedly stuffed it into her purse. The USPS employee looked scandalized and said, "Ma'am, you can't be back here behind the counter. You'll have to go out the side door right now."

The old woman said, "Oh my, I'm so sorry," and limped away from the counter, holding one elbow tight against her ribs. I vowed to think through future experiments with more care. The alligator test had been unnecessary, a variation of hundred-dollar bills blowing over the sidewalks. I had done this one for the fun of it and had injured an innocent woman. Commanding groups had been easy. I needed to tighten my command on a single target without it bleeding over to others. Besides, giving a useless command brought a sense of shame that would wear me down.

When I stepped out of the post office, my shadow fell across the grass like a scar. My experiments were supposed to teach me how to control my abilities, not abuse them. I didn't need the guilt. The video screen in my head ran on automatic, replaying a college history lesson: a Roman general with my face drives his chariot in a triumphal parade, the mob screaming in adoration, and the slave at his back leans over to remind him, "Remember, you are only a man."

Was I merely a man? A person with my powers couldn't

be defined the same way as these insignificant people on the streets of this insignificant town. I was an enhanced man.

I chose the Mosby Artists' Guild shop next. I walked straight to the counter and asked, "What's the most expensive piece you have here?"

The salesman, a man with a pastel bow tie, blinked and pointed to a large abstract canvas near the entrance. I didn't even bother to look. "How much?"

The salesman straightened his tie and in an apologetic voice said, "Eighteen thousand, five hundred."

I pulled a couple of bills out of my wallet and sent a simple command. *I'll give you two dollars for it, but you pay the shipping to Australia.*

A scowl passed over the man's face, mixing the knowledge that this was a disastrous offer with the full realization that he would accept it. He swallowed hard and nodded, unwilling to agree out loud.

I've changed my mind. I'll give you one dollar, and you have to throw in that bow tie.

"All right." He reached up and started to unclip his tie. His voice curled in upon itself so tightly that I reached out to stop him. I sent the release command. The salesman jumped back from the counter, offended that a customer had presumed to touch his neck.

"Sir!" he said. "Is there something I can help you with?"

"No thanks. Just browsing."

I tried one more test. This one had been kicking around in my head ever since Al had joked about it. I crossed the square back to the deli and kept walking to the First Bank of Aintry. The lobby was cool and quiet, a remnant of an institution fast disappearing, doomed by Internet banking. A single teller stood behind the counter. I gave her my best smile.

"I don't have an account here," I said, and I sent my command. *I want to withdraw twenty thousand dollars in cash. Large bills only, please.*

This woman was more perceptive than those I had met so far. "If I do that," she said, "I'll lose my job. They'll probably arrest me, too."

But you'll give me the money.

She looked imploringly at me and said, "But I'll give you the money." She stepped back and squared her shoulders. "We don't keep that much cash out front. If you'll wait here, I'll go into the vault."

Forget it. That was all it took to rescue the voodooed woman. I felt I had done something commendable, releasing her from the damning command. She should thank me. Each time I exercised my power, the shame shriveled a little more.

My tests had taken all morning. I relented and went to Magic Beans for lunch. Cassie stood behind the espresso machine, looking sullen. When I waved for her attention, she drifted in my direction, taking time to speak to a table of diners. When she was good and ready, she spread her palms on my table and bent over to ask, "What do you want to order, Fogger?"

She leaned forward to expose what she imagined were her best assets, but this wasn't a flirtation. "I'm still mad at you for the way you treated my friend Mr. Garrison. Did you really have to be so snotty?"

"I'm sorry, Cassie. Would you bring me a chicken salad sandwich and a glass of water? Then, if you're free, can we talk a bit?"

She straightened her blouse and left with my order. "Yes, we should talk."

I really had nothing to talk about with Cassie. On the surface, she remained the same shallow girl I had known in grade school, obsessed with her looks and unwilling to see beyond superficial appearances. And not that smart. Her friend Garrison was a self-absorbed horse's ass, as false as a circus clown, and she could not see it. The one thing I wanted from Cassie was reassurance that she was not the Hatch Alpha.

So I wasn't much different from the monster who forced fathers to kill their children. Only marginally better than the one who ordered eccentric sisters to hang themselves on a clothesline. My goals depended on the same perverse manipulation as his did. Did I honestly believe I could use my newfound ability to eliminate the Alpha and then give it up? I was a bigger horse's ass than Norman Garrison, ready to use Cassie as a maze rat. The eighteenth-century philosopher Jeremy Bentham said this test was essential: Utilitarianism, justification by necessity, greatest good for the greatest number, all that.

Bullshit. To hell with individual rights.

Cassie returned with my chicken sandwich. She sat down and said, "Well?"

The lunch crowd sat all around us, so I limited myself to simple commands: *Touch your nose. Stand up. Sit down. Laugh.* Cassie's laugh sounded like a camel with a chest cold, but she followed each order. I pulled her strings without a pinch of remorse. She gave no sign that she realized I had governed her every response.

I wanted to believe my test eliminated Cassie Wrenner as the Alpha. Regardless of what Al's DNA tests said, she did not have the power to block me. Or else she was a world-class faker. The anomalous four-lobe marker at the end of her chromosome six probably qualified her as a Hatch, but special powers? Only the remotest chance.

Cleanup was easy: *We've had a nice conversation.* In response, Cassie looked smug. I reassured myself that I was not controlling her body but making suggestions for her mind to filter. If she was the Alpha, she'd block them or find a way to fake it. *We are the best friends,* I reassured her.

"Before you go, Cassie, who owns the old movie house across from the courthouse?"

"Memories and Movies?" she said. "It's not really that old. Two gay boys bought it about five years ago. Fixed the place up, built a wine bar in the back, sold hot dogs and popcorn out of the front. It didn't catch on. They gave up and moved back to Decatur. Not enough audience for nostalgia films in our little town."

"And who owns it now?"

"The boys listed with Mosby Properties. The realty office is right next door to Memories."

It sounded like the ideal place to fulfill Al's final suggestion.

36

I stepped into the Mosby Properties office and gave the agent's gray matter a nudge. The man thought nothing odd about my request for the key to Memories and Movies. He even offered me his flashlight, since the theater had been without electricity for years.

Memories and Movies, the only white stucco building in Mosby, stood fresh and stark among the aged red-brick structures that surrounded the square. Its bleached walls blazed in the afternoon sun. I stepped into the recessed front entrance, apprehension creeping up my backbone, feeling like a prison escapee pinned by a guard tower floodlight.

The theater's glass street-side door faced the post office square and featured a colorized poster of the 1927 German silent film *Metropolis*. There she sat, the character named False Maria, a metallic robot-seductress framed by coils of orphic electricity. In the movie she was programmed to inflame the proletarian mob to violence. How appropriate. False Maria was the perfect poster girl for Mosby.

I pressed my face against the glass door. Afternoon sunlight made the old-fashioned soda fountain stools in the front section too conspicuous. I turned the corner at the courthouse intersection and walked around the building to the miniature parking lot at the rear.

A sign on the theater's narrow back door proclaimed, "Wine Bar." The fringed, funereal awning above the door, bleached and deteriorated by years of direct sunlight, belonged on a horse-drawn hearse from an antique time. Ragged strips of awning canvas lay in the dirt, matted with dried orange mud. Deep scars around the keyhole showed where someone had tried to jimmy the lock. The real estate agent's key worked fine. I shot a quick glance across the street at the darkened rear windows of the courthouse. No one watched. I let myself in.

Darkness closed in when I shut the door; the wine bar had no windows. I switched on the flashlight and discovered an elegant, carved mahogany bar at the back of the room, rescued from a thrift shop or defunct hotel. A single liquor bottle sat on the dusty shelves. There was no furniture. The bar's barren expanse of countertop made the room appear doubly empty.

A padded door behind the bar led into a miniature theater set up to show DVDs on a ten-foot screen. At total capacity, the room could hold about forty people. A small-time operation, even for the 'burbs. The seats themselves were first-class recliners. I sank into one in the last row, at the top of the inclined floor, and switched off my flashlight. All was pitch black, as if I sat at the bottom of a crater on the far side of the moon wearing a hood over my head. An ideal place to contemplate my problematic future.

I drew in a deep, cleansing breath and attempted to

meditate. Kung fu masters always did this in old Hong Kong films. They took that deep breath, closed their eyes, and steepled their fingers. Try as I might, the films that came to mind were not those where Ip Man and Jackie Chan submerge in profound concentration before confronting the enemy, but the Korean revenge movies of Park Chan-wook, filled with severed tongues and dismembered bodies. Had the Alpha come here and sat in this same seat before the theater shut down? Had he searched the screen for new fantasies and then implemented them, confident that no one possessed the power to stop him?

I thought over all the lessons of my short time in Mosby. Furlong Hatch had been born a century ago, gifted—or cursed—with a genetic abnormality that gave him the ability to do what many other animal species had figured out: to communicate instantaneously with his kind. Like those animals, he could influence what the others thought and did. As evolution intended, he had worked overtime to spread his unique genes. Sometimes he had had sex with his children. Did he realize he was screwing his own daughters? Almost certainly. Had he intended to run his own perverse experiment? Unknown. Had he foreseen the long-term consequences? Doubtful.

I was one of those lamentable consequences. The Hatch Alpha was another. There might be more of us, and if I lived through the day, I'd search for them. But not now. My urgent need—my imperative, if I wanted to survive—was to sort out how to predict my half-brother's next gambit. He had to cut my strings now, before I got stronger. Sure, I'd discovered how to block his attacks, but eventually he would wear me down, put together a successful ambush, or smother me with a mob of puppets. The skills I'd learned today gave me a chance. I'd taught myself how to manipulate people as if they were objects.

"I'm not that guy." My voice resonated in the dark theater. "Never that guy."

I wouldn't jerk others around. I'd been governed by doubts my entire life. No one should live like that. I would not play games with people who couldn't defend themselves. I'd stifle my revulsion and use my power to neutralize the Alpha. After that, I'd find ways to make lives better.

All of a sudden, the darkened theater smelled foul. Neutralize him? What a joke. I had to crush him. Only then could I ever engineer a normal life. Lauren would help me metamorphose into a better man. Fogger Grace, version 2.0.

Another option whispered in my ear. Perhaps I could bargain with the Alpha and share power with him. We didn't have to lock ourselves into a battle that concluded with one or both of us brain-dead or just dead. Or I could let him call the shots, take the place of Ronnie Millman; become his super-amplifier. If I went to the Dark Side, I might save myself.

I sat forward, unnerved. Go to the Dark Side?

Oh, he was very good. None of these thoughts sounded like me. The Alpha had tracked me down. The dreams of control and conquest were his. Join him? That would deny all I hoped to be. Fogger Grace was a born-again libertarian. No coercion, no trampling on the basic human right to self-determination. I could change, would change, had changed, but never in that direction. The Alpha was running his own experiment. If the blunt force approach didn't work, go indirect. If he couldn't kill me, he'd subvert me.

I put his planted thoughts behind me, the seductive dream

of controlling everyone. I couldn't defeat the Alpha by becoming his twin. Meanwhile, I had to survive his attacks. He had tried poison, then a manufactured traffic accident. He had attempted to seduce me into a crazed suicide, and when that failed, he had ordered a hapless, half-starved girl to go after me with a steak knife. Well, that last might have been a veiled joke, a demonstration of his power. But it was no joke when he tried to make me the victim of a crackbrained mob. Each time he had used an intermediary, he had failed. The Alpha must be seriously bent out of shape at his lack of success.

What had he not tried? Easy. The simplest approach, the method of jilted lovers and disgruntled employees, of every miserable loser with a grievance. A bullet. Uncomplicated, direct, foolproof. Walk up behind Fogger Grace, keeping your mind cloaked, and plant one in his brainpan. Call the town maintenance crew to clean up the mess. Erase all trace of that aggravating person.

It might have worked before I'd learned to read the signals and intercept the commands. There was a thin, vital window of time between perceiving that the Alpha had given a command and blocking it. Inside that clock-tick moment, I could divert any attack by a physical weapon. The direct approach had failed because he had not met another person with similar skills.

But what if it were the Alpha himself with the gun, the knife, the poison? There wouldn't be a burning sensation. Would I detect my rival's decision in time to freeze his finger on the trigger? I'd only know when the attack played out in real time.

At least I had help. I had Lauren and...and the man who...the man.

Damn. I'd suffered too much stress to remember everything. The attacks. All the new people I'd met. I could see my friend's face, the mashed, cage-fighter nose. Normal, that was it. No, Norman. Norman Garrison. Thanks to Norman, I had survived this long. Without his guidance, I would have been a stain on the park green, washed away with a garden hose. Norman and his lectures about birds. His conversations always came back to the birds. He had wanted to soar, I remembered, to wheel in intricate patterns far above our small-minded human concerns. That was the solution: Climb to the top of the Westin Tower and take flight with...with his murmuring starlings.

And that wasn't right at all. I wasn't making sense. I concentrated and set up a block to push the Alpha's order away. I found the memory of my friend, his lean black face, his thoughtful look behind Harry Potter glasses, his scraggly mustache framing the smiles etched into the corners of his mouth. My brother, Al Amon.

A narrow escape, that one.

The Alpha's attacks had evolved. If I'd bought into his lie and made Garrison my confidant, where would he have taken me next?

Another thought: He had reached me here, alone in the darkened theater. He knew precisely where to find me.

I thought I heard a furtive sound in the wine room on the other side of the padded door. The merest scrape of a shoe on the carpet. I strained to hear him a second time. No telltale sensations burned my cheeks. My overheated imagination conjured up murderous ghosts. But damn, what better place to finish me off? No intermediaries. No messing with commands and false images. Direct action. A bullet in the brain. I sat motionless, listening to the slow susurrus of my breathing. When I felt I could hear the individual air molecules moving across the bronchioles of my lungs, I gave up.

Who wanted me dead? If I went by the DNA analysis, Cassie was the most likely suspect. But when I'd tested her, she'd followed my commands without resistance. It could have been an act, but if she were that adept, she would have eradicated me by now. And there were other candidates. I had met only a fraction of Mosby's citizens. Given Furlong Hatch's insatiable sexual appetites, any of the remaining thousands might be my unknown doppelganger.

Then there was Al. Lauren had valid doubts about him. I liked the man and trusted him, but everything I knew about the Alpha and murmuration came from Al Amon. Could I read an electron microscope photograph? No, and he knew it. I couldn't be certain that the DNA results he'd showed me really belonged to the individuals he claimed. And what about Al's repeated poor-mouthing of his own powers? An adept Alpha could fake anything.

I needed to believe in someone. I put my faith in Al. He was the only person in Mosby who searched for answers.

Days earlier, when I asked Al if the murmurative power might be unlimited, he said, "The energy required would boil your brain." Greater range demanded even more energy. The Alpha got to my mother, all the way off in her Atlanta retirement home. He forced her to forget I ever existed. Okay, he might have planted that message during her short visit to Mosby, but what about my editor, Michelle? Even though she'd never visited Mosby, she'd sent me unearned money and published my old columns as new material. Then I'd disappeared from her memory, too. Could I send a command all the way from Mosby to Atlanta? Unlikely. If that were true, then a couple of hours ago Atlanta would have been awash with people stopping traffic while they searched for imaginary hundred-dollar bills.

There was an easy way to find out. The theater was so dark that I didn't need to close my eyes, but I did anyway. I concentrated on Michelle. *Fogger Grace exists. Send him a text message right now.* I added my cell phone numbers and email address focused on the command. Nothing happened. I waited in silence and darkness for what I imagined must be ten minutes, and my cell phone didn't make a sound. The Alpha would have to travel to Atlanta to plant a blocking command with Michelle. The field of candidates narrowed.

To be doubly sure, I pulled out my phone and checked for messages, but the text that popped up was not what I wanted.

"You must be worn out from worrying, little lemming. Sending a command doesn't work that way. You need line-of-sight to set the target up the first time. After that, proximity. That's the first thing you should have worked out. Admit it—you're outclassed. Might as well dance in traffic."

37

Whatever confidence I'd had in my abilities collapsed. I sat in a dark, deserted room, trapped.

The Alpha knew where I was, and in my rapidly degenerating mental state, the invisible walls of the theater began to close in, and the ceiling, a great sheet of dense metal, ratcheted downward foot by foot. I grabbed my flashlight and wrenched myself out of the seat. A stupid move. Even as I fumbled for the flashlight switch, my knees caught on the back of the seat in front of me, and I tumbled headfirst into the lower aisle. My flashlight flew into the darkness.

I flailed the air and fell sideways. My jaw crunched into a reinforced seat back. My ear slammed against my shoulder. My right hand came down hard on an armrest, which knifed into the space between my middle and ring fingers. Somewhere in my hand, joints separated. The pain was immense.

I levered myself up with my forearm instead of my hand. Even then, the pain radiating up from my fingers made my eyes tear. I had to do something about my injury, so I cradled my throbbing hand as I shuffled my way to a stand, then scurried up and down the aisles until I found the flashlight. Another less-than-smart move; pieces of the shattered lens scattered into the dark. When I flicked the switch, the bulb shone with a glow so anemic that I whimpered in self-pity. Fearless Fogger Grace, ready to confront his arch-enemy.

No, I didn't use the flashlight app on my cellphone. The agony in my hand overwhelmed my judgment. All I could think was, I'd trapped myself in a dark, vulnerable place. My options defaulted to my new powers. If I called Al for help, he'd be easy meat as soon as the Alpha spotted him. I had only one other person I could count on.

I'm in the movie theater. Back door open. Bring bandages and a small splint. And a flashlight.

While I waited, I tried to straighten my middle two fingers and nearly passed out when the ring finger snapped into place. I gave up trying to twist my middle finger into alignment and sat with my doubts and fears until the theater door opened and the bright beam of a flashlight probed the dark.

"Fogger, you here?"

"Right here," I said, and her beam climbed up the rows until it found me.

"What the hell am I doing here?" she said, her voice too much of a growl. "Is this one of your superman's commands? If it is, show me where he's hiding. I'll kill the fucker."

"It's just me, Lauren. Do you have the splint?"

She shone her light on my hand and drew in a breath, then sat beside me and took a firm grip on my middle finger.

I got out, "Wait a . . ." before she gave it a hard yank. When my vision cleared, I held the splint in place and made sucking sounds as she looped the gauze over my fingers. Not my finest moment.

Lauren rattled a bottle of pills in front of my face. "I brought painkillers. We get all the good stuff when we bust the locals. You want a couple?"

"Not now. I need my head straight."

"Seriously, Fogger. I get it now. Your Alpha-man can pull my strings. He's real, and it scares the hell out of me. But where is he; why would he help you?"

"It was me, Lauren. I sent the message."

The beam of Lauren's flashlight wavered, then fixed on me longer than I would have wished. It was too dark to see, but her sharp intake of breath made it easy to imagine the shock and disbelief on her face.

"You?" she said. "You're the goddamned Alpha-man?"

It was the only time I had seen her at a loss. I wasn't sure how to answer, and she said, "You crawled inside my head and made me march over here? Like I was a fucking puppet?"

"Wait, Lauren. No. I'm not the one who's been telling people to kill themselves." I reached into the dark. My hand slipped through the air without finding her. "I'm not that guy. But I have the Hatch gene. I can send commands." I reached for her again, and she thunked the metal flashlight hard into the back of my hand. The good one, thank God.

"Don't you touch me," she said. "You did this. To *me*."

But God, I wanted her touch more than anything. I wanted her phantom digit to brush the back of my neck. To say we were still connected.

"Lauren. Give me a chance to explain."

"You are as deaf as a fish, Fogger Grace, and as cold-blooded.

This isn't something you undo. You don't go inside my body and explain it away."

I grasped the first notion that came to mind. "There's this seventeenth-century play, *Cyrano de Bergerac*. They made it into a movie. Maybe you saw it?"

"You mind-fucked me, and you want to talk about movies? Sick, Fogger. Sick. I wonder why I ever slept with you."

I had dealt myself a bad hand, so I spoke quickly. "This lonely man loves just one woman, and whenever he tries to talk to her, he's afraid to say what he feels, so he hides in the dark and speaks to her so she will listen to his words. Only his words. He wants her to listen and forget everything else, just for the moment it takes to think."

"Oh, I'm thinking, Fogger. The movie *I* remember is *Frankenstein*. You're a monster!"

"'I dare to be myself for once.' That's what he says in the dark. That's all I'm asking."

"Oh, I get you," she said. "Especially the 'myself' part. You hacked into my head and programmed my brain."

"I was never inside. I sent a command, that's all."

"A command! An order from Massa to his slave!"

"No. It's what people do when they need help. We ask the ones we love. I needed you to help me, and you came."

"And when you got inside my brain and looked around, did you see anything else you wanted? Is there some sick, ugly order you want to give me? Maybe I should just bend over and let you hump me right here in the dark. Is that what you want?"

"Lauren . . . ."

The seat creaked as she got to her feet. "You finish your

game with your Alpha boogeyman. Whichever one of you survives, he can come see me. Meantime, you stay the fuck out of my head!"

The heavy flashlight dropped into my lap and, without thinking, I grabbed it with my injured hand. My nerves sent fiery waves up to my elbow. I heard Lauren stumble in the dark, curse.

"Show me the goddam door!" she shouted.

I aimed the beam at the soundproofed door and watched her leave, the back of her blue uniform so woven with slanting shadows that she appeared to be shifting between states of matter, as if a *Star Trek* transporter were beaming her to a distant galaxy. My fumbling excuse had created a dread possibility: that I had lost Lauren. I wanted a new life, and one stupid decision put all my cloud-dreams in jeopardy.

Fogger Grace had changed, all right. The boy I remembered, the man I thought I would become, all that was a set of convenient lies. Fogger Grace was a hole in his mother's memory, a canker in the mind of his grandfather-not-grandfather, a tool his scientist half-brother could use to sort out his identity, a check-mark on Cassie Wrenner's bucket list. His past was all invention.

So? The real Fogger Grace could be whoever he desired to be. His goals were whatever the hell suited his fancy. His ethics were whatever made his goals possible. I wanted only two things: to see the next morning, and that when this war was over, Lauren and I would be together.

38

I stepped out of Memories and Movies into sunlight so blinding it hurt to keep my eyes open. The blowtorch heat radiating from the sidewalk was palpable and disorienting, and the flowers around the base of the World War I doughboy statue were shriveled. Perfect weather for a showdown. Perfect, but I didn't see Wyatt or Doc or Virgil or Morgan anywhere.

To prove how isolated I was, my cell phone buzzed with the call I had been expecting. "Fogger, this is Al. I'm at the coffee shop with Cassie and Norman Garrison. I told you I'd survive this fool's parade. If you'll come over here, I'll show you how."

Thank you, Al, for telling me this message was the trap. You've been so certain your death was unavoidable. The command was *Tell him to come over here. Now!* Being Al Amon, you used your allotted words to warn me of the setup, the Alpha's grand finale. And mine.

I knew there was an audience listening to Al's call, so I

saturated my voice with gullibility. "Great news," I said. "Give me five minutes."

This was the Alpha's endgame. I knew how I'd proceed if I had his advantages. My survival depended on his attacking the way Al had predicted.

I went around the corner to the rear of the police station. With a simple command, I brought someone to unlock the back door. I stepped inside and with a second command picked up the one item I was certain I would need. A final instruction told the officers not to respond to any commotion at Magic Beans unless I asked for help. I retrieved my khaki jacket from the rental car and put it on, despite the oppressive afternoon temperature. Minutes later, I crossed the street and entered Cassie's coffee shop, imagining myself sealed inside a protective field, as armored as Clint Eastwood's Man with No Name. My senses vibrated with anticipation.

Magic Beans smelled stale, a rancid mixture of burnt coffee and flop sweat. Customers sat stiffly at their bare, round tables, their hands folded on the wood surface, or hidden in their laps, No one drank coffee. They didn't turn to look when I entered. My heartbeat raced. Under my jacket, my armpits were damp and clammy.

All the principals were there. Cassie and Al sat stiffly at one table, expectation written in their darting eyes. Every table had customers with their chairs turned so they faced the front of the shop. Some were just extra minds to make my blocks harder to hold in place. But enough of them would be armed. The Alpha was betting on massed firepower.

A single, barked cough rose above the sound of "Hotel California" playing on the shop speakers. It was supremely aggravating that the Eagles got pulled into this showdown. I knew their song by heart. Before this week, it had been a favorite.

Three men sat at a table in front of the baristas' station, their spines pressed flat against the backs of their chairs. They did not speak to each other. I had their complete attention. Two of the men were the guys I had brushed off when they wanted my table at the deli. The other was Norman Garrison. His gaze augured a hole through my head.

Cassie gave a wave and a deadpan smile. "We're over here, Fogger." She patted an empty chair between her and Al.

Al's face was blanched, a shade lighter than the sun-faded slate of his bald head, but damp, as if he wore moisturizer. "I got you a latte," he said, pointing at the cup in front of the empty chair. His pupils pulsed with suppressed energy.

The chair put the brick wall at my back, so I sat down. I picked up the cup of coffee and silently commanded Cassie to tell me if it was contaminated. She fidgeted, but she didn't stop me. I took a sip of coffee while I studied the room. Cold; bitter. My stomach waited a second, then reacted as if I had swallowed spoiled gumbo. Acid bile rose in my throat and burned my sinuses. I swallowed it down.

Oh, I was ready, alright. Which one would it be?

Garrison shifted his weight from one haunch to the other, his eyes never straying from our table. His forehead glistened in the overhead lights. His hands must also have been sweaty, because he rubbed them on the legs of his white slacks, wrinkling the fine linen.

The door of Magic Beans opened and Lauren entered, her face distorted by a fierce scowl. She shoved her sunglasses into a breast pocket and took stock of the room with one sweeping scan. She crossed the room and leaned against the counter. I held onto the desperate hope that, despite my misgivings and deductions, she wasn't already on the opposing side of this attack, so I made a warding gesture with my hand, hoping Lauren would understand and be alert to the menace in the area. Her gaze washed over me without pause.

Cassie squirmed. She played with her water glass, moving it from spot to spot as she kept up a barrage of senseless chatter. She nudged her water glass across the table with her fingertips until it hovered near the edge. Each time I turned toward her, she stalled and leaned over the glass, or looked elsewhere to draw my attention away, but even that deception warned me the setup was deliberate.

I felt no warning signs of the attack I knew had to come. The captive minds in the room waited, primed and programmed; all they needed was the trigger signal. It would play out the way Al predicted. And he was out of the fight, frozen in his chair, his eyes shining with an inner turmoil that could not reach his lips.

Cassie studied her glass the way a terrified zebra might watch a crocodile at the edge of a watering hole, as if the reptile controlled what would happen next. Finally, she nudged it the last quarter inch, and it fell.

The glass hit the floor with a faint thump.

They all drew at the same rushing instant. The men at Garrison's table leaped to their feet. Chairs crashed onto the floor. Cassie's revolver emerged from her lap. Her arm spasmed as the muzzle swung toward my chest.

I sent the blocking command. *EVERYONE STOP!...*

Lauren spun away from the counter. The nickel finish of her SIG Sauer flared so quickly in the light, I thought she'd fired. She took a two-handed grip and leveled the barrel at Cassie. And all this registered in the heartbeat after Cassie's glass fell, clattering ice cubes across the floor.

My command lagged.

People were on their feet all across the room, handguns rising from belts and pockets and handbags.

I sent the murmur command again, hard, and shouted it out loud, "FREEZE DAMMIT!"

A competing command rose to block me. We fought for microseconds, seeking a weakness to exploit. Pale faces laid bare our battle. Some wore a death rictus; others were almost comical in frozen, slack-jawed stupidity. My jaws clenched so hard I heard my teeth crackle. My injured hand throbbed. The pain went deep into my heart with all the shock of a mother's vicious slap.

I struggled to keep my blanketing command while the Alpha and I fought for control of the remaining pawns. His voice kept intruding, scrambling my thoughts, and I lost concentration.

Nearly everyone shut down, but the two men with Garrison took a split-second longer to block, and that was enough distraction for Garrison to get his handgun clear of his concealed belt holster.

Cassie and Garrison moved sluggishly, as if underwater. While I rode down on the will of the men at his table, Garrison swung his heavy revolver up, aiming for my head.

I focused on Cassie and swung her aim to Garrison's chest. I had her fire twice, point-blank. I chose him instinctively, not because I thought he was the Alpha but out of pure malice. Both bullets from Cassie's Smith & Wesson 38 Special hit him square, blowing his body back in a spray of red mist, overturning the table behind him. I felt his resistance snap off like a blown fuse.

Garrison's last synapses connected as he shut down, and he got his shots off on the way. The first took me in the chest just above my right nipple, slamming me and my chair into the brick wall. His second shot ricocheted off the wooden table and struck Al, punching a dark hole in the hollow of his throat.

I couldn't stop to think about that. The competing voice writhed around my blocking order. The pain in my chest fogged my vision and I let Cassie's gun hand waver. I reinforced my order for her to lay down her weapon and not fire. Her Smith & Wesson kept sliding off target, then creeping back to center on my chest. Her eyes flicked from her trigger finger to my face, then back. I rose from my chair, holding my bandaged hand toward her.

CASSIE, STOP!

At first, I thought her resolve had weakened; then she pulled the trigger. The bullet hit me squarely in the heart. I staggered back, tumbling over my chair, my lungs spasming from the second impact.

Lauren's face twisted in anger as she aimed and shot Cassie once in the face. She didn't holster her automatic but looked at me and said, "She's down. Where are you hit, Fogger?"

I rolled onto my left elbow and unsnapped the flaps on the Kevlar covert body armor I'd donned at the police station. My full attention hung on the competing command that still vibrated in the air, the command that kept repeating *SHOOT HIM!* to all the armed people in the room.

My sophomoric dreams collapsed. The deceptions had been obvious. I had even deceived myself.

I bore down on my blocking command, and my shield held. When I was sure the block had stabilized and no one else would shoot, I got to my feet and risked a quick glance at the table. Al slumped against the back of his chair, his arms hanging heavily at his sides, his chin resting on his chest, modestly concealing the hole in his throat. His lips had a slight pucker. It seemed he'd heard an amusing joke and was about to say, "Ah," or perhaps he pondered some indecipherable riddle. His final thoughts had evaporated from his eyes, but I knew they would have been for me and how I would survive the Alpha's unmasking. When the Alpha had captured him and set up the showdown, he had realized how it would smash my dreams.

Al, who'd considered me his younger brother. I would mourn him once I took this next step.

I held my block and stared at Lauren. "Drop the act," I said. "It won't work."

The sadness in my voice surprised me. I clutched the edge of the table and pulled myself upright. My mauled chest ached. Each full breath stretched my bruised ribs. I set my chair back on its feet and dropped into it.

Everything ached. The certain knowledge that Lauren was my adversary, that she had been from the start, was a distinctly separate pain. My attention lasered in on her and I sent a command. *YOUR FINGERS ARE FROZEN.*

Lauren swung her Sig in a short arc and centered it on my face. Her lips drew back, revealing a slash of white, perfect teeth. The green-brown eyes I had thought so mysterious and alluring were in reality pitiless. They sought to tunnel into my skull. Our commands seemed to cancel each other. We breathed in unison, our nervous systems entangled and synchronized, our phantom voices combined in a wordless chant.

I had been too eager to find a woman whose love would never falter. Too shy ever to have earned a woman's genuine love. Too inexperienced to know when it was being faked. What were Lauren's thoughts as we coupled in her bed: farce, revulsion, dominance? The emotion I had imaged was love, was a schoolboy's delusion.

39

"What we have here," said Lauren, "is what us folks in law enforcement call a Mexican standoff."

The confidence in her voice told me she was certain she had won. She only needed to push a little harder to finish me. I was the bird with a crippled wing, she the triumphant cat. She had time to savor the play.

Each breath was agony. If any of the zombies in the room tried to read the contest between our commands, they would think it balanced, hanging in the unresolved space between us. I knew differently.

"Oh, Fogger," Lauren said, "I wish this was easier, 'cause you really are a sweet man. But you just won't let me be in charge, will you?" Her baffling smile made me wonder if she was mocking me or really feeling regret. "I wanted this to work. Really did. It's you who made it too hard.

"I figure I have two ways to go. One, I just take you out like the others. With regret, of course. I package this up as another simple accident, and I'm right back where I want to be. No more annoying half-brothers and half-sisters. No overlooked relatives in far-off Atlanta. Just me and my sandbox."

She raised the nose of her Sig a little to emphasize her point but never let it drift off target.

"Option two'd be a bigger challenge. I could bring you along slow. Find out what it's like to wrap up long-term with someone who's the same as me. Well, not identical, but close. I admit you put on some spanking good moves in bed. I was tempted and I might have taught you, little by little, the fun of having a town to play with. I thought if you got the big picture, you'd agree to keep your place, and we could share. Maybe, down the road, we'd expand our territory."

She shook her head in mock regret. "But you won't go that way, will you? You won't take second place. All your 'I'm the new, improved Fogger Grace' bullshit. Worse, you want to treat normals like they're more than cattle. You have the same tools as me, but you're afraid to use them."

"When did you know?" I asked.

"At first, there was too much background noise at the mill. But even after the cousins all burned up, there was still this strange hum in the air. I couldn't get a bearing on it. Then, when we met here at the espresso shop, I sorted out you were a Hatch. A sleeper."

"Why not eliminate me then?"

"I sent the idea that you helped set the fire. Even with Ronnie helping to push the idea, you didn't bite. I caught on then that you were a special case."

"So why . . ." I said, but she cut me off.

"I might've taught you things I had to learn the hard way."

My sense of calm surprised me. Death breathed down the

back of my neck. I felt nothing but regret. "There's nothing you could teach me, Lauren."

"How about not squeezing your eyes shut when you concentrate? Everybody notices when you do that, but you can't see anything that's going on. Stupid habit. I learned to bite down on my cheek. Works fine to focus your mind."

"So why didn't you finish me before I started learning?" I asked. "It would have been natural."

"I gave it a test shot with the pickup. You countered without knowing you were doing it. Later, we had our red-letter night at my condo. One for the records, huh? It tempted me. I worked to figure a way where I didn't have to waste you, but you fought me, every time."

"Why're you dragging this out, Lauren?"

"Honey, this is our last chance to talk. Let's chew on it."

"So, you ran me through traffic," I said. I balanced my command against hers. "My effort in bed wasn't the show-stopper I thought."

She laughed, and it hurt despite my anger.

"Fogger, honey, it was great, but we got to keep our priorities in line. When I spotted you out for that run, it was too good an opportunity to pass up. Almost worked, didn't it? I parked my car behind the Farm Bureau office, so's I could watch. Damn if you didn't make it through! So impressive. That's when I backed off. I decided to take out your pet professor instead, but you blocked me. That was new. Never had someone interfere with a command before. Pissed me off, big time."

Lauren popped the Sig at me again. To anyone watching from the street—and there was a crowd out there, staring through the coffee shop windows—we might have been two friends talking about anything but mortal threat.

"You gave me a break when you stored those coffee cups in the station," she said. "Easy switch. Cousin Al took my sample and ran with it. Once you homed in on Cassie the Cow, it should have been a slam dunk. But, hell, every time I planted an idea, you blocked it. Didn't take long to see the only way to erase the problem was to go straight at you."

I'd heard enough. Lauren had answered all my questions except the essential one. "Did you ever feel anything for me?" I asked. "Sympathy? Love?"

The smile that crossed her lips was difficult to decipher. I hoped its meaning was regret.

"Love's an emotion for sheep," she said. "People with our powers don't need all that baggage."

Her eyes were as cold as a January wind. "Now lean forward. I don't want to make a mess." The muzzle of her SIG Sauer rose a few millimeters and at the same time, she backed up her words with a command. "Bye, Fogger."

Lauren's eyes widened as soon as I pushed. Her lips drew back tight against clenched teeth, and she hissed. Her desperate attempt to block battered moth-like against my will. I pushed again, harder, and her gun hand began to move in tiny, jerking steps.

It could have gone quick, but I dragged it out. I wanted her to know what the others had experienced: the powerlessness, the shrieking denial of what was about to happen.

Lauren was strong. She couldn't stop my command, but she could still plead. "Ohhhhh, don't," she said through clenched teeth. "Don't do this. I worked so hard. Don't. We can work this out." Her left hand fluttered uselessly in her lap, a wing-shot bird circling before it dropped. It wanted to intercept the gun, but she couldn't make it do her bidding.

I moved the muzzle until it loomed in front of her left eye. I didn't draw out the finish. As much as I wanted to punish her, I was not a monster. She was the monster.

"I'm afraid," she said.

"You are the love of my life, Lauren," I said, and sent the command.

Lauren cried out the beginning of a plea, "Fog . . . ," and as the Eagles sang of voices down a dark corridor, she pulled the trigger.

In that thin sliver of time, as the single 124-grain Hydra-Shok round sped down the barrel and pierced her flesh, the barrier between our wills collapsed, and I saw the unshielded Lauren, a terrified thirteen-year-old, as her stepfather laid his body on hers and tore her, and she reached out with her untested, uncontrolled power and commanded her mother, *Kill him.*

The bullet entered Lauren's skull just above her left eye and exited a split second later, taking much of the back of her head with it.

I couldn't hold that image. When I turned away to look out at the street, the light outside had an unnatural quality. I felt as if I wore a diving mask, and the scene on the other side of the glass was distorted by water pressure and mask squeeze.

A small crowd had gathered outside. They peered in at us, open-mouthed, and their animal fascination sickened me. *A terrible murder,* I sent. *Chief Klout tried to stop Cassie Wrenner from killing Professor Amon and Norman Garrison, and was herself killed. No one else is involved. Only the victims.* They stepped back from my glare, but no one turned to run.

My adolescent dream was wrecked. Screw it. What was love, anyway: a diversion from boredom, a moment of animal release, an escape from routine. I can have that any time I wish.

I can make anyone love me.

I left the Magic Beans coffee shop and walked down the sloping sidewalk to my new home. My condo has a nice view of the town park, and I have special memories here. I will make sure that someone responsible takes over the coffee shop. I'm fond of their creamy lattes. After a rest, I'll map out what to do next. There's a lot to learn.

Lauren finished her painting. It's four feet by three, a sea of heads turned away from the viewer, each head a different color but each shaped exactly the same, staring into the distance at a clean, dark line representing the horizon. A dividing line separates the light green below from the light blue above, and at the middle of the image, the focus of all the attention, a single person stands in silhouette, in a posture of defiance. The painting will always be a favorite.

I remember the small brown bird I glimpsed on the afternoon of my first drive out to Mosby. I would like to believe that it eluded the red-tailed hawk, wound its way through I-20 traffic, and found refuge in the dense woods beyond the fields of sod, its tiny, furtive heart beating out a riff that would challenge the best jazz percussionist. I hope it learned a lesson, because the hawk is back on his perch at the top of a tall pine by the edge of the field, as still as a sculpture, his sun-yellow eye eager for the incautious mistake of his next kill.

That's really all you need to know. You won't remember any of this, anyway.

About the Author

Stephen Huggins is a retired aerospace executive. He has been a rocket engineer, sold aircraft and aero-systems on four continents, and directed an advanced technology group. A holder of five university degrees, including a PhD in history, Huggins has taught world history at the University of Georgia and Georgia Military College. His book, *America's Use of Terror*, published in 2019, explores the history of American terrorism from colonial times to the present. *The Murmur* is his first work of fiction.

CPSIA information can be obtained
at www.ICGtesting.com
Printed in the USA
FSHW011637051020
74430FS